The Storm, the Fish, & the Vine

What Readers Are Saying

ADULTS

Jenny is a skilled wordsmith with a love for truth. Her ability to bring things to life in technicolor testifies to her understanding of both human nature and the Word of God.

—**Pastor Jack and Lisa Hibbs,** Calvary Chapel Chino Hills, CA

I was first introduced to Jenny's powerful storytelling years ago when my daughter and I would snuggle up to read *The Ark, the Reed, and the Fire Cloud.* Now, with *The Storm, the Fish, and the Vine,* Jenny has written a book that will truly change lives. As Gillamon remarks in these pages, "The history of any nation is always dependent upon its youth." This story will inspire the next generation to rise against modern-day slavery, raising new Newtons and Wilberforces who will speak out for justice and cultural redemption. As a pastor and someone working in anti-trafficking ministry, I highly recommend this book. You'll be both inspired and entertained, drawing closer to God while gaining a deeper understanding of His redemptive work in history.

— **Rev. Dr. Chris Haughee,** 51, Mirror Ministries
(an anti-trafficking ministry), Richland, WA

Only Jenny L. Cote can ingeniously explore a connection between the prophet Jonah and slave trader John Newton. Her story gives the readers an opportunity to consider the state of our own souls, the wickedness of man, and the abundant grace given by the Maker to all who call on Him. As Gillamon says, "History and storms do have a way of repeating themselves." If ever there was a time for us to learn from history and storms, it is now. I am forever grateful to Jenny for letting me teach her books, and I am excited to teach young people the power of storms and God's "Severe Grace." I love this book! Jenny is a gift from God to this generation.

—**Beth Cuvelier,** EPIC Homeschool Teacher, Woodbridge, VA

Jenny L. Cote has a God-given gift to see a slightly wider expanse of HIStory than we can. Each of her books dives into one scene of God's tapestry, with her characters highlighting the common threads connecting the whole. This scene, of the prodigal John Newton hearkening to the reluctant Jonah, most successful foreign missionary of all time, will imprint on your children that there is always hope;

because of Jesus, no sinner is beyond the amazing grace of God! As a Harvard graduate, practicing pediatrician, and homeschool mom, I thank God for these historical fiction fantasy books that shine like lights in the darkness, illuminating the past to learn from our mistakes, and pointing to the Way, the Truth, and the Life.

—**Jessica Chi,** Homeschool Mom, Pediatrician, Philadelphia, PA

Jenny breathes new life into this retelling of the prodigal son, beautifully weaving the ancient and modern together in one amazing story.

—**Alex Cote,** 31, ML Consultant, Sandy Springs, GA

The Storm, Fish, and the Vine is an inspirational book for all ages. Jenny reaches back into biblical history to tell the story of God's call to Jonah to go and preach his message to the great city of Nineveh. She compares Jonah to John Newton's conversion as a slave trader who wrote the hymn "Amazing Grace." This is powerful inspiration that reaches the depths of the human soul.

—**Dr. Paul Mims,** 87, Pastor, Palmetto, GA

Jenny L. Cote has done it again with this AMAZING read! Batten down the hatches for this inspiring story of a slave-trading wretch redeemed by God's grace. Jenny's epic prose will transport you from the belly of a great fish to the streets of London with page-turning adventures in between!

—**Libby McNamee,** Author & Speaker, Midlothian, VA

This is a very well-written story behind "Amazing Grace", which comes alive at the turn of each page. Jenny has a way of unpacking the scripture verses she used in the book to have a deeper understanding of God. I saw how God used two men from completely separate times, John Newton and Jonah, to show the consistent character of God—bringing light into darkness with the redemption of God's love, mercy, and forgiveness. The book is hard to put down once you begin reading. God is surely using Jenny to tell the history of the slave trader that has long been forgotten, but still an amazing story of the redemptive power of God.

— **Aaron Wrighthouse,** 44, Albany, OR

I discovered so much about the life of John Newton while reading *The Storm, The Fish, and The Vine* and how truly amazing God's grace is! I even learned ways to imitate the love of Jesus Christ in my own Life! I loved seeing the story of Jonah and how Jonah ties into Newton's Faith Journey. "Amazing Grace" helps us remember how God saves the Prodigal children and calls them back to Him! I finished the book in just two days! Miss Jenny's work is superb, finding the balance between deep historical research and sound theological values—all written with vibrant, descriptive imagery and fun animal characters!

—**Amy Lopez,** 24, Freelance Video Editor, Mount Juliet, TN

KIDS AND TEENS

Waiting for *The Storm, the Fish, and the Vine* to arrive felt like anticipating the sequel to a favorite movie. Jenny Cote has done it again! The newest book in her epic series exceeded all expectations. I was especially moved by the story of John Newton and how his transformation shows the power of God's grace to redeem anyone. Jenny's gift for storytelling and her ability to weave gospel truths through every page is truly remarkable. I hope she never stops writing.

—**Weston Nix,** 17, Homeschooled, Dahlonega, GA

When I was younger, I would have my dad sing "Amazing Grace" to me almost every night. To read the redemptive story behind the hymn was a wonderful experience. It also reminded me that when we hit rock-bottom, God is the rock at the bottom.

—**Judah Barsh,** 14, Classical Conversations, Vista, CA

This is a must-read book for anyone who wants to grow in their faith and enjoys reading historical fiction. John Newton's story shows that no one is too deep in sin to receive God's grace and mercy. This book constantly keeps your attention!

—**Emma Ornelas,** 11, San Gabriel Christian School, Monterey Park, CA

This book was an exciting Epic tale filled with tragedy, pain, and thrill. In the begging, John Newton's mother taught him well, which helped him on various moments in his journey to Christ. After his mother died, he made a colossal mistake by straying away from the Lord but while in his biggest storm returned to his faith. Overall, this was an inspirational story that I can reflect on in the tough times that will come in my life. While reading this book, I felt captured in a different world where I can picture the story clearly in my mind.

—**Evangelene Henschel,** 12, Classical Conversations, Vista, CA

The Storm, the Fish, and the Vine is magnificent! I love the details, and the hard work Mrs. Cote puts into her book. John Newton's life has so many good lessons to learn from and the connections between his story and Jonah's enlightens what God wants the readers to learn. Not only is God's message clearly heard in this book, it is action-packed, adventurous, funny, and exciting!

—**Karaleena Andrade,** 13, Homeschooled, Norco, CA

If I'm being completely honest, lately I haven't enjoyed reading that much, but as soon as I flipped the cover, I was immediately immersed in yet another of Jenny's incredible stories. It's truly inspiring to see how much effort she pours into her work, and it really shows! Her delightfully engaging storytelling really has a way of making you feel like you're right there, experiencing everything for yourself. All I have to say is *c'est magnifique!*

—**Elle Inhoffer,** 11, Homeschooled, Aspen, CO

Mrs. Cote never fails to bring HIStory to life, and she's done it once again with John Newton and Jonah, two people whose faith was born amid a storm. As the waves crash down on John Newton, whose journey to Christ is anything but smooth sailing, and Jonah expresses his raw emotion toward God, the two stories combine themselves in a beautifully poetic way, despite being on opposite ends of the timeline. Truly, this is a story of "Amazing Grace" indeed.

—**Vida Ortiz,** 14, Homeschooled, Rancho Cucamonga, CA

WOW. *The Storm, the Fish, and the Vine* is AMAZING … in more ways than one! I felt like I was actually there with the characters, joining in both their delights and their sorrows (Poor Al!). Every page was clearly Spirit-led, and it inspired and challenged me to go further in my own faith. My whole family loved it! THANK YOU, MS. JENNY!!!

—**Adalynn Krahn,** 14, Homeschooled, Omaha, Nebraska

The Storm, the Fish, and the Vine is a truly beautiful story about a man who had continual difficulties in his life. He grew up in faith, fell down a deep pit of sinfulness, tried to rise back up, only to be worse than before, but found amazing grace. This story, in Nigel's words, "takes the biscuit"! Mrs. Jenny's books are amazing reads, so I highly recommend them!

—**Zoë Fung-A-Wing,** 13, Homeschooled, Marietta, GA

Of all Jenny L. Cote's books, this one is by far my favorite! It is an "amazing" story based on factual events, teaching that God will always be with you in every storm, and that no one is too far from His perfect love and grace. I enjoyed it thoroughly.

—**Evah Maxwell,** 14, Homeschooled at Liberty Education Classical Fellowship, Chino Hills, CA

How amazing! This novel may be small, but it had an enormous impact on my life! Jenny expertly weaves John Newton's pathway from sin to salvation in a well-paced narrative that kept me hooked. She also reveals God's true character of mercy and grace so beautifully, especially in the instances when He enters John Newton and Jonah's life at their darkest moments. Newton's character arc also taught me a great deal about God's immense, unrelenting love for us and the simplicity of having a relationship with Jesus! I give so much gratitude to

Jenny for giving me the opportunity to read this book when I needed it most, and I'm so thankful that grace is amazing indeed!

— **Emma Snyder,** 16, Lake Center Christian School, Canton, OH

This book was incredible (and funny)! I loved seeing and learning about John Newton's crazy life story and how it lined up with events in Jonah and other Bible characters' lives. I didn't know much about John Newton before this, so it was really cool to see how God's grace worked in and through him. An AMAZING read!!!

—**Claire S.,** 15, Silk Road Academy, Dushanbe, Tajikistan

Thank you, Mrs. Jenny, for writing this book—it was my favorite of the entire series. My favorite character is Liz; I love her because she is so smart and always comforting the humans. I love reading her out loud because she is French and I like hearing and learning the French words. I can't wait for your next book so I can go on another adventure with Liz and the gang.

—**Faith Jones,** 11, Homeschooled, Tustin, CA

This book is another fantastic addition to the Epic series. I really enjoyed the similarities between John Newton and Jonah. It's incredible to see how the Maker and his special Epic Order of the Seven team intervened in Newton's life, both the good and the bad. His story of redemption is inspiring and made me reflect on the grace of Jesus in my own life. It was also neat to see what led up to the creation of "Amazing Grace," the hymn that has been repeatedly sung for over two-hundred and forty years. Although this is a smaller book, it does not lack anything. I really love it and can't wait to see whose story Mrs. Jenny writes about next.

— **Bogdana Daniels,** 15, Homeschooled at Daniels Academy, Ozark, AL

The latest adventures of our favorite animal team are just as funny, brilliant, and EPIC as ever in Mrs. Cote's new story about conversion and forgiveness. Huzzah for heroes of the past and the writer who brings them to them to life!

—**Raina Boyer,** 12, Liberty Learning Homeschool, Rancho Cucamonga, CA

Once again, Jenny combines HIStory with fantasy, fiction, and beloved animals! This book is one of her best yet. She brilliantly tells the stories of Jonah and John Newton and combines them with one of her familiar plotlines. It took my knowledge of John Newton to a whole new level, intricately weaving in truth and humor. I will read this book again. Five stars!

— **Nathaniel Gade,** 14, Homeschooled, Franklinton, NC

How does she do it?! Jenny L. Cote weaves together yet another masterpiece with all the elements of her former books…and EVEN MORE! Whether you're looking for Biblical Fiction, Historical Fiction, or even something on a famous composer (like John Newton), *The Storm, the Fish, and the Vine* has it all! Follow the Epic Order of the Seven as they watch John Newton change from being a smart boy to a rebellious teenager to a blaspheming slave merchant, and how he returns to Christ to write the hymn we all know and love: "Amazing Grace". It is inspiring to see how God worked through the life of this 'Jonah.' All I can say is, AMAZING!

—**Jolie Forslund,** 14, Homeschooled, Stanwood, WA

Ms. Jenny has done it again! This book has comedy, tragedy, love, and humor, and Al is funnier than ever! I couldn't put it down. I hope I can love Christ as much as John Newton and make better decisions than Jonah. I highly recommend this book!

—**Piper James,** 10, Homeschooled, Bremerton, WA

The Storm, The Fish, and The Vine is an artfully crafted book. The parallel Ms. Cote beautifully made with John Newton and Jonah showing the seriousness of sin and the seriousness of obeying God's word. I was hooked on every word of Ms. Cote's pen, and I can't wait until the next book!

—**Ruth Dennison,** 13, Homeschooled, Brandon, MS

Mrs. Jenny L. Cote does yet another wonderful job in *The Storm, The Fish, and The Vine!* Jenny brought to life the story of Jonah and John Newton in a way that only she could do. It was my first time reading about John Newton, and while being historically plus Biblically accurate, it was super entertaining and easy to understand. Filled with laughs, sadness, and wonderful HIStory, this book will be an epic read for anyone!

—**Grace Jones,** 14, Homeschooled, Pleasanton, CA

A great journey filled with mystery, peril, and God's amazing grace. Jenny's stories are full of adventure and faith. From Noah to Jonah her books are the ones I reach for over and over. This book truly brings Jonah's story to life. I loved how John Newton's story intertwined with Jonah and how our beloved characters Al & Nigel continue to surprise us with displays of courage, showing that God's grace can find you no matter the period. It showed me how uniquely people are intertwined through history, and while reading I am inspired to live my life in a way where my actions can impact others for good. Thank you, Miss Jenny, for writing beautiful books that teach, encourage, and inspire us all.

—**Eliana Galeano,** 13, Homeschooled, Escondido, CA

The Storm, the Fish, and the Vine is full of treachery, truth, and scripture. It has given me a deeper understanding of the life of both John Newton and Jonah, and it encourages me to remember that God is always with us, no matter where we are. Currently, it is by far my favorite book written by Jenny L. Cote. It has changed my life and made my faith stronger in God. You should read this amazing book! Jenny L. Cote has really outdone herself here. Thank you, Jenny!

—**Gideon Forslund,** 12, Homeschooled, Stanwood, WA

BEST BOOK EVER!!!!! Jenny's book is so well written, and I NEVER wanted to put it down. I love how she connected the life of John Newton and Jonah. Jenny does an outstanding job at weaving characters into history in a fun way. Thank You Jenny for another amazing book. As Nigel often says, "That took the biscuit."

—**Milanah Barsh,** 12, Classical Conversations, Vista, CA

Mrs. Jenny out-did herself again! This book is written differently from all the others, which makes it incredibly gripping. I could not put it down! I have read all of Jenny's books, but this one is my favorite. I especially love how it shows that you cannot run too far from God's grace. It beautifully combines adventure, fantasy, fiction, and a bit of mystery. It is truly amazing!

—**Ruth Baggott,** 14, Homeschooled, Lawrenceville, GA

This is the best book Miss Jenny has ever written, and I say that with confidence! The way she incorporates John Newton, Jonah, and even Lafayette—all different characters across various times and places—is absolute GENIUS! I know that I'll never think of John Newton the same way again. His story is so much deeper than I thought it was, and this book brought that out in the most gripping, exciting way. In previous books, Gillamon and Clarie were always such mysterious characters, but I love how this book finally lets us see what they've been doing behind the scenes all this time. And, of course, I must mention that Al is the funniest he's been in the whole series!

—**Carey Talevski,** 14, Homeschooled, Melbourne, Victoria, Australia

FAMILIES

Jenny L Cote had us hooked from the start, yet again, skillfully blending history, heart, and humour to deliver a powerful message of redeeming love and amazing grace. A compelling read that brings history to life. This has fast become a family favourite already.

—**Mike,** Karen, Tilly (11), Charlotte (10), and Lucy (8) Tenkate,
Longford Victoria Australia

The details of Newton's life are so vivid, it seems Jenny knew him personally! She has such an amazing gift for writing, that our family could not put this book down— delightful and fun read aloud that is historically accurate and engaging for even the youngest family member. The dialogue between characters is our favorite part, as Jenny uses that to bring them to life! As with all of Jenny's books, there are zero hesitations in putting these words before the eyes of children; Jenny wrote the story of John Newton to glorify God and that shines through. This story is such a beautiful reminder of God's providence and that not one of us is too far off to be saved by grace.

—**Family Pickerel,** Gabriel 11, William 10, Samuel 7, Felicity 5, Benjamin 2, Homeschooled, Findlay, OH

EPIC ORDER OF THE SEVEN

The STORM, the FISH, & the VINE

JENNY L. COTE

LIVING INK BOOKS
Writing Worth Reading™

Epic Order of the Seven®

The Storm, the Fish, and the Vine

Published by Living Ink Books, an imprint of AMG Publishers, Chattanooga, Tennessee (www.amgpublishers.com).

Print Edition ISBN: 9781617156182
ePUB Edition ISBN: 9781617156199

Cover and internal illustrations by Rob Moffitt, Chicago, Illinois.
Interior design by Katherine Lloyd, theDESKonline.com.
Editing by Richard Cairnes, Walworth, Wisconsin.
Proofreading by ProofreadingPal LLC, Iowa City.

Internal images: ©Cowper & Newton Museum, Historic Maps from the Library of Congress Maps Division.

Back cover photo by Lorraine Howard Photography, Wichita Falls, Texas.

Printed in Canada.

25 26 27 28 29 MAR 5 4 3 2 1

To Casey

You helped me to understand
the depth of God's amazing grace
amid a storm.

This book contains fact, fiction,
and fantasy—in that order.

For the purely factual accounts of the remarkable history contained herein, please see the book of Jonah and sources listed in the bibliography.

. . . *He marked out their appointed times in history* . . .
Acts 17:26

Contents

Acknowledgments . . . xvii
Main Character Profiles . . . xix
Prologue: First Steps to Liberty for All . . . xxi

PART ONE: A WRETCH LIKE ME
(JOHN NEWTON 1725–1745)

Chapter 1 PREPARE TO BE AMAZED . . . 3
Chapter 2 WHAT GOES INTO THE FIRST OF LIFE . . . 12
Chapter 3 MISSING THE BOAT . . . 23
Chapter 4 THE RINGS OF THE LORD . . . 34
Chapter 5 PRESSED FOR ANSWERS . . . 46
Chapter 6 NEVER DELIBERATE . . . 57

PART TWO: I ONCE WAS LOST
(JOHN NEWTON 1745–1748)

Chapter 7 THE WILLING SLAVE OF EVERY EVIL . . . 67
Chapter 8 IN HUNGER, IN THIRST, AND IN NAKEDNESS . . . 77
Chapter 9 A SERVANT OF SLAVES . . . 86
Chapter 10 A FIFTEEN-MINUTE MIRACLE . . . 94
Chapter 11 WHAT IF THESE THINGS SHOULD BE TRUE? . . . 101

PART THREE: BUT NOW AM FOUND
(BACK TO JONAH)

Chapter 12 WHO IS JONAH? . . . 115
Chapter 13 WHY HAVE YOU DONE THIS? . . . 122
Chapter 14 SEVERE GRACE . . . 127
Chapter 15 THE WITNESS . . . 132
Chapter 16 FORTY DAYS FROM NOW . . . 140
Chapter 17 THE GOURDLESS, GRACELESS PROPHET . . . 148
Chapter 18 THE SIGN OF JONAH . . . 156

PART FOUR: WAS BLIND
(JOHN NEWTON 1748–1764)

Chapter 19 WHEN A STORM OF TERROR SURROUNDS YOU 163
Chapter 20 SAVED BY THE FISH 172
Chapter 21 EVIL AFLOAT 181
Chapter 22 VOYAGES AND VINES 190
Chapter 23 WILLING TO DELIBERATE 200
Chapter 24 UNEXPECTED ENCOUNTERS 210

PART FIVE: BUT NOW I SEE
(JOHN NEWTON 1764–1777)

Chapter 25 FISH AND LACE 219
Chapter 26 NEWTON'S NEW YEAR'S HABIT 229
Chapter 27 FISHER OF KIDS 237
Chapter 28 TWO WILLIAMS OF NOTE 244
Chapter 29 A SWEET VINE 252
Chapter 30 AMAZING GRACE 256
Chapter 31 GRACE NOTES 262
Epilogue: A Fortunate Meeting 269

A Word from the Author 273
Bibliography 287
Glossary of Words and Phrases 291
About the Epic Scribe 295
. . . and Her Books 296
The Next Generation of Newtons and Wilberforces to Fight Modern-Day Slavery 299

Acknowledgments

God You are the reason I write. Thank you for giving me the gifts, passions, abilities, and opportunities to research and write YOUR story for the next generation. Soli Deo Gloria.

Epic Historians and Historical Sites Whenever kids ask me what the best part is about being an author, I always answer with an enthusiastic, one-word answer: "RESEARCH!" I read a ton of books, but books alone are insufficient to drill down to the nitty-gritty details of history. I am heavily dependent on historians who know the subject inside and out. Whenever possible I also visit the places where the history happened, but the only place I was able to visit for *The Storm, the Fish, and the Vine* was North Island, South Carolina. You can only get there by boat, and I'm grateful to Robert "Mac" McAlister for arranging to take me there one brisk November day. I appreciate my friend and Colonial Williamsburg's *Marquis de Lafayette* Mark Schneider for reviewing Lafayette's landing scenes for accuracy. For the rest of the book featuring John Newton's life in England, I am eternally indebted to Marylynn Rouse, who is the foremost authority with the John Newton Project. She corrected several misperceptions that I had about the origins of "Amazing Grace" that caused me to thankfully redirect some fictional plot lines. Marylynn quickly clarified past errors from other books on John Newton that caused me confusion and enlightened me on facts I did not know. She admittedly is not a fan of historical fiction because of such errors that found their way into historical biographies! I may not have won her over yet, but I pray that I have done justice to the real story of John Newton, which will inspire readers to dive into his story who might never have done so.

Family, Friends, Critique Team Thank you for your love, encouragement, prayers, feedback, and inspiration while I researched, travelled, spoke, and wrote: My husband Casey and son Alex, my parents Dr. Paul and Janice Mims, my EPIC muse Claire Roberts Foltz, and my EPIC "spoon sister" and fellow author Libby McNamee.

Publishing Team An EPIC thank you to the people who take what comes out of my pen and turn it into something beautiful to hold, read, and share! Illustrator Rob Moffitt, Editor Richard Cairnes, Interior Designer Katherine Lloyd, and the AMG Publishing Team.

Readers It is my joy and honor to write for you. My passion is to inspire the next generation to know and love HIStory, and I pray I have done so with this book. Thank you for your prayers, encouraging notes, letters, pictures, cards, e-mails, social media posts, and book reviews. They make me smile, and you encourage this author's heart more than you could ever know. I would love to hear how this book inspired you, or about something you learned, at jenny@epicorderoftheseven.com. I'll keep writing as long as you keep reading!

With Epic Love,

Main Character Profiles

Max: A Scottish Terrier from (where else?) Scotland. Full name is Maximillian Braveheart the Bruce. Short, black, with a large head, always ready to take on the bad guys. Faithful leader of the team who started with their first mission on Noah's Ark in *The Ark, the Reed, and the Fire Cloud.* Loves to mess with Al, "encouraging" him to work on his bravery. Can't swim. Immortal.

Liz: A petite, French, black cat from Normandy. Full name is Lizette Brilliante Aloysius. Brilliant, refined, and strategic leader of the team, beginning with Noah's Ark. Loves the study of history, science, the written word, culture, and languages. Prides herself on knowing the meanings of names, and simply adores gardens. Immortal.

Al: A well-fed, Irish, orange cat. Full name is Albert Aloysius, also called "Big Al" by his close friends. Hopelessly in love with his mate, Liz, since Noah's Ark. Simple-minded, but often holds the key to gaining access to impossible places, and figuring out things everyone else misses, including deep spiritual truths. Lives to eat and sleep. Afraid of everything. Immortal.

Kate: A West Highland White Terrier, also from Scotland. The love of Max's life ever since they "wed" on the way to the Ark. Has a sweetness that disarms everyone she meets. Is also a fiery lass, unafraid to speak her mind. Always sees the good in others and sticks up for the underdog. Immortal.

Nigel P. Monaco: A jolly British mouse. Possesses impeccable manners and speech. Wears spectacles and is on the same intellectual level as Liz. An expert Egyptologist who joined the team in *The Dreamer, the Schemer, and the Robe.* Taught Liz all about Egypt, giving her the endearing title "my pet." Travels quickly via carrier pigeon and has an affinity for music. Immortal.

Gillamon: A wise, kind mountain goat from Switzerland. Moved to Scotland, where he raised Max (an orphan) and served as his mentor. Died before the Flood but serves as a spiritual being who delivers mission assignments from the Maker to the team. Can take any shape or form and shows up when least expected.

Clarie: A sweet little lamb from Judea. Shepherds gave her to Mary and Joseph as a gift for Baby Jesus in *The Prophet, the Shepherd, and the Star.* Died enabling the family to escape to Egypt without harm and joined Gillamon as a spiritual being member of the team. Serves as all-knowing guide in the IAMISPHERE when the team goes back in time to observe historical events. Can take any shape or form.

Open your ears to what I am saying,
for I will speak to you in a parable.
I will teach you hidden lessons from our past—
stories we have heard and know,
stories our ancestors handed down to us.
We will not hide these truths from our children
but will tell the next generation about the
glorious deeds of the LORD. *We will tell of his power*
and the mighty miracles he did.

—PSALM 78:1–4

Prologue

First Steps to Liberty for All

NORTH ISLAND, SOUTH CAROLINA, JUNE 13, 1777

Al stretched out across the warm sand, mindlessly tracing the outline of a seashell with his claw. The hypnotic sound of the rolling surf, coupled with the bright sunshine, made the plump Irish cat's eyelids heavy. His beautiful mate, Liz, was in the middle of a lecture about the geography of the beach where they sat, sixty miles north of Charlestown. Al yawned wide—just as a gust of wind blew a clump of dry, sandy seaweed into his gaping mouth. The startled orange kitty quickly sat up, pulling off the seaweed that stuck to his whiskers. "There's not much this kitty don't like in me mouth," Al complained with a frown. He spit out the gritty sand. "PPPPPTTT, but sand and seaweed be on me short list."

Al's Scottish terrier friend Max spied the seaweed on the plump cat's face and chuckled. "That reminds me of the time . . ."

"Do *not* say it, Max," Liz hoarsely whispered. Then, clearing her throat, the petite black feline picked up where she was in her description of North Island. "As I was saying, this is a *barrier* island, of that kind that forms when sand and silt build up at the mouth of a bay. Barrier islands serve to protect the mainland behind them."

"Big Al here be illustratin' how North Island were formed with sand in its mouth," Max snorted, slapping his fluffy friend on the back. "Good job, lad."

Al's ears flattened and he spat out more sand. "Anythin' to help me lass."

The slender French cat shook her head and smiled at her loveable, messy mate. She then pointed to the bay. "Winyah Bay is a very shallow inlet from the Atlantic Ocean, no? It is eleven miles long, and almost one mile wide in some areas. This bay is fed by four rivers: the Pee Dee, the Black, the Waccamaw, and the Sampit."

Al and Max looked at each other and snickered.

"PEE Dee?" Max chortled, raising his hind leg.

"Armpit?" Al jested, putting his paw under his fluffy arm.

"Sounds like a stinky place ta me!" Max laughed.

Liz frowned. Al smiled sheepishly. "Sorry, lass," he grimaced. "What were ye sayin' aboot the rivers?"

The perturbed cat slowly curled her tail up and down, trying to ignore the running jokes between these two lifelong friends. "North Island is nine miles long, with sandy beaches on its south side, narrow creeks and broad salt marshes on its west side, and a second small inlet from the ocean on its northern end, called North Inlet."

Max pointed to Al's wide mouth and chuckled. "Al's got an inlet on his north end, too. It's usually filled with fish."

"*Ahem!* So as you can see," Liz continued, ignoring the Scottie, "North Island is less than half a mile wide for most of its length, but grows to approximately one mile wide at its south end."

Max glanced at Al's backside. "Ye're a lot like North Island, lad."

Al looked behind him and patted his tail area. "Aye, me south side be wider than me north side."

Liz whipped her tail back and forth, trying to contain her frustration. "You two are simply . . . simply . . ."

"INTOLERABLE!" came a British voice belonging to their mouse friend, Nigel. He knew how laborious Liz's lectures were with only Max and Al in audience. He sat on the back of a bald eagle who came in for a beach landing.

The eagle's massive nine-foot wingspan brought another gust of wind, sending more seaweed flying into Al's face. "Jolly good show on sticking such a smooth landing, old boy!" Al wrinkled his brow and slowly wiped off his whiskers with a pout.

"Thanks, Nigel. Hello, all," the bald eagle greeted them, flapping his wings, and wiggling his tail feathers.

"*Bonjour,* Veritas! *Bonjour,* Nigel!" Liz exclaimed, thrilled to have new friends with whom to converse. "Welcome to North Island!"

Nigel walked over and took Liz's paw in his to graciously kiss it. "A pleasure to see you, my dear."

"If you don't mind, I spied some fish over in the bay, and I'm starving after our flight from New Jersey. I'm going to grab some dinner," Veritas told them. "I'll pick you up later, Nigel."

"Splendid! Enjoy your well-earned seafood buffet," the little mouse quipped. "According to Gillamon, we shan't be long."

"Fish? Can I go?" Al pleaded before seeing Liz's frown. He gave a weak laugh. "But who cares aboot fish when me beautiful Liz be in the middle o' a lecture then?"

Max leaned in and whispered, "Nice recovery, lad."

Liz ignored Max and Al and turned her attention to the little British mouse. "Nigel, I have already provided an overview of North Island and Winyah Bay. Can you give us the lay of the land from your aerial report, *s'il vous plaît?*"

"I would be utterly delighted," Nigel answered, straightening his golden spectacles. "Right. Now then, behind the beaches are wind-formed sand dunes and ridges. Some of these sand sculptures are quite extraordinary, reaching forty feet high!"

"Fascinating!" Liz answered.

"Behind the sand dunes and ridges are lush forests comprised of pine, cedar, palmetto, and live oak trees that extend back to the vast salt marshes," Nigel continued. "The only way to travel betwixt the mainland and this island is by ferry—or in my case, via *flight.*" He preened his whiskers with a jolly chuckle.

"*Oui,* the first humans here were the Native Americans, who used dug-out cypress canoes to hunt, fish, and explore," Liz added.

"Wish I could go fishin'," Al whimpered under his breath.

Nigel nodded. "Precisely. The Indian tribes had settlements all along this coastline, but then came the first attempt by Europeans to settle here."

"*Oui,* the Spanish, back in 1521," Liz followed. "Lucas Vázquez de Ayllón's men landed here and explored Winyah Bay as a possible site for a new colony. They captured sixty Indians and took them away to Hispaniola as slaves. Ayllón returned in 1526 with a large entourage of six hundred Spanish settlers and slaves from Africa, but their largest ship struck a sandbar and sunk out there in Winyah Bay."

"Served 'em r-r-right," Max growled, staring out to sea.

"When Ayllón was unable to find a suitable spot here to found their colony, he proceeded to sail south, to what is now the Georgia coast, and attempt his colonization there," Nigel relayed. "But disease and starvation not only killed Ayllón but wiped out all but a hundred and fifty of his people within three months. The survivors subsequently sailed back to Hispaniola."

"Sounds like a deadly expedition," gulped Al. "And it started with first steps here on North Island? This be a deadly place."

"There were, of course, others who came here in the sixteenth and seventeenth centuries. More Spanish, English, and French explorers stepped foot here, but none stayed long," Liz explained.

"But the *English* finally settled the town of Georgetown eleven miles from North Island in 1733, betwixt Winyah Bay and the Sampit River," Nigel concluded.

Max and Al looked at one another and stifled their laughter. Al pumped his armpit with his other paw. Liz rolled her eyes.

"But to bring you up to where we are now in the history of this place, Georgetown developed a thriving shipbuilding and trading town," Liz shared, then frowned. "They discovered that rice would be a booming crop grown on the banks of these rivers."

"Aye, r-r-rice gr-r-rown by slave labor," Max growled, now turning serious.

Al welled up. "Seems like this place be gettin' worse all the time! The Spanish captured Indians for slaves, then brought African slaves here. Then the English brought even more o' the poor lads and lasses here."

"We have dealt with humans enslaving humans from the very beginning. Egypt, of course, was the first nation to perfect the practice of slavery and the slave trade," Nigel noted. "Joseph was sold into slavery by his dastardly brothers before the Maker made him the second-highest ruler in Egypt."

Max nodded. "Aye, although Joseph's slavery were turned ta good for the birth of the nation of Israel there in Egypt, there came a pharaoh who didn't r-r-remember Joseph, an' the Jews became slaves for four hundred years. I were glad we got ta help Moses fr-r-ree them all."

"But then came the Baby-onions," Al added sadly. His face started twitching as he thought about those ancient civilizations. "And those Donkey-yrians—they were the worst o' them all!"

"Babylonians, and *Assyrians,"* Nigel corrected Al, stifling his mirth.

"An' them Gr-r-reeks an' R-r-r-omans, too," Max quickly offered, trying to divert Al's thoughts. "Remember when ye got ta wear that R-r-roman armor, Big Al? Ye looked b-r-rave!"

Al wore a goofy grin and sat up tall to wipe back the fur on his head. "Aye, this kitty looked good then."

"Humans in every nation and tongue have been enslaving each other ever since," Liz lamented, furrowing her brow. "There is sadly nothing new under the sun when it comes to slavery, except for the wicked means of transporting those poor humans."

"Indeed, my pet. Every nation has blood on its hands, and now it has sadly even come to this infant nation of America with the African slave trade via the horrific Middle Passage," Nigel added with a shudder. "Great Britain would not allow the colonies to stop the import of slaves to these shores, so when America gains her independence, we shall see if these United States choose to take the first steps of liberty for all."

"I pray so, *mon ami,"* Liz uttered, closing her eyes. "How I hate this evil scourge of slavery!"

"I know you do, little one," came the wise, comforting voice of their team leader, Gillamon. "Which is why I've called you all here."

"Gillamon!" Liz cried, running up to the majestic mountain goat and nudging him affectionately. "I am so happy to see you in your natural form."

The handsome mountain goat leaned his head down low to hug Liz with his white goatee blowing in the sea breeze. "It is a nice change of pace to be myself instead of a human. But it is an honor to serve General Washington as 'Mister Atticus.'" As the leader of the Order of the Seven team, Gillamon was able to assume any shape or form, as was another team member, Clarie the lamb.

"Aye, lad, I like to know it's really ye when I see ye, and not some statue, or scroll, or donkey, or . . . what else have ye been?" Al asked, scratching his head to remember.

Max opened his mouth to say something, but Liz quickly whispered, "Do not say, 'fish', *mon ami,* whatever you do."

"Don't let me interrupt your history lecture, Liz," Gillamon interjected with a knowing smile to change the subject.

"Ah, *oui, oui,* to conclude then," Liz quickly said, "by 1750, North Island became home to harbor pilots who watched approaching ships to guide them across Winyah Bay to Georgetown. Now, a few of the area rice planters have built summer homes here to escape the suffocating heat and risk of malaria from the standing water of the inland marshes."

"Indeed, so now the primary residents of North Island are a few humans, deer, some nesting sea turtles, waterfowl such as pelicans and seagulls, and those of Veritas's kin," Nigel concluded.

"Thanks for the geogr-r-raphy an' histor-r-ry lessons, Liz an' Mousie," Max offered. "It's always best ta know aboot things when ye be on mission somewhere."

Al went up and kissed Liz on the cheek. "I could listen to me Liz talk aboot anythin'."

"Well, I'm sorry *me* lass missed the lecture," Max lamented, scanning the horizon.

"I'm sure that Liz and Nigel can catch her up to speed, Max," Gillamon assured him. "Here she comes now."

There in the distance was a three-masted ship flying the French flag and pushed along by a strong northerly wind. She wasn't a large ship at seventy-three feet long and twenty-five feet wide. But painted on her stern in big, gold letters was her name: *La Victoire*.

"Kate!" exclaimed Max, Liz, Nigel, and Al at the same time.

"She has finally made it safely from Spain!" Liz cheered.

Al wrinkled his brow. "I thought that Lafayette were French. If he's a Spaniard, he better not step foot on *this* island. We all know what happened to that poor Allony lad after *he* did!"

Max rolled his eyes and playfully bonked Al on the head. "Daft kitty. Of course, Lafayette's a Frenchie!"

"*Oui,* Lafayette escaped France to sail to America but stopped in the Spanish port of Los Passajes, where he evaded capture before setting out on the open sea," Liz explained. "That is where I bid Kate *adieu* in April. *Ooh-la-la,* but it has taken roughly eight weeks for them to reach this shore!"

"Looks like they be gettin' r-r-ready ta dr-r-rop their anchor!" Max exclaimed, wagging his tail as he spotted a little white Westie on the bow. "I see her! I see me bonnie Kate!"

"We must not draw attention to ourselves, Max," Gillamon cautioned him. "Lafayette and his men will look for a pilot to guide their ship into Winyah Bay. When they land, I've instructed Kate to join us. The humans will proceed to their mission, and we will proceed to ours. But for now, we must remain out of sight."

The animals watched as some crew members climbed up through the rigging to quickly lower the sails while others released the massive rope holding the ship's anchor, sending it splashing into the calm waters offshore. They could hear the raucous cheering from the crew celebrating the end of their long voyage.

"Good show! It would appear they are now lowering the jolly boat," Nigel observed.

Al grinned broadly. "Hooray, somethin' good finally be happenin' here! A jolly boat sounds like a happy boat."

"A jolly boat, or a yawl, is a small craft that large ships use to transport their crew to shore," Liz explained with a giggle. "But *oui,* I have no doubt those humans are jolly indeed, *cher* Albert."

The friends watched as seven crew members stepped into the jolly boat, followed by Lafayette, Baron De Kalb, and a few other officers. As they began to lower the small boat down the side of the ship with sturdy ropes, Kate took a daring leap from the ship's railing and landed in the small craft.

"Bibi! You should have stayed on board!" Lafayette scolded her.

Ye be goin' on one mission, but I be goin' on another, Kate whimpered, licking Lafayette's hand.

"I'm sure your little dog is longing to run und stretch her legs after being cooped up for nearly two months at sea," De Kalb offered with a grin.

Lafayette smiled. "As are we all, no? Very well, Bibi. You may run, but do not stray once we are on land."

For the next several hours, the crew rowed the jolly boat the full length of North Island, looking for any signs of life. But they only saw one long stretch of white sandy beach with large dunes covered in swaying sea oats. The only living creatures they saw *were* great white pelicans and seagulls diving in the shallows for fish. Eventually, pink ribbons stretched across the fading blue sky as the sun made its descent. A waning moon appeared, as did the faint light of stars above. Not wishing to be lost in dark water at night, and eager to disembark their jolly boat, the crew pressed on until they finally found the inlet at the northern part of North Island. They wrinkled their noses at the pungent smell of low tide with its exposed marsh grass. It was now 10:00 p.m. A single swinging lantern hung from a hook on the bow, casting a ring of light onto the shallow, murky water as they entered the inlet. But it would be midnight before they set foot on solid ground.

A small group of slaves stood barefoot in their dugout canoe, using long wooden oyster tongs to comb the labyrinth of oyster beds as they scraped through thick tidal mud. The croaking frogs and chirping crickets were so loud that they drowned out the distant sound of ocean waves rolling into shore on the other side of the narrow spit of sand. Fireflies as numerous as the stars above blinked on and off, dancing along the cattails and dark green marsh grass. Mosquitoes and sand flies hovered around the shirtless, sweaty men, who wore pants caked with mud. Sweat dripped down their faces as they hummed a low, soulful tune to pass the time.

Two of the men, both with massive muscular arms, raked the bottom of the riverbed. They repeatedly grabbed the open handles of the tongs and plunged them to the muddy river bottom to find oyster clusters. Closing the sharp teeth of the tongs over jagged clumps of the shells, they jerked the tongs back and forth to release the shellfish. They lifted the closed tongs to scoop the oysters into the canoe as two other slaves gathered and sorted them into baskets, carefully handling the razor-sharp shellfish as they broke them apart.

"You see dat?" one man whispered, pointing to a lantern making its way through the marsh.

"It's a li'l boat!" another answered with alarm. "Maybe dem be British spies!"

"We best get away from here!" another suggested.

As the men hurriedly pulled their tongs into the canoe, they suddenly heard the voice of a man with a strange accent, calling to them. "Vhere are ve?"

"Dat ain't no British," one man suggested. "Don't know what he is, but he ain't no Redcoat." He got to his feet and cupped his hand to his mouth, calling back, "Yuh on North Island, near Massa Ugee's place, up a ways dere on de beach!"

De Kalb looked at the others in the jolly boat. "Must be servants of a local plantation owner."

"Bon! Take us over to those men!" Lafayette instructed.

The crew members began to row in the direction of the slaves, but suddenly got stuck in the mud. They weren't going anywhere. Lafayette frowned and stood to his feet. "Then we shall go to *them!*"

Lafayette rocked the jolly boat as he eagerly walked his hands over the shoulders of the crew members and made his way to climb over the side. His boots sank into the wet mud, but that didn't matter to the young Marquis. He had finally set foot onto American soil, and his heart raced with excitement. Emotion caught in his throat, and he boldly declared, "I shall conquer or perish to aid America!"

De Kalb followed Lafayette, and the two men sloshed their way over to the slaves, trying not to sink into the muck and mire of the river bottom.

"Ve have sailed from France to fight on the side of the Americans, und ve need a pilot to guide our ship through the bay," De Kalb translated to the slaves as Lafayette gave a rapid-fire list of explanations and questions to the small group of oystermen. "Vill you please take us to your Master?"

Suddenly they heard dogs barking in the distance, coming from the Huger home. They could see lights appearing in each window. Warning shots rang out along with muffled shouts.

"Mon Dieu, are they are *shooting* at us?!" Lafayette exclaimed, wide-eyed. "They must mistake us for Englishmen—can you imagine!? *S'il vous plaît,* take us to *Monsieur* Huger at once!"

"We can take a couple yuh, but not all," one man explained. "The tide's ebbin' so yuh best put yuh boat back tuh yo ship 'til morn."

"Very well, *allons-y!"* Lafayette exulted, climbing into the muddy canoe filled with baskets of oysters and four very surprised slaves. For the first people to welcome the freedom-fighting Frenchman to America, liberty was just as foreign as was his accent.

Kate realized that this was her chance. As Lafayette and De Kalb left with the slaves who agreed to take them to Major Benjamin Huger's house, she jumped over the side and ran off into the dark night through the muddy marsh.

PART ONE

A Wretch Like Me

(John Newton 1725–1745)

1

Prepare to Be Amazed

THE WAR ROOM

Soft candlelight flickered from two brass wall sconces hung on either side of a dark, empty panel. A long hardwood table ran the length of the mysterious room used by the Order of the Seven for secret team meetings, research, strategic planning, and communications. Gillamon had created this War Room at the beginning of the team's mission to help the humans with the American Revolution.

For eons, Gillamon had summoned the team to receive their mission assignments in a cylindrical portal soaring seventy stories high. Named for how the Maker views time—past, present, and future, all occurring at once—the IAMISPHERE was filled with rushing wind and moving panels of time. There the animals could not only view but also visit moments in history to learn or relive key scenes that held some bearing on their current or future missions. But the darkened panels of future time were viewable to the Maker alone. While the Maker gave Gillamon occasional glimpses of the future to help guide the team, the wise mountain goat was kept from knowing everything. This team of hand-picked animals had to operate on faith as they served the Maker, just as did the humans to whom they were assigned.

No mortal creatures were allowed inside the IAMISPHERE, with the rare exception of creatures needing emergency transport from one geographic location to another. This surreal portal could access not only moments in time, but places on Earth. Liz once transported a young bald eagle named Cato from London to Virginia in the mission to help young Patrick Henry find his voice.

When on mission to inspire George F. Handel to write his masterpiece *Messiah,* the Order of the Seven had used the IAMISPHERE to revisit the life, death, and resurrection of Jesus. This hallowed portal served the team in monumental ways.

But the team needed a place to serve as a practical gathering hub to obtain resources such as maps, books, spy gadgets, or any items Gillamon deemed necessary for their assignments. So, the War Room became the place where the animals could come and go, leave messages for one another, and of course receive important instructions from Gillamon. And on the wall of this room hung a single panel of time.

Nigel and Liz sat atop the table, poring over some recent intelligence missives sent by General Washington's aide-de-camp. The little British mouse adjusted his gold-rimmed spectacles and shook his head with a frown.

"This simply will *not* do. Washington needs a sophisticated network of informants to pass along secret intelligence," Nigel observed.

"Oui," Liz agreed, "and a fresh cipher to send messages in code."

"I'd like some fresh cider," Al whined. "This kitty's thirsty."

Max wrinkled his brow. "Daft kitty. CIPHER, not cider. Ye sure be a str-r-range cat. I thought ye liked milk, not that sweet apple-y stuff."

"Oh aye, I love milk, too! Do ye have some?" Al asked hopefully.

"Here you go, Al," Gillamon offered, pouring water from a flask into a pewter bowl that sat on the table. The mountain goat was in his human form of Mr. Atticus. He slid the bowl over to Al with a grin.

"Thank ye, Gillamon!" Al exclaimed happily. "Do ye have anythin' to eat?"

"This ain't a tavern, lad," Max scolded the hungry cat. "An' Gillamon ain't yer server!"

"Cher Albert, Gillamon said his briefing will begin when the others arrive, and will not take long," Liz offered. "I am sure you can wait a while longer to eat."

"Hear, hear! Buck up, old boy!" Nigel encouraged, patting his stomach. "You may find that water quenches not only your *thirst* but your hunger as well, for hunger often presents as thirst in disguise."

Al wrinkled his forehead. "Then ye better add water to yer secret spy stuff, if it's such a good disguise."

Liz and Nigel looked at one another with raised eyebrows.

"Why Albert, what a brilliant idea!" Liz exclaimed with a kiss to Al's fluffy cheek, causing him to break into a wide grin.

Just then they heard footsteps and turned to see their lamb friend Clarie walk toward the table and set down in a chair a blindfolded young Scottish terrier named Jock. Clarie was in the human form of an eighteenth-century seamstress. She wore a simple burgundy skirt, cream-colored blouse, and black shoes. On her head was a white mop cap and around her neck was an intricate lace collar. Tied around her waist was a striped apron with numerous pockets holding scissors, needles, thread, and scraps of lace.

Max broke into a broad smile. "Gr-r-reetin's, me gr-r-randlad! I didn't know ye'd be here."

"I didn't either, grandsire!" Jock answered from under the cloth covering his eyes. While Jock was allowed to visit the War Room, because he was not one of the Order of the Seven team members, he could not witness the means of reaching this secret room. But Jock had been given the ability to affect weather and served the team on their current mission of securing American independence. Weather miracles were vital for the patriot cause, and weather dog Jock Frost Knox provided them while faithfully attending to his human, General Henry Knox.

"I wanted Jock present to hear our updates as well as to witness some important history," Gillamon explained, pulling the cloth from the young Scottie's eyes. "Even *weather* history has a way of repeating itself." He leaned over and tapped the young Scottie on the nose. "Plus, I thought it high time that you meet your grandmum. She'll be here any minute."

"Me grandmum Kate?" Jock exulted, wide-eyed. "Finally! I can't wait!"

Liz cupped Jock's chin with her dainty paw and smiled. "And she cannot wait to meet you, *cher* Jock."

"It took a while, but *La Victoire* finally made it across the Atlantic," Clarie piped up. "Lafayette's horse Vercengetorix is ready to stampede off that ship."

"Oui, I am certain that Lafayette's white 'sea horse' could gallop all the way to Philadelphia if let loose," Liz agreed with a giggle. The curious cat then paused and studied the shape-shifting lamb. "Clarie, you sound as if you were on board, but you look nothing like a French sailor, *mon amie."*

"Maybe I was on board," Clarie answered with a wink as she tickled Liz's ear. "Or maybe I was swimming alongside. But now I'm dressed for our mission in Olney, England."

"Ye jest never know with ye two changin' beasties!" Max exclaimed. "Tell us aboot yer mission, lass."

"Oui, but I do hope you will help our anxious Vercingetorix off of Lafayette's ship," Liz opined.

"First things first," Gillamon interjected. "Vercengetorix will get to stretch his legs after we've explained everything to you here today."

"I sure hope this meetin' don't last long, for all our sakes," Al whispered to Liz, his stomach growling.

"Have I missed anythin'?" came Kate's sweet Scottish voice. She instantly spotted Jock, and her eyes brimmed with happy tears. "Oh, this be a happy day! I don't have ta miss seein' me grandlad anymore."

"Grandmum!" Jock exclaimed, jumping down from the chair and running over to nuzzle Kate's head. "I thought we'd never meet, with you in France and me here. We're all so scattered with our assignments that we keep missing each other. But not today—I'm so happy, I could make a rainbow!"

Kate closed her eyes and embraced the young Scottie. "Aye, dear lad. Our work for the Maker be so important that bein' separated from each other happens from time ta time. We not only miss seein' each other but seein' all that each other's been doin' while we were apart."

"Which is why I've called you all to this meeting today," Gillamon told them, sharing a smile with Clarie. "For the past fifty years, you have been spread out across the globe on your various mission assignments, as was Nigel inspiring Handel's *Messiah* and assisting Benjamin Franklin with his kite experiment."

The little mouse humbly bowed with his paw draped across his chest. "It was my supreme honor to wield both violin and key for the cause of humanity."

Liz applauded. "Bravo, *cher* Nigel!"

Gillamon pointed to Liz. "And as with you, Liz, helping Patrick Henry to find his voice, which rallied this infant nation of America to pursue independence."

"An' don't forget how she an' Mousie helped wr-r-rite that Declar-r-ration ta go along with it," Max added.

Liz smiled shyly and batted her eyes. *"Merci,* it was such an honor to serve *Messieurs* Henry and Jefferson."

Gillamon nodded. "And while Liz and Nigel assisted both the Voice and the Pen of the Revolution, Max and Jock have served valiantly to protect the *Sword* of the Revolution, General George Washington."

Max trotted over and wrapped his burly paw around Jock. "Aye! The Br-r-ruce Boys be at the r-r-ready with br-r-rawn an' blusters."

Al's ears flattened. He was assigned to the British. "Seems I always end up on the opposite side o' things."

"But at least King George an' his r-r-redcoats feed ye well while ye're gatherin' all that intelligence under their noses, Big Al," Max added with a grin.

Al patted his belly, which rumbled at the thought. "True, true. This kitty be grateful for that."

"And Kate has faithfully watched over our ambitious young Marquis de Lafayette and the French connections who are lending aid to the patriot cause," Gillamon continued.

"But you and Clarie pop in and out all over the place," Jock noted.

Nigel nodded. "Indeed, I do wonder where you two are the rest of the time."

"Yes, Clarie and I have been elusive over the decades despite helping each of you with your respective assignments," Gillamon admitted. "Thus, we will now bring you up to speed on a crucial mission that we have been working on these past fifty years."

Liz's eyes brightened with anticipation. *"C'est bon!* Do tell us, *s'il vous plaît!"*

Gillamon reached out his hand to tap the dark panel of time. "I want you to become acquainted with a human whom the Maker has purposed to change the entire world for good."

The scene of a large ship anchored off the Ivory Coast came into view on the panel. A jolly boat rowed toward the larger vessel carrying several frightened, shackled prisoners. Up on the ship's deck a group of sailors made ready to receive them, laughing and pointing at the captured African slaves as they were hoisted up to their doom. One sailor in particular burst out into a bawdy chorus as the slaves were pushed into the crowded barricado or secured enclosure, on deck. He used such blasphemous profanity that even the other sailors looked shocked.

Kate covered Jock's ears with her paws, growling at the ghastly human.

"That is a *slave* ship!" Nigel fumed. "Those poor souls are heading to their horrific fate whilst that wretched sailor sings some salty shanty! This is intolerable!"

"I feel sad-sick," Al cried, covering his eyes. "And I lost me appetite."

"Why show us this, Gillamon?" Liz asked, frowning. "Who *is* that foul wretch?"

Gillamon shared a knowing look with Clarie. "That *wretch* is a man by the name of John Newton. This is a scene from his past."

"Well, I can't imagine that pathetic monster havin' much of a future," Max growled with clenched teeth. "I'd like ta bite his buttocks an' r-r-rip his br-r-reeches ta pieces!"

"Oh, his past got *much* worse," Clarie added with a knowing grin. "But you must see how his life unfolded every step of the way to understand the impact of his future."

Liz wrinkled her brow. "But you cannot possibly mean that this John Newton is the one that the Maker has called to change the entire world for good . . . can you?"

"Right!" Nigel protested with a paw raised to the panel. "How could the Maker use *him?*"

"You'll see . . . in time," Gillamon answered with that familiar twinkle in his blue eyes. "Nigel, your experience with music and Liz, your flair for the written word will come into play as never before for humans." He turned and pressed his hands onto the wooden table, locking eyes with each member of the team. "You all should know by now that the Maker's ways are not our ways. And He calls the most unlikely humans to greatness for His purposes."

Liz and Nigel shared a convicted glance.

"Didn't Saul become Paul?" Al asked, daring to peek out from behind his paws.

"Aye, the lad were a wr-r-retch of a Chr-r-ristian-killer before he changed," Max growled. "He said he were the best sinner there ever were."

Nigel crossed his tiny arms over his chest as he watched John Newton shove a slave down into the hold of the slave ship. "Indeed, but that was before *this* vulgar human came along into history."

"How can John Newton change the entire world for good, unless he changes for good, too?" Jock wanted to know.

"Exactly," Gillamon answered with a wink, standing upright and reaching over to swipe the panel to reveal another scene of 1732 east London on the north bank of the Thames River. "Prepare to be amazed."

Nigel's eyes widened as he saw a bustling English wharf packed with seamen delivering cargo from countless merchant ships anchored in the middle of the Thames. Watermen in small boats taxied passengers back and forth across the river. Just up the bend stood the Tower of London, its proud White Tower, built by William the Conqueror, catching the sun's rays. The Old London Bridge was visible a little farther beyond that point on the river. "I say, that's Wapping, one of the busiest wharves on the Thames. We've been there many times!"

"Aye, Al likes ta go there at low tide ta see if any fish be floppin' aboot in the marshes," Max recalled. "All sorts of sea beasties live there—fish, eels, sea horsies, an' even harbor seals lyin' on the shore sunnin' themselves."

Al wore a goofy grin. "So, if ye be a fast fisher-kitty, ye can grab a slow fish if the tide catches it off guard."

"But if ye be a *slow* fisher-kitty, one of them harbor seals might tr-r-ry ta catch ye, ain't that so, Big Al?" Max joked. Al's ears flattened at the unpleasant memory.

"I thought London was inland, but that looks like an oceanside city," Jock noted, watching the harbor full of ships.

"Oui, London is inland, but for ninety-five miles, the Thames River snakes through England as a tidal estuary that empties into the North Sea. Twice daily, the Thames transforms from a slow-moving river with marshes to a 'mini sea' as the North Sea surges inland," Liz explained. "The moon can change the river's height by over twenty feet in six hours!"

"Right, and the tides are strongest just there near the Old London Bridge, which is the only crossing point on the Thames," Nigel explained. "It is also one of the most *dreadful* parts of London, what with pirates, smugglers, and the lowest dregs of society lurking among the honest merchantmen."

Jock sat up excitedly. "Pirates? I've always wanted to see one!"

"I'd rather ye not see one like this," Kate cautioned, frowning as a terrible scene came into view. Down by the waterfront was a green, muck-covered wooden gallows with a dead pirate hanging from a short noose at the low tide mark.

"All seafaring criminals who are caught and sentenced by the Admiralty Courts are brought here to Execution Dock," Gillamon explained. "They might have committed mutiny on the high seas and were brought back to London, or they might have been caught at night stealing cargo from one of the anchored ships right here on the Thames. But they all must walk down those Wapping Old Stairs to the river and meet their fate at the gallows, on which they are hanged."

"The short noose is designed to prevent them from perishing immediately from a broken neck, as traditional gallows afford," Nigel reported gravely. "The wretched criminals suffer slow asphyxiation whilst the rising waters of the Thames claim them."

"Aye, an' their bodies have ta be left hangin' until thr-r-ree tides wash over them," Max added. He wrinkled his nose. "They can get r-r-real stinky after a day."

Liz winced and turned her gaze from the grotesque scene. "But the most notorious criminals are tarred and gibbeted in cages for months or years to serve as a warning for seafarers to think twice before committing crimes.

Captain Kidd was the most infamous privateer-turned-pirate to suffer this fate back in 1701."

"Do we have ta show this ta the wee lad?" Kate protested. "Max, I'd rather Jock not see these things."

Max frowned. "I know it be a br-r-rutal scene, but it also be the r-r-reality of wha' happens ta bad lads. I think Jock needs ta know aboot these things."

"Actually, this is the identical argument that the parents of John Newton had on this day," Clarie added, pointing to the scene unfolding before them. "It didn't seem important at the time, but you had a brief encounter with John Newton as a small boy. Look."

A blond little boy followed a burly seaman carrying a sea chest on his broad shoulders down a cobblestone avenue. They were heading toward the Wapping Stairs to reach the banks of the Thames. Suddenly, Max and Kate went trotting down the street and the little boy stopped to pet them. He squatted down and giggled. "Hello, puppies!" Max and Kate wagged their tails and licked his hand.

"JOHN! Come!" Captain John Newton bellowed. "I will *not* have you dawdle with dogs." As Captain Newton descended the slick, greenstone steps, coming up the steps bounded Al and Liz from the narrow low-tide beach below.

A look of fear gripped the boy's face. "Yes, Father, sir!" he answered, before spotting Liz and Al next to Max and Kate. "Hello, kitties! You must all be friends," the boy whispered with a giggle. He quickly ran a hand along Liz's sleek fur without missing a step, so as not to upset his father. He hurried along to catch up with the man.

"I do not recall this brush with destiny," Liz marveled.

"I were preoccupied," Al noted, watching himself flick mud from his back paws onto Nigel, who hid in the shadows of the alley leading to the Wapping Stairs.

Nigel proceeded to wipe off his spectacles. "This scenario of Al besmirching my spectacles has recurred so often throughout the millennia that I also cannot recall this exact moment in time."

"After this encounter, you soon proceeded on to your mission in Mayfair and Hyde Park, helping Handel to write *Messiah.* Meanwhile, Clarie and I were here on the John Newton mission in Wapping," Gillamon explained.

"Ye mean, ye were workin' on mission for the Maker jest *five* miles away from us?" Max marveled.

"Extraordinary!" Nigel exclaimed. "I say, did 'Mister Gillamon' and 'Lady Clarie' *also* encounter young John Newton whilst in London?"

Liz wore a sad expression after seeing her momentary brush with young John Newton. She watched the little boy climb into a boat to be rowed out to Captain John Newton's merchant ship. "Look how sweet and innocent he was then. What happened to him?"

"You will see, but we must start at the beginning," Gillamon told them, "for what goes into the first of life goes throughout all of life."

2

WHAT GOES INTO THE FIRST OF LIFE

WAPPING, ENGLAND, 1732

"Sir, I must insist that you *not* expose young John to such scenes," Elizabeth Newton admonished her husband. She stood there in the cobblestone street, gripping the little boy's hand as he cowered behind her skirts. "I know you wish for him to follow in your footsteps as a sea merchant, but my hope for his future lies with the church as a minister. I simply cannot bear the thought of him singing bawdy sailor shanties and living amongst the world of thieving, murderous pirates who end their miserable lives with a *short drop* and a *sudden stop*."

Captain John Newton narrowed his eyes at her gruesome reference to hanging. He knew that his wife hated him bringing John down to the wharf where he could see Execution Dock. "What better way to encourage the boy to choose a virtuous path than by showing him what happens to thieving, murderous pirates? And the Holy Writ speaks of my profession in the Psalms. What does it say, boy?"

John stood erect and obediently quoted the passage he had memorized from Psalm 107. "*Others went out on the sea in ships; they were merchants on the mighty waters.*"

The well-traveled, well-educated Captain Newton lifted a hand. "There you have it. The Spanish Jesuits schooled me with strict discipline and hard work at an early age, so I *will* show the young boy how to load and prepare a ship for a long voyage as I've done today. I take care to shield the lad, but if he happens to see a dead pirate or hear a sailor curse, it will not be his ruin."

Elizabeth let go an exasperated breath, knowing she needed to respectfully heed her stoic husband's directive. He was as severe in the discipline of his family as he was of the sailors under his command at sea. John was terrified of him. Captain Newton did not laugh, nor did he exhibit affection. He was a cold, distant father, and John knew that his mother was relieved when Captain Newton sailed to ply his trade in the Mediterranean for months on end, as he was about to do on this day.

"Well, we shall bid you farewell and make our way to church," Elizabeth told her husband. "Godspeed and I pray you have a safe and successful voyage. Tell your father good-bye, John."

Captain Newton looked at his wife. "You may refuse to attend our state Church of England and take the lad to hear your Dissenters, but as to his future, that will be between him and God." He looked down at John and held out his hand. "I keep my religion private, just between me and God. It's easier that way."

John shook his father's hand. "Good-bye, sir."

With that, Captain Newton gave a singular nod to his small family, turned, and headed back to descend the stone Wapping Stairs that led to his awaiting ship on the Thames.

Elizabeth leaned over and cupped John's chin in her dainty hand. "There, there, John, I know your father can be stern, but always remember that he loves you. He just has a difficult time showing it. Now then, when he returns from sea, he'll be proud to hear the new Scripture verses you've learned. Come, we mustn't be late. Doctor Watts will be there today!"

John's chin trembled and he choked back his tears as he looked over his shoulder to see his father walking away. He was sad that his father was sailing off, for they never knew when (or if) they'd ever see him again. It could be months or not at all if a storm, fatal illness, or accident struck while at sea. He held onto his mother's hand as they walked the few blocks to the Dissenting Chapel in Wapping. Dissenters were Protestants who did not conform to the official Church of England, but who chose to worship freely as they saw fit. John was also sad that his parents disagreed and argued. It confused him to hear their differing views on God, life, and worship. His father was a strict Anglican, but John never liked attending their austere, stuffy services that felt as cold as the marble statues lining the front of the ornate sanctuary. There, the people sang one slow, monotone psalm after another; but his mother's church was different. There the people sang songs with joy and feeling. Their hymns were full of meaning and spoke to the young boy's heart. As far as his future was concerned, the six-year-old boy's thoughts didn't extend much beyond the next hour ahead.

DISSENTING CHAPEL, RADCLIFFE SQUARE, WAPPING, ENGLAND

"When I survey the wondrous cross
Where the young Prince of Glory died,
My richest gain I count but loss,
And pour contempt on all my pride,"

John sang as his small finger traced the words printed in the hymn book. His mother had taught him to read by the age of three, and he voraciously read everything he could get his hands on. He liked studying the words and how they were put together on the page.

John looked up to see the small frame of Dr. Isaac Watts directing the music from the pulpit, his arms joyfully swaying in the air. Their Scottish pastor, Dr. David Jennings, was good friends with Watts, whose chapel was only a mile away. Watts came here on occasion to preach and lead music, and John was always enthralled. The sermons might be over his head, but the music always touched his heart.

"Forbid it, Lord, that I should boast,
Save in the death of Christ my God!
All the vain things that charm me most,
I sacrifice them to His blood."

Watts was a revolutionary Dissenter and a nonconformist. He therefore wasn't allowed to attend Oxford or Cambridge, which only accepted Anglican students. He attended a Dissenter school instead and went on to write about logic, philosophy, and science. His passion was in education and teaching, but his poor health limited his abilities as a full-time preacher. So, he poured his passion into changing how music was used for worship. Singing the Psalms began with ancient Israel and David writing words to set to traditional music of the day, but Watts introduced poetry into the lyrics to make the songs relate to the Christian experience. He wanted the people to better understand what they were singing. He had written hundreds of hymns, but this was Elizabeth's favorite. *Singing hymns here feels freer than father's church music—here, it's kind of like sailors singing happy shanties, only with good words,* John realized with a smile.

"See from His head, His hands, His feet,
Sorrow and love flow mingled down!
Did e'er such love and sorrow meet,
Or thorns compose so rich a crown?"

Images filled the young boy's mind as he sang those words. *Jesus was killed and put on public display like that pirate down at Execution Dock,* he thought. *But Jesus was innocent. And He did it . . . out of love?*

Elizabeth's slender arm was draped around John. She squeezed his shoulder as they sang together. John turned to see that she was visibly moved by the words she softly sang, tears welling in her eyes. She was raised as a devout Christian and sought to instill a strong faith in her only son. Elizabeth helped John to memorize verses and full chapters of Scripture, as well as hymns and poems. John had such a keen memory that he seldom forgot what he read. He could even recite parts of sermons he heard. Even though she was only twenty-seven years of age, Elizabeth's health was poor, so she gave her full attention to John's education. In addition to his Christian training and reading, she taught him Latin and mathematics. Being the well-educated daughter of an East London man who made mathematical instruments, she had a way of making learning fun. While other children played outside, John was happier simply being in his mother's company. The boy loved to learn, and the investment his mother made in him ran deep into his heart and mind.

"Were the whole realm of nature mine,
That were a present far too small;
Love so amazing, so divine,
Demands my soul, my life, my all."

"Thank ye, Doctor Watts," Dr. Jennings responded with a smile in his thick Scottish brogue. "It's always a joy ta have ye lead us in worship. Please all, have a seat as we prepare our hearts ta hear from God's Word. Let us now turn ta our first text for today, which is the eighteenth Psalm, followed by the first chapter of Jonah."

John looked around as they took their seats in the simple pews. He noticed an elegantly dressed man sitting in the next pew over. The man had a kind smile and gave him an affirming nod as they took their seats. John noticed that he rested his hands on a beautifully carved maple walking stick with a fish carved for the handle. He stared at the stick and couldn't wait to get a closer look at it after service. Elizabeth opened her Bible and tapped the

Scripture passage to turn John's attention back to the sermon as Dr. Jennings read aloud:

He drew me out of many waters.
He delivered me from my strong enemy,
From those who hated me,
For they were too strong for me.
They confronted me in the day of my calamity,
But the Lord was my support.
He also brought me out into a broad place;
He delivered me because He delighted in me.

Gillamon looked across the table in the War Room to see if Al was awake. The plump cat had nodded off before the sermon—which is exactly what he had hoped, given the subject matter. He had been prepared to halt the viewing of the scene at any moment, should the need arise. He grinned and turned his attention back to the screen to which the other animals were glued.

"Why good morning, Mrs. Newton and young master John!" Dr. Jennings greeted them as everyone exited the chapel.

"Thank you for your wonderful sermon, Doctor Jennings," Elizabeth told him, her arm around John. "Jonah is one of our favorite Bible stories. And thank you, Doctor Watts, for your beautiful hymns. Your words never cease to fill our hearts with joy."

"'Joy to the World' is *my* favorite!" John exclaimed. "Sir, when did you first start writing?"

Dr. Watts clasped his hands in front of himself and humbly bowed his head with a smile. He lowered his gaze to John. "When I was not much older than you, John, I enjoyed making up rhymes. One day at church, when asked why I had my eyes opened during prayers, I answered, 'A little mouse for want of stairs ran up a rope to say its prayers.' So, the good Lord gifted me with a love for putting words together as a young boy."

John smiled and screwed up his mouth. "Seems to me that whoever caught you with your eyes open during prayers had theirs open, too."

As the adults laughed and continued to exchange pleasantries, John looked around his mother's skirts to spy the interesting cane belonging to the well-dressed gentleman standing behind them. He had a book tucked under his arm and smiled, his blue eyes exuding warmth.

"My dear Mister Gillamon, what a surprise to see you here!" Dr. Watts exclaimed, taking the gentleman's hand in his to shake it warmly. "What brings you here today?"

"Good day, Doctor Watts. I heard you would be the guest hymnody leader today, and I just so happened to have recently read your new book. Might I trouble you for an inscription?"

"Why, of course, of course! I'm honored, kind sir!" Watts exclaimed with a hand over his heart. He turned to Dr. Jennings as he took the book in hand. "Allow me to introduce my longtime friend, Mister Gillamon."

"A pleasure to have you join us today, Mister Gillamon. And allow me to introduce Mrs. Elizabeth Newton and her fine son, John," Jennings said, shaking his hand.

"I also enjoyed your sermon, and I happened to overhear that you like the story of Jonah," Mr. Gillamon told John, smiling and leaning over to balance his hands on his cane. "It's one of my favorites as well."

"Is that why you have a fish carved on your stick?" John asked.

Mr. Gillamon chuckled. "Indeed! Can you read what I have carved along the side, just there?" He held up the cane for John to study it.

"*When I had lost all hope, I turned my thoughts once more to the Lord.* Jonah 2:7," John read, running his finger along the carved passage. He smiled, studying the carved fish on the handle.

"How would you like for me to inscribe the book, Mr. Gillamon?" Dr. Watts asked.

Mr. Gillamon pursed his lips and tilted his head as he studied the young boy. "Tell me, young master John. Do you like to read?"

"Yes, sir! I read all the time," John answered expectantly.

"Very well. Doctor Watts, please inscribe the book for Master John, if you'd be so kind," Mr. Gillamon told him. "I especially enjoyed the section on Jonah, so I know he will as well."

"What generosity, Mister Gillamon! Thank you!" Elizabeth exclaimed. "What is the book?"

"*A Short View of the Whole of Scripture History*," Dr. Watts answered. "I wrote it to help young persons learn the truths of the Bible with a question-and-answer format."

John's eyes lit up with excitement and he bounced on his toes. "Thank you, Mister Gillamon!"

"There you are, Master John," Dr. Watts told the boy, handing him the book. His eyes danced with excitement to hold a book signed by the author himself.

"You are most welcome," Mr. Gillamon answered, putting a hand on John's shoulder. "I believe children should always be taught in ways that they can best understand God's Word. I pray you will never forget the lessons that Jonah teaches."

"I won't, Mister Gillamon. But I hope I won't get swallowed by a great fish," John answered.

Mr. Gillamon chuckled. "Well, if you are, know that you are loved, and you are able."

Weeks passed, and John devoured Dr. Watts' book, memorizing the answers to many of the questions, especially those from Jonah. Elizabeth was grateful for the book, not only because it taught so many wonderful lessons, but also because it kept John occupied when she was too ill to attend to his lessons. Her glistening red cheeks, coughing spasms, and sudden weight loss confirmed her worst fears. She had contracted tuberculosis, for which there was no cure. She was encouraged to go stay with her distant cousin and best friend Elizabeth Churchill Catlett, in Kent, to benefit from the sea air. Dr. Jennings had helped Elizabeth make arrangements for John to stay with an older couple from their church who lived nearby. This would be their last night in the house together before Elizabeth rode away in the carriage to Kent tomorrow.

John hopped into bed and pulled the covers up. Elizabeth began coughing and pulled a handkerchief from her pocket. John could see the blood as she wiped it from her mouth. "Mother, I'm scared to lose you."

"And what verse from Psalm 56 do we use when we're fearful?" Elizabeth asked, tucking the covers under John's chin.

"*Whenever I am afraid, I will trust in You,*" John answered softly. A tear rolled down his cheek.

"That's right, dear one," Elizabeth told her son softly. She wiped his face and smiled sadly.

"Why can't I come with you?" John asked tearfully.

"Please trust that you'll be well taken care of while I'm gone." Elizabeth swallowed the lump in her throat to put on a brave face for her little boy. She didn't want him to watch her decline and be traumatized by her possible death.

"Will you be back for my seventh birthday in July?" John asked hopefully.

"I hope so," Elizabeth offered with a burdened smile. She patted his chest and swallowed hard. "But if not, remember to never put your happiness in people or things you can lose—only in the One who has promised to never leave you nor forsake you."

WAPPING WHARF, ENGLAND, 1733

Captain Newton hefted the sea chest to his shoulders before climbing the slick green Wapping Stairs, casting a glance at Execution Dock to see if any pirates had been hanged lately. A seagull landed on top of the waterside gallows that stood there with an empty noose swaying in the breeze. *At least things have been quiet here of late,* he thought. After nearly a year at sea, he was eager to get home to his own bed but already anticipated how he'd sway with his eyes closed, the rhythm of the sea following him home. He wended his way through Wapping from block to block, exhausted but glad to be back. He walked up the steps to his house and jiggled the handle, finding it securely locked. He frowned and set his sea chest down when he saw the faded black ribbon draped over the front door.

"No tears, boy," Captain Newton brusquely told John, who appropriately wore a black mourning coat and breeches. The seven-year-old trailed behind his father from the neighbor's house where he had stayed since his mother left. Elizabeth never made it home, dying two weeks shy of John's seventh birthday. He struggled to fight back the renewed tears of grief over his mother, mixed with tears of joy at his father's return, mixed with tears at his father's cold reaction to the news that Elizabeth was dead. Not to mention the fact that there was no physical embrace of sympathy to comfort him, which a loving father should provide.

"Yes, sir," John answered with a broken voice as he followed his father into their cold, empty house.

THE WAR ROOM

Liz wiped the tears from her eyes. "Now I see what happened to that sweet little boy."

Kate sniffed. "Aye, the wee lad lost his mum, an' all the while his father were at sea."

"An' then his father were as cold as ice ta the lad aboot it all," Max growled, feeling sympathy for young John Newton.

"Sadly, this was only the beginning of John's woes," Clarie told them as Gillamon reached out to reveal another scene.

MARSHFOOT HOUSE, AVELEY, ENGLAND, 1733

"Shoo! Go outside and play with the other children. I'm too busy to attend to you," Thomasin scolded John, who simply wanted to stay in the kitchen as she made bread. She placed a weary hand on her stomach, nauseated by her pregnancy.

"Do as your mother says, boy," Captain Newton called from the other room as he pored over maps to chart the course for his next sea trading voyage.

"Yes, sir," John answered with a lowered head. He quietly slipped out the door of this house where they now lived in the Essex countryside, fifteen miles east of Wapping.

"She's *not* my mother," John angrily murmured through gritted teeth. He kicked a rock on the path leading to the town, looking back at this grand farmhouse belonging to his stepmother's father, who was a wealthy grazier of Italian descent. Captain Newton wasted no time in marrying again following his return home, and decided to move the family here so they could be looked after while he was at sea. Soon John would have a stepbrother or sister who would no doubt consume every bit of time and attention from Captain and the new Mrs. John Newton. *And this will never be my home.*

John meandered down the street and caught sight of two boys crouched behind a split-rail fence, whispering. He recognized them from when they walked to the parish church on Sundays. These boys never darkened the doors of the church, but were always laughing and running down the street unattended.

"I dare you to take one, Billy," the boy named Edward teased, nudging his friend. "Come on, the old man won't even know it's gone."

Billy heard John walking up behind them and motioned for him to squat down so they all wouldn't be seen. "Ye're the new boy who lives in the Italian's house, aren't ye?"

John nodded and squatted next to them as instructed. "Yes, we just moved here from Wapping. I'm John."

"Pleased to meet ye, John. I'm Billy, and this here is Edward," Billy said, shaking his hand.

John smiled and brightened to be instantly welcomed by the neighborhood kids. "What are you doing?"

"Stealing pumpkins," Edward explained with a laugh.

John wrinkled his brow. "Stealing isn't right."

Billy blew a raspberry. "But it sure is fun! Wait here."

John and Edward stayed behind the fence while Billy quickly darted from tree to tree over to the patch of young pumpkins. He crept out and ran over to rip one of the squashes from the vine and ran back to climb through the fence. Together, the three boys ran off, laughing as they smashed the pumpkin in the street.

THE WAR ROOM

Nigel crossed his arms over his chest and frowned. "You need not show us any further shenanigans with this trio of boys, Gillamon. I can already surmise that young John Newton falls prey to their negligent, irreligious behavior, quickly forgetting his mother's instructions for godly conduct and common decency."

"And they act like bad lads, too," Al added sadly.

Gillamon nodded and turned to face the animals. "John was left to roam the streets unattended with bad company, and quickly became the unloved stepson. His parents sent him off to boarding school from eight to ten years old."

"The poor dear!" Kate lamented.

"It was terrible!" Clarie told them. "John's schoolmaster was such a cruel tyrant that he almost broke John's spirit and enthusiasm for books. He not only derided him constantly, but he beat the boy with a rod. John even forgot the most basic principles and rules of arithmetic that his mother had taught him. If it hadn't been for Gillamon stepping in as his new teacher during his second year, I fear what would have happened to him."

"C'est tragique! How terrible for young John!" Liz cried. "What did you do, Gillamon? Were you 'Mister Gillamon?'"

"No, I took on the common identity of a country teacher. I simply treated John with kindness and patience and steered him to his penchant for Latin that his mother had already given him," Gillamon explained. "He quicky excelled, and became the top of his class, reading Virgil with perfection."

Nigel clasped his paws behind his back. "I'm most pleased to hear it."

"But sadly, I may have pushed him forward too quickly," Gillamon followed. "Because John's grounding was so unstable, he would soon lose all he learned as the next phase of his life arrived."

Al covered his eyes. "Do it get worse? I'm not sure I wanna watch."

"I take it the lad jest became a hoodlum with those bad laddies in the neighborhood," Max grumbled.

"Not full time, at least," Gillamon answered. "At age ten, Captain Newton decided that John's schooling was over, and decided it was time to take him to sea. On his eleventh birthday, John stepped aboard for what would be his first voyage to Spain. He took five voyages with his father over the following six years."

"So, I presume that instead of the path to enter ministry as his mother had wished, Captain Newton's desired course for John unfolded," Liz surmised with a furrowed brow.

"It would appear so," Clarie agreed. "Although Captain Newton was careful to protect John's morals among the crew while aboard, he worked the boy very hard. His stern, distant treatment only discouraged and intimidated the boy."

"'Tis a tragedy for all that hard work his mum poured inta him ta go ta waste," Kate observed, shaking her head. "Seems like his beliefs didn't hold fast then."

Gillamon nodded. "Even the best education may fall short of affecting the heart. Although children may stray from their upbringing in the faith, those truths instilled in them at a young age will return to their minds again and again. When the Maker finally opens their eyes, they will return to bless the prodigal."

"What goes into the first of life, goes throughout all of life, no?" Liz reminded the others hopefully.

"*Train up a child in the way he should go, and when he is* old, *he shall not depart from it*," Nigel quoted from Proverbs.

Max frowned, expecting the worst. "Aye, but for John Newton's in-between years, ye best batten down the hatches."

3

MISSING THE BOAT

AVELEY, ENGLAND, 1737

"What shall we do with a drunken sailor,
What shall we do with a drunken sailor,
What shall we do with a drunken sailor,
Ear-ly in the morning?
Put him in the bilge and make him drink it!
Put him in the bilge and make him drink it!
Put him in the bilge and make him drink it!
Ear-ly in the morning!"

John Newton sang at the top of his lungs, holding a hand to his brown leather three-cornered hat as he threw back his head. He had just returned from a voyage with his father and happily walked down the country lane to meet up with his friends.

"Welcome back, Johnny! What're ye singing?" Billy asked, running up to join him.

"Thanks, Billy! Just a sailor's shanty," John proudly answered, continuing to hum.

"Why do sailors like to sing shanties anyway?" Billy asked, never having been to sea.

John curled up his arm with a balled fist and pointed to his bicep. "See this? Muscles are what make ships *move,* and shanties are songs that help a ship's crew do its work. A shantyman leads the song with a call, and the crew sings back a chorus. The rhythm of the song helps the sailors with a pace as they do things like haul the halyards to raise the topsail, raise the anchor by walking around the capstan, or even while they swab the deck. But shanties are *only* sung for work. Sea songs are what sailors sing when they're off work and enjoying a dram in the forecastle." The young boy was proud of his vast, worldly experience, even though his father did not allow him to mingle with the crew in the forecastle. "Sea songs can be whatever the men want them to be."

"So, ye're a regular old salt now, hey?" Billy asked as the boys walked on this early spring day that bordered the farm along the hedgerow belonging to John's step-grandfather. The thick, vine-covered hedge served to keep fattening sheep grazing within the farm's boundaries. Freshly sharpened stakes had been added all along the hedgerow to shore up the thickening growth.

John wore a smug grin. "Aye, I've sailed all the way to *Spain.* The sea's in my blood, mate."

"Blimey! Do ye get to handle the ship's wheel?" Billy asked, wide-eyed.

"Aye, of course! My father *is* Captain Newton," John answered proudly, his changing voice cracking. "I get to run all over the ship." The twelve-year-old neglected to add that his father worked him like a sea dog with whatever he needed him to do. He helped the galley cook with clean-up duty, scrubbed the deck, served as messenger boy, or stowed the ropes and rigging.

The boys suddenly heard a horse galloping up behind them and turned to see Edward with a half-excited, half-scared look on his face. "Ahoy!"

John rolled his eyes at his ridiculous friend. "You're such a landlubber! We're in the *country,* not at sea, Eddy!"

"WHOA!" Eddy shouted, pulling on the reins of the nervous brown horse that stomped on the ground, kicking up dirt.

"Where'd ye get this horse?" Billy wanted to know, putting his hand on the horse's muzzle.

"I borrowed it," Edward confessed with a mischievous grin. "I'll return it after we've had a ride or two. The squire will never miss it."

Billy and John exchanged expectant glances. Billy nudged John. "Are ye a sailor or a country squire today, hey? Ye can steer a ship, but can ye steer a horse?"

John felt a nervous jolt, but wanted to ride this handsome steed. "I'll give it a go."

Edward slung his leg over the horse and stepped down from the saddle. He held the reins for John and patted the horse's muzzle. "Just put one foot in the stirrup and lift yerself up into the saddle."

"Here I go!" John exulted, climbing up into the saddle. Edward handed him the reins.

"Squeeze his belly and kick yer feet into his side," Billy told him—although, never having ridden a horse, he really didn't know.

John kicked the horse, and it lurched forward before something darted out in front of it. The frightened horse suddenly rose up on his hind legs, sending John flying off his back. The young boy screamed as he flew right over the sharp, newly trimmed hedgerow, nearly landing squarely on top of a pointy, razor-sharp stake. He landed on the wet ground so hard that it knocked the wind out of him.

Edward went running after the horse, who took off back toward the farm where he belonged.

"Blimey, ye were almost impaled! Missed it by inches!" Billy exclaimed, holding his thumb and finger up to show how narrowly John missed the stake. "Are ye all right, Johnny?"

John groaned, holding his stomach. He slowly sat up with a sprig of green vine in his hair, and dirt smeared over his face. He looked up at the pointy stake and his heart dropped when he realized that he could have been killed instantly. A wave of fear washed over him at the thought. He suddenly felt sick and slowly rose to his feet. "I'm going home," he told Billy, walking away back toward the farmhouse.

Billy cupped a hand to his mouth and shouted, "Better stick with sea horses, hey?"

John ignored his mischievous friend as fear gripped him. *What if I had died and had to stand before God today? What would he think of me after all the trouble I've gotten into?* He turned his gaze upward as he walked along. "Thank you for saving me, Lord. I didn't deserve it," John whispered as he walked through the field.

THE WAR ROOM

Liz sat with the others as they watched the scene of John Newton's divine protection. She frowned. "I am relieved that John was spared, although I am none too pleased that one of my fellow felines was the cause."

"The *r-r-real* cause were the lad bein' with them hoodlums," Max grumbled. "They've moved on from smashin' pumpkins ta stealin' horses!"

"Utterly dreadful behavior!" Nigel agreed.

"You'll be pleased to know, however, that after this incident, John broke off his bad behavior and tried to follow God again," Clarie told them. She then frowned. "Unfortunately, it didn't last. John entered a cycle of sinning followed by a guilty conscience, followed by repentance and trying to act better. He repeated this often, but every relapse sank him into greater depths of bad behavior."

"Oh, me," Kate sighed sadly. "Sounds like he were tryin' ta do everythin' in his own strength."

"At least the Maker were watchin' out for the boy when he were makin' bad decisions," Al noted. "He even saved him from a bad kitty."

Liz frowned. "Just how long did this cycle continue?"

"For years," Gillamon told them. "The more he went to sea and was surrounded by godless, cursing sailors and then came home for extended periods to his mischievous friends, the more he mimicked their behavior. He dug himself into a very deep hole. Shortly after John turned fifteen, his father arranged a promising position for him in Alicant, Spain. But he was undisciplined, easily angered, and rebellious on board. He returned home to face his father, carrying the shameful report from the Spanish captain that John was not worthy of the Newton name!"

"This is intolerable!" Nigel fumed, pulling on his whiskers.

"John wasted that opportunity, and once again became the repentant backslider," Clarie told them. "Thankfully, since he was a child, he was greedy of books, so he picked up Lord Benet's *Christian Oratory.* He decided to attempt a life of piety by praying, reading the Bible, and even keeping a diary. He wrote that he 'felt religious,' but religion on its own is worthless, as we know."

"Oui, he struggled like most humans do with the unholy trinity," Liz observed.

Jock cocked his head. "I've heard of the Holy Trinity. What's the *unholy* trinity?"

"The world, the flesh, and the evil one," Nigel explained. "All three conspire to undermine one's character whilst one attempts to live a holy life."

"But it's not like humans don't have a choice in the matter," Kate suggested. "Ye can either choose Jesus or yerself ta be Lord of yer life. Sin never be the first issue, but wha' ye do with yer heart in tryin' ta play lord of yer life." She put her paw on Jock's arm. "When ye allow Jesus ta help ye say an' do everythin', He sets ye free. Life becomes full of meanin' an' joy."

"Well put, Kate," Gillamon agreed, bringing another scene into view. "So, it was in the middle of this cycle that the Maker provided yet another moment of Divine protection. I was instructed to simply detain John for a few moments following a service at his family's local parish. Observe."

ST. MICHAEL'S CHURCH, AVELEY, ENGLAND, 1740

John Newton nervously bounced his right leg up and down, and let go an exasperated breath through his nostrils, crossing his arms over his chest from excruciating boredom. The fifteen-year-old drew a stern look from his stepmother, who held onto her beloved four-year-old son, William. She tried to keep the young child quiet as the Anglican pastor droned on and on. She didn't need to keep an adolescent quiet, too. Captain Newton was off on a voyage, and had left John at home. But John didn't care about the sermon. Billy and Edward were waiting for him two miles away at the waterfront at Long Reach to go on a grand adventure, and he was not about to miss it.

A couple of days earlier, the trio of teenage boys had been mudlarking down at the harbor at Long Reach, scavenging for trinkets or treasure in the tidal zone of the Thames. They'd sometimes find pieces of broken pottery, or an old clay pipe tossed away by a sailor. Of course, they always hoped to find an ancient Roman coin or some sort of real treasure amid the flotsam and jetsam. While the boys looked for treasure, they had seen a sailor rowing toward them from a seventy-gun man-of-war galleon moored in the harbor. Rumors of another war with Spain filled the air, so British frigates were made ready in every port, including Long Fleet. It had three masts and two decks, and John Newton just had to get on board to see what a real Royal Navy ship was like, as opposed to the smaller merchant vessel his father captained. The sailor had promised to row the boys out to tour the ship on Sunday afternoon. So, here John sat, dying to jump up from the pew as he stared at the curved naves of this six-hundred-year-old Norman church. When the vicar finally ended his sermon, John sighed and quickly rose to his feet with the rest of the congregation. It was then he spotted Mr. Gillamon, lifting a hand of greeting to him from a nearby pew box. He still held onto his maple stick with the carved fish on the handle.

As the congregation filed out, Mr. Gillamon made his way quickly to John and his family. "Why, could it be Master John Newton all grown up? I thought I recognized you." He reached out his hand to John's stepmother. "Allow me an introduction. I am Mister Gillamon, and I met young Master John years ago in Wapping."

"Ah, how lovely. A pleasure to meet you, MisterGillamon," Thomasin replied, her four-year-old pulling on her skirts. "Welcome to Saint Michael's."

"Good day, Mister Gillamon. I'm surprised you recognized me," John said flatly, irritated by this delay. "I see you still have your fish stick."

Mr. Gillamon chuckled. "Indeed. Some things never change, just like some of the historic artifacts in this old church. I'm fascinated by that brass carving of the knight over there."

"John, show Mister Gillamon our beloved Knight Ralph while I tend to William," she instructed. "Please excuse me."

John gripped his hands in frustration but lifted a hand toward the tall rectangular brass plaque on the far wall. Together they meandered around the pew boxes to reach the knight, every step in the opposite direction of where John needed to go. Gillamon asked him about his schooling and John told him about his sea voyages with his father.

"Radulphus de Knevynton," Gillamon read the Latin inscription as they studied the intricate carving of the knight dressed in full armor. "I see he has his faithful dog at his feet. Or is he putting his foot on an enemy dog?"

"I'm not sure, sir," John answered mindlessly, casting a glance back to the church's front door. "We don't know much about this knight. He was just from around here."

"I recall that you were quite the learned scholar at your mother's knee, voraciously reading," Mr. Gillamon recalled. "Did she also teach you to read Latin?"

John recalled an image of his mother's face pronouncing some Latin phrase. "Yes, sir. And I became quite proficient at it in boarding school, but I don't remember much of it now."

"How unfortunate," Mr. Gillamon uttered with a frown, pointing to his head. "But those things you learned early are still in the recesses of your mind." He turned to read the plaque. "Now then, it reads, 'Hiere lies Ralph de Knevynton, who died on the Thursday before the feast of Saint Nicholas the Bishop, in the year 1370.' Isn't it sobering to think that this knight died nearly four hundred years ago? He must have been a brave man to be so beloved by this church."

A feeling of familiarity came over John as Mr. Gillamon read. "You remind me of my Latin teacher from school." He glanced back at the door.

"Am I keeping you, Master Newton?" Mr. Gillamon pointedly asked him.

"I . . . uh, well, yes, Mister Gillamon," John answered. "I am to meet some friends at Purfleet jetty."

"I see. Well, I don't wish to delay you any further," Mr. Gillamon responded with a kind smile. "Please escort me outside and I shall bid you good day."

John was happy to escort the older gentleman but was irritated as he took his good time to exit the church, using his fish stick to point at a tapestry here, a beautiful wall sconce there. When they exited the church, bright sunlight nearly blinded them.

Mr. Gillamon slowly reached out his hand. "It was good to see you, Master Newton. I wish you a good afternoon with your friends. I hope our paths will cross again soon."

John gave a hasty nod of respect and shook his hand. "Thank you, Mister Gillamon. Indeed. Good day." With that, he turned and started running toward the Thames.

PURFLEET, LONG REACH, 1740

An out-of-breath John Newton leaned over to rest his hands on his knees. He had run the entire way from the church to the waterside and had to catch his breath. He wiped the sweat from his brow with the back of his arm and looked for the jolly boat where the sailor told the boys to meet him. It wasn't there. John put a hand out to shield his eyes from the sunlight and survey the harbor. He soon spotted the sailor, Billy, Edward, and a couple of more men in the jolly boat, rowing out to the man-of-war.

"Sink me! I've missed the boat!" John exclaimed in surprise. He then began to curse, furious that he had been delayed at the church by Mr. Gillamon. He waved his arms wildly in the air, trying to get their attention. "I'm here, boys! Come back!" he shouted, hoping his friends could hear him. But it was no use. They were quite a distance away, and the brisk wind snatched his voice away from their ears. John picked up a rock and hurled it into the water, cursing with every word he had ever heard from the seamen or from his friends.

Suddenly, as the jolly boat neared the massive ship, it struck something beneath the waves. The boat overturned and everyone aboard fell into the Thames, thrashing about. John's heart sank. Billy and Edward didn't know how to swim. John shouted for help, but no one was nearby. It was no use. He watched his friends slip into the depths of the river and drown before his eyes, but he didn't notice the odd ripple extending fifty feet from the horrific scene.

THE WAR ROOM

I was furious at Mr. Gillamon for delaying me those few minutes, but that delay saved my life, John thought, convicted to his core. *What an ungrateful wretch I am!*

"C'est tragique!" Liz exclaimed as the animals looked at John. He sat

once more in a pew at the church, but now to attend the funeral for his best friends. He leaned over to rest his elbows on his knees, overcome with grief.

"The poor lads!" Kate lamented.

"Aye, but John were saved with Gillamon's help," Max noted.

"Surely the adolescent's woeful experience led to yet another time of repentance," Nigel assumed. "I have no doubt he again realized the Divine hand of providence."

"Yes, but once again, his seeming goodness had no solid foundation and he tired of the effort," Clarie reported. "John gradually gave up and finally acted out worse than before. His prayers turned to cursing and blasphemy. He repeated the cycle about three or four times before he was sixteen."

Al frowned. "So, it were Bible, blasphemy, Bible, blasphemy, Bible, blasphemy."

"John Newton were blind an' daft!" Max grumbled.

"He seems to get ambrosia a lot," Al pointed out.

"You mean *amnesia,* old boy," Nigel corrected him.

"Sadly, throughout this tumult, John Newton's heart was insincere," Gillamon told them. "He understood the necessity of religion as a means of escaping hell, but he loved sin and was unwilling to forsake it. But finally, he made a valiant effort to be pious. It lasted two years, but he was miserable." He pointed to another scene of John sitting alone in a darkened room, reading the Bible.

"John became a hermit and began living the strict life of a pragmatic Pharisee," Clarie pointed out. "He did everything possible to live a moral life as defined by human rules and regulations. He even gave up eating meat for three months and became depressed."

"That would depress me, too," Al muttered at the thought.

"Aye, this jest goes ta show that ye kin do all the right things, but none of it matters if yer heart doesn't belong ta the Maker," Kate offered.

Max gave a solid nod. "R-r-right, me Kate! The Maker doesn't want ye ta give up things jest so He can keep ye from good things. He jest wants yer heart so He can *give* ye more good things than ye could ever imagine."

"You two Scots have summarized the heart of things perfectly," Gillamon affirmed with a smile. "So, our John Newton practiced a 'poor religion' and became a miserable, antisocial, apathetic wretch for two years. He hardly ever answered a question for fear of uttering a wrong word. During these teen years and early manhood, John ran away from the truths he had been taught as a child. They remained buried in the depths of his soul. He just couldn't reach them for a time."

"So, what happened to this depressed teenager?" Liz asked.

"Poison happened—on a voyage to the Dutch port of Middleburg," Gillamon answered, tapping the panel of time.

"Poison!?" Max asked. "Wha' do ye mean?"

John walked up the wharf from his father's ship into the town, and stopped in front of a shop selling maps, books, and other items of interest. There in the front window was a beautiful map. He went inside the store and asked to get a better look at the map. He was greeted by a strange-looking man, evidently the store clerk.

"Dis is called de Carta Marina, or de map of de sea. De Svedish geographer and historian Olaus Magnus drew dis in 1539 in Rome. It is vone of de earliest accurate cartographic depictions of de Scandinavian peninsula," the man explained.

John was instantly drawn to the beautiful artwork. He then spotted a grotesque sea creature attacking a ship. There were more beasts scattered around the map. "What are all these strange monsters?"

"Sea monsters come in all shapes and vorms—serpents, dragons, lion-headed vish," the man explained. "You are a sailor? Hafe you not seen deese monsters on your voyages?"

John wrinkled his brow. "I can't say that I have, no. Are they real?"

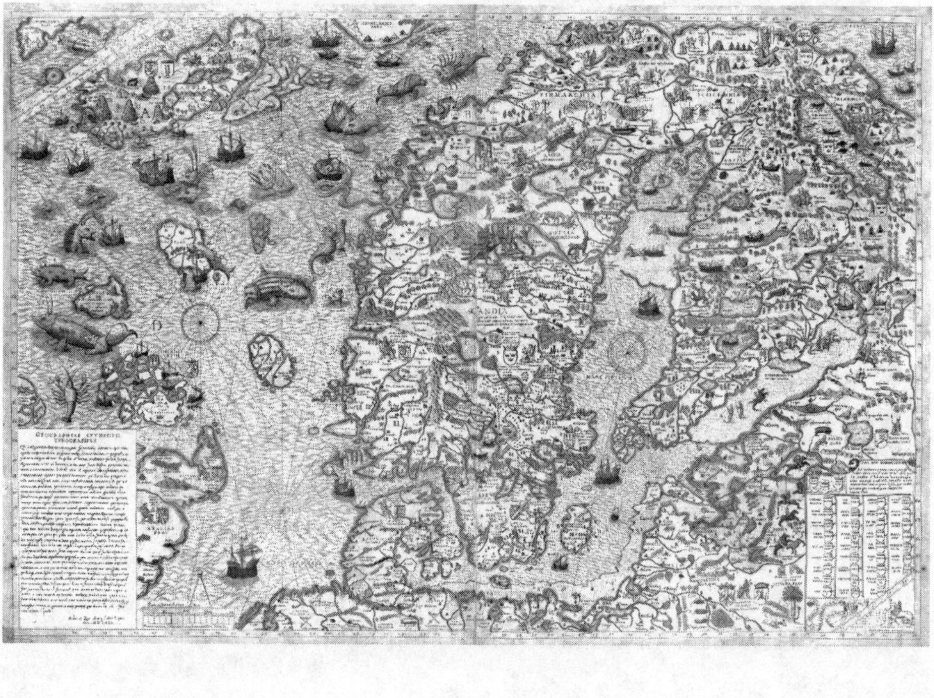

The man's eyes narrowed. "Of course dey are real! As long as man has sailed de sefen seas, dere hafe been sea beasties to terrify and drag men to de depths. Bevare of dem." He pointed to a giant lobster holding a man in its claws. "Dis kind vill cut you in two."

John gave an uncomfortable smile, but didn't know if he believed in such folklore. Still, there were strange things that happened at sea. "I shall beware. That is a bit unnerving. Anyway, I would like to find a good book for my voyage home."

"I have someting dat vill do de trick," the man told him, walking over to a table of books. He handed a volume to John.

John wrinkled his nose at the odd stench coming from the man. He was intrigued as he thumbed through the book. Handing the man a few coins, he left and walked back to the ship, his nose in the book.

Nigel held his spectacles as he read the spine of the book John had purchased. "*Characteristics,* volume two, by the third Earl of Shaftesbury." The little mouse's eyes widened. "Poison indeed! This is a dreadful development!"

"Why, Mousie?" Kate asked.

"That horrid, godless book encouraged the evil idea that God's laws could be easily adjusted to suit men's *failings,*" Nigel answered, shaking his head. "It's filled with every sort of rot, wrapped up with romantic words of eloquence and pompous discourse."

"Poison," Liz whispered, thinking as she slowly curled her tail up and down. "How odd that a book published thirty years earlier in English would be sitting on a shelf in the Netherlands, no?"

"John thought the author was a religious man, so he felt that all he needed to do was follow exactly what Shaftesbury said in order to be happy," Gillamon explained. "The author wrote of God, but never about Jesus Christ. He was a Deist who wrote that truth was only an opinion, and every man must form his own truth, which of course is exactly what John wanted to hear. He eagerly memorized an eighty-eight-page section entitled, "The Moralists: A Philosophical Rhapsody." It was a blueprint for a lost, free-thinking degenerate. Its effects were not immediate but acted like a slow poison on John's soul."

Nigel preened his whiskers before reciting Proverbs 5:22-23. "*His own iniquities entrap the wicked man, and he is caught in the cords of his sin. He shall die for lack of instruction, and in the greatness of his folly he shall go astray.*"

"Aye, the lad hasn't had *anyone* ta help guide him between truth an' error!" Kate wailed. "Wha's ta become of this lost lamb?"

"Captain Newton's fury came to the rescue, believe it or not," Gillamon said. "In December of 1742, he told his son that enough was enough. He would not have his eldest boy spend such endless days being useless to himself and to the world. Captain Newton arranged a position for John with a merchant in Liverpool by the name of Mister Joseph Manesty. John was to sail to Jamaica and become the overseer of slaves at a sugar plantation. This was the opportunity of a lifetime. He was promised that if he worked hard, within five years he could earn a fortune and possibly return to London a wealthy man worthy of even a seat in Parliament."

"So, this is how he entered the slave trade?" Liz surmised with a frown.

Gillamon smiled at Clarie. "Actually, no." He tapped the time panel, revealing the image of John knocking on the door of a lovely country estate. Suddenly the door opened, and there before him stood a beautiful young lady with dimples, smiling shyly. John smiled back.

"*Was this the face that launched a thousand ships*?" Nigel asked, quoting Christopher Marlowe's description of Helen of Troy from his 1604 play *Doctor Faustus*.

"Hardly," Clarie replied with a coy smile. "It was actually the face that made John Newton miss the boat . . . again."

4

THE RINGS OF THE LORD

MARSHFOOT HOUSE, AVELEY, ENGLAND,
DECEMBER 1742

"Are you about packed, boy?" Captain Newton asked John, who folded a set of long clothes for his upcoming adventure to Jamaica.

"Almost, sir," John answered, reaching for a woolen coat. He was seventeen years old now, and no longer a boy, but he was not about to correct his father.

"You won't need many woolen layers once you reach the Caribbean, but the voyage across the Atlantic will be bitter cold," Captain Newton advised. He handed John a piece of paper. "Before you leave, I need for you to conduct business for me down in Maidstone. It should only take you three or four days."

"Aye, aye, Captain," John answered on reflex, before catching himself. "I mean, yes, sir."

Following a final voyage to the Mediterranean that ended with a jaunt north to the Netherlands, Captain Newton retired as ship's captain. He was ready to take a shore post, and given his vast experience quickly landed a position with the Royal African Company. The massive trading company dealt in gold and silver, but the slave trade was its largest source of revenue. His business dealings would involve coordinating the trade of goods across England, of which Maidstone boasted one of the largest agricultural markets. Maidstone's Saturday market drew buyers from all over southern England. The city was in Kent, with the Thames Estuary to the north, and the White Cliffs of Dover to the south. Kent had been used as a strategic location by the Romans and then the Normans; Julius Caesar considered its people to be "by far the most civilized inhabitants of Britain." Maidstone was only half a day ride from the farm in Aveley, so John could go there and be back in time to catch his ship to Jamaica.

"John, this letter just arrived for you," John's stepmother told him, walking into the room to hand him an envelope embossed with a red wax seal. "The courier had some of the most remarkable blue eyes I've ever seen."

John took the letter in hand but didn't recognize the handwriting. "Who could this be from?" he wondered, taking a letter opener to break the seal. He unfolded the beige parchment, and his eyes widened as he read its contents. He looked up at his father with surprise. "It's from Elizabeth Catlett in Chatham in *Kent*. It's been ten years, but . . . she's invited me to visit them. How strange that you've just asked me to go to Kent as well. What do you think, sir?"

Captain Newton raised his eyebrows and placed his hands on his hips, casting an unfavorable glance at his wife. John's mother Elizabeth had died in the home of her distant relations, the Catletts, while he was at sea. They didn't approve of his hasty marriage to Thomasin, so contact with the Catletts became strained before it eventually grew silent. "The timing is indeed an odd coincidence. But the Catletts can at least provide you a meal along your journey. Go if you wish."

John nodded and resumed his packing. "I probably won't go. I'm anxious to get back here, after all. I've got a ship to catch."

MAIDSTONE INN, ENGLAND, DECEMBER 12, 1742

John Newton rubbed his cold hands together and blew into them while his horse ate oats from a leather pouch. He had completed the errand for his father and couldn't wait to get home. "By this evening, you'll be in your barn, and I'll be in my warm bed and out of this bone-chilling weather," he told the horse as he packed the saddlebag.

Suddenly his hand felt the letter from Elizabeth Catlett, and he pulled it out, rereading her kind words of invitation. He heaved a sigh of uncertainty. "We should just head home." Just then, a servant girl came walking into the barn with a basket draped over her arm to collect eggs from the chicken coop. She smiled and nodded to John. "Hope yer horse is havin' his fill of breakfast," she said. Her eyes were a remarkable shade of blue. "Where're ye headed today? No doubt rain is comin'. It will make for a miserable ride, hey?"

John frowned. The cold was bad enough, but riding a horse in an icy rain was even worse. He opened the letter and read the address to the servant girl. "Do you know where this is in Chatham?"

"Aye, of course! The Catletts live only about a mile off the main road," she answered happily. "If I were ye, I'd pop in for a bit to warm up by the fire, hey?"

What could it hurt? John thought. *I'll get warm and then be on my way.* "Thank you, Miss." He readied his horse and left the barn. As he headed to the main road, he glanced up at the stormy skies and felt the first drops of rain. *That lass was right about the rain.* He furrowed his brow. *I didn't mention the Catletts by name. I wonder how she knows them.*

The cold rain was heavy, and the horse kicked up mud onto John's breeches and coat as he trotted down the lane toward the Catlett's house. Water dripped from his three-cornered hat as he dismounted and tied the horse to the iron post ring. John didn't expect to be so nervous, but as he walked up the steps to the front door and spotted the brass ring door knocker, he suddenly felt a wave of emotion. This was the house where his mother came and died. He wondered if she, too, used this door ring. He reached his hand up and gripped the ring for a moment, closing his eyes to imagine her here. He knocked on the door and waited, his breath rising like an icy puff of smoke. Within moments, John heard someone fiddling with the latch. The door opened and there stood the loveliest sight he had ever seen. A thirteen-year-old girl with dimples and brown eyes and hair stood there smiling at him, holding a baby boy on her hip.

"Uh . . . good day, miss . . . I'm . . ."

"JOHN NEWTON!" came a voice behind the girl. Elizabeth Catlett ran up to envelop John with a warm hug, unconcerned about his wet clothes. She gripped his upper arms with her hands and looked intently at his face. "I could never forget that precious face." She hugged him again. "You must have received my letter. Welcome! Come in, come in!

As they entered the foyer, children surrounded them, giggling. "Dear ones, this is our beloved John Newton, my best friend's son. You must make him feel welcome." She turned to point to each child. "This is John, eleven, Sarah, four, Susanna, two, baby George," she named off, taking the baby into her arms. "And this is Mary, thirteen."

"But you can call me Polly, like my family does," the girl quickly offered with a shy smile. "Nice to meet you, John."

John removed his hat and humbly nodded his head in greeting, unable to stop staring into Polly's eyes. He immediately felt warm inside and out and slowly reached for her hand, his heart jumping as they touched.

"Here, let me take those," Elizabeth insisted, handing George back to Polly. She took John's soggy hat and wet cloak. A tall man walked into the room and John's mind instantly recalled the sad day when this man knocked at their home in Wapping to take his mother away. "George, it's John, all grown up!"

George Catlett reached out his hand and warmly took John's in his. "Welcome, John. It is so good to see you, lad. It's been a long time."

"Yes, sir, it has," John answered. "Thank you for your kind invitation."

"You are to call us Uncle George and Aunt Elizabeth, understood?" George instructed with a broad smile and a gentle yet firm hand to John's shoulder.

"Yes, s—, I mean, Uncle George," John answered, glancing over at Polly, who shared his smile.

"Come get warm by the fire," Elizabeth ordered. "We'll add another place setting to the table for supper. How long can you stay? The Maidstone market is on Saturday which we *never* miss, and next week our church will have a nativity play for Christmastide."

"I'm a shepherd!" young John exclaimed.

"And he'll get to hold a real baby lamb!" Sarah followed excitedly, gripping her big brother's arm proudly.

Is this how a family is supposed to act? They show such love for one another and for me, John marveled, hungry to be part of such a family. From the moment he set foot in this house, he had seen and felt nothing but warmth. All he had ever known since his mother died was cold-heartedness that dripped from the walls in his own house. It was as if he had arrived at a safe haven he had only dreamed about, but here it was real. Love was real. And Polly—Polly was real. John had never been in love, but in an instant, he knew it was real, too. *So, this is what it feels like.*

"How *wonderful!*" John exclaimed with delight for the children. He turned to Polly with a grin. "And will you be 'Mary'?"

Polly blushed and gave him a sideways glance. "Yes. I hope you can stay."

Uncle George nodded. "Is there any reason you need to rush home?"

John gazed at Polly's sweet face and slowly shook his head. "No reason at all."

THE WAR ROOM

"Ah, *c'est l'amour!* I would recognize it anywhere," Liz said dreamily as the animals observed the beautiful scene of this loving family gathered around the dinner table. They were laughing and enjoying each other's company while they ate a bountiful feast.

"For both John an' the lassie," Kate agreed. "Did ye see how they were lookin' at each other?"

Clarie beamed. "It was a beautiful sight to behold."

"I suspect that you were playing the role of Cupid, what?" Nigel surmised with a jolly chuckle, twirling a whisker. "Might you have been a courier *and* a certain servant girl who happened to dispense directions to our *uncertain* John Newton?"

Clarie turned her eyes at the ceiling with a coy grin. "Maybe."

"Jest how long did the lad stay?" Max wanted to know.

"Three weeks," Gillamon told them, tapping the panel to skip through scenes of John's extended stay with the Catletts over the Christmas season. They loved hearing John's stories from his exciting sea adventures, especially young John. "Of course, John missed the boat to Jamaica, but he did so *intentionally.* From the moment he met Polly, he was smitten and determined that nothing would keep him away from her."

"Did he profess his love to the lass?" Al asked, laying his head on Liz's shoulder. "Like this?"

"No, he couldn't let anyone know," Gillamon answered. "Polly was far too young, and John had no money or position since he had literally thrown away his prospects by staying with them in Chatham."

"What did John tell his father?" Liz worried. "He must have been furious!"

Clarie closed her eyes and nodded. "He was indeed. You should have heard him roar when John returned home. Captain Newton's relief that John had not been killed or press-ganged lasted only a minute before he tore into the lad. But John couldn't tell his father the real reason for his delay; that he had fallen madly in love with a thirteen-year-old girl. He just stood there, giving no real excuse."

"Oh dear, whatever happened next?" Nigel asked with a paw to his chin. "Did Captain Newton escort young John down to Execution Dock himself?"

"Mousie!!" Kate shouted.

"Actually, he did just that, down the Wapping Stairs, but not to the gallows," Gillamon explained, showing the scene of John boarding a merchant vessel a week later as a common sailor. "As punishment, Captain Newton put John on a merchant vessel bound for the Mediterranean, telling him he would no longer have the protection and comfort as the captain's son or stay in his plush quarters. John would now learn discipline as a 'Jack Tar.'"

MEDITERRANEAN SEA, APRIL 1743

"Come all you young sailormen, listen to me
I'll sing you a song of the fish in the sea,
and it's . . ."

"Windy weather boys, stormy weather, boys
When the wind blows we're all together, boys
Blow ye winds westerly, blow ye winds, blow
Jolly sou'wester, boys, steady she goes."

"Up jumps the lobster with his heavy claws,
Bites the main boom right off by the jaws!
and it's . . .

Windy weather boys, stormy weather, boys
When the wind blows we're all together, boys
Blow ye winds westerly, blow ye winds, blow
Jolly sou'wester, boys, steady she goes.

John's calloused hands gripped the holystone as he scoured the wooden deck of the ship in a back-and-forth rhythm with his fellow sailors. They sang chorus after chorus of "The Fish of the Sea" in answer to the lead sailor who belted out verses about eels, sharks, fish, and of course,

"Up jumps the whale . . . the largest of all,
'If you want any wind, well, I'll blow ye a squall!'
and it's . . .

John envisioned the map of sea monsters he had seen at the bookstore in the Netherlands. He had learned a great deal about such sea beasties since being aboard this ship with these scurvy dogs. As the rum flowed, and the sailors got squiffy, they told tales that, if true, would scare any seafarer.

When they left London, John had kept to himself, trying to quietly do his chores as they sailed down the coast of France, turned east at the Strait of Gibraltar and entered the Mediterranean. But little by little, his defenses broke down, and he blended in to indeed become a common sailor. They would sail up the Adriatic Sea to Venice, Italy, and then back through Greece before sailing west along the southern tip of Spain through the Strait of Gibraltar. From there they'd sail north, hugging the southern coast of France before crossing the English Channel and returning to their home port.

They would be gone one year, but that didn't bother John. It was only one year away from Polly, not the *five* years it would have been if he had sailed to Jamaica. Not much bothered John if he kept his mind on her dimpled face. The damp, smelly, hot, cramped quarters of the forecastle where the crew slept in swinging hammocks didn't bother him. Neither the foul body odor and rum-soaked breath of his bunkmates, the profanity-scented air from cursing, shanties, and sea songs, nor the fourteen-hour days of back-breaking, exhausting work bothered John Newton. He slowly joined the crew by once more loosening his tongue, throwing away every thought of God and the moral behavior he had labored so hard to perform. John continued to absorb every word of *Characteristics*, filling his mind with the freedom to do whatever he felt the impulse to do. But he stopped short of joining his fellow sailors in seeking the company of ladies onshore, as he wanted to remain true to Polly. It mattered not that she didn't know of his love for, and devotion to, her. John knew it, and she was the only one who motivated him to retain a shred of restraint in his behavior.

VENICE, ITALY, MAY 23, 1743

A pink sunset gave the harbor of Venice a magical glow of color that extended beyond the city to the high, jagged mountain peaks of the Alps in the distance. It was the perfect ending to what had been a colorful day in this port city with the annual "Marriage of the Sea" ceremony. The Venetians commemorated this event every Ascension Day, which was always thirty-nine days after Easter. But this pagan ceremony posed a striking contrast to the ascension of the Resurrected Christ.

The Duke of Venice (called the Doge) and his nobles embarked on an elaborately decorated ship called the *Bucentaur* built specifically for this occasion. They ventured a little way into the Adriatic Sea, where they threw a gold ring overboard to signify the marriage of Venice to the sea and their maritime dominion. The ship's pilot took an oath to bring the vessel safely back again in defiance of wind and weather.

John and a crewmate leaned over the ship's railing and gazed at the *Bucentaur* as it reflected the last rays of the sun across its golden hull. The vessel was 115 feet long and covered in carved sculptures painted gold. Mars, the Roman god of war, sat above a wing-headed lion of St. Mark, emblem for the patron saint of Venice. Its two decks were covered in red velvet and seated ninety, with an immaculate throne for the doge at the stern. The ship was propelled by 168 oarsmen and manned by forty sailors.

"Blimey, can ye imagine bein' one of them crew, hey?" the sailor asked, wiping his nose with his shirt sleeve.

"I don't think you'd be suited for wearing their frilly dress clothes, mate," John teased with a laugh.

"Aye, it's all a fancy to do that's a bit over the top to the likes of us. But it does seem a bit foolhardy to throw a perfectly good ring of gold into the sea," the sailor answered.

John nodded. "I don't think the sea cares what men think or do. These Venetians think they can tame the sea, but no man can."

"I've heard of One who can," another sailor piped in, joining them at the railing. "Both wind and weather are at His command, and He can calm storms with a single word."

"Who?" the sailor asked with an unconvinced look.

"Don't you know?" the sailor asked with a grin, pointing to the sky. "He's the One who flew up to Heaven on this day."

A faint memory stirred in John's mind of his mother reading him the story of Jesus calming the storm on the Sea of Galilee. *Hush, be still!*

"Oh, aye," the sailor replied, chagrined that he couldn't think of who it was. "Well, I'm guessin' the good Lord wouldn't approve of this ring-tossin' ceremony, hey? But I can't judge the pagans today." He snickered and jabbed John in the ribs. "I'm goin' to act like one meself tonight by drinkin' a clap of thunder!"

John laughed and pointed at their gathering crewmates. "Looks like our mates are ahead of you."

The crew had labored for several days hauling cargo aboard, and now were given shore leave for a night of carousing. A group of sailors were laughing and heading to the ramp.

"Come on, Johnny! Come drink with ussshh!" a drunken sailor slurred. He jabbed John in the ribs with his elbow and a wink. "Maybe you'll meet a bonnie Italian lassh of yer dreamsh!"

John laughed and steadied the sailor. "I'm taking the first shift for night watch, bucko. Drink a nipperkin for me, hey?"

The drunk sailor made an exaggerated, slow nod and poked his finger into John's chest. *"That,* I can do, mate!"

John shook his head and gave a low chuckle as the group of sailors escorted their tipsy friend down the gangplank to the pier. He held his breath, hoping the sauced sailor wouldn't step off into the water below.

Hours passed and John slowly walked the gangway around the ship, thinking about Polly. He looked up at the full moon and wondered if she was thinking about him, too. *Someday I'll give Polly a ring.*

ZAKYNTHOS, GREEK ISLES, IONIAN SEA, JUNE 1743

Leaving Venice, John's ship sailed south through the Adriatic Sea into the aquamarine blue waters of the Ionian Sea. Beautiful white sandy beaches gave these Greek islands the aura of paradise. John pondered all he had seen and experienced over the past few weeks, especially their time in Venice. He often opted to take the night watch where he could walk the gangway in peace from his boisterous shipmates and think. It was late, and John yawned, glad to see a man coming to relieve him for the second watch of the night. He made his way down to the forecastle, climbed into his swinging hammock and quickly drifted off to a deep sleep. It wasn't long before he began to have a strange dream.

> He was once again back on deck, making his night watch rounds back in Venice. He noticed a loose rope out of place and took a moment to set it in order. When he looked up, there before him stood a cloaked man. John couldn't see his eyes, but his shadowed face revealed a smile of goodness that set him at ease. The man held out his hand, and in his palm was a gold ring.
>
> "This is for you. Take it," the man told John.
>
> John took the ring and slipped it onto his finger, overjoyed that he owned something so beautiful and valuable.
>
> The man held up a hand of caution. "Preserve it carefully, mind

you. If you do, you will be happy and successful. If you lose it or part with it, you can expect nothing but trouble and misery."

"I accept your terms willingly, sir," John answered confidently, admiring the ring as it caught the light of the moon. "I have no doubt I can do as you say."

While he continued to look down at the ring, admiring its beauty, another man appeared next to him. John looked for the cloaked man, but he had vanished.

"Nice ring ye have there, hey?" the man told John. "Where'd ye get it?"

"A kind and generous man gave it to me freely and explained that it will bring me happiness and success," John explained. "I only need to ensure that I don't lose it or part with it."

The man looked at him with squinty eyes, his voice dripping with irritation. "Oh? And what exactly will happen if you part with this *precious* ring?"

John frowned, rubbing the ring. "He said I will have nothing but trouble and misery."

"Ha! And you *believe* him?! What, are you a *child* to believe such fables?" the man scoffed. "Can't you see what a lie that is? Aren't *you* the one who controls your destiny? You're honestly going to tell me that some free gift from someone you've never met will give you all you long for without you lifting a finger to work for it? Ha! Nothing in this life is free, mate. You don't need that ring. Just toss it overboard. Show what an independent freethinker you are. You are free to make your own way."

This confused John. "I . . . I don't know."

"Are you such a weak man? Throw it away!" the tempting man spat. He then proceeded to harass John for several moments until all that John had read in *Characteristics* started to align perfectly with the man's argument. John couldn't take it anymore and on impulse plucked the ring from his finger and tossed it overboard.

Just as the ring hit the surface of the water, fire instantly erupted off the distant Alps behind Venice, setting the hillside ablaze. As John gazed in horror at the scene, he heard sinister laughter behind him.

"You fool! You have made the experiment indeed, for all the mercy God had in store for you was shot up in that ring, and you have foolishly thrown it away," the man mocked, pointing to the fiery mountains in the distance. He slowly reached a grimy hand to grip John's shoulder. "You *willfully* threw the ring away, so you must now go with me to those mountains. Those flames are burning because of *you*."

John began to tremble as terror struck his heart. He dropped to his knees in despair. "Have I no hope? No way to plead my case?" He hung his head and writhed in agony over what he had done.

The tempter suddenly backed off, as another pair of feet appeared next to them. John looked up to see the cloaked man who had given him the ring.

"Why are you troubled, John?" the cloaked man asked.

John swallowed back the lump of regret in his throat and shook his head. "I'm a miserable wretch. I failed. I've willfully ruined myself. I threw the ring away, and now I deserve no pity." He cast his gaze down to the deck.

The cloaked man didn't reply immediately, and in that pregnant pause, John felt the weight of a thousand fiery mountains falling over him to crush his spirit. "You were foolish to throw away the ring. Look at me, John."

John lifted his gaze with tears streaming down his cheeks.

"Would you be wiser if you were given the ring again?" the man asked.

John swallowed hard, hope rising in him. "I . . . I could have the ring back?"

The cloaked man immediately turned and jumped overboard with a mighty splash. John ran to the deck's railing and saw the pool of rippling water where the man descended beneath the surface. Within moments, he stood next to John as water spread over the deck from his drenched cloak. In his hand he held the ring. As he lifted the ring in the air, the flames on the far mountains were instantly extinguished, and the tempter slunk out of sight. John's heart surged with hope, and he happily reached out to take the ring, but the man shook his head.

"No, John. You have already proved how unfit you are to keep it," the man told him in a firm voice. "If I should return it to you now, you would soon lose it again. It shall remain with me; then it will be safe, and I will take care to produce it when it shall be wanted."

John woke with a start and sat up, covered in sweat. He grabbed the edges of his hammock and slowly put his feet on the floor to get his bearings. His heart was pounding, and the storm of emotions from the dream filled him with great uncertainty over what he *should* feel now that he was awake. Fear? Joy? Regret? Elation? John took a deep breath and slowly let it go. He held up his trembling, ringless hand and furrowed his brow.

"It was only a dream," John whispered to himself. He closed his eyes, then suddenly opened them. "Or was it?"

5

PRESSED FOR ANSWERS

THE WAR ROOM

"Brilliant! It was an utterly brilliant dream, I must say," Nigel cheered. "It was a perfect combination of John's ring encounters in Chatham and Venice blended with his current spiritual struggle to hold onto his faith. I couldn't have written one better myself for the lad! This dream must have had quite the lasting effect on the old boy."

"I'm sorry to tell you that the dream's effects only lasted three days," Gillamon told the animal team with a frown. "John couldn't sleep, eat, or function very well as he pondered the dream. But soon reality crept back into his conscience and drove the dream from his thoughts. By the time John climbed the Wapping Stairs in December 1743, it was forgotten. And this dream was John's final warning."

Nigel pulled on his whiskers. "Blast it all! How incredibly *obtuse* must one be to not see the meaning of this powerful dream?"

"*Oui,* and also not to see who those men were in John Newton's dream," Liz agreed. "Jesus was clearly the cloaked man who gave John the ring of salvation, and Satan was the tempter who convinced John to throw it away."

Jock cocked his head in question. "So, the tempter tried to convince John that salvation is worthless?"

"Which is the evilest lie that could ever be," Kate told him. "His arguments were the same thing he told Adam an' Eve in the Garden."

"An' it's always been that serpent's first an' favorite play ta use on humans from his black-hearted, evil gamebook," Max growled. "We've seen it over an' over acr-r-ross time, lad."

"Of course, pride is at the heart of it all, and was the cause for Satan's fall from grace," Liz offered. "He wanted to be his own god, and has been trying to convince each and every creature to join him in his miserable existence ever since."

"Aye, but did ye see how kind Jesus were ta John even after he failed?" Kate interjected hopefully.

Max nodded. "Aye, Jesus be holdin' on ta the r-r-ring until John can keep it for good then."

Liz thought back to the scenes with Polly. "Polly is the only thing that John now cares about, which is concerning. Desperate love can cause humans to set up even *good* people as idols on the thrones of their hearts. Gillamon, did John see Polly when he returned from his voyage?"

"Yes, and history repeated itself, for the most part," Gillamon answered. "John dropped his sea chest home at Aveley and got Captain Newton's hasty permission to go see Polly for the second time."

"Did the bud of romance blossom betwixt John and his fair maiden?" Nigel asked, preening his ruffled whiskers.

"Yes and no. It blossomed further for John, but since he still did not reveal his true feelings to Polly, it was not reciprocated," Gillamon told them. "But Uncle George may have suspected John's true motives for visiting, as he pointedly asked about his plans and ambitions. To which John could only offer his hope to one day become a merchant captain with his own ship."

"That's because John was sabotaging his own plans while he stayed under their roof!" Clarie added. "Once again, Captain Newton had secured another position for John with another merchant vessel departing in January. And once again, John overstayed his sojourn with the Catletts through Christmas and past the New Year until he missed *that* boat."

"He sure do miss the boat a lot for bein' a sailor," Al noted, scratching his head.

Liz grimaced. "I do not wish to see the scene of John's return home from his overstay with the Catletts."

"I didn't think you would, Liz," Gillamon agreed. "It was an ugly scene, for John had again shown nothing but irresponsibility and ingratitude for what his father had arranged. Captain Newton threatened to disown John and kick him out of the house."

"What happened, what happened!" Jock implored, worried. "Did his father make him walk the plank?"

Kate looked at Jock with shock. "Where did ye get that kind of piratey idea, wee Jock?!"

Clarie gave Jock an assuring pet. "You'll be glad to know that John finally convinced his father to give him yet another chance. John confessed that his year at sea as a common sailor gave him much needed experience and convinced him to follow in his father's footsteps. That was enough to cause Captain Newton to search for another ship for John to sail. But he warned John that until he secured a position with a merchantman, he had to be *extremely* cautious walking about at the Thames, especially wearing his unmistakable sailor clothes with their signature checkered shirt."

"Ye mean, clothes can be dangerous?" Al asked in fear, patting his fluffy backside. "I'm glad I wear fur."

"Albert, sadly there were rumors at the time that my beloved France was about to attack England, so the Royal Navy would be looking for merchant seamen to press into service against their will," Liz explained. "If John was wearing his sailor clothes in public, he would be a walking target, no?"

Max nodded. "Gr-r-reat Britain may be a powerful country, but they've never had enough soldiers an' sailors ta fight their wars. So, they'll hire soldiers from other countries like them Hessians that Washington's army be fightin' alongside them R-r-redcoats. But they also gr-r-rab poor lads in England an' force 'em ta serve."

"Quite right. The Royal Navy has held the legal authority to impress able-bodied fellows into service in times of war ever since the Middle Ages," Nigel further offered. "But press gangs *cannot* touch seamen who possess a certificate of protection proving that they are employed on a merchant vessel."

"Aye, so without them papers, John could be taken against his will ta serve on His Majesty's Ships," Max added.

"But at least he got out of trouble with his father, right?" Jock reasoned.

"Yes, but because he didn't *listen* to his father he walked right into far worse trouble," Gillamon said, pointing to the time panel of John walking along the wharf of the Thames dressed in his heavy wool sailor's coat and long white breeches. "And this final disobedience against his father would alter John's life course forever."

"Oh, dear me!" Kate cried. "Why didn't he listen ta his father's warnin'?!"

"Woe is he upon whom the press gang's shackles hang!" Nigel exclaimed dramatically.

"I'm beginnin' ta think our John Newton be more daft than Big Al when he's depr-r-rived of fish," Max told the group.

Liz frowned and shook her head. "Will that boy *ever* learn to listen to words of wisdom?"

"Speakin' aboot wisdom, I been thinkin' aboot what ye said and have a question aboot John's dream, Gillamon," Al said. "What were John's dream a final warnin' aboot?"

Gillamon tapped the panel. "Missing the eternal boat."

THAMES FERRY, KENTISH SHORE, MARCH 1, 1744

Uncle George is pressing me for answers about my future, so I will tell him what I've learned since January, John thought as he stepped off the ferry in Kent. While his father sought him a new position, John spent his time walking along the docks at the Thames, asking questions and studying the most efficient methods used by merchant vessels to load and unload cargo, and how they determined trading partners, supply routes, and the like. In their discussions around the dining table in January, Uncle George explained that he supplied bread and flour for the Royal Dockyard at Chatham, where His Majesty's Ships restocked food and provisions. George stored supplies on a hoy (a bulky barge) near their house at the waterfront.

John didn't tell his father, but he was heading back to Chatham to surprise Polly for a quick visit. He decided that on the way he would walk along the waterfront to see Uncle George's operation. He could then speak intelligently and perhaps share how he'd seen other merchants transport their foodstuffs. *I will tell him that in short order I will become a captain of my own merchant vessel. He needs to find me worthy of Polly before I can think of revealing my true intentions.* The eighteen-year-old lifted his chin in the air, certain of his plan. *At least I'll look the part of a captain in training when I knock on Polly's door.*

"Well, well, well, will ye look at that? I think we've got a new *volunteer,*" the young lieutenant leader of the press gang remarked as he spotted John strutting at the wharf in his checkered shirt. He jabbed his two fellow sailors and pointed at John. The other two muscular press gang members laughed, and one rattled the chains.

"There's a Jack Tar what must want to join His Majesty's service, hey?" one of the sailors sarcastically asked.

"But what if he's carryin' papers?" the other followed.

"There's only one way to find out," the lieutenant replied, pulling a club from his belt.

John breathed in the salty air and smiled as he saw a ship unfurling its sails to depart the harbor. He envisioned himself at the helm, imagining what orders he'd be calling out to the crew. Suddenly he heard the unmistakable sound of rattling chains behind him.

"Slowly turn, mate," the lieutenant ordered.

John's stomach dropped and he turned to see the press gang encircling him. They were seasoned sailors with the telltale mark of leathery skin carved from the sun and winds of countless days at sea. Their massive bulk communicated formidable strength, and they towered over John's smaller frame.

"You're obviously a sailor, so which ship here is yours?" the lieutenant asked, pointing his club out to the ships there in the harbor.

John stammered. "I . . . uh, I'm currently . . . I will soon sail with a merchant ship."

"Soon? Well then, show us your papers," the lieutenant asked, getting right in John's face.

The other men gripped the manacles, ready to use them.

"I . . . I don't have any, but my father will soon get them for me when he finds a ship . . ." John tried to explain.

The lieutenant made a mocking pout and spoke with dripping sarcasm. "Well, since daddy hasn't found you a ship yet, you'll be coming with us." He nodded to the two men holding the chains. "Welcome to His Majesty's Royal Navy."

The bulky sailors laughed and grabbed John, clasping his wrists in iron, roughly pushing him down the street toward a waterside inn. John's mouth was dry with fear.

John sat next to some crates on a cold stone floor in the storage room of the old inn and listened to voices on the other side of the door. The press gang told the innkeeper that they would be quartering John there while they rounded up nine more "volunteers" for the Royal Navy. His mind raced in a panic over what was happening. He had to get word to his father to get him out of this. "Please, please! I need to send a message to my father! Please, help me!"

No one answered, and John heard the voices trail off as they left him alone. John drew his knees up under him and wrapped his manacled hands around his legs. He put his head down in despair. *I didn't listen! How could I have been so foolish?*

Suddenly, a piece of paper and a charcoal pencil were shoved under the door. "Write your message," came a girl's voice. "I'll see that it's delivered."

John caught his breath with a glimmer of hope from this unknown angel of mercy. "Oh, thank you! Yes, right away, yes!"

Within moments, he had scribbled a pathetic explanation to his father about what he had done along with his current predicament. He addressed the note and slipped it back under the door. "You'll find Captain Newton at the Marshfoot House in Aveley. Thank you. I'm forever in your debt!"

Clarie smiled on the other side of the door, picked up the note, and rushed off to Aveley.

Over the course of the next day, the storage room filled with other men who had been pulled from the streets by the press gang. John knew that when they reached ten men, they would be taken away to a ship. If his father didn't reach him in time, all hope would be gone. The door opened and the ninth man was thrown into the room.

"One left," the lieutenant declared as he slammed the door.

Soon John heard a familiar voice talking with the press gang and the innkeeper on the other side of the door. It was his father! The conversation lasted a while, and John couldn't hear all that they were saying. He could make out words here and there: French fleet, Dunkirk, imminent.

"Please, I implore you, allow me to speak to my son," Captain Newton finally loudly insisted.

Another moment passed, and the door creaked open. John scrambled to his feet and rushed to the door. "Father! Father, I'm sorry! I should have listened to you! Are you able to free me?"

Captain Newton tightened his mouth and shook his head sadly. "I cannot, son. War is imminent. No amount of influence will release you."

John's face writhed in anguish. "What is to become of me?"

"You are to do your duty and serve your king," Captain Newton told him resolutely, glancing at the other men in the room. He handed John a small money pouch and a leather knapsack with a bit of bread and the few items that John had requested, including writing materials and his favorite books. "At least you are far more experienced at sea than most of this lot. Godspeed . . . John."

HMS HARWICH, MARCH 4, 1744

"Welcome to the *Harwich*," Captain Philip Carteret formally greeted the men after they were stripped, inspected by the ship's surgeon, and found fit for duty. John and his fellow forcibly impressed sailors stood in the captain's quarters, looking around in awe at the oiled mahogany wood paneling, elegant brass wall sconces, and oriental rug lining the floor. Captain Carteret sat in a red leather chair at the end of a long mahogany table with carved lions on its legs. Every inch of these distinguished captain's quarters oozed prestige, down to the tidy stack of papers held in a silver tray that he pulled from as he examined each man.

Captain Carteret was a man of long naval experience and great reputation, being kin to one of the King's Secretaries of State, Lord Carteret. He would see to it that this newly commissioned man-of-war would be governed with a fair but disciplined hand. It was a fifty-gun warship spanning 140 feet and crewed by 350 men. John had only ever served on a merchant ship with twenty or so other men. Now, he was crammed into tight quarters below decks with hundreds of men, many of whom were convicted criminals assigned to naval duty, ruined men who had nowhere else to go but from the filthy gutter to the navy, or fellow press-ganged men. Few had any previous sailing experience, so at least John had that in his favor.

"Clerk, please list John Newton, John Craven, and James Wheeler as Able Seamen," Captain Carteret instructed, looking at the line of men. "The rest of you will be Ordinary Seamen."

"Yes, sir," James Mitchell replied, locking eyes with John and the others as he made note of who was who. John made a point to give this man a nod of respect.

"Now then, we shall be patrolling the English Channel and escorting convoys to Scotland and Norway on the eve of war. You shall work hard and obey orders without question, or you will experience the wrath of my master at arms, Mister Hedge, who wields unmatched skill with a cane and a whip," Captain Carteret told them with a stern look. "That is all."

With that, John and the rest of the men were taken below deck to then begin their duties. A heavy rain had begun, but it was to be disregarded, as the crew would work at double speed in all weather, doing whatever their superiors ordered them to do. Serving in the Royal Navy was a harsh, brutal existence of pain, exhaustion, fear, and hunger. Sailors would be broken physically and mentally by fear of the whip or corporal punishment if they shirked their responsibility for even a moment. Their meager food rations consisted of tough salted beef or pork and hardtack biscuits that groaned for iron teeth. Their sleeping quarters reeked with the smell of bilge water as rats scurried about. In these conditions, dysentery could spread among the men as quickly as lice. Filth, body odor, overturned mess pots, and sailors sick with vomiting onto the floor greeted John. In addition to the miserable work and living conditions, John would be submerged in the debauched, profanity-riddled behavior of the crew, some of whom he quickly grew to hate. *Welcome to the* Harwich *indeed.*

After an agonizing month in the biting March winds that felt as if they could cut a man in two, Captain Carteret assembled the crew on April 3 to read aloud the official Declaration of War with France. The gravity of this voyage only deepened as the reality of combat on the open seas filled the men with a new level of fear.

"Newton, follow me," James Mitchell shouted; John looked up from where he scoured the deck with a row of shipmates who continually teased and ridiculed him, especially the sailors named Cullpack and Tarrant.

"Oooooh, no one's called to the cap'n unless he's in trouble," taunted Cullpack. "We might be in for a good flogging, boys!"

John gripped the holystone until his knuckles turned white, clenching his jaw as he rose to his feet. His anger mixed with his uncertain fear of why in the world Captain Carteret had called for him. Had one of these vile men spread a lie about him? He slammed the holystone down next to the unruly sailor and glared at him but said nothing as he turned to follow Mitchell.

"Ah, Newton, come in," Captain Carteret greeted him, fiddling with his stack of papers and pulling out a letter. "I understand that your father is Captain Newton with the Royal African Company?"

A jolt of surprise went through John. "Yes, Captain, sir."

"Captain Newton and I have a mutual acquaintance who has requested that you be shown favor while aboard," Carteret explained. "I have discussed your performance thus far with Mister Mitchell and others and have decided to promote you to Midshipman. You will promptly move to the quarterdeck.

Mister Mitchell will review your new assignment and see to your change of uniform."

John couldn't believe what he was hearing. His father had come through for him! Not for his release, of course, but at least for release from the horrid company of the ship's bottom dwellers. He would now be a sub-officer in training and would dine with the other officers on the quarterdeck. If he performed well, he could quickly work his way up to being a Lieutenant. But one of the most gratifying benefits to John was the power he immediately gained over the common sailors, especially those he hated. "Aye, aye, Captain Carteret, sir! Thank you, sir!"

Carteret gave a decisive nod. "Very well, Newton. Carry on."

John restrained a lump of exultation in his throat and shared a nod and smile with James Mitchell. As John passed Cullpack and Tarrant, their smiles vanished and they fearfully cast their eyes down to the deck, having heard that John Newton would now be their superior. John couldn't wait to get started. He could taste the sweetness of revenge in his mouth. The power was already going to his head, but the gratitude for what his father and Captain Carteret had done would soon escape his mind.

HMS HARWICH, OFF THE COAST OF THE NETHERLANDS, JUNE 1744

"A lobster that cuts men in two? A serpent swallowing a man? You can't be serious, John," Mitchell said, throwing his head back with laughter and tapping the back of his ring on the deck railing as was his habit. "Surely you don't believe in sea monsters and such childish illusions. Come now!"

John gave a self-conscious laugh and pointed toward the Dutch port of Middleburg as he and Mitchell stood on the stern of the ship, watching the wake swirling behind them. "I saw those beasts painted on an old map of these very waters in a shop right in that port. That's where I bought *Characteristics.* Those sea monsters might not be real, but what I've learned from that book surely is real."

"Ah yes, your *new* glorified 'bible,'" Mitchell teased. "We've been discussing that book and your beliefs for several weeks, but it's time for me to speak plainly, John."

James Mitchell was about six years older than John and quickly became John's mentor in all things. John had never had any kind of mentor and aspired to be as witty and quick on his feet as Mitchell. His mentor was extremely intelligent and talented in many areas of life, not just as a naval officer. His strengths and passions involved debating beliefs and destroying arguments, especially if his opponent was unsure or misinformed. He relished leaving his opponents a bit confused, for it gave him a feeling of intellectual superiority. Mitchell was so charming and likable that he never had a shortage of men wanting to have lengthy discussions, and John Newton was no different. Over the past few weeks, John had sought out Mitchell's company because he was so knowledgeable and well read. John was ecstatic when he learned that Mitchell had read his favorite book, *Characteristics.* For a while, Mitchell allowed John to share his enthusiasm and insights into the book. Mitchell even spoke favorably about religion at first, biding his time to gain John's confidence. But that was about to change.

John wrinkled his forehead. "Speak plainly of what, sir?"

"You have truly never understood *Characteristics* and what Shaftesbury was out to do," Mitchell began with a smug grin. He locked eyes with John. "He wasn't writing to support religion, but to *depose* it. Don't you see? Religion is simply a tool that men use to impose their beliefs, promising either hope for a joyous life eternal or an eternal judgement to hell if you don't agree with their opinions. But the truly wise man only adheres to beliefs that are his *own,* based on as much experience as he can obtain in this life. After death there is nothing else, so a grown man ought to do whatever he pleases in thought, word, or deed. This is the only life you will have to live, my friend. So don't suppress your desires. Let them have free reign and live! Don't allow all those guilt-ridden, absurd fears to keep you from the things that men were meant to know and do. Isn't it logical that if sin doesn't exist, then nothing is forbidden? Come now, don't you agree? Why shouldn't you embrace freedom as a freethinking man?"

John stood there in shock to hear such thoughts from his mentor, but the more Mitchell talked, the more he absorbed every word like a sponge. Yes, he wanted freedom and to throw off the shackles of guilt. Trying to adhere to religious rules always left John exhausted and feeling worse than he did before. What if he could throw all caution to the wind? He felt his "bible" slowly begin to shift now from *Characteristics* to Mitchell's way of thinking, just as it had shifted from the real Bible to *Characteristics.* How liberating it would be! "You've given me much to consider."

"Splendid. I won't press you for an answer . . . *now,*" Mitchell teased with a wink, tapping the railing with the back of his ring one last time. "That is for you alone to do as a *freethinking* man. I must check in with the captain, so I shall leave you with it, Mister Newton."

With that, John stood alone on deck and watched the sun setting on the distant mountains. Just as with the ring from his dream, he mentally tossed the final remnant of his Christian beliefs overboard. Like an unwary sailor who leaves his port just before a rising storm, John Newton renounced the hopes and comforts of the Gospel at the very time when every other comfort was about to fail him.

Little did John realize it, but sea serpents were indeed very real. He had just been swallowed by one.

6

Never Deliberate

THE WAR ROOM

No one spoke a word for a moment. They had just witnessed a grave turning point in the life of John Newton, and it left them devastated for the young man.

"To watch a human who has been given repeated chances and still makes one poor decision after another leaves one feeling angry, frustrated, and helpless," Nigel finally announced. The little mouse threw his paws up into the air, then snatched the spectacles from his nose to polish them with a cloth on the table.

"John Newton was also left feeling angry, frustrated, and helpless," Gillamon told him.

"Please tell us this is the lad's low point," Kate pleaded.

Clarie shook her head. "Unfortunately, no. Some humans have a very low bottom to reach before they can begin to climb up again."

"That Mitchell lad were a bad influence on John," Al spoke up, his bottom lip pursed in a frown. "Did John miss the eternal boat ye were talkin' aboot?"

"John certainly *had* missed the eternal boat at this point in his life. The enemy used Mitchell to cut the lifeline to which John's drowning faith clung," Gillamon explained, tapping the panel of time to reveal a ship getting battered in a storm. "But you need to see who *did* miss the eternal boat of salvation. Years later, Mitchell was on a ship that got caught in a violent storm off Lisbon, Portugal. A massive wave swept him overboard and into eternity."

"Quel dommage!" Liz exclaimed with a paw to her face. "While I am angered by his godless influence on our John Newton, to think of that young man lost forever is so very sad. He ridiculed the salvation of Jesus and 'tossed his ring overboard,' as it were."

"Aye, Mitchell were the one that went ta them fiery mountains," Max added with a furrowed brow. "Jock, this always be the last play in that old serpent's gamebook. When he's done usin' humans for his purposes, he loves seein' them destr-r-royed. We've seen it happen ta lots of humans. Always beware when bad characters tr-r-ry ta get ye ta doubt the tr-r-ruth."

Jock rested his chin on the table. "So, all that John's mum had poured into him about God, Jesus, the Bible, and faith didn't matter?"

Clarie put her hand on Jock's head. "Of *course* it mattered! But its effects wouldn't be fully realized until later in John's life. All souls must choose for *themselves* what they believe, not just what their parents, family, or friends believe. They can learn every bit of truth and all the Bible verses there are to learn, but if they never give their heart completely to Jesus and hold onto that precious ring themselves, they will end up like James Mitchell, eternally lost."

"Oui, everyone must make their faith their *own,"* Liz added. "So, back to John Newton. After he was pressed into the Royal Navy, what happened next? Did the *Harwich* endure sea battles?"

"No, even though war was declared between England and France, the *Harwich* only had one encounter with a French ship with some shots fired, but ultimately that action did not amount to much," Gillamon explained.

"I almost hate to ask, but I suppose we must hear about John Newton's sordid spiral into the abyss," Nigel presumed, pacing down the table with his paws clasped behind his back. "Let's get on with it!"

"Very well. John became arrogant, profane, and abusive to those under his authority as midshipman," Clarie reported with a downcast expression. "He even began to compose songs about the sailors he despised, insulting them with any turn of phrase he could invent. He sat down in the chair of the scorner, so to speak. John made it his business to revile and despise the Bible, and all who adhered to it."

Gillamon nodded and revealed another scene of John ordering the lowly sailors to scrub the deck while he sang one of his vile songs about them. "Not only that, but he became very much like Mitchell in trying to turn others away from the Maker's sure salvation. He sadly succeeded, too. A fellow midshipman named Job Lewis looked up to John and had come from a Christian home. John made it a point to tear down Job's faith and turn him toward atheism."

"Wha' a r-r-real loser," Max grumbled. "I don't like this version of John Newton."

"But while he was passionate about tearing others down, he was *not* passionate about his work. John became foolishly negligent, disobedient, and even provoked his superiors," Clarie further told them. "He gradually lost all respect from others and was on bad terms with everybody. He even disobeyed Captain Carteret. While his ship was moored near Chatham for a few weeks that summer, John left the ship without leave to go see Polly while she was at boarding school! He was forgiven each time, but even the longsuffering Captain Carteret had his limits."

"John had developed a new motto for life: 'Never deliberate.' He acted on emotion and impulse, not giving much thought to his actions. As the 'freethinking' man he had become, his decisions only went from bad to worse." Gillamon tapped the panel to reveal John riding a horse up to the Catlett's house at Christmastime and slipping inside.

Kate shook her head. "Don't tell me. He did it again, didn't he? He went ta Polly's house an' overstayed his time."

"Yes, but *this* time, he abused his approved twenty-four-hour leave from Captain Carteret and overstayed *ten* days," Gillamon told them.

"That's like one o' them vuja de things," Al announced, counting slowly on his paws.

"I think you mean '*déjà vu*,' old chap," Nigel corrected him.

"Well, however ye say it, this be the *third* time the lad's started a New Year by gettin' in trouble. Seems like he'd want to start off a New Year with a fresh start by doin' something good."

Gillamon and Clarie shared a smile at Al's remark.

"Did John finally profess his love to Polly? Did he tell her that he was now an atheist?" Liz wanted to know. "Like Nigel, I almost hate to ask, but what were the consequences that John experienced this time?"

Gillamon revealed the scene of John talking to Polly's parents and then storming off angrily. "He hid his atheism from Polly and the family. And he did indeed profess his love to Polly. He asked if he had permission to write to her, as was the proper custom," he explained. "Her parents refused, saying he must first get permission from Captain Newton. It devastated John that the one family where he felt unconditionally loved set conditions on his behavior with Polly. He felt betrayed by the Catletts—which was selfish on his part, of course."

"He wrote the lass, anyway, didn't he?" Kate surmised, sharing a look with Liz, who nodded.

Clarie nodded. "John and Polly arranged for one of her aunts to serve as courier. John wrote that he was afraid of losing her to a local lad and felt that his voyage ahead would either destroy him or bring him riches that he could lay at her feet. Gillamon, show them John's letter."

Gillamon showed John hunched over a lap desk with a small candle, furiously penning a long letter at one in the morning on January 24, 1745:

> *The first day I saw you I began to love you; the Thoughts of one day meriting you (and I believe nothing less could have done it) roused me from a dull insensible melancholy I had contracted, and pushed me into the world. Had it not been for you, I had till this Time remained heavy, sour, and undesirable.*

"I don't think the lad's much improved," Al proposed. "Now he's *light,* sour, and undesirable. Doesn't sound very appetizin' to be around."

"Oui, humans think that they can be rescued by other humans," Liz agreed. "Other humans can help, of course, but ultimately only the Maker can provide the rescue that a human needs."

"So, he was allowed back onto the *Harwich,* but what happened when he returned?" Jock wanted to know. He wasn't as interested in the romance part of John's story. "Did the captain hang him from the yardarm?"

"Jock!" Kate shouted, wide-eyed.

"Well, isn't that what happened to deserters?" Jock protested.

"Ye can be hanged for eatin' dessert?!" Al whispered to Nigel, growing worried. Nigel rolled his eyes and ignored the word-challenged feline.

"Aye, but he hadn't *deserted,"* Max corrected him. "The disobedient lad at least r-r-returned ta the ship."

Gillamon tapped the panel again and John stood before Captain Carteret with his hands clasped in front of him and his head hung low while his superior commander gave him a stern lecture. John explained that he had done everything because of love, and although Captain Carteret let John's violation of shore leave go one last time, he had finally lost the captain's favor forever."

"That means he did it again, don't it?" Max grumbled. "I kin see a storm a-bre-r-rewin'."

"Storm clouds formed—not just with Polly and her family, but also along the coast of Cornwall that February," Gillamon told them, revealing a scene of a violent storm bashing an entire fleet. Ships were tossed about on the waves and collided with each other. "The *Harwich* was assigned to sail with a convoy of Guinea ships under Commodore George Pocock. The ships were battered, with some losing their mainmasts, sails, and bowsprits. Thankfully, the *Harwich* escaped without much damage, but the entire fleet limped into Plymouth Sound. About a dozen of the crew were so terrified from having nearly died in the storm that they deserted the ship when it was moored for repairs. But then came the news that would cause John to join them."

Nigel held a paw to his mouth. "Oh dear, what news?"

"Captain Carteret had announced to the crew that instead of sailing to the Mediterranean for one year, they would be sailing to the East Indies and be gone for five years," Gillamon explained.

"Which of course was impossible for John Newton. He would refuse to be separated from Polly for five years," Liz determined. "It is logical to assume that he would not only likely lose her to another, but he could also lose his health or even his life on such a difficult voyage, no?"

Clarie crossed her arms over her chest. "While repeating his new motto 'never deliberate,' John convinced himself to deceive Captain Carteret. The captain had ordered him ashore with a group of men to get fresh vegetables and provisions. He was to closely guard them and make sure *they* did not desert."

Al leaned over to Nigel and whispered, "The captain ordered that they could have vegetables but not dessert?"

"But then *John Newton* deserted!" Jock exclaimed as Gillamon showed the unfolding scene of John getting apprehended by some Redcoat marines. "Uh-oh, this is bad."

"Ye're tellin' me," Al muttered under his breath.

"When he heard his father was thirty miles away in Torbay to arrange for the repair of some merchant ships damaged in the storm, John hatched a plan. He'd go ask his father to find him a position with a merchant ship in the Royal African Company. But he had to stealthily walk the entire way, taking care not to ask for directions or talk to anyone lest they ask him for papers."

Gillamon nodded. "Yes, but instead of a press gang, he walked right into a patrol of marines looking for deserters. He was only two hours away from his father."

"The marines put John in chains and marched him all the way back to Plymouth where they threw him in a guardhouse for two days," Clarie added. "He was ridiculed by townspeople as they paraded him back to the *Harwich,* taunting him with hate-filled jeers that he was a coward." She turned to Jock. "John thought for sure he would be hung from the yardarm of the ship because that was the usual punishment for deserters."

Jock's eyes widened with fear as Kate put her paw around his shoulder. Al put a fearful paw up to his neck. "Sailor clothes *and* desserts be dangerous now! I think I jest lost me sweet tooth."

"But Captain Newton came to John's rescue again, having heard of John's arrest from a message delivered by a blue-eyed courier," Gillamon told them with a smile, lifting a hand to Clarie. "Captain Newton contacted his friend, Admiral Medley, who petitioned Captain Carteret to allow John to be exchanged for a midshipman from a merchant vessel. This was a common practice that the Royal Navy utilized to rid themselves of troublemakers."

"What happened!?" Jock asked eagerly. "Did he get traded?"

"No, Captain Carteret determined that he would extend grace to John in letting him live, but he still ordered brutal punishment," Clarie told him. "Not only was John stripped of his rank and demoted to the lowest rank of Ordinary Seaman, but he was stripped and flogged while the entire ship looked on."

The animals watched in horror as John's back was beaten, bloodied, and bruised with a cat o' nine tails whip made of knotted rope. Drums rolled between each furious strike by the bosun's mate, and John moaned in agony as the whip found its mark. When it was over, they poured salt water over his back, adding to his pain.

Al covered his eyes. "I can't watch!"

"John spent two days with the ship's surgeon before he was cleared for duty," Gillamon told them with a furrowed brow. "He then went down to the belly of the ship with the very men he had abused as an arrogant midshipman. He was mercilessly taunted and bullied, rejected by the lowest of the low. But then he was soon abandoned by his former colleagues who at first pitied him and tried to speak out on his behalf."

Liz's tail whipped back and forth. "Pfft! So even James Mitchell, who made John abandon his faith, wanted nothing more to do with him."

"Captain Carteret warned the midshipmen and officers not to help John Newton, but they deserted him anyway when he lashed out at anyone who tried to interact with him at all," Clarie reported sadly. "All the while, John blamed everyone but himself. He was a miserable wretch. He was filled with bitter rage and consumed with black despair over his future. He had no friends, and everyone now despised him."

Kate slowly shook her head. "But beyond all that, the poor lad's worst fear were losin' Polly forever, weren't it?"

"Indeed," Gillamon responded. John's mental state deteriorated so rapidly that he contemplated revenge by possibly murdering Captain Carteret, or . . ." Gillamon touched the panel. A battered and bruised John Newton leaned over the ship's railing as the *Harwich* sailed away from England, keeping his eyes fixed on the shore until it disappeared. He then cast his gaze down into the sea, gripping the railing and looking around him.

Nigel pointed in alarm to the scene of the distressed young man. "Oh dear, he's going to jump and end it all!"

"To John's new atheistic way of thinking, he would simply then cease to exist and could escape his agony!" Liz assumed, holding a paw to her mouth as John leaned over to assess the fall.

"Did either of ye r-r-run ta his side an' gr-r-rab him before he jumped?" Max asked, sitting on the edge of his seat.

"No," Gillamon answered with a smile. "The secret hand of the Maker Himself restrained John Newton."

Jock closed his eyes and exhaled. "I'm glad the Maker didn't deliberate, for John's sake."

Everyone gave a sigh of relief as John left the railing to go sit on a barrel by himself, hanging his head in despair.

"Surely *this* must have been the miserable wretch's low point, what?" Nigel asked.

Gillamon shared a knowing look with Clarie and answered, "John Newton's troubles had only just begun."

PART TWO

I Once Was Lost

(John Newton 1745–1748)

7

The Willing Slave of Every Evil

HMS *HARWICH*, MADEIRA, MAY 13, 1745

The Portuguese sent Colonies here in 1425 who found it covered with wood which they mostly burnt, the ashes fertilized the soil and rendered it very productive on Vines with a surprising luxurience of Grapes which they have cultivated ever since and made prodigerous quantitys of Wine.

James Mitchell took a sip of the local Madeira, a favorite wine of England and her North American colonies. He swirled it around in his mouth and dipped his quill in the inkwell while he read over his log entry. After nearly three weeks' voyage from Plymouth, the *Harwich* moored here in Madeira to gather an ample supply of wine, water, and wood while readying the ship to sail to the East Indies. Anchored in this bustling harbor were three other Royal Navy and merchant trader ships in their convoy as well as those heading down the Guinea Coast as West Africa was called.

Mitchell always kept to his log, making daily notes of their voyage, including the history and practical information about their ports of call, weather conditions, storms, and ship damage such as they sustained off Plymouth. He would note the activities of the men such as catching sharks, which they ate for "a very strong and course repast indeed." He would describe everything from "a cooling cheerful gale," the flying fish that jumped from the depths and flew alongside them, or a massive dead whale floating on the surface of the ocean, which they had mistaken for land after crying, "Land ho!" He wrote of the games and amusements of the men singing songs or telling stories as well as somber events such as "committing to the deep" sailors at sea who succumbed to fever. Mitchell needed to make the final notes describing their time here in Madeira. It would be a busy day ahead as they prepared to embark.

> *The Island abounds in Oranges, Limes, Pineapples, Bananas, &ca, Roots and Vegetables . . . Funchiale the Capital is situated on the South East side of the Island, the streets narrow and dirty; the Church much tho' not elegantly ornamented; the Convents neat and Nuns allowed to come to the Grate at certain hours to sell their manufacture of curious artificial Flowers, Baskets, &ca. In a small Chapel of one of the Convents the sides and ceiling were decorated with human Sculls and other Bones.*

The ship was fully provisioned, and tomorrow they would get underway with the convoy, so nearly the entire crew were on shore for one last stretch of their legs and romp through civilization before going to sea. The men meandered through the colorful market, flirting with the beautiful ladies, sampling the local spirits or trying one of the five types of bananas sold in Madeira (including some as red as their signature wine.) Some sailors tried eating prickly cactus fruit despite the nuisance of the fine spikes piercing their mouths. But while the sailors took advantage of their shore leave with their fellow shipmates, one sailor did not.

Drool slipped from the corner of nineteen-year-old John Newton's open mouth as he lay in his swinging hammock, fast asleep. He had slept through the boisterous clambering of the others who stowed away their hammocks and rowed to shore. Such deep sleep resulting from the exhaustion of working like a sea dog was the only peace he ever had. In his hand was a copy of Euclid's *Elements of Geometry,* one of his favorite books; he had picked it up in Plymouth. Since he wasn't welcomed in the circle of messmates, he sought the company of triangles and trapezoids.

> *The Beech is shelving and consist of large Pebbles, very dangerous for Boats where there is a Surf, which frequently happens.*

Mitchell looked out the window of Captain Carteret's cabin where he sat at his clerk's desk and noticed a jolly boat approaching from a Guinea trader. Two seamen sat clutching their sailor bags in the bobbing boat that sliced through the choppy turquoise waves.

"Our two new seamen are arriving from the *Levant,* ," Mitchell informed Captain Carteret.

"Ah, very good," Captain Carteret mindlessly answered. He, too, was busy with paperwork from the business completed here in Madeira. "The Guinea captain expressed his concern that he would not receive able seamen in return, but he shall receive what we send. See to it that our transfers are set to go, Lieutenant."

"Yes, sir," Mitchell answered, rising from his chair. He tugged on his jacket and first tidied the desk.

"Wake up, Newton!" Job Lewis shouted, juggling John's hammock ropes with a grin. He and John had once been close before John's fall from grace with the captain and crew. He missed their friendship, but there was nothing to be done.

John grunted but kept his eyes shut, uninterested in waking. Job furrowed his brow and reached for his knife. He gripped the hammock ropes and sliced through them with his blade, sending John crashing to the floor. John winced from the still-healing wounds on his back. He opened one eye and sat up slowly, looking a mess with his hair askew.

"Looks like you didn't hear the bosun's whistle, Newton," Job pointed out. "Just because you didn't go to shore doesn't mean you can laze about here all day. Get up and get on deck. Don't hang the jib. There are always chores to do!"

John exhaled and slowly nodded, getting to his feet. "Aye, sir. I'm up." He angrily stood but said nothing disrespectful to Job, giving a singular laugh about yet one more thing to go wrong in his world. Now he'd have to retie his hammock to hold his weight before he fell asleep tonight. As Job walked on to continue his morning inspection rounds, John picked up his volume of Euclid and shoved it into his knapsack before quickly dressing and running up on deck.

The two new Guinea seamen brushed passed John, and he saw one of his shipmates tossing a bag down into the waiting jolly boat as he readied to climb down the rope ladder. "What's this?" John asked the sailor.

"Swapping mates with a Guinea ship," Henry answered brusquely. "Commodore Pocock ordered two Jack Tars from the *Levant* brought 'ere to *Harwich*. I'm one of the two blokes what's got ta be a merchant seaman now. Here comes the other bloke." He pointed to another sailor walking toward them with a bag slung over his shoulder.

John's heart immediately caught in his chest. This was his way out of the Royal Navy and out of his living nightmare. *Never deliberate!* "Please, please! Hold the boat!" he called down to the Guinea sailor. He turned to the two sailors. "Please allow me to see if I can replace one of you. Give me just a few minutes, I beg you!" His shipmates shrugged their shoulders and leaned against the ship's railing. They didn't really care on which ship they sailed. They would remain on the bottom rung of any crew's ladder no matter which jack flew from a ship's halyards.

The Guinea sailor lifted a hand and nodded his agreement to wait, smiling after John turned to run to the officer's quarters.

Mitchell saw John hastening toward him in the passageway. "Newton, what's your hurry?"

"Sir, please! Please, may I be permitted to transfer to the *Levant* instead of one of the men preparing to row over as we speak?" John pleaded, taking a quick breath. "I know Captain Carteret disallowed my transfer at Plymouth with Admiral Medley's request, but perhaps he will reconsider it now. Might he prefer to keep a crewmember in better standing here aboard the *Harwich?"*

Mitchell lifted his chin and thought for a moment. *Able Seaman.* "Wait here, Newton."

John gripped his fists excitedly, anxious for an answer while Mitchell spoke with Captain Carteret. His heart and mind were in a race to grasp all that this transfer could mean. *I will be free from this uncomfortable voyage and head to a different corner of the world! Maybe I can be home in a year so I can return to Polly!*

Within moments, Mitchell returned and nodded. "Captain agreed. Get your things, Newton. Good luck—and hurry up so we don't keep the *Levant* waiting."

John's face lit up with excitement. "Thank you, oh thank you, sir! Please give Captain Carteret my thanks, as well!" With that he turned and ran back down to the lower deck. He grabbed his knapsack holding only his Euclid and his writing materials and left all else behind. There was no time to pack anything more. He didn't want to miss *this* boat.

It had only been twenty minutes since he fell to the floor with that rude awakening, but John Newton was now excused from the Royal Navy and was now part of a Guinea crew. He threw his bag into the jolly boat below and climbed down the ladder, taking his seat next to Henry and giving a happy nod to the Guinea sailor.

"Welcome aboard. Name's Jonah. What's your name, sailor?" the Guinea sailor asked with eyes that matched the color of the sea. John saw a hint of familiarity about him.

Jonah. John gave it a passing thought, but didn't allow his mind to dwell on the name. "John Newton, from . . . London," he answered haltingly as he further thought what this transfer would mean for him. Aside from this fellow *Harwich* sailor whom he didn't know well, no one had to know who John really was. They didn't have to know about the press gang, his desertion, or his demotion from midshipman. And they certainly didn't have to know what he believed before he began his journey to the mid-Atlantic Ocean. He was a freethinking atheist who didn't have to impress anyone with respectful Navy decorum or decent Christian behavior.

As he looked up at the craggy green mountain soaring 1900-feet above the blue waters surrounding Madeira, he squashed his reflex thought of jumping from its heights. *I no longer must think about murdering either myself or another. I'll be with complete strangers. I can appear without disguise and now be as abandoned as I please, without any control! I will finally be free . . . from everything!*

ABOARD THE *LEVANT* GUINEA TRADER SHIP

"Welcome 'board *Levant.* I'm Cap'n James Phelps," the plump captain greeted John and Henry in a thick Liverpool Scouse accent, not bothering to stand. His thick red hair was tied back with a head scarf, and he had white streaks at his temples and throughout his bushy eyebrows and beard. He and his first officer were in the middle of a late breakfast. Phelps tucked a large brown napkin sloppily in the neck of his shirt. He leaned on thick forearms and tapped a boiled egg on the dark wood table bearing numerous burn marks from hot clay pipes and faded rings from overspilt mugs of ale. His messy Guineaman quarters were a far cry from those of the impeccable Captain Carteret. "The Royal Navy obviously didn't propa *ask* permission ta press two of me men, so I 'ad norra choice. I've 'ad a cob on about this transfer." He peeled off the eggshell with his thick sausage fingers. "I *expect* ye ta pull yer weight and not swing the lead, understood?"

"Aye, aye, Captain," John and Henry both agreed.

"Ta. This 'ere be Mister William Miller, me first mate," Phelps announced, pointing to a man eating a banana who gave a silent nod to the two men. "Youse'll fare well if ye keep yer daily chores as ye ough' and ye migh' even get flush in the pocke' from our trades. Fancy some scran and a bevvy?" Phelps asked in a high nasally tone. He held out a pudgy hand to the open chairs. "Tell me about yerselves." He took a bite of the boiled egg, and a piece of yellow yolk fell into his beard. "Cackle fruit?"

"Thank ye, Cap'n, sir. Name's Henry Parker," Henry responded with a nod to Captain Phelps as he reached for an orange.

"Yes, thank you, Captain," John answered, eagerly taking a fresh boiled egg, which was a delicacy compared to hardtack biscuits. "I am John Newton."

"Newton?" Phelps answered, talking with his mouth full of boiled egg. "Sink me! Don't tell me ye're the son of Cap'n John Newton! Our ships crossed maps many times."

John's eyes widened to hear that Phelps knew his father. "I am, indeed! Amazing that you know him!"

"Aye, that's bosh, 'ey?!" Phelps exclaimed with a slam to the table, rippling the ale in the pewter mugs. "Wha' be the odds that I meet the boy of me mate down 'ere near in these wa'ers?"

The men joined in as Phelps broke out in a hearty laugh and brusquely grabbed John's shoulder with surprised delight. He was a colorful, long-winded yet likeable man. He whispered in John's ear, "Yer father's a good man. I pledge ye me friendship an' protection."

John nodded and gave a wide grin as Phelps winked at him and patted his back so hard that John winced.

"What a remarkable coincidence!" another man exclaimed, scooting back a chair to join the table. He reached for a banana. "Welcome aboard, gents. Name's Evans."

Phelps pointed at Evans. "Evans be part owner of the *Levant.*"

"So, what is your primary trade?" John wanted to know, giving a singular nod to Evans.

"The golden triangle," Evans answered with a dark smile and a chuckle as he peeled the banana.

"We trade goods like cloth, muskets, and baubles along the Windward coast for slaves," Phelps explained. "Then we ship those slaves across the Middle Passage to the West Indies and fill our coffers with plenty of sugar and rum before heading back across the ocean ta home port in Bristol." He patted his belly. "I've made plenty of rum runs, jyano wha' I mean?"

John chuckled. "So, slavers can make a good livelihood then?"

"Aye! Evans 'ere went from not 'avin' a copper in 'is pocket ta wealth enough ta marry an African *princess!*" Phelps told them. "Tell 'em yer business bit."

Evans shared a laugh with Phelps and nodded. "I run a slave factory in the Banana Islands off the coast of Sierra Leone. I came here with nothing from London but now five years later I've grown quite the lucrative business. My operation sails upriver in shallow draft shallops to reach the up-country where tribes supply us the slaves in exchange for our goods. We specialize in service and *convenience* for the traders. In fact, I'm heading to Plantain Island to build a new factory so ships can barter for slaves there. Hope to have it operational by next year."

"I see, and you married an African *princess?"* John asked Evans, fascinated by this surprising culture shock.

"Aye, from the Bombo tribe," Evans answered with his mouth full.

"Swept 'er off 'er feet, 'e did!" Phelps teased. "The Bombo's be some of the best slave suppliers in West Africa. So, lads, we'll spend the next six months goin' from river ta river ta pack the belly of this ship with black gold. Then we'll sail west. A'right?" He lifted his pewter mug.

"To the golden triangle!" John exclaimed, lifting his pewter mug and clanking it with Henry's, Phelps's, Evans's and Millers's, sloshing ale across the table.

John already felt an exhilaration with this new venture and couldn't wait to get started in the slave trade with this boisterous, godless crew. Never had he felt freer!

THE WAR ROOM

"Ye were that sailor who r-r-rowed John over ta the *Levant,* weren't ye?" Max asked. "At jest the r-r-right time. I see wha' ye did there with yer name of . . ."

"I was, indeed, Max," Gillamon interrupted him.

"That's why finally John didn't miss the boat," Al noted, eyeing the table of food. "It looks smaller than the *Sandwich*."

"Harwich," Nigel corrected him with a chuckle. "You must be hungry, old chap."

Al's stomach rumbled. "I can't help it with all them bananas!"

"The *Levant* was a two hundred fifty-ton galley with twenty-four guns and sixty men, so it was quite a bit smaller, Al," Gillamon explained. He tapped the panel and the very first scene they ever saw of John Newton and the crew bringing slaves on board came back into view. "I kept watch over John on board for six months."

"So, it was on the *Levant* that John Newton entered the slave trade," Liz realized with a frown. "He must have gotten along well with Phelps, since the captain knew his father and offered him friendship and protection."

Gillamon sighed and revealed a panel of John teaching a song to the crew, banging on the table as they laughed uncontrollably. "One would have thought that would be the case, but not so with John Newton. It's as if the young man resolved *not* to have friends. Captain Phelps' temper and John's willful character frequently clashed in angry disagreements. John reached the point where he neither feared God nor regarded man—and before long, he made Phelps his *enemy.* John not only became careless and disobedient, but he foolishly devised songs to make fun of the *Levant* and Captain Phelps himself. He didn't mention names in his mocking lyrics, but the whole ship knew exactly whom he meant. John became exceedingly vile and profane, and tried to bring others down to his level of poor behavior as well."

"Oh me, were he completely daft?" Kate asked, shaking her head.

"Wha' in the name of Pete were his problem?!" Max growled.

"John was running from the Maker, and from the pain he had experienced since childhood, no?" Liz offered.

"Indeed, all of that was magnified by his forced servitude that had separated him from his beloved Polly," Nigel added. "She was the only thing in this life he cared about, yet she was taken from him."

"I bet Captain Phelps was sorry he brought John on board," Jock assumed.

Clarie nodded. "He was, Jock. But sadly, Captain Phelps died just as the *Levant* was getting ready to sail to the West Indies. First Mate William Miller succeeded him as captain, but he equally despised John and John knew it."

"What happened?" Jock asked. "Did Miller trade John with another ship?"

"Not exactly, but he did get John off his ship," Gillamon explained. He tapped a panel showing John and Evans being rowed over to a white sandy beach island covered in swaying palm trees and banana trees. "Since John expected that Miller would trade him again when they reached the West Indies, he figured out a way to stay in Africa. Thinking he could improve his fortunes by learning the slave trade, he asked if Evans would take him on as an apprentice as he built his new slave factory. So, the *Levant* dropped them off at the Banana Islands before they sailed twenty-four miles south to tiny Plantain Island."

"I'd love to go to the Banana Islands!" Al exclaimed. "Sounds like a paradise!"

"Daft kitty," Max grumbled. "That ain't no paradise with wha' goes on there."

"Gillamon, while it will be difficult to hear, in order to understand what is next for John Newton, we must understand exactly what happens at a slave factory," Liz offered, swallowing hard.

Jock frowned. "How do these poor humans get to be slaves in the first place?"

"Very well. Jock, first understand that slavery is the universal way of the world for humans, with every civilization across time enslaving others," Gillamon began. "We've seen it with Egyptians, Assyrians, Babylonians, Persians, Chinese, Indian, Romans, Greeks, and now with Portugal, Europe, and the Ottoman Empire."

"Indeed. Twenty percent of Romans and *forty* percent of Greeks were enslaved," Nigel pointed out. "It has been a horrific practice with humans from the very beginning."

"Tragically so. But I will explain the way slavery takes place here in Africa," Gillamon told them. "The Africans enslave their fellow people for three reasons. First, most slaves are convicts who break tribal laws for things like theft or adultery. Second, warring tribes will enslave those that they defeated in battle, thus sending away their enemies to reduce threats to their territories. Third, some slaves are kidnapped for sheer greed to acquire goods that traders offer, whether they be from Christian nations in Europe or distant Muslim nations like Turkey. Traders such as Captain Phelps and Evans travel up and down the coast, going upriver to trade with tribal chiefs for slaves. Once they make their deals, slaves are processed in factories." Gillamon revealed the scene of a shed with a thatched roof packed with frightened men, women, and children.

"This be so hard ta watch," Kate lamented, putting her paw around Jock.

"This is a barracoon, where new slaves are stripped, branded, and put in irons," Clarie explained gravely. "They separate families, and men from the women and children. The men fight to escape, so they are brutally chained together and whipped into submission. The slaves are rowed out to the slave ships for the horrific eight-week voyage over the Middle Passage. Slaves are confined below deck in horrible, cramped conditions where they can hardly move. If the weather is good, they bring the slaves outside and chain them to ring bolts on the deck while they air out and clean the cabin below. If the weather is bad, however, those poor souls are kept in the hold of the ship with foul air, sometimes for days. Fever and disease can then spread rapidly among the slaves, as well as the crew."

"Pure evil," Nigel muttered as the other animals looked on in horror.

"There is no justification for slavery," Liz declared. "But I presume that Captain Phelps himself succumbed to the fever? Sometimes the very act of participating in the slave trade leads to the death of those involved with it."

Gillamon nodded. "Slavery leads to death in some form or fashion for every person involved. If not physical death, then the death of a society or a soul."

"So, by running from the Maker, becoming an atheist, and giving his life now to slavery, John Newton has become the willing slave of every evil," Nigel summarized.

"If you willingly give your life to anyone other than the Maker, it will ensnare you," Gillamon pointed out. He brought a panel into view. John Newton was dressed in rags and lying alone in a slave hut on a mat, drenched in sweat and shivering from fever. "The consequence is that you become a slave to that which you thought would serve you."

8

IN HUNGER, IN THIRST, AND IN NAKEDNESS

PLANTAIN ISLAND, AFRICA, SPRING 1746

"GET UP! Princess P.I. demands your presence!" a tall, muscular black man roared at John, poking him in the back with his wooden stick, which was covered in numerous tribal markings. He was one of the princess's attendants who acted as both bodyguards and messengers. His fierce appearance of a burn scar armband and burn scar dots under his dark eyes was enough to make anyone heed his commands.

John Newton blinked with bloodshot, sunken eyes, and ran a dry tongue over his cracked lips. He attempted to swallow but coughed against his parched throat. He didn't recall the last time he had had a sip of water. He gradually sat up, his head throbbing and the dusty room spinning. He felt ready to throw up, but as the bodyguard got ready to strike him again with the stick, John rolled over onto his knees and forced himself to slowly stand. He shook all over from weakness and dehydration as his feet shuffled across the dirt floor of the slave hut where the princess had placed him.

As John stepped outside into the bright sunlight a searing jab of pain hit him in the eyes. He squinted to view the flat sandy beach out to the water but did not see Evans's shallop. It would be another day without his master's protection from his cruel wife who had summoned him. John gazed beyond the blue sea two miles to the coast and saw the distant mountain range of Sierra Leone—an Italian cartographer's spelling for the Lioness Mountains, so named by the Portuguese. Princess P.I. was the undisputed lioness of Plantain Island and wanted nothing more than to rip John to shreds. Instead, she toyed with him as a cat treats its prey.

John had begun the New Year of 1746 by setting foot onto Plantain Island with Evans and some slave workers brought from Evans's home base on the Banana Islands. He was determined to work hard and prove his value to his new master, while setting his mind to learning the slave trade. The island was only two miles in circumference but covered in palm trees. They began the hard work of building lodging for themselves as well as for slaves, felling tall palm trees and using banana leaves to thatch the roofs. All was going well until two things arrived on the island: Princess P.I. and a life-threatening fever.

Evans had married this tribal princess, whose name was pronounced "Pee Eye," in a savvy transactional move with his chief slave supplier. She was a powerful woman who possessed an almost hypnotic power over Evans. She quickly adopted a love and desire for all things European, including food, comfortable surroundings, and beautiful gardens. John and Evans labored endlessly to make sure things were perfect for her arrival, but when Princess P.I. first laid eyes on John, it was hate at first sight.

Always accompanied by her masked spiritual advisor who continually whispered in her ear, P.I. bristled at John's presence. She was angry that Evans had brought another white man into their operation. Evans was the only white man she tolerated, beyond the traders with whom she conducted business. She would charm those white men with her beauty and smooth tongue that dripped promises about the finest stock of slaves available in all of Africa. But that was necessary business. The presence of John Newton was not. It didn't matter when Evans argued about the expansion of their operation and the need for another able-bodied overseer to run their new factory. P.I. seethed with prejudice and was convinced that Newton would take away from their profits and stab them in the back at the earliest possible occasion.

When fever struck John a month after his arrival here, he no longer could prove his worth through hard work, or even show how he could contribute to their operation. P.I. complained that he was just lazy. But John was helpless, as his fever-wracked body left him confined to his mat. Evans had no choice but to leave John behind as he sailed away in his shallop on a slave-trading excursion up the Rio Nuna River. He gave instructions for P.I. to take care of John, but she soon tired of the task, moving him from comfortable quarters to an unoccupied slave hut to suffer alone. John's bed became a mat spread across a chest, with a palm log for a pillow. P.I. neglected John and left him almost starved, without even a little water to drink, for days at a time. He was too weak to fetch it himself, and she knew it.

Miraculously, John survived the fever and knew he needed some kind of nourishment. P.I. sent him mere trash to eat while she lived in plenty. When she felt generous, she would send half-eaten scraps from her plate after she had dined, but they were not enough to sustain a young man. Today she was in a high good humor and sent for John.

As John shuffled barefoot through the hot sand, he winced as he stepped on the sharp broken shells lining the path. The bodyguard prodded him forward to the lovely entrance of P.I.'s outdoor terrace lined with palm trees. She sat under a vine-covered arbor draped with white gauzy linen that caught the gentle breeze and shielded her from the intense sun. She wore an immaculate multi-colored dress, and a matching headdress adorned with gold-fitted jewels. Around her neck was a large black-and-purple amulet suspended by a thick gold necklace, and on both wrists several gold bracelets clanged as she moved. The princess was draped across a lounging bed with a pewter plate in her hand. Surrounding her were several young female servants adorned in gold earrings and wearing colorful clothes and headwraps.

P.I.'s fierce-looking spiritual advisor wore a helmet mask covering his entire face and head. Carved of wood painted black, it depicted a face of distorted features painted red: bulging eyes, a long nose, a twisted mouth with pointed teeth and forked tongue, and large horns curved behind its head reaching its jaws. Long straw hair crowned its head down to the shoulders. The mysterious man's dark black body was painted with tiny white markings resembling scales, and he wore a wide straw necklace, armband, and leggings. In his hand he held a staff topped with a carving of a snake.

The West African peoples believed in two worlds that continually talked to one another: the visible physical world of land, water, sky, and animals, and the unseen spiritual world. God was too vast for humans to know, so was assisted by many gods and goddesses representing the natural world, who much more accessible to humans. Below those were the oracles, who could explain the past and predict the future. Whenever a human put on a mask, they became that entity or spirit, and could foretell the future, relay messages from dead ancestors, or determine necessary judgment on humans to drive away bad spirits. They believed countless spirits surrounded them, which were also too many for humans to know and understand, so spiritual advisors helped to explain everything. This was the dark world into which John Newton had now entered.

The masked man leaned over and whispered in P.I.'s ear. She gave a devious grin as John approached.

"Look who is up and about!" P.I. mocked with a laugh. Everyone in her company immediately joined her laughter. She tilted her head and looked at

John from head to toe. "You look thin, Newton. Here, have a bite." Her bracelets jingled as she moved her plate back and forth, enticing him to come over to her.

John's mouth watered as he walked past the platters of food spread out across the table: baked fish, roasted fowl, fresh pineapple, caramelized plantains, coconut rice, roasted cassava root, and an assortment of nuts, cakes, breads, and wine. He shuffled over to P.I. and kept his gaze down, not wanting to ignite her ire if he looked into her eyes as an equal.

"That's it, come and get it," P.I. teased, jiggling her plate of scraps.

John gave a nod of grateful respect and reached his shaky hand to take her demeaning gift. But as he took the heavy plate, his weak hand trembled and he dropped it to the ground, spilling his much needed allotment of food everywhere. The masked man again whispered in P.I.'s ear.

"How clumsy of you! Pity, but we won't make you clean it up, as that would be beneath you," P.I. insisted. "Guard, take him back to his mansion. He will have to think about being more careful on an empty stomach tonight."

John wanted to cry at seeing a servant quickly pick up the scraps and put them on the plate, only to scrape them off into the brush for animals to later find. The guard shoved John, and he fell to the ground as everyone broke out into laughter.

"Get up, worthless, indolent creature!" P.I. screamed. She motioned for her attendants to mimic John's motions as he struggled to rise to his feet. The masked man picked up a lime from a bowl and threw it at John, followed by others who were eager to heap on the abuse.

John shook as he got to his feet and was shoved back to the ground again by the guard, generating a fresh round of laughter. The servants clapped their hands and threw more limes at him while P.I. continued to scream for him to get up. Finally, he stood on his shaky legs and turned to walk back to his hut. The masked man picked up a small stone and hurled it at him. John winced and put a hand to the back of his head, feeling warm blood. He took a deep breath and willed himself to continue taking one more step across the broken shells and the hot sand back to his hut. He collapsed onto his mat and was once again left alone as he wept, wrapping his arms around his stomach that screamed for food.

John waited until stars filled the night sky before creeping out of his hut. He quietly made his way in the blackness down to the grove of cassava plants they grew for food. Considered a delicious staple of the Sierra Leone diet, this root was boiled or roasted through a long series of steps to make it edible. But John didn't have that luxury. Terrified of being caught stealing, he quietly dug up a root from under the plants and eagerly began chewing it. Within a matter of minutes, he could feel his stomach wanting to expel the undigested root. He quickly covered the soil and stumbled back toward his hut, vomiting in the bushes along the way. Once more he collapsed on his mat, starving, thirsty, and alone.

As he lay there exhausted from sickness, hunger, and physical and mental abuse, he heard the soft clanking of chains outside his hut. Fear gripped him. Was the princess now sending a slave to murder him in the night? He lay there motionless and listened as the clanking halted for a moment, then trailed off. Why was a slave shackled with iron fetters outside his door? He was too weak to investigate and mercifully drifted off into a deep sleep. A faint memory played from his subconscious mind.

"And what verse from Psalm 56 do we use when we're fearful?" Elizabeth asked, tucking the covers under John's chin.

"Whenever I am afraid, I will trust in You," John answered softly. A tear rolled down his cheek.

"That's right, dear one," Elizabeth told him softly. She wiped his face and smiled sadly.

John slept only an hour or two before waking, but he didn't remember the dream. He was desperate for water. Shivering from weakness, he crawled over to the entrance of his hut and made a shocking discovery.

That slave had left a small amount of food and water at John's door.

WEEKS LATER

John heard shouts of joy and revelry outside, coupled with the unmistakable voice of his master. *Evans is back!* John got to his feet and was a bit more stable as he had slowly begun to recover. The scenario of P.I. sending him half-chewed scraps and even coming to his hut simply to ridicule him with her attendants had continued. He learned to take the hurled limes and a rock or two, but the degrading verbal abuse was almost more than he could bear. Surely, Evans would straighten all of this out and set things right again.

"Please, Mister Evans, sir, I don't know how I offended your wife, but she has taken such a hatred to me and left me without food or water!" John cried. "I'm innocent of any wrongdoing, I assure you!"

P.I. stood there with her hand slipped under Evan's arm. Her venomous eyes narrowed as John recounted all that had happened while Evans was away.

"Are you finished?" Evans calmly replied after John ran out of things to recount.

John looked from Evans to P.I. and back to Evans. "Yes, sir."

"Then speak of it no more. Return to your quarters. I've got to make up lost time with my wife," Evans said coldly, giving P.I. a kiss on the cheek. She leered at John with a look of spiteful satisfaction. Together they turned to walk back to their grand house and left John standing there alone. Evans not only didn't believe him, but he didn't care even if it was all true.

TWO WEEKS LATER

"Grab those fetters, Newton," Evans instructed, pointing to a pair of leg irons hanging on a nail near the barracoon that was slowly filling with slaves. "I want to make sure we have extra irons if we need them."

"Yes, Mister Evans," John answered quickly. He ran over to the barracoon and locked eyes with a despondent slave who sat under the shade of the open-air hut. *Could that be the slave who fed me?* he wondered. There was no way to know, as they would never acknowledge such a thing. If anyone was caught defying P.I. in any way, they faced severe punishment. John grabbed the fetters and ran back to wade into the shallow water where the shallop waited.

Evans had restored John's meager food rations and was even taking him on a trading excursion. Although he had not acted on any of the accusations against P.I., perhaps this trip would prove restorative to their working relationship and to John's status as his apprentice. Hope filled John as he climbed into the boat, eager to sail away from the evil woman. They'd be gone for two months, and John welcomed it. As they hoisted the single sail and left the beach, the masked man watched from the shore, pointing his staff at them.

"Pass the rum!" Evans asked another local slave trader as they sat around the fire at dusk. "This day has been a complete success, for *both* of us!"

The man stumbled over to Evans and slapped a cloudy glass bottle into his hand. "And we desherve it! Drink up, drink up! You desherve your own bottle. I'll gets another." The man lifted the lid to a wooden box with a squeaky hinge. He rummaged around in the box before slamming it shut. He stumbled over to another box and did the same, slamming it shut and cursing. He came back to the fire and sat down on the log with a grunt, snatching the bottle back from Evans's hand. "SOMEONE'S been pilfering the supplies. Not only the rum, but some foodstuffs are missing, too."

Evans frowned. "Who could possibly be taking our supplies?"

The trader pointed at John with the bottle. John was tidying up the deck of the shallop while they sat onshore. "I saw him sneak some food out here last night. He had a bottle in his hand, too. I wouldn't be surprised if he took from yer purse, so best check yer coin. He's a baddun."

Evans furrowed his brow and shot to his feet. "Newton! Get over here!"

"Coming, sir!" John quickly answered. Their trading had been going exceptionally well over the past week, and Evans had more than once commended John for his quick thinking in their trade discussions with local chieftains, making *them* agree to deliver the slaves to Plantain.

"What's this about you stealing from our trade supplies?" Evans accused him angrily, rummaging through the wooden boxes.

John couldn't believe what he was hearing. "I haven't stolen anything! I may be many bad things, sir, but one thing I am *not* is dishonest. I am no thief! I've taken nothing! Please, you must believe me!"

The drunken trader wore a sinister expression of delight as a heated argument ensued. There was no evidence, but Evans believed the accusations against John, just as he had *not* believed the accusations John had hurled at his wife. The light from the fire danced and reflected in the trader's red eyes as Evans finally grabbed John by the wrists and ordered the other servant to put the iron fetters on John's ankles. Within moments, John's legs were shackled, and he was locked onto the rings of the deck of the ship like a slave.

As Evans and the trader kept at their rum by the fire, John felt the cold iron against his skin and spiraled in despair from the repeated injustice shown to him. Before long, rain began to fall, and Evans made his way back on board. "Good thing we brought those extra fetters, hey, Newton?" With that he descended into the dry, warm cabin, leaving John alone. All John had on was a thin cotton shirt, sailor breeches, a handkerchief tied around his head, and a swath of cotton cloth tied around his waist. The rain pelted him like needles and quickly soaked him to the bone. Drifting from the shore he heard low laughter mixed with the fire's sizzle as it was extinguished by the rain.

Your rations, Newton, Evans had told John matter-of-factly, leaving a pint of rice on the deck near to where John was chained. Evans had given him enough slack to move a short distance around the deck, his chain dragging behind him. *We'll return in a day or so.*

The rice was long gone, and John had been locked out in the elements for nearly thirty hours. He shivered, both from the cold rain and from the sunburn he had received earlier in the day when the brutal sun beat down on him. This was the rainy season, when the weather changed from scorching heat to violent thunderstorms in a matter of minutes. John had opened his mouth to the rain and was grateful to at least have something to drink. But his stomach felt as if it would eat itself. *How am I going to survive?*

Suddenly a shadow flew overhead, and John turned to see a seagull swooping down toward the deck before quickly turning up when it saw him. It swooped down again, skirting the deck. John looked to see what it was after and noticed some bloody entrails lying on the deck next to the small cooking brazier where Evans's servant had prepared a wild duck they had shot for dinner. The guts remained wet from the constant rain. "Maybe I could catch a fish!" he exclaimed to himself, getting up and dragging his chains. He shooed away the seagull and picked up the guts. "I need a hook." He looked around the brazier and stuck in between two planks was a single hook on an old bit of string. "Oh!" John's heart leaped with hope. His hand shook as he took the bloody entrails and threaded them onto the hook. He looked overboard and saw that the tides were changing. John knew he had a small window of time to try to catch a fish while the currents were still.

John slowly lowered the hook over the side of the boat and scanned the muddy river water for the shadow of a swimming fish. After a few moments a shadow darted by, investigating the baited hook. "Take it, take it," he urged the fish through clenched teeth. The shadow disappeared and everything was still for a few moments. John's face fell, and he thought of eating the entrails himself.

Suddenly he felt a tug against his hand and pulled the string taught, hooking the fish. His heart raced as he slowly lifted the fish from the water and onto the deck. He hadn't felt this happy since he was sitting next to Polly at the Catletts' house! The fish flopped on the deck as John lit the few coals in the brazier with the flint stored there in the mess box. He picked up the fish and kissed it, overjoyed to have something to eat. He used a small knife from the mess box to gut the fish, reserving the tools for a later catch. He placed his catch on the hot coals. He didn't care that it was charred and that he had no sauce or seasoning. He devoured every bite with tears of relief.

Within moments of finishing his fish, rain pellets plinked across the deck and the temperature plummeted, ushering in a new storm. John curled up next to the brazier to soak up the last bit of warmth before the coals died away. Tornadic winds suddenly blew with such ferocity that he had to hang on to the ship's gunnels for dear life. Lightning lit up the darkened sky and thunder crashed above him. In mere moments he was drenched and chilled to the bone. But while the storm growled, at least his stomach did not.

He had hope that he could make it one more day, because of one single fish.

9

A Servant of Slaves

PLANTAIN ISLAND, AFRICA, FALL 1746

The full moon gave John Newton enough light to make his way down to the beach where the incoming tide gently washed back and forth over a cluster of rocks. His shirt was now frayed at the edges, but it was the only one he had, and it was filthy from his long day of hard work. His ankle irons clanked against a boulder as he sat down and removed his shirt to scrub it on the rocks. While he washed away the grime, he gazed up at the moon, thinking about Polly. *I'm glad she can't see me like this.*

Earlier in the day some men from a ship that was anchored offshore rowed to the island. John hid in the woods until they were gone, as he was too ashamed to be seen by anyone. After their return to Plantain Island from the two-month trip upriver, Evans promptly took John to the blacksmith and had him fitted with a pair of ankle irons. Why Evans did so seemed pointless, except for serving to further humiliate John by displaying his new status. John couldn't swim, so he certainly wouldn't escape by swimming the two miles to Sierra Leone. Perhaps Evans reasoned that John might try to steal a canoe at night and row to freedom. Either way, John was resigned to his fate. He was now a servant of slaves.

John was assigned to work for a slave who was the overseer of this growing plantation. His task was to dig row upon row of holes and plant young lime trees. It was backbreaking, solitary work in the hot sun. No one was allowed to speak to John Newton other than his supervisor.

Of course, Evans and P.I. spoke to him, mockingly. One day, they came to the lime orchard to inspect John's progress.

"Who knows, Newton?" Evans said, rubbing a leaf between his fingers. "Who knows but by the time these trees grow up and bear, you may go home to England, obtain the command of a ship, and return to reap the fruits of your labors? We see strange things sometimes happen." P.I. shrilly laughed at the idea and together they walked away, arm in arm.

John was twenty-one years old now. It seemed a lifetime ago that he was sailing the Mediterranean to Venice or singing bawdy shanties with the men on the *Harwich* or the *Levant* or sitting with Polly on a bench in Kent. Gone was the haughtiness he once possessed. His heart was now brought low, but not to a wholesome repentance or even to the language of the prodigal son. His spirits were sunk like the poor sailors who had perished from fever and were committed to the deep with weights tied to their feet. He had lost all resolve to conquer his world, along with almost all reflection about anything with meaning. Even the lofty ideas of his once-admired *Characteristics* held nothing of value for him to ponder. He had lost the fierceness that fired him on board the *Harwich* to make him capable of the most desperate attempts. Still, he was no more changed than a tiger tamed by hunger: if his circumstances were to change, he would be as wild as ever.

John was indeed tamed by hunger. His meager rations continued, as did the anonymous gifts of food from fellow slaves. But he was numb to life, unable to even feel gratitude for what had been given him by a sympathetic house servant or by those heading to a fate worse than death aboard a slave ship crossing the Middle Passage.

But Polly. The thought of her was the only thing that made him feel *anything*. The seemingly impossible hope of seeing her again was the only motivation he had to take a risk when an opportunity presented itself several weeks later.

A house slave who was responsible for ensuring that Evans's mail was transferred to passing merchant ships bound for London approached John with an unspoken idea. Well, he didn't speak with words, but with actions. He kept his distance on the far side of the lime grove. He pointed at John, wrote in the air, and then tapped the canvas mail bag. He looked both ways and then walked over to a tree to put his hand in between two branches, indicating the spot where John could place a letter. This servant was risking everything to give John a lifeline to the outside world. His reason for doing it was beyond John's understanding. He gave little thought to the servant's motives, and he didn't hold much hope that a letter would reach his father or Polly, but what could it hurt? It might take half a year to arrive in London or never arrive at all if the ship was lost at sea, or the mail bag pilfered and tossed overboard. John still had a few pieces of paper and a charcoal pencil in his knapsack, so he scribbled one letter to his father and one to Polly. He left the letters in the tree early next morning, and noticed they were gone shortly thereafter, even though he never saw the servant retrieve them.

John wrote to his father about his condition and asked for assistance. But he also told him that he had resolved not to return to England unless his father was pleased to send for him. And what was he to tell Polly? That he was now a servant of slaves? There were no grand exploits of adventure or the possibility of laying riches at her feet. Still, he promised her all he had to give, and that was his undying love.

As John gathered the writing materials, he saw his copy of Euclid tucked away in his knapsack. It was the only thing he possessed, and it might pass the time and allow him to get lost in mathematical equations. Anything would be a welcome relief from this meaningless existence.

John yawned. It was late and he couldn't wait for sleep. He wrung out his shirt the best he could before putting it back on wet so it would dry while he slept. He lumbered back to his hut dragging his ankle fetters and lay down on his mat, falling right to sleep.

After weeks, it became a daily ritual for John to work hard all day and then retreat to the far end of the island with his book. He took a long stick and wrote out equations in the sand to visualize what he read. Doing these mathematical exercises gave him a strange sort of mental solace. He escaped from his hopeless world into one where there was order, clarity, and consistency. The principles of geometry that Euclid described were steadfast and proven across centuries. If only other books held such dependability and steadfast truth! Before long, he had mastered the first six books within this volume of Euclid as a self-taught student of the ancient Greek master.

One evening as he was writing out an equation in the sand, a white man came walking toward him, stunned by what he saw. Here was a white slave in rags, wearing shackles, and standing in the middle of a sandy peninsula covered in mathematical equations. John didn't hear him approach so jumped in surprise when the man spoke to him.

"Who *are* you?" the man asked, surveying John's appearance with pity.

John quickly turned and dropped his stick in the sand. No one had spoken a word to him in so long. He had almost forgotten how to converse like a normal person.

"I . . . I am no one," John mumbled, rubbing his bony, filthy hands together nervously with his eyes cast to the sand. He was ashamed of his appearance and his predicament.

The man took a few steps closer and stared intently at John's gaunt face and the dark circles under his eyes. He could tell the young man was obviously malnourished and emotionally traumatized. "You're from London. So am I. I'm Patrick Clow, here to do some trading on the island, separate from Evans's operation of course. What's your name?"

"John . . . Newton," John told him, not offering anything further.

"How is it that you know how to do all of this?" Clow asked him, pointing to the equations in the sand.

John looked at his work, shrugged his shoulders, and leaned down to pick up his book. "I read this."

"Well, you're obviously very intelligent," Clow told him with a warm smile. He didn't want to press the young man about his situation just yet. "Are you hungry? I have some biscuits and a bit of dried ham."

John's mouth watered at the thought of ham. He nodded. "Thank you."

"Have a seat," Clow offered with a hand to the sand. He sat down and opened his knapsack, removing a flask of water and a cloth holding the biscuits and ham. He spread it out for John.

John eagerly took a bite of ham and struggled to not well up with tears at something so delicious. He didn't recall the last time he had eaten something so hearty. He eagerly drank from the flask, closing his eyes, and wiping his mouth with the back of his arm.

Clow wrapped his arms around his knees and looked at John's rags. "What happened to you, John?"

John. How long has it been since someone called me that? he thought as he swallowed another bite. "I came here to apprentice with Evans in the slave trade, but the princess hated me the moment she met me. Now I'm planting her lime orchard." He didn't want to say much more, or risk saying something that would cause punishment from P.I. when Clow next spoke with her.

"So instead of being a slave *master,* you are a *servant* of slaves," Clow realized, furrowing his brow as he stared at the rags and chains. John simply nodded, not saying more. "Well, you obviously have much more value than planting lime trees." He brushed off his hands and got to his feet. "We'll speak again soon, John. I'll bring you more food later, yes?"

John gave a slight smile. "Yes."

As Clow walked back toward the main part of the little island, John sat there in the sand eating a biscuit and stared out to sea. The sun was setting, and the sky became streaked in brilliant hues of red, orange, yellow, and pink. He didn't know what to think of this encounter.

THE WAR ROOM

"Because you did not serve the Lord your God with joy and gladness of heart, for the abundance of everything, therefore you shall serve your enemies, whom the Lord will send against you, in hunger, in thirst, in nakedness, and in need of everything; and He will put a yoke of iron on your neck until He has destroyed you," Gillamon read from Deuteronomy 28 as they looked on at the unbelievable scene.

"This is wha' it looks like when ye run away from the Maker, jest like Israel," Kate told the others sadly. "Look how far the lad has fallen by makin' so many bad choices! But he *still* hasn't had a change of heart ta make him turn an' run back ta the Maker."

"He must have a low backside," Al noted with great seriousness.

"I believe you mean he has a low *bottom* to hit before he can make an upward turn," Nigel clarified.

"I knew what you meant, Al," Jock whispered to the simple-minded cat.

"But it is *quite* astonishing to see the depths of John Newton's depravity," Nigel suggested. "Yet, evil has always swirled around humans, both good and bad. I recall when David penned the fifty-sixth Psalm:

"Be merciful to me, O God, for man would swallow me up;
Fighting all day he oppresses me.
My enemies would hound me all day,
For there are many who fight against me, O Most High.
All day they twist my words;
All their thoughts are against me for evil.
They gather together,
They hide, they mark my steps,
When they lie in wait for my life."

Liz silently shook her head in shocked disbelief. "I do not know where to begin in discussing the things that have happened to John on Plantain Island."

"Aye, well, I know one thing. There be evil there with that poisonous pr-r-rincess. An' if I didn't know better, I'd say that were Charlatan himself whisperin' in her ear behind that fr-r-reaky mask," Max suggested.

"Oui, and there is actual poison as well! John ate *raw* cassava roots!" Liz exclaimed. "Unless cassava roots are boiled and dried by the sun, they are toxic! The entire plant is poisonous—its roots, leaves, and peels. John was essentially consuming cyanide!"

Jock's eyes widened. "So, he's not only *eating* poison, but he's surrounded by poison and evil?"

"But at least he were saved by a fish," Al offered for a bright spot.

"It is of course obvious that John is suffering the consequences of running from the Maker, but I also see a pattern of evil intervention here," Liz suggested. "There is no logical reason for P.I. to have instantaneously reacted with such hatred and to treat John with such inhumane cruelty."

"Aye, she acted jest like Potiphar's evil wife in accusin' Joseph back in Egypt," Max agreed. "Joseph hadn't done anythin' wr-r-rong, but Potiphar thr-r-rew the innocent lad in pr-r-rison."

"That's when ye worked for the jailer and I lived with Pharaoh," Al remembered. "I had to wear all sorts o' jewelry like the princess do."

"You are all correct," Gillamon told them. "As we've seen across time, whenever the Maker has a special calling upon a human He intends to use in a great way for His purposes, evil opposition is all too obvious in attempting to thwart those plans. Although John Newton willingly turned his back on the Maker and has experienced the consequences of his decisions, evil actors are indeed at work to maximize those consequences."

"Poison. Kakia!" Liz exclaimed in alarm. *"She* was the smelly bookseller that sold that evil book *Characteristics* to John, no? And what better way for her to kill John than to make sure he's starved and desperate enough to eat poison?"

"It would appear that's exactly who it was," Clarie offered. "Since Kakia is a cat that can take any shape or form, like me or Gillamon, she appears to have been very active on the John Newton mission from the beginning."

"I say, was *she* the feline that startled John's horse that sent him flying to narrowly miss the hedgerow?" Nigel posed. "The boy could have died instantly!"

"Of course! And what exactly caused the boat to mysteriously overturn and drown all of John's friends on that fateful Sunday when Gillamon delayed him at the church?" Liz asked. "I presume she became some sort of sea monster."

"Sea monsters be real for *real?"* Al asked fearfully with his paws up to his mouth.

Gillamon nodded. "I knew you would eventually detect the pattern of evil. Evil always overplays its hand to proudly reveal itself."

"Wha' aboot that James Mitchell?" Kate asked.

"Sadly, Mitchell was just a lost human who completely rejected the Maker and unknowingly did Satan's bidding to lure John into atheism."

"So, were that masked man Charlatan whisperin' evil suggestions in that evil lass's ear?" Max asked in a low growl. "He always comes himself for the most important missions, ever since his first assignment in the Garden with Adam an' Eve."

"Oui, and of course Charlatan then struck at Noah's Ark, doing the evil one's bidding," Liz followed. "He has slowly been building his minion team of evil *chaos* to counter our team of *order* as we work on mission for the Maker to help humans."

"Indeed. Charlatan also took the form of the drunken trader with Evans who accused John of stealing supplies," Gillamon answered. "Charlatan and Kakia have worked in tandem to destroy John Newton from the beginning."

"John hardly survived those two months chained to that shallop," Clarie reported. "Evans left him there exposed to the weather sometimes twenty, thirty, or nearly forty hours. Although a young man at the time, the severity of that weather exposure broke his health to such a degree that he suffers to this day, getting easily chilled and unable to tolerate cold."

"But weren't you both there to help him on Plantain Island?" Jock wanted to know, looking at Gillamon and Clarie.

"Not to the degree we would have liked," Clarie answered. "Understand it was important for John to experience the full effects of his choice to reject the Maker. It may seem shocking but not doing anything is one of the kindest things the Maker does to bring lost humans back to Himself. Still, we've aided in small ways where we could ease John's suffering, which is also part of the Maker's kindness."

"Were ye that seagull that dove for them duck guts?" Al wanted to know.

Clarie put her arms out as if she were flying. "That was me! It didn't take much to help John figure out what to do after I stashed the fishhook on the string."

"Like I always say, fishes saves lives," Al testified with a goofy grin, patting his fluffy belly. "I should know."

"Wha' aboot all them slaves bringin' John food?" Kate asked.

"That wasn't us. Those were slaves acting out of genuine kindness and pity for John," Gillamon told them with a smile. "Isn't it astonishing to see the capacity of goodness in the human heart, even when in the depths of despair?"

Nigel cleared his throat. "*To be the sport of slaves, or what's more wretched yet their pity.* Of course, that is from Shakespeare."

Al and Jock looked at one another and shrugged their shoulders.

"C'est incroyable!" Liz exclaimed, her eyes swimming at such amazing kindness. "But what about the slave with the mail pouch? Was that you?"

Gillamon nodded with a grin. "I'm happy to say it was. And Clarie was the one who pointed Clow in the direction where he discovered John on the beach to see how smart he was with all those calculations."

Liz's eyes lit up with excitement as she thought this through. "Clarie, might you have been a *good* bookseller who convinced John to buy that book of Euclid in Plymouth?"

"Yes, and that book was truly anti-poison for John on that island," Clarie answered with a smile. "It seemed odd at the time, but as you'll see, the Maker knew what he was doing with that title. It saved John's life."

"Books and fishes. Both be lifesavers," Al theorized.

"Brilliant! What a jolly good idea for the young chap to send word to Captain Newton!" Nigel cheered. "And I must say, it was a double stroke of genius to reunite John with his Euclid, what? I'm quite pleased as to John's self-taught geometric prowess. It shall serve him well in life."

"If he ever gets off that island," Jock added. "So, did John's letters arrive?"

"Oui, and what happened with this Clow fellow?" Liz eagerly asked.

Max nodded. "Aye, an' wha' else did ye do ta help the lad?"

Gillamon tapped the panel and grinned. "You'll see. Sometimes making history comes down to a fifteen-minute miracle."

10

A Fifteen-Minute Miracle

SIERRA LEONE, AFRICA, FEBRUARY 1747

It was a good day for business, with stunningly blue skies and gentle breezes wafting through the palm fronds above the open-air trading house positioned by the turquoise water. A pair of green monkeys frolicked atop the thatched roof, causing the trader to frown and step out from under the canopy to shoo them away. He didn't want one of his best customers to be irritated while he looked over the items for trade, but the monkeys stayed put for the transaction.

Captain Anthony Gother lifted a soft bar of beeswax to his nose and breathed in its mildly sweet fragrance before replacing it in the box. He rubbed his thumb and fingers together and nodded. "I'll take the lot."

"Excellent! No better beeswax in all West Africa!" the trader claimed excitedly. "Are you sure you do not want one or two slaves to take with your ivory?"

Gother watched a line of five barefoot African slaves carrying heavy eight-foot elephant tusks toward his longboats to row back to his merchant ship *Greyhound.* He knew this trader wanted to get double the profit for his combined ivory-slave business. Ivory had long been the "white gold" of Africa ever since the ancient Romans exported North African elephants for the games in Rome. The ivory tusks were extracted from the slain gentle giants in the bloody Colosseum and used for numerous carved items desired by the wealthy class. Such brutal hunting nearly drove the elephants to extinction, halting the ivory trade for several centuries; the trans-Saharan traders of the Middle Ages then brought ivory from West Africa to the Middle East and Europe. In the fifteenth century, demand for ivory drove

Portuguese explorers to increase the West African elephant ivory trade, soon depleting the population of African elephants near the coast. Hunters now had to search farther inland to find herds, requiring more human labor to transport the massive tusks back to the coast. In an act of cruelty to both men and beasts, traders decided they would first capture slaves whom they could then use to haul the ivory. This solved the transport problem and brought a double profit for them to trade with both the slaves and the ivory.

"No slaves. We only seek gold, ivory, beeswax, and camwood on this voyage. But speaking of slaves, I'm looking for a man by the name of John Newton. He works for a slave trader named Evans. Do you know him?"

The African trader frowned with a pout, shaking his head. "Evans? Maybe he's on the Bananas. You look there."

"Very well, we will venture to those islands on our way down the coast," Gother answered.

KITTAM, AFRICA, FEBRUARY 1747

John Newton sat drinking late afternoon tea on the beautiful veranda outside the factory with his junior associate McCraig. The two young men had just assessed their inventory of trading goods in the warehouse for John to transport upcountry. "We need more rum, cotton, and gunpowder." He set down his pen and picked up the china cup, taking a sip and staring the distant mile out to the sea. "The cotton and powder are not as important to the tribal chiefs, but they always want the rum. Plus our trades are much improved after allowing them to try *plenty* of samples."

"Amazing how it all comes full circle, isn't it, John?" McCraig observed. "The African chiefs supply the slaves who go to the West Indies to work the sugar plantations for producing the rum that is brought back here for them to drink before they go out to capture more slaves."

"It's a strange world, but it's business," John answered with a smile, replacing his teacup in the saucer. "*Good* business."

"I'm sure they'll accuse you of watering down the rum *after* they've sampled it," McCraig joked. "But don't let them cheat you either, John!"

"You tink I am a *white* man?" John joked back with an exaggerated African accent.

The African slave trade thrived on shrewd cunning and deception. Both sides tried to take advantage of each other to maximize profits. So, the blacks would denigrate the white men as cheaters, but after enough years at the trade the white men would strangely "grow black." This of course didn't refer to skin color, but to adopting the personalities, customs, and ceremonies of the natives. Some would even succumb to the pretended black magic with amulets, divinations, and all mysterious manner of witchcraft and voodoo.

It had only been a few months since John left Plantain Island, but he was already back to full vigor, and prospering in partnership with Patrick Clow. After their first meeting on the beach that providential afternoon, Clow sought to take the good-with-numbers John Newton with him to work for his slave factories. It took Evans and P.I. a while to agree to Clow's proposal, but they eventually relented, and the servant of slaves was liberated from planting a lime orchard in chains.

John soon was well clothed, eating his full at Clow's bountiful table as a companion, and entrusted with all Clow's domestic affairs involving the management of several thousand pounds. Clow was far more successful than Evans, owning several factories with white servants in various places along the Guinea Coast. He decided to take John to the thriving factory in Kittam where the vast river system ran parallel to the coast and split into endless waterways to reach inland tribes. John was given a joint share in the management of the business with McCraig, so they had the right to own a certain number of the captured slaves and sell them to trading captains for personal profit.

Life was good now, and John Newton thought himself to be quite happy. He had already begun to grow fond of the customs of the country and contented himself with the thought of living and dying among the Africans. Thoughts of returning to London and Polly were pushed further and further from his mind; not for lack of desire, but for his despair of ever seeing them again. It was easier to bear the disappointment by accepting where he was and just moving forward. If that meant giving himself completely to Africa and growing pitch black, he thought, then so be it.

"So, what do you want to do about the missing items for trade?" McCraig asked, taking a sip of tea.

John ran his fingers through his hair and clasped his hands behind his head. "I know merchant ships pass this coast, even though I haven't seen one since I've been here." He thought a moment more and threw a hand down to slap the table. "Let's give it until tomorrow afternoon, and if a ship doesn't pass by, I'll just head upriver with what we have."

"Very good, John," McCraig agreed. "Who knows? Perhaps we'll get lucky and a ship laden with rum will enter these waters!"

"For now, let's get busy like white men and pack up my wagon," John laughed.

McCraig was awakened early in the morning by a screeching monkey outside his window that would not let him sleep. Frustrated, he threw back the covers and decided to take a couple of slaves with him down to the beach in case a ship happened by. As soon as they got down to the water's edge, he pulled out his spyglass and couldn't believe what he saw. "A ship! Hurry, light the smoke signal to let them know we want to trade!" he ordered the slaves. He kept an eye on the ship as it kept sailing off. "They've got a fair wind, and they've already passed by. Still. . ."

As the slaves lit the signal, a plume of thick black smoke rose into the air.

"Sir! Smoke signal from shore!" a sailor cried from the bosun's nest at the top of the mast. "They want to trade!"

Captain Gother pulled out his spyglass to see the signal, then looked up at the *Greyhound's* taut sails. They were clipping along at fantastic speed from the excellent winds. At this rate, they could make up lost time today. They had looked for John Newton and Evans in the Banana Islands, but the locals there told him that the boy was probably somewhere upriver a couple of hundred miles south. Gother collapsed his spyglass with a frown, uncertain if they should stop. He didn't want to waste any more time.

"Captain, what if that signal leads you *straight* to Newton?" posed a crew member named Daggdul. "Now *that* would be a fanciful tale to tell, as well as a feather in your cap with Mister Manesty, hey?"

"Hmmm," Gother mumbled as he thought a moment. "It would indeed."

He had been given the unlikely assignment of finding a needle in a haystack by his employer, Joseph Manesty. As soon as John's letter to his father miraculously arrived in London, Captain Newton went straight to his friend Manesty's Liverpool office. He implored Manesty to please have his ship *Greyhound* look for his son and bring him home. The ship just so happened to be leaving for the Guinea Coast as they spoke. Although John had previously thrown away his opportunity to sail with Manesty to Jamaica and make his fortune, Captain Newton hoped his friend would nevertheless help the wayward boy. Manesty knew how desperate his friend was to bring his son home, fearful and appalled at the boy's predicament. He remembered that once upon a time, he too had been a headstrong, unwise youth. He agreed to help and ordered Captain Gother to exhaust his efforts to find John.

Suddenly, Gother gushed out orders, "COME ABOUT!" sending the crew into action to turn the ship around. "Let's see if we'll have a tale to tell or not."

"They're turning!" McCraig exclaimed as he saw the ship now sailing back toward them. "Get the canoe ready. I'll go out and see what they have for trade."

Within thirty minutes, McCraig had rowed out to the *Greyhound* anchored offshore. As soon as he reached the top of the rope ladder, Daggdul extended his hand to help him onto the deck with a smile. He had striking blue eyes. "Welcome aboard."

"We saw your signal," Captain Gother told McCraig. "Tell me, do you know John Newton?"

McCraig looked from the captain to Daggdul, his mouth hanging open in disbelief. "Newton? You mean *John* Newton from *London?* Why yes, we're partners here in Kittam! He's on his way upcountry this afternoon but was hoping to obtain a few more items from a passing ship before he left. It's as if the timing of you sailing by Kittam was all planned!"

Gother turned to share a broad grin with the Daggdul who had encouraged him to stop.

"Then we had better catch him before he leaves, shan't we?" Gother said, walking over to climb down the ladder.

"Mister Newton, at last! I'm Captain Gother of the *Greyhound,"* Gother told a very surprised John Newton, reaching out his hand. "We've been looking for you *everywhere."*

John gave a confused look at a smiley McCraig and took Gother's hand to shake it. "What do you mean, sir?"

"Your *letter,* of course! It reached your father who then asked Mister Manesty if our ship could inquire about you on our travels here," Gother explained excitedly. "What a remarkable turn of events! We've sought you at several places in Sierra Leone and the Banana Islands while we traded for ivory and beeswax. At the speed we were sailing, had your smoke signal gone up just fifteen minutes later, we would *never* have seen it and would have sailed on. But here we are!" He held out his hands wide, delighted at their mission accomplished. He could just hear the praise from his employer. Perhaps this would lead to a promotion, or at the least a handsome bonus. "We're now heading south along the Ivory Coast to trade for gold and camwood before sailing west toward Brazil where we'll turn north to Newfoundland and sail back over to Liverpool. We should have you home within a year. The wind is fair today, so how soon can you be ready to depart?"

John felt numb. This shocking development was something he never dreamed would happen. He had lost all hope, which left his heart seared against ever hoping again. If the *Greyhound* had arrived while he was in fetters on Plantain Island, he would have been overjoyed with the idea of freedom. But now, he was happy here . . . wasn't he?

"I'm not going with you," John flatly informed Gother whose face fell as if he'd been put in fetters himself.

"Not *going?!* My dear Mister Newton, but you *must* come!" Gother implored, suddenly determined to not lose his reward now that he had obtained his objective. "Mister Manesty clearly commanded that I use half of his cargo if need be to secure your release, as your father is anxious to have you return home."

John shook his head. "I have a successful partnership in the trade with Mister Clow. My life is here now."

Gother's mind was racing for a convincing reply. He placed a hand over his heart and attempted a heartfelt look of joy. "Forgive me, but I haven't told you the most *important* news. In our hurry to embark Liverpool, I missed bringing a large packet of letters and papers for you. But I heard it straight from your father's own mouth, as well as from Mister Manesty, that some distant relation has passed and left you a substantial inheritance," he explained, trying to read John's face. "An inheritance of . . . four hundred pounds sterling per year. That is the salary of a *gentleman,* Mister Newton. Just think of the future you could have with that tidy sum."

Polly, John immediately thought, his heart stirring. It wasn't the thought of his father's care and desire to see him that carried any weight in this moment. That wasn't sufficient reason to make John leave his new life here in Kittam. *Oh, but my beloved Polly! There is new hope of seeing you again. And with this inheritance, I might be able to finally gain your hand!*

Gother tried to see if he had sold John on the idea. *One more incentive,* he thought. "Plus, you shall lodge in my cabin, dine at my table, and be my constant companion, Mister Newton. You will be treated as a gentleman passenger with no responsibilities on our voyage. How does that sound?"

John was still thinking about his future with Polly. The captain's offer was a bonus, but highly unnecessary given hope restored to marry the girl of his dreams. He broke out in a grin to the captain.

"I'll take that as a *yes,* Mister Newton," Gother winked. "Very well, shall we?"

The conversation lasted no more than fifteen minutes, but it ended his fifteen months of captivity. Within an hour, John Newton was aboard the *Greyhound* and bound for home. But as Kittam disappeared from view a few hours later, John didn't see the invisible chains that snaked around his soul with his newfound freedom.

11

WHAT IF THESE THINGS SHOULD BE TRUE?

THE WAR ROOM

"Huzzah, John's been rescued!" Jock cheered. "He must *really* be thankful for the Maker's help by now."

"Quite so, with such *undeniable* Divine intervention to lead the *Greyhound* to Kittam whilst John was in residence, following his Divine deliverance from that dreadful island of horrors," Nigel added.

"Plus, the *Greyhound's* arrival before John departed on his trading journey inland," Liz followed.

"An' McCraig bein' on the beach at jest the right time," Kate further agreed.

"And he's gettin' all that hair-i-tance, whatever that is," Al offered. "Plus eatin' at the captain's table!"

"So, the lad must be r-r-returnin' back ta the Maker now," Max concluded with a wide grin.

Gillamon and Clarie shared a knowing look and shook their heads, simultaneously declaring, "Not yet."

"Unfortunately, John's conscience is so incredibly seared that he is completely blind to see the connections between these incredible events and the Maker's Hand in them," Gillamon explained. "He sees them all simply as coincidences and thinks nothing about the meaning behind them."

"I say, is the old boy *blind?"* Nigel asked, adjusting his spectacles.

"Aye, an' daft?" Max grumbled. "Ye're tellin' us he no more thought aboot wha' happened ta r-r-rescue him than Al here thinks aboot geometry?"

Clarie shrugged her shoulders. "John is like a wave of the sea driven with the wind and tossed, and only reacts to events as they happen. He doesn't look any farther than the present moment. But He who is eyes to the blind is leading John in a way that he doesn't realize . . . yet."

"But the Maker is so very patient and gracious with blind and foolish creatures, no?" Liz suggested.

Jock cocked his head to the side. "I have a question. John was made a servant of slaves, right? I understand that Clow taking him away from Plantain Island to work in another factory was how John escaped, but when given the chance to go home and leave the slave trade, he didn't at first. Why did he want to keep working as a slave trader, doing the same thing to others that was done to him?"

"When ye're lost, it's hard to find yer way out o' things, jest like that time I got lost in the king's haze next to Tim's River," Al offered. "I panicked and didn't know which way to turn. I thought this kitty would never be seen again."

Liz stifled a grin. *"Oui,* Albert, that was on our Handel mission at King George II's palace of Hampton Court on the *Thames* River. You got lost in the *maze."*

"Well, there were haze in that maze," Al remembered.

Nigel gave a jolly chuckle. "I shall never forget your expression when your bride went in to find you and you emerged from the puzzle of green vines, exclaiming, 'I once were lost, but now I be found!'"

"Sure, and it's a grand feelin'—maybe better than fish and bananas," Al recalled. "I were right then."

"And you are right now, *cher* Albert," Liz told him with a nuzzle to his cheek. "John Newton is so very lost, and he does not know which way to turn, which leads to his poor decisions."

"So, once he's found, he'll know which way to go?" Jock asked.

"Aye, lad. That's how it works with the Maker," Max affirmed. "Lost humans make daft decisions an' stumble in their confusion inta all sorts of evil."

"So, if John wants ta get out of his maze, he needs ta follow the voice of the Maker ta lead him out," Kate added. "The Maker will give the lad grace for all he's done."

"That's what I'd call a*maz*ing grace, what?" Nigel quipped.

"Bon analogy. Now, I assume that Captain Gother came up with that tale of John's inheritance to convince him to return with them?" Liz asked.

"Correct, there was no inheritance," Gillamon confirmed. "But John did indeed get to sail as a first-class passenger with no responsibility, eating at the captain's table and staying in his comfortable quarters."

"Right, well, I must inquire about the assistance you two rendered for these events," Nigel posed, pointing to Gillamon and Clarie. "I suspect you were that pair of green monkeys to keep tabs on where the *Greyhound* stopped as well as rousing McCraig out of bed on that fateful morning to get him to the beach?"

"I'd like to be a monkey!" Al interrupted with a paw in the air. "I would eat every banana in sight!"

"He don't need ta be a monkey for that," Max whispered to Jock with a chuckle.

"Yes, it was necessary to make sure the timing and communications played out perfectly," Clarie answered with a grin.

"And of course, Gillamon you were the crew member Daggdul," Liz surmised, curling her tail up and down as she pondered the name. "Hmmm, Daggdul."

"Also, true, Liz," Gillamon told her. "It was vital that I be aboard for every moment of this journey until . . . well, until I needed to be elsewhere."

"So, that means ye can tell us all aboot the voyage," Kate shared happily. "What happened next?"

"I'm sad to tell you that for the *fourth* time in a row, John managed to destroy the good graces of his ship's captain," Clarie reported. "It didn't take long for him to offend Captain Gother."

"At least the lad's consistent," Al remarked awkwardly.

Max bonked Al on the head. "Daft kitty!"

"I won't burden you with the sights and sounds of the prodigal John Newton, but suffice it to say, he daily violated Parliament's Blasphemy Act 1697 and the Profane Oaths Act 1745, so he was a law-breaking blasphemous passenger from the moment he went aboard the *Greyhound,*" Gillamon told them.

"How utterly despicable!" Nigel spat, a paw to his forehead.

"What do those acts mean?" Jock wanted to know.

"See here, in their effort to foster good, Christian behavior of the citizenry, Parliament passed these two acts," Nigel began to explain. "The Blasphemy Act made it an offense for anyone educated in or professing Christianity to deny the truths of Christianity, such as the Holy Trinity or the Bible as the divine authority, or claim there to be more than one god. Of course, it has *rarely* been enforced but is meant to keep the Crown's citizens mindful of proper Christian conduct."

"Wha' aboot the Profane Oaths Act?" Kate asked with a frown.

"Well, its preamble refers to the 'horrid, impious, and execrable vices of profane cursing and swearing' abounding in the kingdom that 'may justly provoke the divine vengeance to increase the many calamities these nations now labor under,'" Nigel relayed. "The new act established a system of fines and possible imprisonment. Of course, offenders must be reported within four days of the act, so John Newton is safe from the law whilst at sea, as are the other sailors whose salty tongues wax profane."

"So, he were a foul-mouthed scoundr-r-rel," Max growled. "Wha' else, Gillamon an' Clarie? We might as well know the full of it."

"I can honestly say that no human has kept us busier with providing protection more than John Newton!" Clarie told them. "The *Greyhound* spent the next year sailing a thousand miles south of Kittam along the coast of Africa. The types of goods they sought took longer to find than slaves or other goods. They traded for camwood, which is a lightweight wood used for dyes, along with ivory, gold, and beeswax. Sometimes the trading took them deep into the jungle, and John would go along for the adventure."

Gillamon chuckled. "Adventure is an understatement. We had help from angels more than once at Cape Lopez, with the many dangers and snares surrounding John when they went hunting for wild buffalo. Night fell and they became lost without a compass or moonlight to guide them. Tigers, poisonous snakes, wild boars, crocodiles, venomous spiders, and all other manner of beasts tracked John and the group of men with him. They journeyed waist-deep in rivers and walked further inland in the opposite direction of the sea. I even had to wrangle a rather large python when John wasn't looking."

"If I'd been there, I'da wr-r-rangled him for ye, Gillamon!" Max exclaimed.

"But finally, the Maker pulled back the clouds, so the moonlight returned, and they found their way back to the shore," Clarie followed.

"Were zebras after them too?" Al asked, wide-eyed and worried.

Everyone looked at Al, saying nothing.

"The biggest danger for the entire crew was one of Captain Gother's making," Gillamon told them. "The *Greyhound* had been at sea for over a year and was in critical need of repairs and refurbishment. Over time, and especially in warm equatorial water, every part of a ship wears out. Sails get thin, rigging becomes worn, and wooden timbers rot. All ships leak and take on water, but if a weathered ship isn't properly caulked and painted, it can lead to disaster."

"So, rather than spend a few weeks in port where the *Greyhound* could have all of these repairs made for the voyage home, Captain Gother decided to make a non-stop voyage of seven thousand miles back to England in a leaky, rotten, unraveling, threadbare ship," Clarie continued. "They made one last stop at the small volcanic island of Annobón in the Gulf of Guinea to fill the ship with food, water, and provisions to last the journey. They couldn't have fit one more cask of water or flour on the ship. Cages of sheep, livestock, and poultry packed the outer deck."

Liz frowned. "This does not bode well for such a long winter voyage through the tropics, up the Atlantic seaboard and across the Northern Atlantic. So, besides John's poor behavior, the episode in the jungle, and the poor condition of the ship, what else happened while you were protecting him?"

"Show them the night he almost drowned, Gillamon," Clarie suggested.

"Very well, but I warn you that it was not a pretty sight," Gillamon told them, tapping a panel. "After that scene, we will look at the final stop in Newfoundland before venturing across the North Atlantic to England."

"Are we ever going to get to see the part where John becomes good again?" Jock asked sadly. "I've about given up on him."

"Like I said, the lad has a low backside," Al reminded him.

Gillamon smiled. "Hang on, little one, it's coming."

GREYHOUND AT ANCHOR, GABON RIVER, NEAR THE EQUATOR,1747

Four sailors sat on the deck lit by lanterns, clay pipes in hand laughing as John belted out his latest bawdy song with lyrics profaning the Christian beliefs held by Daggdul. When he was finished singing, he plopped two large bottles holding gin and rum onto the deck.

"I propose a competition!" John shouted. "Let's see who can remain standing the longest from drinking drams of rum *and* gin!"

"Take a swig and pass the bottle!" one sailor suggested with a laugh.

John shook his finger. "Not from the bottle, but from *this!"* He brought from behind his back a large seashell. "The man to your right has to pour your dram!"

"Show us how it's done, Newton! You're first, mate!" the sailor to his right teased, holding the bottle of rum.

"Very well!" John exclaimed, holding out the shell for the man to pour.

John gulped down the rum and then held out the shell for the sailor to pour the gin, some of it trickling down his chin as he chugged it down in one swallow. When he finished, he shook his head, already feeling dizzied, and handed the shell off to the next man. They all took turns, laughing and soon getting very drunk. But no one got drunk faster than John. He was never fond of drinking but got amusement from getting others drunk. Tonight, however, he took it too far. The joke was on John Newton.

As the drunken sailors started singing in slurred voices, clapping and stomping their feet on the deck in rhythm to a sea shanty, John proceeded to dance around the deck. He moved like the Africans he had seen dance around the fire in a drugged state of delirium in one of their voodoo rituals. Suddenly his hat blew overboard, and John ran to the railing. In his drunken state he thought his hat fell into the longboat right next to him, but it was tied and bobbing in the swift current twenty feet behind the ship. Like most sailors, John couldn't swim. If he landed in the water while sober, he would likely drown, but if he landed in the water drunk, it was guaranteed.

"I hash to gets my hat!" a very drunk John Newton slurred as he staggered along the deck with an outstretched hand. As he put his foot up to jump over the side of the boat, Daggdul appeared out of the shadows, grabbed him by the back of his shirt and pulled him down onto the deck. The other sailors were so drunk they thought that John just slipped and fell. The rest of the crew were fast asleep. John lay on the deck, laughing as the masts above him appeared to spin and spin and spin.

"Come, Mister Newton," Daggdul told him with a frown, picking John up to drag him to his bunk. "We don't need you swimming with the fishes tonight."

GREYHOUND, NEWFOUNDLAND, MARCH 12, 1748

"We'll only spend half a day here, men," Captain Gother told the crew as they dropped anchor off the banks of Newfoundland. "Our expert fisherman Daggdul assures me these are prime fishing waters for cod."

"Aye, Captain. The cod are so abundant now that they might jump into the longboat," Daggdul told the crew with a broad smile, getting a round of cheerful *huzzahs* from the men. "We'll catch scores of fish with the nets, then gut and salt them for the voyage home."

"Captain, we made sure to fill the holds of the ship with plenty of provisions in Annabón to see us home," First Mate Randy Jackson sourly noted under his breath with a nasally tone. "Is it necessary to spend time fishing in this frigid weather?"

Gother slapped Jackson on the back with a hearty laugh. "Indeed, we have provision enough to make it home, but a bit of diversionary fun and exercise is good for the men before we make our final run across the open sea."

"We'll feed the cod to the livestock," Daggdul suggested, pointing to the wooden crates of pigs, chickens, and sheep. "They'll enjoy the fish."

"Very well, make ready the longboat!" the captain ordered, sending the crew into action to lower the longboat over the side and into the chilly water below.

"So now we want our pigs to be happy before we slaughter them?" Jackson scoffed under his breath as Gother walked ahead of him.

Daggdul gave a singular laugh and readied the fish cleaning station to prepare the fish.

"Sir, I notice everyone is here to help except that John Newton," Jackson told Captain Gother with a sneer as they watched the crew below toss out the nets.

Gother frowned. "Newton was told he would have no responsibility on board. He evidently cannot handle this cold weather after his time in Africa, so he prefers to stay in the cabin. But *I* prefer it this way. Better to not have that Jonah around the men. He's been nothing but trouble since we picked him up in Kittam. His wicked influence on the crew is more than I can abide. All those bawdy songs and that blasphemous cursing! I am no religious man, but even *I* fear the judgment of God with him aboard. It's not safe to sail on the same ship as John Newton."

Jackson lifted his chin and looked down his bright red nose with a smug look on his face. "Agreed, Captain. Newton's arrogance has even caused the crew to grow weary of his dreadful daily 'expressions' to quote throughout the day."

Gother gave a snort as he pointed at Jackson's large, bulbous nose. "Newton made a veiled mockery of you after your night of heavy drinking brought on by Newton himself."

Jackson frowned at the insulting memory. John Newton had laughed, exclaiming, "Beware the jaw-me-dead snoach if he's been in the sun! Vice-Admiral of the Narrow Seas makes shoes run yellow with rum!" The insult described a talkative person who speaks through the nose, gets drunk, and then pees on other's shoes under the table—all of which described Jackson. Newton never mentioned anyone by name, but everyone always knew exactly who he meant with his daily digs at the crew.

"If only Newton hadn't agreed to come aboard in Kittam, but the idea of that *inheritance* was too good to pass up," Jackson jeered.

Gother winced. It was because of his fabricated lie of the inheritance that John Newton was even aboard the *Greyhound.* "Well, we'll be rid of him soon enough when we arrive in England."

"Unless you decide to toss him overboard now and save us the trouble of a storm," Jackson jested.

"The thought had occurred to me," Gother retorted, half-serious.

John Newton stood behind the mizzenmast close to where the two men stood. He had heard every word. He folded his arms tightly across his chest and shivered against the conversation that was as cold as the arctic air. It wasn't lost on John that as they approached England, he was returning home twofold more a child of hell than when he went out.

GREYHOUND, NORTH ATLANTIC, MARCH 20, 1748

John ran his hand along the few books he had borrowed from a couple of men aboard. With no responsibilities on this voyage, he had little else to do but read when the crew were busy with their chores. It had been a draining, cold day, and no one felt like expending their little remaining energy on drinking and bawdy songs. John had continued to amuse himself with mathematics, but his volume of Euclid was so used that he felt he had little else to learn from it. The crewman Daggdul had let him borrow a New Testament and Stanhope's edition of *The Imitation of Christ* by Thomas à Kempis. *What an odd name that mate Daggdul has,* John thought with a grin as he pulled the well-worn à Kempis from the shelf. He had thumbed through it a few times before tonight to pass the time, but its lofty words about faith and Jesus Christ never affected him any more than a romance novel. Still, it was something to read, so he proceeded to flip through various underlined portions of the book that Daggdul had evidently found meaningful.

> *Happy is he to whom truth manifests itself, not in signs and words that fade, but as it actually is. Our opinions, our senses often deceive us, and we discern very little. We have eyes and do not see. What, therefore, have*

we to do with questions of philosophy? He to whom the Eternal Word speaks is free from theorizing.

Wherever you are, wherever you go, you are miserable unless you turn to God.

He who seeks anything but God alone and the salvation of his soul will find only trouble and grief.

The beginning of all temptation lies in a wavering mind and little trust in God, for as a rudderless ship is driven hither and yon by waves, so a careless and irresolute man is tempted in many ways.

John furrowed his brow and squirmed. For the first time, the words he read started to act like a mirror. He didn't like what he saw.

When a man desires a thing too much, he at once becomes ill at ease. A proud and avaricious man never rests, whereas he who is poor and humble of heart lives in a world of peace. An unmortified man is quickly tempted and overcome in small, trifling evils; his spirit is weak, in a measure carnal and inclined to sensual things; he can hardly abstain from earthly desires. Hence it makes him sad to forego them; he is quick to anger if reproved. Yet if he satisfied his desires, remorse of conscience overwhelms him because he followed his passions, and they did not lead to the peace he sought. True peace of heart, then, is found in resisting passions, not in satisfying them. There is no peace in the carnal man, in the man given to vain attractions, but there is peace in the fervent and spiritual man.

As iron cast into fire loses its rust and becomes glowing white, so he who turns completely to God is stripped of his sluggishness and changed into a new man.

"New man? *Puh!*" John sneered to himself, growing more uncomfortable. He forcefully flipped the book to another page.

When Jesus is near, all is well, and nothing seems difficult. When He is absent, all is hard. When Jesus does not speak within, all other comfort is empty, but if He says only a word, it brings great consolation. For what, without Jesus, can the world give you? Life without Him is a relentless hell, but living with Him is a sweet paradise. If Jesus be with you, no enemy can harm you. The man who lives without Jesus is the poorest of the poor, whereas no one is so rich as the man who lives in His grace.

John stopped reading as a thought occurred to him. "What if these things should be true?" The question hung in the air, unanswered. John couldn't diagram these words or fit them into a tidy formula as he could his Euclid. He slammed the book shut. "True or false, I must abide by the consequences of my own choice. Enough of this reflection." He shoved the book aside and got up to join a chat with the crew over some vain matter or other to clear his head. By the time he crawled into his bunk that night and blew out his lantern, he thought no more about what he had read. But his subconscious mind mulled over the words even as he slept.

If you knew how to free yourself entirely from all creatures, Jesus would gladly dwell in you.

NORTH ATLANTIC OCEAN, MARCH 21, 1748, 3:00 A.M.

What felt like a thousand ice picks stabbing him made John bolt upright from a deep sleep. His eyes shot open, and he sucked in a desperate breath, in shock from the cold water that now drenched his body and his bed. He saw water pouring down the rungs of the ladder from the deck above into the cabin. Jumping to his feet, he grabbed hold of whatever he could to steady himself to reach the ladder. The *Greyhound* was being tossed about like a cork in the middle of a violent storm.

John reached the ladder and looked up to see shredded sails flying wildly in the wind, illuminated by a crack of lightning that lit up the night sky. They were tangled in the rigging, and he could hear them ripping apart. Just as he started to climb the ladder, Captain Gother's face appeared over the hatch and called down to him. "Newton! I need the large knife from my chest in the cabin! Find it, hurry!"

"Understood, Captain!" John shouted back, stumbling to locate the chest. Everything was out of place from sliding around the floor.

Suddenly Daggdul ran down the ladder into the cabin. "I'll help you look, John!" Within minutes, he had located the knife and turned to climb back up on deck. John stumbled, but followed behind him up the ladder.

As soon as Daggdul stepped out onto the deck ahead of John, a massive wave as tall as the Tower of London crashed over the ship, sweeping him off his feet and washing him overboard into the sea.

"NO!" Captain Gother screamed.

John's eyes widened in horror at seeing Daggdul swallowed by the raging sea. Gother clung to the tangled rigging and pointed at John. "If only *you* had come up that ladder first, Newton!" Captain Gother shouted above the roaring wind. He was overcome by grief at the loss of Daggdul but had no time or ability to retrieve him during this violent storm. "YOU, Newton, are a *Jonah!* A curse attends you wherever you go! All the troubles we're experiencing are because we brought *you* onto this ship! I should toss you overboard right now!" he raged. All Gother's pent-up anger and revulsion at John's wicked behavior came gushing out of him without restraint.

John's face filled with fear.

PART THREE

But Now Am Found

(Back to Jonah)

12

Who Is Jonah?

THE WAR ROOM

"GILLAMON!" Jock screamed. "You were washed overboard! And who is J . . . ?" he started to ask before Nigel quickly interrupted him.

"J-J-JUST look at the time!" Nigel shouted with a nervous chuckle after glancing at Al, who sat there transfixed on the angry scene of Captain Gother accusing John of being a "Jonah" in the middle of the storm.

The whiskers on the right side of Al's face started to twitch and he mindlessly muttered, "I thought time stopped in here."

Nigel locked eyes with Liz, who hurried over to get right in Al's face with a forced giggle. "Ah *oui, cher* Albert, obviously, we are in a timeless portal, but your *stomach* is not. You must be famished by now!"

"Aye, why don't ye go get some vittles, Al?" Kate suggested, putting a cautionary paw on Jock's leg. "We'll wait for ye."

"I were jest thinkin' aboot fish," Al confessed, suddenly blinking as if to clear away any other thoughts floating around in his mind.

"Ye're always thinkin' aboot fish, kitty," Max chuckled. "Go on, then."

Gillamon and Clarie shared a wink. Jock's eyes narrowed and he looked around the table at the other animals. "Something fishy is going on here."

"Ye kin say that again, lad," Max muttered under his breath.

Gillamon cleared his throat and walked over to the moving globe that sat at the end of the long table. "I seem to recall that you have a special affinity for South Carolina flounder, Al." He moved the metal Order of the Seven seal on the globe's cross dial to hover over North Island. "Go enjoy a snack and we'll be here when you return." He smiled and held out his hand for Al to come press the seal which would instantly transport him from the War Room to North Island.

Al's stomach rumbled, and he broke out in a goofy grin. "Don't mind if I do!" He hopped up onto the table, kissed Liz on the cheek, and sauntered over to the globe. "Be back in a flounder o' three."

"Cheerio and happy fishing, old boy!" Nigel exulted.

Clarie put her hand over Jock's eyes so he wouldn't see Al's departure. The big orange cat reached out his fluffy paw, pressed the seal, and immediately vanished from the room. Everyone let go a collective sigh of relief.

"What is going on?!" Jock protested as Clarie lowered her hand from his eyes.

"Ye see, lad, we can't talk aboot Jonah when Big Al's around," Max explained. "It sets him off somethin' fierce."

"Aye, it took him *decades* ta get over that mission," Kate quickly added.

Nigel placed a hand over his heart. "That was a close one, but the crisis was averted!"

Jock grumbled and barked, "WHO IS JONAH?! And why did the Captain of the *Greyhound* accuse John Newton of being one?"

Liz sat calmly with her tail wrapped around her legs. "We do owe you an explanation, little Jock. For you need solid answers to these important questions, no?"

Gillamon walked over to the panel of time and touched it, revealing a middle-aged man wearing a blue and white tunic hurrying along a bustling dock at the ancient port of Joppa. He walked down a row of Phoenician ships as their hulls filled with cargo, scurrying from one to the next to determine its next destination. "This is Jonah. He was one of the Maker's prophets for the ten northern tribes of Israel, about eight hundred years before Jesus was born. Max, Liz, Kate, Al, Nigel, and I were assigned to help him on this mission."

Clarie's face lit up and she sat down next to Jock. "I'm excited to see this history myself, Jock! This mission was way before my time."

"He was a different kind of prophet," Liz interjected.

"And defiant," Nigel added with a finger raised in the air.

"An' difficult," Kate chimed in.

"An' *delicious,"* Max said with a snicker. "Ain't that r-r-right, Gillamon?"

Jock's eyes widened. "What *is* a prophet anyway?"

"A prophet be someone ta whom the Maker gives a message for sharin' with a specific human or groups of humans," Kate explained. "They give warnin's or hope, an' tell things that will happen in the future, either good or bad. Ye always know if they be true prophets when their words happen jest as they said."

"For instance, Isaiah prophesied that the coming Messiah would be a baby born of a virgin, and Micah prophesied that he would be born in Bethlehem Ephrathah," Liz explained, smiling. "That's when we met Clarie, when Jesus was born."

Clarie reached out to give Liz an affectionate scratch behind the ears. "So, what made Jonah different from other prophets?"

"The Maker sent Jonah to give a message to Israel's most hated enemy—the Assyrians," Gillamon answered. "Normally, the Maker sent messages to His own people within the borders of the Hebrew nation. He never sent missionaries to Gentiles out in the world, but rather used Israel as an epicenter for the world to come and see His glory, as was the case with King Solomon. And the Maker most certainly never sent prophets to warn Israel's enemies to turn away from wickedness. So, Jonah did not wish to be the first prophet to do any of those things. That made him quite different."

"An' he were the first pr-r-rophet ta r-r-refuse the Maker's assignment," Max added with a growl. "That made him defiant. Instead of obeyin' like other pr-r-rophets, the lad r-r-ran in the opposite direction from where the Maker were sendin' him!"

Jock's mouth hung open. "Jonah actually disobeyed the Maker?"

"Dear me, yes! And not just in his actions, but in his *heart,* which made him consistently difficult," Nigel answered. "I suggest we read about our subject straight from the source." The little mouse walked over to the closed Bible sitting on the table in front of Clarie. "My dear, if you would be so kind, please open the Holy Writ to the book of *Jonah."*

"My pleasure, Nigel," Clarie answered with a smile as she opened the book and flipped the pages until she found it. She turned the Bible around and pushed it toward Nigel.

"Thank you, Clarie. Now then, the book of *Jonah* contains only forty-eight verses," Nigel explained.

"So, at first glance, his story may not appear to be very *deep,"* Liz interjected with a coy smile. But *au contraire,"* Jonah's story is quite the opposite, in more ways than one, no?"

"Indeed, my pet!" Nigel chuckled, preening his whiskers as he walked up onto the page and began to read:

> "Now the word of the Lord came to Jonah the son of Amittai, saying, 'Arise, go to Nineveh, that great city, and cry out against it; for their wickedness has come up before Me.' But Jonah arose to flee to

Tarshish from the presence of the Lord. He went down to Joppa, and found a ship going to Tarshish; so he paid the fare, and went down into it, to go with them to Tarshish from the presence of the Lord."

Jock's gaze drifted to the panel of time. He saw Jonah pull out a leather pouch to pay the captain of the ship. Jonah nervously looked both ways and cast a glance skyward, pulling his cloak over his head before he walked down the ramp and quickly disappeared below decks. "Well, Jonah must not have been a very smart prophet. Doesn't he know the Maker is everywhere? You can't run from Him! Even I know that."

Kate put her paw on Jock's shoulder. "Humans have been tryin' ta hide from Him ever since Adam an' Eve sinned in the Garden an' then hid themselves. But there be more than one way ta run from the Maker besides hidin'. We've been watchin' John Newton run as far from Him as he can. Creatures can hide jest by ignorin' the Maker an' actin' like they didn't hear wha' He told them ta do."

Jock wrinkled his brow. "So, where did Jonah come from, and where is Nineveh? And where is Tarshish? I don't know any of these things."

"Never fear, we were there!" Nigel exclaimed, with a confident fist in the air. "Before we travel onward with our wayward prophet down Living History Lane, I believe it would benefit our young friend to hear the story behind Jonah's story."

"C'est un bonne idée, Nigel," Liz agreed. "Jonah was from a little town called Gath-hepher in Galilee, very near Jesus' home in Nazareth. His father's name 'Amittai' means 'firm, faithful, and true.' Jonah's name means 'Dove.'" Liz frowned. "I've always wondered if something tragic happened to Jonah when he was younger. Something must have driven him to defy the Maker and refuse to go to Nineveh. There is always a reason behind all behavior, *n'est-ce pas?"*

"Hear, hear! I fully concur, my dear," Nigel agreed. "Jonah served as a prophet during the reign of King Jeroboam II in the northern kingdom of Israel, from 793 to 753 B.C. Allow me to present a brief history of Israel's kings, as it tends to get a bit muddled, what?" The little mouse started walking up and down the table, in full lecture mode, gesturing with an outstretched paw as if pointing to an invisible timeline.

"Right, now then, Israel's first king was Saul, followed by David, and then Solomon," Nigel began. "This was Israel's golden era, with the Maker's favor upon His chosen people. But sadly, this unified kingdom of the twelve tribes only lasted a century before it split into two kingdoms, around 931 B.C. The northern kingdom, with ten tribes, became known as 'Israel' and the southern kingdom with the two tribes of Judah and Benjamin, became known as 'Judah.' These two kingdoms would continue their separate ways for two hundred years before each of them was torn asunder by external enemies."

"It were so sad ta see," Kate sighed. "All that work ta birth the nation of Israel, only ta see it ripped ta shreds."

"C'est tragique," Liz agreed, closing her eyes. "And it all began when they took their eyes off the Maker and went after worthless things. Then with internal strife came division."

"Indeed," Nigel continued. "And just as the Hebrew nation divided, their worst enemy rose to world dominance: the Assyrians. Although ancient Assyria dated its beginnings to around 2600 B.C, with the rise of the unstoppable Neo-Assyrian Empire around 911 B.C. they became a menacing lion ready to devour Israel by slowly surrounding them."

"Aye. First divide, then conquer," Max noted with a frown.

"So, during this time of the divided kingdom, the Maker had to deal with His defiant people as they slowly drifted from worshipping Him as they should," Liz offered. "They even began to worship false gods! He therefore sent prophets to both kingdoms to warn them they would be conquered if they did not return fully to Him."

"Precisely. But first, the Maker tried to get their attention to avoid such a predicament. He punished Israel by reducing her size on the northern border in conflicts with Damascus. This is where our Jonah enters the scene. He was not only a prophet but *quite* the patriotic statesman, fiercely loyal and proud of Israel's heritage," Nigel enthused. "The Maker loved Israel and remembered His land of promise. So, in His goodness, the Maker sent Jonah to assure King Jeroboam that He would restore the land they had lost to the King of Damascus."

"But instead of bein' gr-r-rateful ta the Maker, Israel got all puffed up an' thought they were immune from judgment as the Maker's chosen people," Max further explained. "The more they pr-r-rospered, the more they fell away from the Maker."

Kate furrowed her brow. "Plus, they wanted the Maker ta wipe out other nations while they received His blessin'."

"The Maker had surprisingly even used *Assyria* to attack Damascus, which not only got Israel's northern land back, but allowed Israel to see what could happen to them if they didn't heed His warning," Liz added. "Perhaps if Israel had returned to the Maker at that point, the Assyrians would have never been able to invade their land. But Assyria remained the real threat to Israel, making probing raids, and bullying Israel's kings into paying tribute to them for years."

"The Assyrians were a nasty business!" Nigel exclaimed with a shudder. "They were the cruelest nation that had ever existed. When they attacked other nations they would maim, torture, kill, plunder, and carry off survivors who had witnessed unimaginable horror."

Jock looked at Clarie in shock. "I'm glad you missed being there for that part of history, Clarie."

Clarie nodded and mussed Jock's fur. "The Romans weren't much better, little Jock. Humans have always found a way to be cruel and to hate each other."

Nigel clasped his paws behind his back and shook his head. "This is precisely the attitude that Jonah had about the Assyrians. The old boy *hated* them! He didn't want them to repent and be saved. He wanted them to be destroyed! It's quite the conundrum—Jonah was called to *prolong* the life of an enemy which was already in the process of trying to destroy Israel! Yet the Maker actually *postponed* the captivity of Israel with this mission of our wayward prophet."

"But around this time, the Maker also sent the prophets Amos an' Hosea ta warn Israel that He'd send them far away ta Assyria if they didn't turn from their own wicked ways an' worship Him in truth," Kate informed the group with sad eyes. "They were true prophets because the Maker did jest that. By 722 B.C., the Assyrians had taken all the ten tribes of Israel away into captivity."

Nigel nodded. "Of course, after the Assyrians took Israel into exile, Babylon later took *Judah* into exile. While Judah eventually returned from Babylon, I'm sad to report that the ten northern tribes never recovered from their Assyrian exile.

"Assyria's reign of terror lasted three hundred years, but they themselves fell when Babylon then crushed them in 612 B.C., becoming the new world power," Liz followed. "So, to summarize, when God's people stopped obeying Him, they became divided, and their enemies conquered them. It was a difficult time, but this is where Jonah entered history."

Jock blinked and shook his head. "I'm very confused. Now I don't blame Jonah for running away from his assignment! The Maker wanted him to warn his dangerous enemies and betray his own country. It just doesn't make any sense to me!"

"Aye, gr-r-randlad, at the very least, Jonah's chances of success were likely zero, an' his chances of death were high," Max informed the younger Scottie. "It were a confusin' mission for us, too."

"Until this side of the Cross," Liz told them with a sad smile, drawing a cocked head from Jock. "Because Jonah could not *see* a good reason for the Maker's command, he decided there must not be one. But Jesus had much to say about Jonah, and we will get to all this later. For now, understand that Jonah lived five hundred miles southeast of Nineveh, but he travelled fifty miles in the opposite direction to board a ship to sail twenty-five-hundred miles to Tarshish, which was in Spain. It was the farthest known point of the world back then."

"Jonah must have been very afraid of the Assyrians!" Jock surmised.

"But that wasn't the *real* reason he ran in the opposite direction, as you will soon see," Gillamon told him.

"If Jonah was disobeying the Maker, why didn't the Maker stop him?" Jock wanted to know. "Why did He allow Jonah to get on that ship and sail away? Looks like he got away with it."

"Jest because ye can buy a ticket an' get on board doesn't mean ye're in the Maker's will," Max told Jock with a grin. "When ye deliberately disobey the Maker, ye're always out of His will."

Kate closed her eyes and nodded. "Aye, things might look good for a while when ye're runnin' away from the Maker, but don't ever assume that if He doesn't stop ye, it means ye have His permission. An' ye always end up bringin' harm ta yerself an'others in the process."

"And just as Jonah paid the fare to go down into the ship, one must always pay the price and go down with every disobedient move," Liz added. "The Maker never allows His children to sin with success, whether they be one prophet like Jonah, or a nation like Israel."

Jock grew silent for a moment, trying to process all of this. He then cocked his head. "You haven't told me why your mission with Jonah was so terrible for Al. Why did it take him decades to recover? What happened?" He turned to Max. "And why exactly did you say that Jonah was 'delicious'?"

Max warmly chuckled and patted Jock on the shoulder with his burly paw. He nodded to Gillamon, who touched the panel of time. "Ye'll understand when ye see wha' happened."

13

Why Have You Done This?

THE PHOENICIAN SHIP, MEDITERRANEAN SEA

"I have a surprise for your birthday, Jonah," Amittai teased, holding something behind his back. "But you'll have to come out of hiding to get it."

Amittai looked at his wife and they shared a knowing grin as they heard scuffling from behind some crates stacked in the corner. Their son loved to play hide-and-seek. Soon a skinny young boy emerged from under a canvas tent-cloth, his hair sticking up in every direction. He grinned broadly and ran over to his father. "What is it, Father?"

The kind father stretched out his hand and the boy's eyes danced with delight. It was a little dove with a reed in its mouth, made from clay and painted with vibrant colors. Jonah took the toy in hand and smiled. "A dove!"

"To remind you of the meaning of your name, and of the hope that God gave to Noah after the mighty flood," Amittai answered. He leaned down and looked Jonah in the eye, placing his hand on his son's shoulder. "You are to bring peace and hope to others, true? Of course, true!"

Young Jonah clutched the toy dove to his chest, and then gave his father a smothering hug. "Thank you, Father! I will"

Jonah's mother kissed her son on the cheek. "Happy birthday, my little dove!"

Suddenly a huge wave hit the ship, causing it to heave sideways. Rolls of purple cloth tumbled off a stack of crates next to where Jonah lay dreaming on the lowest level of the ship. He was in such a deep sleep that he didn't hear the muffled shouts of sailors desperately manning the oars a deck above. Another wave sent some clay amphorae full of olive oil rolling around the juniper wood floors. Jonah stirred briefly before turning over on his pallet. He continued to dream, oblivious to the storm. But he twitched and moaned as the scene in his dream changed from one of joy to one of pain.

They'll never find me in here, Jonah thought. He grinned and wrapped his fist tightly around the sturdy vine that grew across the family's well, lowering himself out of sight. He was quite small for his age, so the thick vine that trailed along the wooden crossbeam over the well would easily support his weight. Jonah braced his feet against the stacked stones, knocking a pebble into the cool water far below. He heard a *plop* that echoed off the circular walls and looked down into the darkness. His heart jumped as he realized what would happen if he fell into the depths of the water. He quickly turned his gaze upward and tried not to think about it. His pride was at stake, after all. He told his friends that *this* time, no one would find him. No one would think of looking for him in the well. He clung to the vine. It would hold him.

Jonah smiled as he heard his friends running around, calling his name while they tried to find him. But after a few moments, their voices stopped, and he then heard harsh voices shouting instead. He heard the thunderous hooves of horses, the sounds of metal clanking and people screaming. *What is happening?* His heart raced and he immediately froze, but he dared not lift himself from the well to peer over the edge.

"WE'RE ALL GONNA DIE!!!!!" Al screamed at the top of his lungs as his claws dug into a grain sack. Another wave caused the ship to lunge forward, sending cargo sliding down the corridor. "AHHH!!!! GOODBYE, CRUEL WORLD!"

"Get a hold of yourself, old boy! We are most *certainly* not going to die!" Nigel shouted above the roar of the wind howling outside. He was holding on to a thin rope tied around a bundle of barley, his back legs flying in the air. "We *can't* die! Besides, Gillamon gave us explicit instructions to stay with Jonah wherever he goes until Gillamon meets us somewhere along the voyage, and that is *precisely* what we shall do!"

The wide, rounded Phoenician ship was tossed about like a cork on the sea in this violent storm. Its carved wooden horsehead on the bow gave the ship the appearance of a stallion rising on its hind legs to buck off its rider. High winds struck from out of nowhere, tearing the red and white-striped square sail from its rigging. Two sailors clung to the steering oars at the stern of the ship, while two rows of oarsmen on double decks below battled the waves that repeatedly sent them reeling in every direction. Wave after mighty wave washed over the deck, tearing off the wicker fence that served as a railing to hold ropes, tools, and rigging. Everything washed overboard as the men cried out to their gods to save them. Suddenly the crew heard a loud crack before the sturdy cedar mast came crashing down onto the deck. The captain and crew could easily see that the vessel was about to break apart.

"Great Ba'al, save us from this tempest!" one sailor screamed, his eyes wide with fear as he clutched his little wooden idol of Ba'al to his chest.

Another sailor, trembling with fear, kissed his carved idol of Yamm, god of the sea. "Yamm! Save us, we beg you!"

"We've got to further lighten the ship!" the captain shouted to his crew who finished tossing everything off the upper deck. "We must toss the cargo stored below decks as well!"

A group of mariners stumbled down into the cargo hold and set up a chain of men to heave one crate after another to toss overboard.

"Well, them pagans sure be afraid!" Al protested. "Jest listen to them screamin' and holdin' their little wooden dolls!"

"Idols, not dolls!" Nigel retorted. "Of *course* they are afraid! They've placed their hope in worthless blocks of wood carved by human hands!"

The captain hurried to the lower deck to assess the cargo they needed to heft overboard before they sank. He then spotted Jonah, sound asleep. He rushed over and gripped the prophet's bony shoulder, his dripping tunic splashing water onto Jonah's face. "How can you sleep at a time like this?" he shouted angrily. "Get up and pray to your god! Maybe he will pay attention to us and spare our lives!"

Jonah abruptly woke from his deep sleep and stared at the captain in confusion. It took him a moment to remember where he was before he could process what was happening. But he said nothing in reply to the captain.

Several of the drenched crew members rushed down the ladder to find the captain. "Let's get to the bottom of this," an out-of-breath sailor urged, holding out a bundle of small sticks. "Let's draw straws to identify the culprit on this ship who's responsible for this disaster!"

One by one, each man drew a stick as they struggled to maintain their balance. The sailor held the bundle out to Jonah, and he reluctantly pulled out a stick. It was the shortest stick in the bundle, meaning the lot fell to Jonah as the guilty one.

"You! What have you done to bring this awful storm upon us?" one sailor shouted, pointing at Jonah.

"Who are you? What is your work?" another sailor asked, clutching his idol in one hand while he held onto a beam to remain upright.

The captain got in Jonah's face with a scowl. "What country are you from? What is your nationality?"

Jonah looked from one man to the next and lifted his chin. "I am a Hebrew; and I fear the Lord, the God of heaven, who made the sea and the dry land."

The pagan sailors looked at one another, now more awash in fear than in water.

"Those pagans are terrified, as their entire belief system is founded upon the powers and processes of nature," Nigel told Al, who still clung to the grain sack. "If Jonah's God created the sea and the dry land, they know He also created this storm."

Jonah hesitated and then told them exactly what he had done. "I have fled the Lord's presence, for He commanded me to go where I could not bear to go."

"Why have you done this?" the captain asked incredulously through gritted teeth, his gold earring shaking as he spoke.

"Even the pagans know ye shouldn't run from God," Al observed, finally opening his eyes.

The crew looked around at each other and then at Jonah. Another wave sent the ship reeling. The men fell to the floor, knocking the wooden idols out of their hands. Their gods tumbled about, lifeless.

A terrified sailor screamed and grabbed Jonah's tunic, pleading with the prodigal prophet. "What should we do to you to stop this storm?"

Jonah looked at the fear and desperation of these men, and he knew that it was all his fault. "Pick me up and hurl me into the sea. Then the sea will become calm for you, because I know that on account of me this great storm has come upon you."

The captain shook his head. "No, that we will *not* do! Everyone, to the oars to relieve the men!"

Together the seamen scooped up their fallen idols and scrambled back up the steps to where the two rows of exhausted oarsmen had labored against the storm thus far. They took the place of the weary men and put all their might into rowing against the storm.

Jonah slowly and resolutely climbed the steps to watch the sailors' futile attempts at rowing against the storm that only increased in its ferocity. Nigel and Al scrambled up behind him, not letting him out of their sight.

"Remarkable! Jonah refused to go on mission to warn the pagans in Nineveh of their impending doom, and here *this* group of pagans have defied Jonah's instructions to do all they can to save *him,"* Nigel realized.

After a while, the men grew exhausted as the ship continued to lurch and plunge into waves that towered above them.

"It's no use," Jonah calmly told them as he climbed to the upper deck. The rain stung his eyes, and the wind whipped his tunic violently against his legs.

The crew followed Jonah above deck, and the captain clenched his jaw with a defeated nod of surrender. "Do it. Toss him overboard."

The sailor with the Ba-al idol fell to his knees on the slippery deck and cried, "O Lord, don't make us die for this man's sin!"

The other sailor with the Yamm idol quickly added, "And don't hold us responsible for his death. O Lord, you have sent this storm upon him for your own good reasons."

Two other sailors each grabbed Jonah by the arm and lifted him to the railing. Jonah closed his eyes, ready for his fate as the men threw him overboard.

As Jonah disappeared beneath the waves, the storm suddenly stopped, and the wind calmed to a soft breeze. All that could be heard was the gentle lapping of the waves against the hull. The clouds parted and the sun burned so brightly on the aquamarine water that the sailors had to shield their eyes from its blinding brilliance. In that moment these pagans knew that Jonah's God was real. Their mouths gaped in awe at what they had just experienced.

No one spoke a word as the two sailors with the wooden idols got to their feet. They looked at one another for a moment and knew exactly what they needed to do. They tossed their Ba'al and Yamm idols into the sea, followed by every other pagan on the ship, who ran below to get their worthless gods to hurl overboard. Each man vowed from that moment to only worship the one, true God. As the ship sliced through the calm sea back to port, it left a trail of bobbing, worthless idols in its wake.

14

SEVERE GRACE

MEDITERRANEAN SEA

Al's head popped up from below the waves and he pawed the water's surface, digging his claws into one of the wooden idols that floated by. He coughed up saltwater and flattened his ears, spying Nigel with one stinging eye closed. "Sure, and I can't believe ye pushed me, Mousie!"

Nigel blinked hard to peer at Al through the sea spray covering his spectacles. Saltwater dripped from his white whiskers, and he also grabbed hold of a wooden idol as he and Al bobbed along. "I'm terribly sorry, old boy, but there was simply no time to convince you to jump as the sailors pushed Jonah overboard," Nigel explained. "Gillamon gave us explicit instructions to follow Jonah no matter where he went."

Al looked around, but all he saw were the floating wooden idols and the Phoenician ship sailing away. "Well, Jonah ain't anywhere around. Now what?"

Nigel furrowed his brow. "I am not quite sure. Jonah must have drifted off and we can't see him betwixt the billowing sea swells. Sometimes, following orders can lead to moments of uncertainty, but I know we have acted correctly. An answer shall assuredly come after Gillamon's preparations are complete."

"What preparations?" Al wanted to know.

"Again, I am not certain," Nigel answered. "Gillamon simply stated that the Maker would be preparing him for his part in this mission."

"Well, I guess those pagan lads didn't need their little dolls anymore," Al observed, grabbing another idol so he could float with one under each arm.

"Indeed, it was an extraordinary turn of events!" Nigel agreed. "Once the pagan sailors saw the Maker's power first to create, and then to *calm,* the storm, they realized that He is the only God they need."

Al thought a moment. "Seems like them pagan lads used these dolls jest for emergency religion. But then they sure did start actin' Jewish by trustin' the Maker, while Jonah were actin' like a pagan by *not* trustin' Him."

"Splendid observation, old boy!" Nigel cheered. "Idols need not be made of wood or stone. They can be anything that turns our hearts from the Maker and makes us run away from Him, including religious rituals, what?" The little mouse tapped the idol he sat upon and began to chuckle. "These idols aren't *completely* worthless. They make splendid buoys." He stood on his hind legs as the idol bobbed up and down, scanning the area for any sign of Jonah. "Blast these water spots! I have nothing with which to clean my spectacles. I cannot see a thing."

Suddenly Al's eyes grew as big as saucers when he glimpsed an enormous, silvery shadow swim under them. "That's probably a good thing." The waterlogged orange cat's face filled with fear as the massive creature breached the surface. It was larger than the Phoenician ship, and its side was lined with countless rows of silvery white scales that glistened in the sun. The gigantic fish came falling toward them with its pink mouth wide open. Al screamed, "We be fish food!"

Assyrian raiders were ransacking Jonah's village. This enemy of Israel had begun to make sporadic attacks as they probed the northern reaches of Galilee, testing the defenses of this Hebrew nation they sought to conquer. Jonah had overheard his parents talking about such a raid that occurred in Damascus weeks ago. The Assyrians brutally slew the men and children and took the women away with them back to Nineveh.

Suddenly Jonah heard his mother's voice trailing off, instructing him in their Hebrew dialect, "MY DOVE! Stay where you are!"

"IMA!" Jonah whispered hoarsely, fear enveloping him. He shut his eyes tightly and held onto the vine, willing it all to stop. Within moments, everything grew still. He stayed frozen a long while, choking back the tears and remaining as quiet as possible. As dusk settled in, Jonah knew he had to get out of the well. He slowly pulled himself up and peered over the edge. He didn't see or hear anyone.

Jonah felt something nudge him and he immediately awoke from his recurring dream. His eyes fluttered open but he quickly shut them, his heart racing with crushing, inescapable fear. Forget the dream! He was in a living nightmare. He could hardly breathe. His movements were confined with his arms pinned to his sides while warm water swirled around him. He could feel some sort of slimy substance all around him as he lay on a soft bed made of . . . what? What was it? Where was he?

Darkness. Seawater. Oppressive heat. Rotting fish, he thought slowly, word by word. Suddenly he felt nauseated and struggled to turn on his side, vomiting out seawater. "Seaweed," he hoarsely whispered, slowly sliding his hand up to feel it wrapped around his head. Jonah struggled to use two fingers to pull the seaweed from his face. His mind raced, replaying scenes that he struggled to remember so he could piece together what had happened.

Running from God. Joppa. Ship to Tarshish. Storm. Pagans. Jonah took in a quick breath of foul air that burned his lungs. "Oh, God! Oh, God! Oh, God!"

Tears stung his eyes. Now he remembered. *The sailors tried to save me. They had to toss me overboard. The waves covered me, and I immediately began to sink. I stretched out my hand and the last thing I saw was the faint shafts of sunlight penetrating beneath the waves. But I couldn't reach the surface. I sank and sank, and my breath gave out.*

"In my great trouble I cried to the Lord and he answered me," Jonah muttered from a throat choked with saltwater, bile, and grief. He opened his eyes, willing himself to see God. That's all he wanted to see!

"From the depths of death I called, and Lord, you heard me! You threw me into the ocean depths; I sank down into the floods of waters and was covered by your wild and stormy waves. Then I said, 'O Lord, you have rejected me and cast me away.' How shall I ever again see your holy Temple?'" Jonah gushed out in a soulful prayer. His lip trembled at the realization of what had happened.

"I sank beneath the waves, and death was very near. The waters closed above me; the seaweed wrapped itself around my head," Jonah recounted. He trembled as he relived the horror. "I went down to the bottoms of the mountains that rise from the ocean floor. I was locked out of life and imprisoned in the land of death."

Jonah reached out his hands to feel around him, and then he knew. As impossible as it seemed, and as undeserving as it seemed, he knew exactly where he was. He was in the belly of a great fish. "But, O Lord my God, you have snatched me from the yawning jaws of death!"

The wayward prophet began to sob and sob and sob. He had thought he was going to perish as he sank to the depths of the sea. But God! He didn't deserve to be saved after his flagrant disobedience to the Creator of the seas and the dry land, of the heavens and of creatures and of men—all men. He didn't expect to live. He expected to die. But he was alive. He didn't know if he would yet live, but he was alive right now. And that was enough to give praise and thanks to God.

David wrote in the Psalms that God inhabits the praise of His people. Oh, God, I cannot reach you, but you have reached me! Jonah realized. His spirit brought another Psalm of David pouring into his mind. He understood it as never before. *Where can I go from Your Spirit? Or where can I flee from Your presence? If I ascend into heaven, You are there; If I make my bed in hell, behold, You are there. If I take the wings of the morning, and dwell in the uttermost parts of the sea, even there Your hand shall lead me, and Your right hand shall hold me. If I say, 'Surely the darkness shall fall on me,' even the night shall be light about me; indeed, the darkness shall not hide from You, but the night shines as the day; the darkness and the light are both alike to You.*

"When I had lost all hope, I turned my thoughts once more to the Lord. And my earnest prayer went to you in your holy Temple," Jonah gratefully, mournfully prayed in a broken voice. He continued to sob and sob until he grew so exhausted that he passed out.

Jonah drifted in and out of consciousness for hours. Finally, he felt something hard bump against his leg. Startled, he reached down and struggled to push it away. His skin now felt raw and stung as he moved his hand toward the object. The tips of his fingers brushed against it. *Wood?* He felt all along the object and could tell that it was carved. He soon realized what it was—a carved idol. *The pagan sailors must have thrown it overboard and the fish swallowed it, along with me. But did they throw it away intentionally? Do they now believe in the one, true God?*

"Those who worship false gods have turned their backs on all the mercies waiting for them from the Lord!" Jonah cried out. Thoughts swirled in his head until he was suddenly struck by a humbling truth. *I didn't deserve grace. I turned my back on all the mercies you give, but you gave them to me, nonetheless. Just as you gave them to those pagan sailors. They responded to your fierce storm by believing in you and your mighty power, so you calmed the sea and preserved their lives. You sent the storm to stop me . . . but were you also trying to save those pagans?*

A final cry of praise spilled out of Jonah. "I will never worship anyone but you! For how can I thank you enough for all you have done? I will surely fulfill my promises. For my deliverance comes from the Lord alone."

As those words left his lips, Jonah suddenly felt completely at peace. He had been given grace despite his running from God. The Hound of Heaven would not let him go. He pursued Jonah by sending a storm to stop him in his tracks, and He then sent a fish to rescue the disobedient prophet. He had been given grace—severe grace—but that's all that *could* have saved him. Jonah realized he wasn't just saved from the sea. He was saved from his own rebellion. He didn't know if he'd get out of this fish or not, but He knew that the God who sent the fish knew. And suddenly, that's all Jonah needed to know.

15

THE WITNESS

OFF THE COAST OF TYRE

"He passed out again," Al whispered in the darkness.

"I am not surprised, given the extreme trauma Jonah has endured," Nigel whispered in reply. He was nestled next to Al's belly and wondered at the diminishment of the fluffy fur normally abounding there. Of course, they were all completely drenched. "I know you can see in the dark, Al, but perhaps it would be best if you kept your eyes shut for now."

Al whimpered. "Too late. I can't unsee everythin', Mousie. I had no idea me tummy were such a dungeon o' terror for the fish I eat. Or for the bananas, or for anything else on me menu."

"Now, now, old boy. You mustn't equate your natural and *necessary* food consumption with this great fish's consumption of Jonah," Nigel consoled him.

"And us," Al added.

Nigel cleared his throat. "Right. We are not intended to be on the *menu du jour.* We shan't remain in here much longer. The digestive processes of a big fish break down its food into organic matter with powerful acids coupled with a methodical grinding of the stomach walls. This is not a hospitable environment for a human to survive for long. What has happened here is simply the Maker's way of saving Jonah from being lost at sea."

"So, a place o' death has become a place o' rescue?" Al thought out loud. "Have ye ever noticed how the Maker likes ta start everythin' with water and end up with dry land?"

"How so, Al?" Nigel asked.

"Well, Liz told me the Maker started with water when He made the Earth, then he added the dry land," Al began. "Babies float around in water before they're born to live on dry land. And when the humans ruined everythin', the Maker had to start all over again by floodin' it with water. The humans and animals were rescued in the belly o' Noah's Ark until all *that* water went away and we landed on dry land. And when Jonah ruined *his* mission, the Maker had to use water again. So, how are we supposed to get back on dry land so Jonah can start all over?"

"Astounding revelations, old boy!" Nigel replied, marveling at the simple cat's ability for philosophical thought. "Indeed, the Maker certainly has a pattern of using water for new life and new beginnings." Suddenly Al's belly rumbled. "Oh, dear."

"Did ye feel that?" Al asked, sitting up in alarm.

"I most certainly did, but I'm afraid you're going to have to wait to eat, old chap," Nigel told him.

"Not me, Mousie, the *fish!*" Suddenly there were powerful vibrations throughout the fish as it emitted a low moan, causing the standing water to slosh back and forth. "I think it's gonna hurl!"

"How much farther do you want us to go, little kitty?" Jenny the hinny asked Liz.

Liz was perched atop a light brown hinny who trotted next to a dark brown mule. Max and Kate ran next to them. Liz looked behind and saw the man following in the distance. She then looked ahead and could see a white sandy beach with lush green palm trees and crystal-clear water lapping the shore. Turquoise blue water spanned this coastline of beaches at Tyre along the Mediterranean Sea with breathtaking beauty. "You obviously must stop when you reach the water, *mon amie.*"

"Not necessarily. Me and Jenny are excellent swimmers," chuckled Davy the mule. "In fact, after this chase I think I'll take a dip. I'm HHHHOTTTTTTT!"

Max wrinkled his brow at the sound of this beast and grinned. "Ye sure make a funny sound there, horsie."

"I'm a MMMUUULLLE!" Davy protested.

"Ye can lead a mule ta water, but ye can't make him sink," Kate joked.

Davy snickered with a hilarious honk-laugh, his long ears pivoting in all directions as his big teeth projected from his mouth. "My whinny is a cross between a neigh and a bray. You could say I'm bilingual."

Max chuckled. "Heh-heh, so when Jenny whinnies, it be a Jenny hinny whinny?"

Kate giggled and studied the thin legs and small narrow hooves of the mule and the hinny. They were tall with long necks and faces like horses, but they had long ears, short manes, and wide eyes like donkeys. "Davy, why are ye called a mule an' Jenny lass called a hinny?"

"My mom was a mare, and my dad was a Jack," Davy explained. "A Jack is a male donkey."

"And my dad was a stallion, and my mom was a Jenny," Jenny explained. "A Jenny is a female donkey."

"I see, well, thank ye kindly, Jenny the hinny and Davy the mule," Kate answered with a perky grin. "We're not sure why our team leader Gillamon gave us such strange instructions. He jest told us ta get ye ta run ahead of yer human so he'd be here at the beach when we all arrived."

"I have a theory, given your human's occupation, but it still isn't quite clear to me," Liz posed. "He is a spy and a circuit rider for the Assyrian government, no?"

"Yeeeeeeesss, not no," Jenny whinnied with a laugh, not understanding Liz's French mannerism. "Davy and I make up one of the mule teams they have posted on the King's Road for five hundred miles all the way to Nineveh. The Assyrians figured out how to send messages quickly by putting rest stops all along the route so humans could stop and then get another waiting pair of mules for the next leg of the journey."

"Why do they use mules an' not horses?" Kate wondered.

"We're a lot stronger, sure-footed, resilient . . ." Jenny answered.

"And smarrrrteeerrrr!" Davy chortled. "We can do this job for twenty years and remember every place we've been. We can carry heavy loads of supplies. Plus, we're so lovable that the humans can't resist us." He grinned with an exaggerated smile, his chunky teeth showing.

"I hear ye're stubborn, too," Max followed with a chuckle.

"Not stubborn, but headstrong—because we're *cautious,*" Jenny explained. "We know if a certain path is dangerous, so we have to stop the clueless humans before they hurt themselves."

"So how quickly can this communication system send a message from here to Nineveh?" Liz asked, thinking about her theory.

Davy and Jenny looked at one another and flicked their long ears back and forth, counting. "I'd say anywhere from five to seven days, depending on if one of the humans has a breakdown," Jenny determined.

Liz raised her eyebrows. *"C'est incroyable!* I have never heard of humans sending messages so fast! Tell me, do the humans send letters or verbal messages with their couriers?"

"BOTHHHH!" Davy bellowed. "If the humans send a letter, it's sealed with an official signet ring engraved with the picture of the Assyrian king killing a lion. Only the magnate governors and ambassadors of the provinces have such rings and can use the system. If a human brings a super-secret message himself, he may or may not have a letter. Just depends."

"Fascinating. What kind of messages do the humans typically send with this system?" Liz asked.

"Most of their letters deal with unexpected matters that a magnate can't answer himself," Jenny answered. "Usually problems or catastrophes, that kind of thing. But spies such as our human report back anything their Assyrian authorities need to know about lands they already possess, or lands they plan to invade."

Suddenly Liz spotted movement in the water. Something was rapidly swimming toward the beach, kicking up a huge wake. Gillamon had not told Max, Liz, or Kate what would happen with Jonah, Al, and Nigel, so they were unclear why he told them to meet him here.

"Max, Kate, keep your eyes on the water," Liz instructed. She gently patted Jenny's neck. *"Merci* for the ride, *mon amie.* I must get off now." She proceeded to jump to the sand and together the animals walked to the edge of the water, gazing out to sea.

Just then, the fish gained speed and caught a wave to surf into shore, its silvery white scales glimmering in the sun.

"Do ye see wha' I see?" Max asked. "It's big like a whale beastie, but it's more of a fish beastie."

"Aye, an' it's comin' right at us!" Kate added.

Just then the fish turned sideways and spotted the animals standing there on the beach.

"And it has blue eyes!" Liz exclaimed. "That can only mean . . ."

"GILLAMON!" Max, Liz, and Kate shouted in unison as the fish winked at them.

The Assyrian spy came running up behind Davy and Jenny, breathless and grabbing their reins. "Got you!"

Suddenly the massive fish opened its mouth and spit out Jonah, who rolled into the beach-landing surf, covered in seaweed and muck. Al and Nigel soon followed, and the fish slipped back out into deeper water. The threesome desperately splashed in the water, gagging as they struggled to get to dry land.

Jonah slowly crawled out of the surf on all fours, coughing and shaking as he reached the sand where the waves stopped. He collapsed on his back, breathing heavily and weak from shock. The Assyrian took a step back, not believing what he just witnessed. His face filled with fear, and he dropped to his knees to mumble a prayer to his pagan god, raising his arms up and down toward the sea. After a moment, he heard Jonah moan and saw him cover his eyes from the blinding sun. The man slowly stood and carefully walked over to Jonah. His expression screwed up in horror as he looked over the skinny man dressed only in blue rags.

"Who *are* you?" he asked Jonah in Aramaic, the common language at the time.

Jonah didn't appear to be totally human. Not only was he devoid of any hair, eyebrows, or eyelashes, but his skin was bleached a sickly shade of neon yellow. Jonah couldn't yet speak but motioned for a drink of water. The man pulled out a leather flask and gently lifted Jonah's head to help him take a sip.

Over where Max, Kate, and Liz stood, Al came scrambling out of the water, scooping up the sand as if to hug the beach. "Dry land! Come to me, me beauty!"

Nigel gently coasted onto the beach and shook off the water before straightening his spectacles. "Blast it all, I can't see a thing!"

"That might be a good thing at the moment, Mousie," Max told the little rodent.

Max, Liz, and Kate stood there with their jaws hanging open at the shocking sight of Al and Nigel. Kate held her breath. Liz couldn't speak. Davy started guffawing, his tongue hanging out as he snorted, honked, brayed, neighed, and laughed.

Just like Jonah, Al and Nigel were completely bald with skin bleached to a neon yellow.

"Poor Mousie, what happened to ye?" Al exclaimed at seeing the little bald mouse next to him. The oblivious cat was caked with sand, so he hadn't noticed his own condition.

Liz swallowed hard and wore an expression of shock, pity, and dismay. "*Cher* Albert, it is . . . good to see you and Nigel . . ." she began, struggling to come up with what else to say.

"How'd ye get naked, Big Al?" Max blurted out. "Ye an' Mousie look like bananas."

Al looked down at his furless belly in horror. Then he peered at his furless legs, paws, and tail. "First the revenge o' the fish, now the revenge o' the bananas!" he screamed, running off to hide in the grove of palm trees.

"Ye be wha' ye eat, lad!" Max joked, drawing stern looks from Kate and Liz.

"MAX! How could you tease poor Al at a time like this?" Kate scolded him. "Can't ye see Al, Mousie, an' Jonah have been through somethin' traumatic? Ye owe Al a big apology! Now get over there an' take care of yer best friend!"

Max frowned and lowered his head. "Aye, that weren't very kind of me, lass. I jest couldn't help meself in the moment. I'll go check on the lad."

As Max trotted off, Liz and Kate surrounded Nigel. "Whatever happened, *mon ami?"* Liz asked, afraid to touch the little mouse for fear of hurting him. *"Je suis vraiment désolé!*

Nigel held his paws up to study them. "Unfortunately, I am unable to see through these sea-sodden spectacles, but I presume that we have collectively lost our fur. Fascinating!"

Liz and Kate shared an awkward glance. *"Un moment,* Nigel. I shall go retrieve a bit of cloth to clean your spectacles."

"Thank you, my dear." Nigel touched his arm. "Ouch! I am a bit tender, what? Presumably, the digestive properties of that fish did their dirty work on us whilst we were in the belly of the aquatic beast."

"Ye mean *Gillamon,"* Kate informed him. "He winked at us with blue eyes before he spit Jonah out on shore."

Liz handed the mouse a scrap of cloth in Jenny's saddlebag. "Here you go, Nigel."

"Most kind, Liz," Nigel replied as he removed his spectacles to clean them. He began to chuckle. "I say, I never knew the old boy had it in him! When Gillamon told us that the Maker was preparing him for the Jonah mission, we scarcely could have envisioned him to be prepared as a great *fish!* Extraordinary—he became Gillafish!"

"You are taking this all rather well, Nigel," Liz told the mouse with a smile. "But how exactly did this all come about?"

Nigel put the cleaned spectacles atop his nose. His eyes widened as he now studied the condition of his skin. "By Jove, I *do* look like a banana!" He grabbed his belly and laughed.

"NIGEL!" Kate and Liz exclaimed, dying for answers.

"Right, sorry, well you see, Gillamon instructed Al and me to go undercover as a typical 'cat-and-mouse' duo that sea merchants would expect to see on board, what with using felines to keep their food stores free of *revolting* rats," Nigel explained. "But soon after the ship left port, the Maker sent a devastating storm. Didn't you see it from here?"

"No, *mon ami.* Things here were sunny and beautiful," Liz explained. "It must have been a localized storm."

"Extraordinary! Well then, the pagan sailors drew straws and determined that Jonah was the guilty party responsible for said storm," Nigel continued. "After a thorough interview with the wayward prophet, and despite their attempts at rowing the ship, they relented and followed Jonah's instructions to throw him overboard. I knew Al wouldn't take the leap; thus, I was forced to push him overboard so we could do exactly as Gillamon instructed and stay with our human."

"Bravo, Nigel! So, then I assume Gillamon came along to rescue you all in the form of this great fish," Liz realized. "What an unusual yet thrilling form of rescue, no? I am glad we were all here to see Gillamon's delivery!"

"I am TOOOOOOO!" Davy whinnied with a snort as he and Jenny walked up behind them.

"That's got to be the most amazing thing any human's ever seen, much less we animals," Jenny agreed. "I know our human was terrified enough to drop to his knees and pray to Dagon."

"Dagon?" Kate asked.

"The Assyrian fish god," Davy explained, matter-of-factly. "He's half man and half fish. The Assyrians worship Nanshe, daughter of Ea, the goddess of fresh water and Dagon, the fish god."

Liz's eyes suddenly brightened. *"C'est ça!* Now I see! Gillamon wanted us to ensure that this Assyrian spy messenger was here to witness Jonah's miraculous delivery from the fish onto this beach. It is logical that he will send word immediately back to Nineveh about this supernatural event!"

"I see where you're going with this!" Nigel exulted. "If the Maker has determined for Jonah to deliver a message to the Ninevites about their impending destruction, what better way to get their attention than from a skinny, bald, yellow, freakish-looking prophet who came forth from the mouth of a fish?! Utterly brilliant!"

"Not only can this Assyrian deliver a message *about* Jonah's miraculous arrival, but perhaps he can deliver Jonah as well," Liz thought out loud. She turned to Davy and Jenny. "Does this Assyrian communication system allow passengers to travel with the messengers?"

"Not usually," Jenny answered.

"But this sure ain't USUSAL!" Davy brayed with a big toothy grin. "I bet he'd carry Jonah with him. Me and Jenny might even get to travel the entire length of the King's Road."

Kate glanced over at Jonah and saw the Assyrian helping him to his feet. Together they slowly made their way over to the shade of a palm tree. "Jonah looks to be in bad shape. It may take a bit for him ta recover before he can head ta Nineveh."

"That is, IF he still heads to Nineveh," Nigel pointed out. "Remember that he refused the Maker's first order to go."

Liz's tail whipped back and forth as she studied the prophet and the Assyrian. "Something tells me that Jonah will comply this time."

"Indeed. Jonah has learned a hard lesson about disobedience and running from the Maker, and I shall tell you all about his mournful prayer within Gillamon's gastric nether regions," Nigel promised, holding a hand up to greet Max, who had trotted back down to join them at the water's edge. "How is our furless feline?"

"Looks like yer mind be unfazed, Mousie," Max told Nigel with a grin. "Big Al's not doing too well. He said he don't want ta ever leave them bushes again, but I'm sure he will when he gets hungry enough."

"Which should be any minute now," Kate noted with a chuckle.

"Oui, but I fear that Albert shall still suffer from severe PTSD," Liz worried.

"PTSD?" Nigel asked.

Liz stifled a grin. *"Poisson* traumatic stress disorder."

No one said anything for a moment before Davy let loose a deafening, honking guffaw and fell to the sand, laughing until he couldn't breathe.

16

Forty Days from Now

THE KING'S ROAD

Jonah quietly climbed out of the well and crept toward the house, which had been ransacked. Broken pottery littered the floor, chairs were overturned, and everyone was gone. The young boy trembled as he walked from room to room. The Assyrians had taken everything—including his toy dove.

From then on, whenever anyone in Israel mentioned Jonah, son of Amittai, people knew exactly who he was.

GET UP AND GO TO THE GREAT CITY OF NINEVEH AND DELIVER THE MESSAGE I HAVE GIVEN YOU.

Jonah's eyes fluttered open and his body shuddered all over at hearing the voice of God interrupting his dream. Reality came crashing into his mind as he looked up to see sunshine dancing between the palm fronds swaying above him in the sea breeze. He put a hand to his aching head and slowly sat up. There, sitting next to him, was the Assyrian. He was cooking some flat bread on a hot stone over a fire, staring at him.

"What day is it?" Jonah asked. His voice was raspy and weak.

"The first day of the week," the Assyrian answered.

Three days in the belly of that fish, Jonah thought.

"Where did you come from?" the man asked, handing Jonah the water flask.

Jonah reached out a shaky hand and took a swig. He wiped his mouth with the back of his hand, then looked at his yellow skin with revulsion. "I am Jonah, son of Amittai, from Gath-heper."

The Assyrian raised his eyebrows in surprise. "You are *Jewish,* from Israel? I am Ninos, one of the King's messengers from Nineveh. I chased my two mules down to the beach where I witnessed . . . what happened to you. How did you . . .?" he started to ask, not really knowing how to phrase the question.

Jonah slowly shook his head in surreal disbelief. *Yes, Lord, I will go to Nineveh as you have commanded. You clearly arranged for a fish, and now for two mules to take me there,* he thought. Jonah cleared his throat. "The Lord God, creator of the seas and the dry land, commanded me to go to Nineveh with a word of warning to the city, but I disobeyed him and boarded a ship to Tarshish," Jonah admitted. "God sent a storm to stop me, and a great fish to save me. He again commands that I do as He told me before, and travel on to Nineveh."

Ninos's eyes widened in fear. "What word of warning?"

Jonah just stared at the Assyrian, wanting to toy with this man whose people were his most hated enemy. It sickened Jonah to have to drink this man's water or ask anything of him, but Jonah knew he needed him. Jonah had no money, no shoes, no clothes, and no transport. The prophet wagged a finger and shook his head. "I will not tell you until you bring me to Nineveh."

Ninos swallowed hard and nodded. "So be it. I will take you. But first, eat. Regain your strength." With that, he took some bread from the hot stone and handed it to Jonah.

The animals stood by in the green scrub brush listening to Jonah and Ninos.

"Sounds like Jonah has decided ta go ta Nineveh an' deliver the message," Kate observed.

"Indeed, the Maker must have come with a word to Jonah a second time," Nigel agreed.

Max chuckled. "The Maker pr-r-robably started with, 'As I were sayin' . . . go ta Nineveh!'"

"And Ninos has readily agreed to transport our disobedient prophet," Liz added, glancing over at Al, who remained curled up in a fetal position, looking pitiful. She frowned and walked over to the forlorn cat. "Albert, we will be leaving soon, so you must eat to regain your strength."

"I'm not hungry." Al sniffed and his lip trembled. "I'm not yer noble famous warrior anymore, lass. Ye go on without me."

"Do you say this because of what you do not have on the outside?" Liz frowned and got right into Al's face. "Listen to me, Albert. It is the armor that you wear on the *inside* that makes you my noble famous warrior. Fur has nothing to do with it, no? And *mon cher,* your fur will grow back." She kissed his bald head.

Al lifted his head. "Ye mean that, Liz?"

"Oui, I am so very proud of your bravery in battling the storm and getting swallowed by the great fish," Liz told him.

Al blinked a few times. "I mean, will me fur grow back?"

Liz giggled. "But of course it will!" *At least, I believe it will,* she thought.

A slight smile appeared on Al's whiskerless face as he stared cross-eyed at his nose. "And me whiskers, too?"

Liz cupped Al's cheek. "And your whiskers, too." *I hope.*

Al closed his eyes in relief. "I were worried ye wouldn't want me anymore since I don't look like me handsome self."

"Nothing could make me love you any more or any less, *cher* Albert," Liz assured him.

"I love ye, too, me black beauty, even if ye were bald like me, although I might not recognize ye," Al told her, suddenly sniffing the air and detecting the fresh baked bread. Drool slipped out of his mouth.

"And you should know that you were not *technically* swallowed by a fish. It was Gillamon in the form of a fish, sent to save Jonah," Liz explained.

Al's eyes widened. "Ye say GILLAMON were the fish?! So, I weren't really swallowed by a regular swimmin' beastie? Well, that makes me feel lots better." His stomach growled. "I think I could eat somethin' now, but please—no fish or bananas, lass."

"I understand," Liz answered, pleased to see her mate acting like himself, but surprised to hear that he did not want his favorite foods. "Stay here and I will get your *petit déjeuner."*

"I recommend that we stay out of sight whilst we follow Jonah to Nineveh," Nigel told the animals. "Al and I wouldn't want to upstage Jonah with our shocking display. No need to distract from the prophet's already difficult assignment."

"I agree, Mousie," Max concurred. "We'll jest tail them at a distance."

Liz grabbed some bread from the hot stone while Ninos was occupied with finding a clean garment for Jonah to wear. She gave the bread to Al, who eagerly devoured it. "Now then, Jonah has his renewed marching orders, provisions, and transportation. Nigel, might I suggest that you ride hidden along with Davy or Jenny to listen in on their conversation?"

"Splendid suggestion, my pet!" Nigel agreed. "I imagine it shall be quite the interchange, what with our reluctant prophet and his necessary yet unwelcome travel companion."

Kate walked up to Davy and gave him a stern look. "An' no more laughin' at Al. He's in a fragile state right now, so be kind ta the naked, yellow kitty. Swallow yer whinnies or I'll give ye somethin' ta whinnie aboot!"

Davy bit his flappy lip and nodded thoughtfully, "Mm-hmm."

Jenny whinnied. "I think Davy's assignment will be harder than Jonah's."

Jonah and Ninos slept at a stopover point halfway to Nineveh. Ninos had decided to keep Davy and Jenny as his two mules for the entire journey so Jonah wouldn't have to get used to different animals along the way. The sturdy mules were up for the challenge.

"It would appear that the Maker has made far more preparations for this Jonah mission than we had anticipated," Nigel reported. "He has been softening up the Assyrians, so to speak."

"How so, Nigel?" Liz asked.

"Dear me, where do I begin?" Nigel exclaimed. "For starters, despite their continual bullying of Israel, Syria, and other territories, Assyria has experienced a long period of internal decline. The ruling crown is terribly weak, and the nation is being governed by magnates in each province, making decisions that best suit local interests. No one dares threaten to supplant the king himself, but he holds weak authority outside of Nineveh."

"Ye'd think the empire would collapse on itself," Max surmised. "Jest like Israel. Divide, then get conquered."

"But that's only the beginning of the empire's woes!" Nigel replied. "Assyria has experienced no fewer than five revolts, two plagues, AND a recent solar eclipse!"

Liz's eyes widened. "And of course, the pagans believe that an eclipse portends doom from the gods."

"Aye, but this time, it be the R-R-REAL God doin' the doomin'," Max noted.

"C'est bon! This will make the Ninevites even more willing to listen to what Jonah has to say," Liz enthused.

"Well, like I always say, the Maker goes ahead of ye, an' be there waitin' for ye when ye arrive," Kate offered.

"Speaking of arriving, allow us to give you all some background on the land of Assyria and the city of Nineveh," Liz suggested. "Of course, we know that Noah's son Ham had a son named Cush who fathered Nimrod. After the humans scattered from the Tower of Babel, Nimrod took over four cities including Babel to begin his kingdom. From there, he went into the land of Noah's grandson Asshur, which is called Assyria. Nimrod then built four more cities, including Nineveh."

"Indeed, but Nimrod's story takes a dark turn, I'm afraid," Nigel added with a furrowed brow. "Nimrod was first known as a mighty hunter, then as a king and conqueror of the surrounding lands. But his descendants sadly elevated him to a godlike status and worshipped him as 'Bel' or the more common 'Ba'al,' and that dastardly religion spread across Mesopotamia."

Al's eyes widened. "Ye mean, that pagan sailor's doll were really supposed to be Noah's great-grandlad?!"

"Shocking, I know, old boy," Nigel answered. "Nimrod's godlike monikers also became 'Marduk' or 'Merodach.'"

"Jest how many names do false gods need, then?" Kate lamented. "Humans always take evil too far."

"Oui, this is sad but true," Liz agreed. "When the one language spoken by the humans split into multiple languages at Babel, many of those early patriarchs naturally became known by various new names. For example, 'Nimrod' was also called 'Ninus,' which is where the humans got the name *Nineveh.* So, you see that the confusion of language also confused the names of humans, gods, cities, and even nations."

"Daft humans," Max grumbled.

"Case in point, all that name-muddling led to the Assyrians' original founding city of Assur being named for their main god, Assur, which is just missing an 'h' from Noah's grandson," Nigel explained. "Now then, to bring us up to the current state of things, the Assyrian ruler is considered the human agent of Assur, thus he acts as the godhead of political and religious authority. And he must be perfect in every way! Now the Temple of Assur where their main god resides is quite busy, as the entire empire serves to 'feed' him daily. They go to extreme measures to import food from each province, and Assur supposedly consumes the food by 'smelling' it. Any food then not consumed by their temple servants is distributed back across the empire and the humans must ingest it regardless of it being stale, as an act of worship to Assur."

Al's eyes widened. "'Tis a shame to think o' all that good food goin' to waste."

"One more note on Assur and the Assyrian beliefs before I tell you about the great city of Nineveh," Nigel told them. "They have seven principal gods, but when they conquer other nations, the Assyrians believe in 'god-napping,' as it were! They bring back seized statues of defeated enemy gods to serve as Assur's *guests* in his temple. This shows the defeated people groups that their gods have submitted their allegiance to Assur's sovereignty."

"Assur's Temple must get pretty crowded, then," Al surmised.

"I'd like ta see them tr-r-ry ta god-nap the r-r-real God!" Max grumbled. "The daftness jest keeps spr-r-readin'!"

"Of course, we know that this belief system is based on false gods, so it is therefore untrue. But sadly, this is a powerful way to subdue nations they have defeated militarily through army sieges," Liz noted. "The Assyrians certainly believe in psychological warfare by making other nations believe their 'gods' have deserted them so they will simply give up."

"If only the humans would jest believe in the one true Maker, their lives would be so much happier," Kate lamented.

"And easier," Al added.

"Now then, whilst the city of Assur begat the Assyrian civilization, Nineveh is their premiere city of today," Nigel told them. "It is situated at the meeting of the Tigris and Khoser Rivers. Greater Nineveh is approximately thirty miles long and ten miles wide and protected by moats and walls one hundred feet high. In fact, those walls are broad enough for four chariots to drive abreast of one another, for a circuit of eight miles!"

"That's a big city!" Kate exclaimed. "How is Jonah supposed ta cover all that ground?"

"Maybe he'll get to ride in a chariot," Al suggested with a chuckle.

"Well, the heart of Nineveh *proper* is only three miles long and about one-and-a-half miles wide, thus Jonah shan't have as great a distance to traverse with his message of warning," Nigel explained. "Once word reaches the king and court, it could spread easily throughout the region."

"Hmmm, I estimate that it will take Jonah three days to walk across the city," Liz surmised.

"An' then what'll he do?" Al wanted to know.

"It depends on whether the people of Nineveh believe Jonah's message,"

Nigel determined. "One thing is certain. If they do *not* believe him, his chances of leaving Nineveh alive are very low."

NINEVEH, ASSYRIA

As Ninos and Jonah approached the entrance to Nineveh, two massive statues stood, one on each side of the main gates. They were each carved in the form of a muscular, winged bull's body, with a human head of curly hair and a full beard.

"What be those things?" Al asked fearfully.

"Those would be Lamassu, Assyrian deities," Nigel answered. "The Assyrians are known for their finely crafted statues and reliefs depicting victorious battles lining the walls of the imperial city. Lions are a horrendous problem here, so the king likes to show his dominion over them with hunting scenes as well."

"No wonder they have such high walls," Al gulped. "I don't care if we be related or not—I don't like lions."

"They also have an extensive collection of literature and possess vast scientific, architectural, and horticultural knowledge to build their monumental palaces, temples, houses, parks, and lush gardens," Nigel continued. "These Assyrians may be dastardly in battle, but they are quite brilliant in their construction, to include extensive aqueducts for fresh water supply and indoor plumbing!"

"I have heard they even have menageries of exotic animals and plants they have captured in the far reaches of their conquests," Liz explained. "These gardens serve to show their people a miniature representation of the vast Assyrian empire, no?"

Max nudged Al. "Ye best stay hidden, Big Al. I have a feelin' they'd want ta put ye on display."

Jonah felt sick in his gut, but not from what he'd been through physically. An overwhelming sense of evil enveloped him, and his nightmarish encounter with these people long ago toyed with his emotions. Jonah clenched his jaw, once again in utter disbelief that God had called him to come here with a word of warning to these people he hated. He didn't want to warn them. He wanted to see this city up go in flames and be flattened by the hand of God. Jonah's emotions were boiling like the storm on which his ship had been tossed. He closed his eyes and took a deep breath. He would do as God commanded, but he would hate every minute of it.

"We are here," Ninos told Jonah as he took Jenny by the reins. He looked around them, and people were already pointing at the bizarre-looking prophet, whispering.

Jonah nodded, yet didn't bother to thank Ninos for bringing him here. He had told Ninos very little about himself or his story. Jonah hadn't wanted to engage with the Assyrian unless it was absolutely necessary. "Very well, now you can hear the message the Lord has given me." He walked to the first street corner and exclaimed, "Forty days from now Nineveh will be destroyed!"

"That's it?" Kate asked.

"Short and to the point," Nigel remarked.

Ninos watched the reaction of the people who looked at one another and began asking who this odd man was to exclaim such things. Ninos was the only one who believed Jonah at first, because he had witnessed the true power of Jonah's God. As Jonah continued to the next street corner, Ninos gathered a group of people together and told them about the great fish spitting Jonah onto shore. Word spread like wildfire throughout the city, and soon everyone was rushing out to hear the prophet from Israel.

"Forty days from now Nineveh will be destroyed!" Jonah shouted, scowling all the while as he walked from one street to the next. He didn't care what the people of Nineveh thought or said. He was here to deliver God's message as instructed and was unconcerned about giving them one more word of explanation or comfort. If God wanted to comfort them, that was His business.

The skinny, bald, neon-yellow prophet continued his sojourn through Nineveh for three days. But much to Jonah's shock and dismay, the people believed God's message. From the greatest to the least of them, the people declared a fast and dressed in humble burlap to show their sorrow.

As Jonah saw the people respond to God, his anger only grew, and despite the blistering Assyrian heat, his heart grew cold.

17

The Gourdless, Graceless Prophet

NINEVEH

"WHY DO I HAVE TO WEAR THIS?!" Davy brayed and honked as Ninos put sackcloth over his back. "IT ITCHES!" Ninos ignored the mule's protests as he scratched his own chest from the itchy burlap he also wore. He led Davy by the reins over to the stable where Jenny was tied. She, too, was covered with the same rough garment. Davy pulled against the reins toward the watering trough. He was thirsty. "No water. None of us are to eat or drink by order of the king," Ninos told the mule, even though he knew the beast couldn't understand him.

"WHAT IS GOING ON?!" Davy bellowed as Ninos closed the gate behind him to go back inside the house.

"Good things are happening, *mon ami!"* Liz answered happily, sitting on the stone wall. "The entire city of Nineveh has responded to the Maker's message from Jonah!"

"And once the king of Nineveh heard what Jonah was saying, he humbled himself before the Maker, stepped down from his throne, and took off his royal robes," Nigel added. "You must understand that this just *isn't* done, old boy! It is a severe breach of royal protocol for a king to *ever* be seen without his royal attire whilst sitting upon the throne."

"Oui, and the king then dressed himself in burlap and sat on a heap of ashes!" Liz further explained. "Although the people had already begun to repent, the king intensified the actions of the people to avert the Maker's wrath. He and his nobles sent this decree throughout the city:

No one, not even the animals from your herds and flocks, may eat or drink anything at all. People and animals alike must wear garments of mourning, and everyone must pray earnestly to God. They must turn from their evil ways and stop all their violence. Who can tell? Perhaps even yet God will change his mind and hold back his fierce anger from destroying us."

"So, you see, your scratchy garments are meant to show genuine repentance on behalf of the Ninevites to the Maker," Nigel relayed. "All evil and violence has ceased within the city limits. Jonah's words have literally scared the Hades out of the people, what?" The mouse preened his whiskers and gave a jolly chuckle at the surprising turn of events.

"Well, that's a good reason!" Davy exclaimed, rubbing his rump on the stone wall. "But I still don't have to like wearing this stuff."

Nigel chuckled. "I daresay I can't blame you!"

"What about you all?" Jenny asked. "Do you have to wear this burlap, too?"

"Since we are not part of the Assyrian empire, we are excused," Liz answered. "Now, we must return to Max, Kate, and Al. They're keeping an eye on Jonah, but we wanted to come see first-hand what was happening here."

"Well, Jonah must be happy about this! The wicked Assyrians heard him LOUD AND CLEAR!" Davy bray-honked.

"Not at all happy, old chap," Nigel told him. "Our prophet is about as angry as we've ever seen him."

Jenny shook her head with a whinny. "But people responded immediately! He sounds like he was an instant success with his message."

Liz nodded. "*Oui,* normally a prophet would be happy with such an overwhelming, instant response, but Jonah rather considers himself to be a failure precisely *because* the Ninevites responded."

Davy shook his head and snorted. "Let me get this STRAIGHT. Jonah ran from the Maker, but the Maker saved him anyway, so he repented, was rescued, and was grateful. Now the Ninevites are also repenting, and it looks like the Maker is also going to save them, but Jonah is upset? What kind of prophet is he, anyway?"

Liz and Nigel looked at one another and frowned. "A graceless one," Liz answered.

Nigel furrowed his brow. "It sadly appears that Jonah loves grace if it applies to *him,* but not to *them.*"

"This is *exactly* what I thought you'd do, Lord, when I was there in my own country, and you first told me to come here. That's why I ran away to Tarshish," Jonah fumed with a hand in the air, pacing back and forth on the eastern outskirts of Nineveh. He was alone, for everyone had gone inside to humble themselves and stay in continuous prayer. The animals stayed within earshot of Jonah to see what he would do.

Jonah kept venting out loud to get everything off his chest. "I *knew* you were a gracious God, merciful, slow to get angry, and full of kindness; I *knew* how easily you could cancel your plans for destroying these people."

"Sounds like the lad needs a time out," Al reckoned. "He's havin' quite a tantrum with the Maker."

"At least Jonah also knows that he can be totally honest with the Maker in expressin' his feelin's," Kate offered. "He's right in that he knows the Maker very well."

"Aye, lass, ye have ta give it ta Jonah for that anyway," Max agreed. "At least he's not tr-r-ryin' ta hide anymore. But if he thinks gettin' swallowed by a fish were bad, that ain't nothin' compared ta bein' swallowed by anger an' bitterness."

"Please kill me, Lord," Jonah wailed, gripping his chest. "I'd rather be dead than alive when nothing that I told them happens."

"Jonah sounds disappointed aboot how things be turnin' out," Al announced sadly.

"*Disappointed* is rather an understatement for our difficult prophet," Nigel quipped. "Whenever we set our will against the Maker's will, we shall *always* be disappointed."

Suddenly the animals could hear God speak audibly to Jonah. "IS IT RIGHT TO BE ANGRY ABOUT THIS?"

"The Maker is not condemning Jonah's anger," Liz observed. "The Maker understands Jonah's pain and anger for what the Assyrians have done to Israel. But He is gently trying to get Jonah to honestly *think* about what he's saying."

"Quite right. Anger itself is not wrong, but when it overtakes everything else, it most assuredly is wrong," Nigel agreed. "Jonah knows God all too well. He knows that He is the *living* God who doesn't change. *Ergo,* He is also the *loving* God who will always forgive. And this is Jonah's sticking point."

Jonah stood there in the middle of the road, gripping his fists and clenching his jaw. His blood pressure rose as his cheeks flushed red.

"At least he's got a little more color in his face besides yellow," Al observed with a weak grin.

Suddenly Jonah turned and stomped off, not answering God. He turned his back on both God and Nineveh and walked up a hillside above the city to sulk.

"He is not ready to talk about this, even though the Maker is trying to help him work through his emotional distress," Liz deduced as she watched grumpy Jonah kick up the dust, sending pebbles flying.

Kate nodded as the animals followed Jonah up the hillside. "Aye, but somethin' tells me the Maker's jest gettin' started on this heart-ta-heart chat."

"An' if the lad won't listen ta words, the Maker jest may have ta use somethin' else ta keep him talkin'," Max predicted.

The sun was blazing hot; the temperature was nearly one hundred degrees. Sweat dripped off the tip of Jonah's nose as he angrily ripped another leafy vine from the dry hillside. He dragged it over to the temporary shelter he had built on the side of the hill, threading the vine through the dry tree limbs he'd found on the ground. He plopped down on the ground under the shelter, and wiped his dirty, yellow hands on his borrowed tunic. He was hot, bothered, and miserable. He gathered his knees to his chest and wrapped his arms around them. He sat there for hours, staring down at Nineveh.

"What's he waitin' on?" Al asked. The animals were perched behind some scrub brush to keep an eye on Jonah.

"I believe that he is hoping the Maker will yet smite Nineveh despite the fact that He has seen the people's true repentance and relented from bringing calamity upon them," Nigel answered, straightening his spectacles.

"The lad's aboot ta melt inta his sandals," Max observed. "His little shelter's already startin' ta shr-r-rivel up in this extreme heat."

Kate frowned and panted. "An' no one's talkin'."

Over the course of the next few days, Jonah's vine-covered shelter dried up and he was left sitting in a pile of brown leaves. The sun beat down upon Jonah's head, and his garments were saturated with sweat. He was hot, smelly, grimy, exhausted, angry, isolated, discouraged, and depressed. He rested his weary head on his arms and closed his eyes, unsure of what to do.

That night as Jonah slept, a broad-leafed vine emerged from the ground. It slowly grew up and along the wooden lean-to that Jonah had pieced together. The vine curled around and around the structure, and fresh, green tendrils popped out in every direction.

As dawn came, Jonah lifted his head and felt coolness for the first time in days as shade covered his bald head. The vine above him was thick, green, and alive. He broke out into a wide smile and stretched his arms wide, reveling in the shade of this plant that God had provided. "Ah, this feels good!"

"That's the first time I've seen the lad entirely happy the whole time we've been with him," Al noticed. "O' course, he should be happy with all that shade."

"Look how good the Maker be!" Kate smiled, wagging her tail. "He's given Jonah a gourd vine!"

"Oui, Jonah certainly did not deserve such kindness from the Maker given his argumentative behavior," Liz agreed. "But the Maker's grace keeps pursuing our wayward prophet."

Kate smiled at seeing Jonah so happy. "Aye, the Maker doesn't jest give savin' grace. He gives comfortin' grace, too."

"It would appear that no word exchange is happening at the moment," Nigel observed. "Perhaps the Maker is softening up Jonah just as he softened up the Ninevites, but in a positive way."

"It's only a matter of time before the Maker starts him talkin,'" Max noted. "An' He always has the last word."

Al's ears perked up. "What's that crunchin'? I hear crunchin'."

Liz yawned, her eyes barely opening to see that it was still nighttime. "Albert, it is the middle of the night. Go back to sleep."

Al frowned and his stomach rumbled. "I can't sleep when I hear crunchin'. Crunchin' means somebody's eatin'."

"GO BACK TA SLEEP, KITTY," Max huffed, rolling over to stretch out his legs.

Al's ears flattened and he rolled over with his back snuggled up next to Liz. He whispered to himself. "Wish I were crunchin'."

With the dawn came a hot, eastern sirocco wind. The humidity dropped and the temperature rapidly rose twenty degrees. Jonah was curled up on his side when he felt sand kick up in his face. It was a rude awakening, and he sat up abruptly. Not having eyelashes to block the swirling dust, he used the back of his tunic to wipe his eyes and blinked rapidly. He looked up and noticed that a worm had bored into the vine, causing it to wither away.

"Told ye somethin' were crunchin'," Al wined with a harrumph. "Now Jonah's gourdless."

"Oui, Albert, you were right," Liz agreed, nudging Al playfully. "We should always trust your eating senses. It would appear that the Maker sent a worm to gobble up Jonah's shady vine last night."

The sun beat down on Jonah's head and he started to faint. He lifted his weary head and let go a wailing prayer of desperation to God. "I'm better off dead!"

"Once again, the Maker got Jonah's attention, and he indeed got the old boy to speak again," Nigel quipped. "I know these are terribly wretched conditions, but Jonah is being a bit dramatic, don't you think?"

The animals tingled from head to tail as they heard the authoritative voice of God in reply to Jonah: "IS IT RIGHT FOR YOU TO BE ANGRY BECAUSE THE PLANT DIED?"

Jonah crossed his arms over his chest and frowned. "It *is* right for me to be angry, even to death!"

"If only we could see the Maker's face aboot now," Max pondered, rolling his eyes.

God spoke aloud again to Jonah: "WHAT'S THIS? HOW IS IT THAT YOU CAN CHANGE YOUR FEELINGS FROM PLEASURE TO ANGER OVERNIGHT ABOUT A MERE SHADE TREE THAT YOU DID NOTHING TO GET? YOU NEITHER PLANTED NOR WATERED IT. IT GREW UP ONE NIGHT AND DIED THE NEXT NIGHT. SO WHY CAN'T I LIKEWISE CHANGE WHAT I FEEL ABOUT NINEVEH FROM ANGER TO PLEASURE—THIS BIG CITY OF MORE THAN A HUNDRED AND TWENTY THOUSAND CHILDLIKE PEOPLE WHO DON'T YET KNOW RIGHT FROM WRONG, TO SAY NOTHING OF ALL THE INNOCENT ANIMALS?"

Jonah tightened his lips but said nothing. What could he possibly say?

"It would appear that the Maker has now given *Jonah* much to chew on," came a tiny voice behind the animals.

They turned quickly and there sitting on a dry branch was a white, hairy caterpillar with blue eyes.

"Gillamon?!" Max exclaimed, trotting over to get his nose right up next to the caterpillar. "At first, ye were a huge fish beastie, an' now ye be a wee worm beastie?"

"I say, you have been prepared across a wide spectrum of size and appetites for this mission, old boy!" Nigel marveled with a chuckle.

"YE did all that crunchin'?!" Al asked, getting his nose close next to the caterpillar. "I'm sure glad ye didn't crunch like that when I were in yer belly." The cat shook his head. "I can't believe I were eaten by a caterpillar."

"Bonjour, Gillamon," Liz greeted their leader happily. "The Maker has worked in miraculous ways with Jonah, and with you, no?"

Kate smiled. "Aye, an' He's had ta get firm with the lad, but I know it's all been wrapped in grace. Even the lesson with this gourd vine. It seems like the Maker did ta Jonah wha' Jonah wanted ta see done ta the Ninevites."

"Something Jonah loved withered and died as quickly as it came," Gillamon told them. "The Maker showed mercy to make the idol of self-righteousness in Jonah's heart wither and die. Jonah's desired vindication against the Ninevites would be as short-lived as the vine and ultimately leave him just as miserable. Extending grace might be hard in its first moments, but ah, what a restorative, refreshing relief it immediately then brings to the soul."

Liz's heart caught in her chest. "Look who is coming to see Jonah!"

Ninos was walking up the hill, holding the hand of a little boy. They were both still dressed in humble sackcloth. The Assyrian waved to Jonah with a broad smile. Jonah's heart fell. He suddenly felt his self-righteous pride slip from its entrenched pedestal. It was easy to hate a nation. It was much harder to hate an individual, especially one who had come under the grace of God with genuine repentance. It was one thing for God to say he cared for a nation, but God had just told Jonah that His love and care reached to every individual, and even to every animal. God knew each creature from the inside out and was concerned for every detail of their lives. Jonah knew that as the heart of one person changed, change could then come to one family. Then to one city, and then to one nation. *You love Ninos just as much as you love me,* Jonah prayed silently.

THAT'S RIGHT, JONAH. I DO, God answered his heart.

"This is my son. We've brought you some food and water," Ninos told him, placing a basket at Jonah's feet.

Jonah nodded quietly and suddenly felt very small from their act of kindness. He lowered his head in shame, knowing the thoughts he had wished for the destruction of these human beings.

The little boy pulled on Ninos's sackcloth garment excitedly. "We have something else for you," Ninos said with a smile, his hand on the little boy's back. "My father gave this to me long ago. He said it came from Israel. I thought you might like to have it. We are grateful for the hope you have brought our city. Please, accept our gratitude with this small gift."

The little boy walked up to Jonah holding something wrapped in a silk cloth. He smiled and handed the item to Jonah.

"What is this?" Jonah asked as he unwrapped the gift. Instantly, hot tears stung Jonah's eyes. It was a little dove with a reed in its mouth, made from clay and painted with vibrant colors. *His* toy dove. Jonah shot a dumbfounded glance at Ninos, who smiled with a lump in his throat, even though he had no idea of the gift's origin or significance to Jonah.

Jonah's father's words echoed in Jonah's mind: *"You are to bring peace and hope to others, true? Of course, true!"*

Jonah wiped his eyes, nodded, and with a trembling chin patted the boy's head. "Thank you, little one."

"My father said he saw you spit out of a great fish!" the boy exclaimed. His eyes danced with curiosity as he studied Jonah's odd features. "Can you tell me the story of what happened, please? What happened to your ship? And how did you end up inside of a *fish?"*

In that moment, the words Jonah uttered in the belly of the fish about forfeited grace came rushing back to his mind. *Those who worship false gods have turned their backs on all the mercies waiting for them from the Lord! I didn't deserve grace. I turned my back on all the mercies you give, but you gave them to me, nonetheless. Just as you gave them to those pagan sailors.* Jonah looked into the eyes of this little boy who belonged to the nation of pagans that Jonah had been sent to warn. *You, Lord, have extended grace to the sailors, to the Ninevites, and to me,* Jonah prayed. *And this little boy and his father have in turn extended grace to me. It is now time for me to do the same.*

For the first time, Jonah smiled at Ninos and his son. "Let me start by telling you what I learned inside the belly of that fish, so perhaps you can learn from my story as well." He motioned for Ninos and the little boy to take a seat on the ground next to him.

"Know this," Jonah began with a bony yellow finger raised in the air. "All sin has a storm attached to it."

18

THE SIGN OF JONAH

THE WAR ROOM

Liz wiped away a joyful tear at the scene. *"Merci,* Gillamon, for showing us all that happened to Jonah as a youth. I understand him far better now."

"Did Jonah forgive the Assyrians?" Jock wanted to know. He rattled off question after question, trying to understand all they had seen with the life of Jonah.

Gillamon smiled. "What do you think, Jock? Why would Jonah write a book about his running from God and how poorly he behaved, if he did not wish to share his amazing story of grace?"

Jock nodded. "I think he forgave them. Maybe he finally realized why it would be good for Israel if the Assyrians repented."

"How so, lad?" Max asked.

"Well, seems to me that the best way to stop an enemy from attacking is to take away their reason to hate," Jock reasoned. "Wouldn't terrorists *stop* being terrorists if the Maker took over their hearts?"

Max and Kate looked at one another, beaming with pride. "That's our grandlad!" Kate shone, hugging Jock.

"Aye, we be so pr-r-roud of all ye learned, lad," Max echoed with a wide grin.

"I'm glad Jock and I got to see this incredible story of Jonah," Clarie added. "The Maker was so smart to use that vine to teach Jonah an important lesson. It appears that Jonah's vine was his security blanket in the well and later when it comforted him."

"Brilliant observation, my dear," Nigel remarked happily. "The Maker wanted Jonah to learn that he needed *Him* for security."

Kate piped up. "Jesus also taught His disciples a lesson aboot the vine an' the branches the night before He went ta the cross."

Clarie closed her eyes to recall Jesus' words. "He told them, 'I am the vine, you are the branches. He who abides in Me, and I in him, bears much fruit; for without Me you can do nothing.'"

"Liz, didn't you say that Jesus also said something about Jonah?" Jock asked.

"Oui. Gillamon, would you please show Jock that scene?" Liz asked.

"Certainly," Gillamon said. He tapped the panel of time, revealing a scene of Jesus with a group of Jewish scribes and pharisees.

"Oh, aye! I r-r-remember this," Max recalled. "Them puffed-up phar-r-risees kept tr-r-ryin' ta catch Jesus, but he outsmarted them every time."

> "Please, Master. Show us a miracle," one of the unbelieving Pharisees asked Jesus with a sneer.
>
> Jesus looked at them and shook his head. "Only an evil, faithless nation would ask for further proof; and none will be given except what happened to Jonah the prophet! For as Jonah was in the great fish for three days and three nights, so I, the Messiah, shall be in the heart of the earth three days and three nights. The men of Nineveh shall arise against this nation at the judgment and condemn you. For when Jonah preached to them, they repented and turned to God from all their evil ways. And now one greater than Jonah is here—and you refuse to believe him."

Jock's eyes grew wide.

"You mean, the evil Ninevites are going to judge the Jewish leaders in heaven? Whoa! They truly must have changed their ways for that to happen!"

"Well, at least those who heard Jonah repented and believed God," Nigel noted. "But sadly, their repentance as a nation did not last. Remember that the Assyrians ended up taking Israel captive."

Jock frowned. "What happened to their faith in the Maker?"

"Aye, the Assyrians believed for a time, but it didn't last," Max frowned. "The enemy likes ta come an' snatch away goodness when humans turn ta the Maker. But even if only one generation found gr-r-race, it were worth it."

"Oui, and those who repented will be in heaven according to Jesus," Liz offered. "But the Maker gives free will to each lost soul to choose to become found."

"And the Maker knows how to reach every generation across time," Gillamon explained. "We have witnessed revival happening in different nations, but it will always be up to the next generation for revival to last. Therefore, the history of any nation is always dependent upon its youth."

"If I may, I was also struck with a thought I had never considered before with Jonah and Jesus," Nigel said. "Isn't it fascinating how Jonah went outside of the city to a hill, just as Jesus went outside of the city to a hill? But whilst Jonah didn't wish to extend grace, Jesus Himself *became* grace, taking the sin and evil of mankind on Himself, including all the evil of the Assyrians."

"That's pr-r-rofound, Mousie," Max affirmed to the little one. "Ye should write that down."

"Nigel, how long did it take you and Al to grow back your fur and whiskers?" Jock asked.

"I will answer this question, Nigel," Liz offered. "My affinity for herbs and plants allowed me to experiment with many forms of treatment over the years. I tried numerous combinations of lavender, horse tail, red clover, rosemary, peppermint, ginseng, aloe, hibiscus, sage, and even jellyfish. I eventually found the perfect combination to apply to Albert and Nigel, but I believe the Maker decided He would grace them with their natural coverings to be more comfortable."

Just then, they heard Al coming into the room. "Haloo, I'm back!"

"Gillamon, hurry and put the scene back to John Newton and the storm, no?" Liz implored.

"Right, Liz," Gillamon chuckled. He touched the panel, and there was the *Greyhound,* tossed about in the violent storm.

Merci, Liz mouthed, relieved, as Al jumped up to the table. His belly sloshed as he walked down the table toward Liz. "Hello, me beauty!" the fluffy cat exclaimed. He plopped down next to Liz and proceeded to pick his teeth with a fish bone.

Liz's nose wrinkled at the smell of fish all over Al. "I take it you found some fish, Albert?"

Al let loose a loud burp and patted his belly. "Aye, I think I'll be good for a few hours. What'd I miss?"

Jock was about to burst out laughing, thinking about the bald version of Al. Kate gave him a stern look of warning and he bit his lip.

"Nothin' but a bit of fur," Max jested, now drawing the stern look of Kate and Liz. "But ye be jest in time ta see wha' happens with the *Gr-r-reyhound* in this tempest."

Al looked at the scene as another wave came crashing over the bow of the ship. "I sure hope those sailor lads figure out how to keep that boat afloat." Suddenly Al blinked a few times. "I have a faint memory o' sailors and a storm . . ."

"Oui, well, ha-ha," Liz interrupted him nervously, "I am certain that John Newton and the sailors will survive this storm, for Gillamon and Clarie have been helping Newton in England for quite some time, isn't that right?"

"Yes, but just wait until you see how *fish* saves the crew!" Clarie offered. She put a hand to her mouth, worried that Al might think about a *great* fish.

Al pointed his fish bone to the panel of time. "I were jest saved by fish meself. I were starvin'."

"Good for ye, kitty," Max cheered with a wink to Clarie.

Nigel put a paw to his head, and he leaned over to whisper to Liz, "I think we have averted yet another crisis."

"Very well," Gillamon announced, clearing his throat. "Let us return our attention to John Newton. History and storms do have a way of repeating themselves."

PART FOUR

Was Blind

John Newton
(1748–1763)

19

When A Storm of Terror Surrounds You

NORTH ATLANTIC OCEAN, MARCH 21, 1748, 3:00 A.M.

The sudden unmistakable sound of timbers being torn away from the upper bow of the *Greyhound* filled the crew with terror. Instantly the ship began to fill with the sea, not only from towering waves, but also from a massive hole in its side. It wouldn't take long for the ship to fill with water and sink.

"Go man the second pump before the ship is completely swamped, making us ALL dead men!" Captain Gother shouted. "NOW!"

John gave no reply to Captain Gother but made his way to the pair of chain pumps positioned on deck near the hold of the ship, where water flooded down into the cargo hold. The sailor operating one pump had tied himself securely with a rope so he wouldn't be swept away like Daggdul. John also tied a rope around his waist before grabbing the long crank handle to begin the arduous task of pumping hundreds of gallons of water out of the ship before it sank. The cranks lowered a chain with leather cups to scoop up water in the hold. Using a pulley, the chain returned with full cups of water that drained into wooden tubes on the deck and over the side of the ship. With two men working, they could pump about 230 gallons per minute.

As John and the other sailor pumped, the rest of the dozen crew members bailed. It was a frantic race against time before the ship was lost. The *Greyhound* rose upward to crest over a towering wave only to plunge downward with such force and speed that it felt as if it would dive beneath the waves and down into the depths of the sea. The cold North Atlantic water felt like sheets of ice slamming into John. It was difficult to keep his eyes open against the stinging rain and he shivered from indescribable cold. The exposure he had suffered while chained to Evans's shallop magnified his misery from his inability to handle the cold and wetness. But he had no choice but to suffer. He was held captive at the pump, and equally by his thoughts. No matter how hard he tried, he was unable to escape the hounding truths he had read in Thomas à Kempis. It stirred things in him that were long buried, as a shipwreck left for centuries on the ocean floor.

> *Very soon your life will end; consider, then, what may be in store for you elsewhere. Today we live; tomorrow we die and are quickly forgotten. Oh, the dullness and hardness of a heart that only looks to the present instead of preparing for that which is to come! If you are not prepared today, how will you be prepared tomorrow? Tomorrow is an uncertain day; how do you know you will have a tomorrow? Learn to die to the world now, that then you may begin to live with Christ. Ah, foolish man, why do you plan to live long when you are not sure of living even a day? How many have been deceived and suddenly snatched away? How often have you heard of persons being killed by drownings . . .?*

John thought of Daggdul, but then immediately remembered Billy and Edward. *They were suddenly snatched away and drowned that Sunday I was delayed at church by Mr. Gillamon. Did God save me that day? Why was I the only one?*

John then thought back to his first encounter with Mr. Gillamon and their conversation about Jonah and Dr. Watts's book. *Daggdul's eyes were almost identical to Mr. Gillamon's.* Young John devoured the book and of course knew the entire biblical account. John was no godly man, so the captain's likening him to the prodigal prophet had only to do with the storm.

Another wave crashed over the ship, ripping apart the frayed ropes that tied a crate of pigs to the deck. The pigs squealed when another wave crashed into the crate, washing them overboard.

"Now the swine have been drowned in the sea!" the other pump sailor shouted.

A distant memory of pigs drowning stirred in John's mind, but he couldn't quite remember where he'd heard about it.

4:30 A.M.

As daylight approached, the gale-force winds began to abate, bringing hope and relief to the crew. The light slowly allowed them to see the extent of the damage to the ship. Everything had been washed overboard, including all the livestock, extra rigging, and supplies. The mizzenmast back on the stern had cracked and splintered onto the poop deck, and the shredded sails looked like canvas pennants. But amid the destruction, there was a miracle. Their light cargo had saved them. If they had been carrying the usual heavy cargo of rum, tobacco, or sugar, they would have readily sunk. But as Captain Gother peered down into the hold where men frantically bailed, he saw a miraculous sight. The beeswax and camwood floated about everywhere.

As they continued to pump and bail, some crew members stuffed clothing, bedding, and anything else they could find to cover the holes, nailing wooden planks atop them. New leaks appeared, and men removed their coats to plug the holes as quickly as they could. But with the wind and now the water abating, John felt a surge of hope.

"Just wait!" John shouted at his pump mate with a smile. "In a few days we'll be sitting at the tavern toasting our good fortune with a glass of wine and telling stories about this storm!"

"No! It is too late now," the sailor answered, his eyes full of bitter tears. "You don't understand, Newton. This is far from over. We may be no better off than those pigs that drowned in the sea."

John's smile faded and he lowered his gaze, continuing to pump while no one said another word, a cloud of doom over them. He pumped and his mind tried to remember. *Pigs drowned in the sea. Where did that happen before?* As he pumped and thought, Captain Gother's words echoed in his mind: *"Go man the second pump before the ship is completely swamped, making us ALL dead men!"*

Storm. Swamped ship. Pigs drowned in the sea. John spent the next few exhausting, terrifying hours trying to remember. It was something from his childhood.

9:00 A.M.

Cold and spent from pumping for six hours, John stopped to catch his breath and shake out his hands and arms. He wanted to view the miracle of the cargo where Captain Gother and First Mate Jackson worked with the crew to patch up holes and monitor the water levels in the hold of the ship.

"Captain, the shredded sails are of no further use," John told him. "Might I suggest the men use them to plug the holes?"

Captain Gother nodded but didn't say anything. Why would he want to listen to the man he thought was responsible for this storm? Still, it was a valid point. He ordered the men to gather whatever shredded sails they could.

As John walked away from the captain, he exclaimed, "If this will not do, the Lord have mercy on us." He was immediately struck by his own words. This was the first time in years that he had breathed a desire for mercy. *What mercy could there be for me?* he thought as he resumed his pumping.

1:00 P.M.

John pumped until noon but was too spent to continue. Captain Gother ordered him to briefly rest and catch his breath. John lay down in his cold, soggy bunk for thirty minutes, but he didn't care if he woke up. As he slept, the memory he had been searching for poured into his dreams.

> *It was evening and Jesus was sitting in a boat in the Sea of Galilee. He'd spent the day there teaching multitudes of people. He taught one parable after another—a sower spreading seed that fell along the wayside or into rocky, shallow, thorny or good soils; of the uselessness of putting a light under a basket; of the growing seed that the farmer plants but doesn't understand how it gradually grows, step by step. And he taught the parable of the tiny mustard seed that grows up to become greater than all herbs, with branches large enough for birds to nest under its shade. Jesus spoke to the people about seeds and plants because that was their existence. They understood tilling the soil, sowing the seed, trimming the vines, and gathering the harvest. It was often a long process to plant a seed and wait to see what it would become.*
>
> *Jesus was exhausted, and told His disciples, "Let us cross over to the other side." So, the disciples launched the boat along with some others into the sea. And a great windstorm arose, and the waves beat into the boat, so that it was already filling. But He was in the stern, asleep on a pillow. And they awoke Him and said to Him, "Teacher, do You not care that we are perishing?" Then He arose and rebuked the wind, and said to the sea, "Peace, be still!" And the wind ceased and there was a great calm. But He said to them, "Why are you so fearful? How is it that you have no faith?"*

"NEWTON! WAKE UP! TAKE THE HELM!" Captain Gother shouted from the top of the hatch leading to the cabin.

John had to shake his head to remember where he was. *North Atlantic Sea. Storm. Swamped ship. But what about the wind?*

As John stepped outside, he saw that the wind had abated but his pump mate was right: This was far from over. The waves were still threatening the ship as the crew fought against new leaks.

"Keep the starboard side of the ship out of the water, no matter the course heading," Captain Gother instructed him. "We've got to keep that hole above sea level."

John nodded and gripped the ship's wheel, fully expecting to be washed overboard with each crashing wave. His knuckles were white as he continually braced for impact. Once more, he was bound to the helm and to his thoughts. Following his dream, John slowly felt more memories arise within him from the depths of his childhood.

"How is it that you have no faith?" Jesus asked after he calmed the storm that was swamping the boat. John recounted this scene from the Bible that his mind was trying to remember. *But there is more to this story. Something about pigs drowning in the sea.* He momentarily closed his eyes and envisioned his mother reading to him from the book of Mark:

> *Then they came to the other side of the sea, to the country of the Gadarenes. And when He had come out of the boat, immediately there met Him out of the tombs a man with an unclean spirit, who had his dwelling among the tombs; and no one could bind him, not even with chains, because he had often been bound with shackles and chains. And the chains had been pulled apart by him, and the shackles broken in pieces; neither could anyone tame him.*

John was struck by the words. *He had often been bound with shackles and chains. Neither could anyone tame him.* He looked down at the white scars that remained on his wrists from his time as a servant of slaves on Plantain Island. But that was only one time of being bound with shackles and chains. He had also been bound when he was press-ganged, when he deserted the ship and was brought back to be flogged, and when he was chained to the shallop. But once released, he was still wild, if not wilder than before, with his wicked behavior. He had alienated every single ship's captain who had sought to help him. *Neither could anyone tame him.*

John shut his eyes against what he had become. *How did this happen to me? How is it that I have no faith?* His thoughts returned to the scene of Jesus and the man.

> *And always, night and day, he was in the mountains and in the tombs, crying out and cutting himself with stones. When he saw Jesus from afar, he ran and worshiped Him. And he cried out with a loud voice and said, "What have I to do with You, Jesus, Son of the Most High God? I implore You by God that You do not torment me." For He said to him,*

"Come out of the man, unclean spirit!" Then He asked him, "What is your name?"

And he answered, saying, "My name is Legion; for we are many." Also, he begged Him earnestly that He would not send them out of the country.

Now a large herd of swine was feeding there near the mountains. So all the demons begged Him, saying, "Send us to the swine, that we may enter them." And at once Jesus gave them permission. Then the unclean spirits went out and entered the swine (there were about two thousand); and the herd ran violently down the steep place into the sea, and drowned in the sea.

Pigs drowned in the sea. There it was. There was too much about this biblical account that John couldn't escape. He felt as if it was repeating itself in the middle of the North Atlantic. The storm swamping the ship. The winds calmed. The pigs drowned in the sea. *But what of Jesus facing off with Legion? Is that happening here as well?* John's eyes brimmed with tears. *Jesus left the multitudes and sailed through a storm to reach one tormented man, freeing him from the demons that drove him. But when the man saw Jesus, he ran toward him from afar, because he had run far away from him. Just like me.*

Seeds. His mother had planted seeds in his heart as a child. A memory flashed across John's mind.

Elizabeth sat with her hands folded on her lap as six-year-old John stood before her to recite the verses he had memorized. She had been teaching him about the dangers of falling away from the truth of God's Word. She gave him an affirming smile. "I know these are hard passages, John, but I want you to know them so you will never lose your way. Go ahead, my love. Start with Proverbs 1:24–31."

Young John nodded and cleared his throat:

"I have called you so often, but still you won't come. I have pleaded, but all in vain. For you have spurned my counsel and reproof. Someday you'll be in trouble, and I'll laugh! Mock me, will you?—I'll mock you! When a storm of terror surrounds you, and when you are engulfed by anguish and distress, then I will not answer your cry for help. It will be too late though you search for me ever so anxiously.

"For you closed your eyes to the facts and did not choose to reverence and trust the Lord, and you turned your back on me, spurning my advice. That is why you must eat the bitter fruit of having your own way and experience the full terrors of the pathway you have chosen."

"Very, very good, John," Elizabeth told him with a nod of affirmation. "Now the New Testament."

Young John nodded. "Hebrews 6:4–6:

"There is no use trying to bring you back to the Lord again if you have once understood the Good News and tasted for yourself the good things of heaven and shared in the Holy Spirit, and know how good the Word of God is, and felt the mighty powers of the world to come, and then have turned against God. You cannot bring yourself to repent again if you have nailed the Son of God to the cross again by rejecting him, holding him up to mocking and to public shame.

"And 2 Peter 2:20," young John continued:

"And when a person has escaped from the wicked ways of the world by learning about our Lord and Savior Jesus Christ and then gets tangled up with sin and becomes its slave again, he is worse off than he was before."

Elizabeth clasped her hands together to her mouth as tears quickened in her eyes. She quickly got to her feet and enveloped John in a tight embrace, kissing the top of his head. "Let us pray you never experience these things, yes? Stay close to Jesus, always."

Mother, but I am *experiencing them! These verses describe ME.* John shut his eyes at the conviction he felt. *If the Scriptures are true, there is no hope for me according to these verses. I have willingly opposed them.* Still, he was only half-convinced they were true. The sobering reality of full truth became a greater threat than the waves to wash him into oblivion. If he simply chose to believe that they weren't true, then dying in this storm would mean he simply would cease to exist. But deep down, John knew that argument no longer held any water.

John attempted to think about other things, but he inevitably circled back to the extraordinary turns in his life—the calls, warnings, and deliverance he had met with, the wicked course of his conversations, especially in making the Gospel the constant subject of profane ridicule. *There never was or could be such a sinner as myself. I'm both Jonah and LEGION, running away from God! My sins are too great to be forgiven. Scripture even says so.* An icy wave crashed over the deck and the crew shouted to one another to keep manning the pumps. John's mind was diverted momentarily to the events at hand but then returned to the debate over his soul.

6:00 P.M.

At 6:00 p.m., a cry of hope rose from the crew that the *Greyhound* was free from water for now. It appeared they were going to make it.

Is this the hand of God displayed for our favor? John thought. He felt his icy heart begin to thaw with a burning desire to know if all the Scriptures and what he read about them were indeed true. He knew he wasn't in a place to approach God and call him "Father," but he suddenly began to utter a prayer like the cry of the ravens. *Please, help me.* His thoughts turned to Jesus, whom he had long derided. He thought about Jesus' life and death. *It was a death for sins not your own, but for the sake of those who in their distress should put their trust in you.* He became obsessed with an urgency to know. *I must have evidence that I am not beyond all hope.*

MIDNIGHT

John stood at the ship's wheel for eleven hours, lashed by the storm without and the storm within. Captain Gother finally sent another sailor to relieve him at the helm, and John weakly made his way back down into the cabin to rest awhile. Although shaking from cold and exhaustion, he reached for the New Testament. After reliving the scene of Jesus, the storm, and Legion, he had a driving need to know the truth. With a shivering hand he found one of Daggdul's dogeared pages and started reading. Luke 11:13: *If you then, being evil, know how to give good gifts to your children, how much more will your heavenly Father give the Holy Spirit to those who ask Him!* he read. He sat there for a moment shivering and pondering its meaning. *Spirit. If this book is true, the promise in this passage must likewise be true. I have need of this Spirit. Jesus said He will give it to those who ask. I must therefore pray for it; and, if it be of God, He will make good His own word.*

John's fingers rubbed the edge of the testament and slid into the book of John. He turned to John 7:17: *If anyone wills to do His will, he shall know concerning the doctrine, whether it is from God or whether I speak on My own authority.*

He set the testament down, folded his arms over his chest and leaned his weary head back against the wood paneling, closing his eyes. *I may not be able to say from my heart that I believe the Gospel, but I will for now assume it to be true. If this Spirit wishes to help me believe that there is a way for a righteous God and a sinful soul to meet, I am willing to keep studying. Every other way surrounds me with black, unfathomable despair.*

John rubbed his eyes and lay down on his side, pulling his knees into his chest to try to gather warmth and a moment of much needed sleep. As he drifted off, the end of the story of Jesus and Legion filled his dreams.

> *Then they came to Jesus and saw the one who had been demon-possessed and had the legion, sitting and clothed and in his right mind. And they were afraid. And those who saw it told them how it happened to him who had been demon-possessed, and about the swine. Then they began to plead with Him to depart from their region.*
>
> *And when He got into the boat, he who had been demon-possessed begged Him that he might be with Him. However, Jesus did not permit him, but said to him, "Go home to your friends, and tell them what great things the Lord has done for you, and how He has had compassion on you."*

The seeds that had lain dormant in the heart of John Newton since childhood slowly, finally began to sprout. They had been planted so deeply into the soil that they were protected from birds that would snatch them away, or from the scorching sun that would burn them up. *"Go home to your friends and tell them what great things the Lord has done for you, and how He has had compassion on you."*

He was heading home, but time would tell if thorns would grow up and choke the vine emerging from the soil of John Newton's heart.

20

Saved by the Fish

NORTH ATLANTIC OCEAN, MARCH 22, 1748

"Everythin's gone, Cap'n," a weary sailor named Hardy reported in a defeated voice, wiping his brow. He pointed at the cargo hold and dropped his hand by his side. "All our food provisions were destroyed from sea water breakin' up the casks and crates. All's we got left are a week's worth of pig feed bread, a few casks of water, some brandy, and the salted cod we caught off Newfoundland."

Captain Gother frowned. This was dire. Not only did he have no idea where they were in the middle of the North Atlantic, they had little to feed the crew of a dozen hungry, exhausted men. Although the storm had passed and the wind had abated, until they made it to port—if they made it to port—these men would be required to continually pump, bail, and plug leaks to keep the ship afloat. They were now dressed in little more than thin cotton shirts and breeches, as their other clothes and outer garments were stuffed everywhere in the ship to keep it from sinking. The sails were destroyed beyond use and the ship so wrecked that all they could do was allow the wind to push the vessel where it would. They couldn't head for any port, as they had to keep the right bow up and out of the water, positioning the ship in whatever direction that took them.

"If I had to guess, I'd say we'd be about three hundred miles from land," First Mate Jackson whispered in Gother's ear. "But wherever we are, it will take more time than we have food to make port. All the men know what this could mean, Captain. When the food runs out, someone must be sacrificed to save the crew."

Gother clenched his jaw. "The storm is gone, but the curse remains." He looked over and saw John Newton standing off by himself, reading his New Testament and getting warm in the welcomed respite of sunshine. "Perhaps our Jonah needs to be thrown overboard to save us all."

THE WAR ROOM

Everyone braced for impact from the Jonah comment, nervously looking over at Al, who sat there with a fearful expression, his paws up to his mouth.

"Uh, so Gillamon," Max quickly spoke up, clearing his throat with a diversionary tactic. "Things be lookin' r-r-real dire for the ship an' the cr-r-rew. Maybe ye should just skip ta the next part an' tell us wha' happened."

"Very well," Gillamon answered with a grin. "As you've seen, the *Greyhound* was a floating wreck, with no useful sails left to propel the ship. They were dependent on whatever winds blew to push them along but they always had to keep the wind on the broken side of the ship to keep out the seawater. About five days after the storm, the crew was awakened one morning by the joyful shouts of the watch upon deck proclaiming the sight of land. Everyone scurried up on deck to see an uncommonly beautiful dawn. The daylight was just strong enough to make out distant objects, and they thought they saw a mountainous coast, about twenty miles off, ending with a cape and two or three small islands rising out of the water. They thought the land resembled the extreme north-western coast of Ireland, where they hoped they could make port."

Al's ears perked up. "Me home o' Ireland?"

"Yes, the Emerald Isle, Al," Gillamon replied. "The crew cheered and congratulated each other, thinking that if the wind continued, they would safely arrive to anchor by the next day.

"The crew passed around the small pint of brandy they had left. Captain Gother exclaimed, 'We shall soon have brandy enough.' They also ate up the last bit of bread for the pigs, and were overjoyed at the turn of events."

"Something tells me this was a premature celebration," Liz surmised, her tail whipping back and forth as she studied the horizon.

"Correct, Liz. Unfortunately, what the crew saw were not mountains, but clouds," Gillamon told them.

"Oh, me, how their hearts must've sunk then!" Kate lamented.

"Not only had they finished their brandy and bread, but that very day, their fair wind subsided into a calm," Clarie added. "The next morning, a steady gale sprung up from the southeast, directly against them, and continued that way for two weeks."

Nigel shook his head. "Their dire situation then grew worse with provisions now down to just fish and water."

"I could live on fish and water," Al muttered to himself.

"That was the fish they caught off Newfoundland, right?" Jock asked. "Good thing you suggested that fishing excursion, Daggdul Gillamon!"

"Yes, but Captain Gother kept having to reduce their rations down to a handful of fish per man per day," Gillamon explained. "Meanwhile, the crew was still working hard to keep the ship afloat but grew weaker without enough food for such physical demands. Their bodies quickly wasted away, and their ragged clothes loosely hung on them."

"This is all so very terrible! But in the midst of it all, look at the wonderful things that happened to John Newton!" Liz pointed out. "He came back to his faith in the middle of the storm. *C'est magnifique!*"

"Indeed, this stormy sea rescue takes the biscuit!" Nigel cheered. "The Hound of Heaven doggedly pursued Newton and would *not* let him go! Brilliant!"

"Aye, the Maker *Gr-r-reyhounded* John Newton r-r-right back ta Jesus!" Max echoed happily.

"I'm so happy about that, even with all the bad things happening," Jock repeated with a smile.

"Yes, throughout the month after the storm, John continued to read the New Testament, Thomas à Kempis, a book of sermons, and every other book he could find about the truth of the Gospel," Clarie shared. "John was moved as he studied the Passion of Jesus and was struck with passages from Luke 13 on the fig tree, Paul's transformation in I Timothy, but especially the parable of the Prodigal in Luke 15. He thought he had never been so perfectly mirrored as in the story of the Prodigal Son coming home. So, although he had no one on board to talk to about these spiritual things, by the time they reached Ireland, John had moved slowly but surely from doubt to a willingness to believe to fully embracing the gospel of Jesus. He stood in need of an Almighty Savior, and he found him in the New Testament. From that day on, he never cursed again, as Jesus completely delivered him from swearing."

"*If any man be in Christ, he is a new creature: old things are passed away; behold, all things are become new*," Liz quoted from 2 Corinthians. "I remember watching Paul's transformation from Saul. There is nothing more beautiful than watching a lost soul become found in Jesus."

"Aye, an' especially a prodigal like John, who were raised ta believe Jesus, but strayed away from him," Kate agreed. "I know his mum would be so happy ta see her boy comin' back."

"Yes, John was sorry for his past misspent life and decided that he would have a complete reformation of himself," Gillamon told them. "But while this amazing thing was happening to John, the circumstances grew even more dire for the rest of the crew. They were blown so far north that they did not encounter any vessels that could rescue them. Meanwhile, provisions then grew desperately short. One half of a salted cod was a day's ration for *twelve* men. They thought they had plenty of fresh water, but nothing more. The clothes on their backs were threadbare, and they had no warm outer clothes to endure the bitter cold weather. In these terrible conditions with their never-ending work to keep the ship afloat, one man died. They knew they wouldn't last long like this, and their fears of starving to death grew by the hour."

"The horror!" Al exclaimed, awash in fear. "The poor laddies!"

"I suppose that *one* crew member aboard also suffered repeated allegations and threats by the captain, Gillamon?" Liz posed, inferring Captain's accusations of John as a Jonah.

Gillamon cleared his throat. "Yes, Liz, the allegations and threats continued, sometimes hourly, leading that crew member to nearly feel he was indeed responsible for this calamity. But because of faith, that crew member began to have a hope greater than all of his fears, just as the rest of the crew was ready to give up all hope."

"So, what happened next?" Jock asked expectantly.

"Would you believe it? At just that point, John Newton saw the wind come about to the exact angle they needed," Gillamon answered. "The wind blew perfectly to keep the broken part of the ship out of the water, and it blew so gently that their few remaining sails could handle it. They were able to continue with ease until they glided right into the west coast of Ireland and anchored in Lough Swilly on April nineteenth."

"*And* there they had the very last fish in the boiling pot, and drank up the last bit of water," Clarie told them. "But two hours after they were safely anchored, the wind rose to a violent gale and would have sent the ship to the bottom of the sea had they not made it to the safe haven in time!"

"That's what I call cutting it close!" Jock exclaimed.

"Of course, the Maker's perfect deliverance is clear from these miraculous factors of the perfect timing, the perfect wind, and the perfect number of fish, but I believe there was another factor that you have not yet told us *beneath the waves, n'est-ce pas* Daggdul?" Liz teased. "Should I interpret your name for everyone, Gillamon?"

Gillamon chuckled and touched the panel of time to reveal the *Greyhound* limping into the waters of Ireland. Suddenly the vantage point plunged under the water beneath the ship. Slowly, an enormous, silvery shadow swam up to the ship, nearly the same length as the *Greyhound*. Its side was lined with countless rows of silvery white scales, and it had blue eyes and a pink mouth. The great fish carefully pushed the ship into safe harbor, protecting its broken starboard side.

"Voila!" Liz exclaimed with an outstretched paw. "I give you *dagg dul*, otherwise known as 'great fish' in Hebrew!"

"So, that's where you went when you were washed overboard!" Jock exclaimed.

"Well, I'll be a Scottie's uncle! Ye mean ye were swimmin' along with the ship the whole time?" Max asked in amazement.

"Astounding good show, old boy!" Nigel cheered with a fist in the air. "I say, Gillamon, it was utterly brilliant of you to reprise your role from our mission to help J . . ."

"DON'T SAY IT!" the group collectively shouted.

Everyone quickly grew silent, all eyes on Al to see if the memories of Jonah would set him off.

Al sat up and clapped his fluffy paws. "So, if the Maker sends ye a storm, ye can be sure He'll send ye a fish or two, too." Everyone looked around in shock, based on what Al said. "Sure, He did it for Jonah *and* for John Newton."

Liz couldn't believe what she was hearing. "Albert? You . . . you just referenced . . . Jonah?"

"I thought Jonah still bothered ye, lad," Max followed, then turning and whispering to Nigel. "Best keep an eye for any panic attack signs, Mousie."

"Indeed, old boy," Nigel chuckled nervously, studying the orange cat's face for any sign of breakdown. "Remarkable to hear you reference such ancient history. Are you quite sure you should be talking about . . . Jonah?"

Al stretched out long and hard, extending his back foot on the table. "Why shouldn't I, Mousie? I were there."

"But I thought talking about Jonah sets you off, after what happened to you in the great fish," Jock piped in with a grin.

Al waved off his paw. "Aye, it took me a long time ta get over that trauma, but the Maker done healed me o' those fishy emotions. Jest like He healed Max from his fear o' water by havin' him walk all over it."

Jock turned to Max with wide eyes. "You were afraid of water, grandsire? And you walked on top of it?"

Max gave Jock a wink. "Aye, but that's a long story I'll tell ye aboot another time."

Liz kissed Al on the cheek. "I am so relieved to hear that the Maker healed you of your PTSD, *cher* Albert!"

"Now we can talk about Jonah any time without worryin' aboot it!" Kate cheered. "'Tis a grand thing ta be healed by the Maker!"

"Quite so, for *all* of us," Nigel quipped with a jolly chuckle. "Well done on the reprisal of your role as *Gillafish,* old boy! But I am *terribly* glad that no furry creatures had to join your nether regions for this mission."

"Aye, and I'm glad Mousie and me didn't have to be swallowed again," Al added redundantly. "It were a happy choice o' ye to help guide the ship into Ireland, though. No safer place to land when it comes to serpents."

"I decided that landing John Newton in Ireland rather than in England would be most beneficial," Gillamon told them. "Indeed, there were no *physical* snakes to greet him, Al."

"I do have one question," Al added. "Why were the back side of the *Greyhound* called the poop deck? Were it because . . . well, because of most back sides?"

Liz giggled. "No, *cher* Albert. The 'poop deck' is so called on ships from the French word *'la poupe'* which is the term for the stern, or back of the ship."

Al gave a goofy grin. "Well, I hope John Newton finally reached the end of his poop deck then."

"Again, you infer that Newton has reached his *bottom,* Al," Nigel clarified.

Kate gave her peppy grin. "Aye! So, now that John Newton found his way back ta Jesus, did everythin' start lookin' up for the lad?"

"Aye, did he walk the str-r-raight an' nar-r-row after this then?" Max piped up.

Gillamon and Clarie shared grimaces. "Not exactly," they said in unison.

"It took several weeks for the ship to get repairs, and John stayed in the kind care of people in Londonderry, recovering his health. During that time, he faithfully went to church prayers twice a day," Clarie told them. "He continued to read as much as he could, but he had no one to guide him, so he frequently chose poor books. He didn't have a single Christian friend or faithful minister to help him understand how to live the Christian life. He no longer made a mockery of sin or holy things, or questioned the truth of Scripture, or lost the touch of the Holy Spirit to prick his conscience, but he would soon stumble."

"John felt that this was the beginning of his return to the Maker, or rather the Maker's return to *him*, but it would take a few more years for him to fully understand how to live out his faith," Gillamon added. "One morning he went to the church and made a genuine vow to live completely for the Maker as he took communion. But the subtle serpent tempted him to forget the vows he made to the Lord that day."

"But just as He has done all along, the Maker immediately got John's attention," Clarie told them with a grin. "The very next day after John made his vow, he went out with a shooting party of gentlemen including the mayor of Londonderry. As he climbed a steep bank, he pulled out his fowling piece and it went off, nearly grazing his face and shooting off the corner of his hat!"

"John immediately recognized that the Divine hand of Providence saved him, once again," Gillamon told them.

"Good gr-r-rief!" Max exclaimed. "So, we have ta keep holdin' our br-r-reath in watchin' the lad's life play out then?"

"Please don't tell us he's just getting started!" Jock pleaded.

"Don't worry, the worst is behind John Newton physically," Gillamon told them. "Well, almost. But a great challenge to his spiritual life was coming, to see if he could hold onto his infant faith. He didn't yet understand that he couldn't keep his vow to Jesus in his own strength. No amount of 'promising to do better from now on' ever helps humans who proceed to try to live up to a list of 'dos and don'ts' by their self-will. John didn't yet understand that living the Christian life must come through Jesus, who does all the living through a believer, giving them the strength."

"Aye, we've seen this in lots of humans across time," Kate remembered, nodding her head.

"Ah, yes, our baby faith Newton has not yet discovered the secret that Paul discovered when he thrice begged for his thorn in the flesh to be removed," Nigel recalled. "He penned to the Corinthians in his second letter that, *'My grace is sufficient for you, for My strength is made perfect in weakness.' Therefore, most gladly I will rather boast in my infirmities, that the power of Christ may rest upon me. Therefore, I take pleasure in infirmities, in reproaches, in needs, in persecutions, in distresses, for Christ's sake. For when I am weak, then I am strong."*

"The lad may need a steady thorn ta r-r-remember where his str-r-rength r-r-really comes fr-r-rom," Max suggested.

"Perfectly stated, Max, and a thorn has been planted," Gillamon told him. "John doesn't feel its convicting sharpness yet, but it will most assuredly come. Just as with Paul, John will never be able to escape it, but it will keep him close to Jesus for the rest of his life."

"Gillamon, did John write to his father and to Polly about his safe return?" Liz wanted to know. "I am anxious to see their response, no?"

"Yes, and as you can imagine, they were overjoyed," Gillamon answered. "Captain Newton had given up hope of ever seeing John again. The *Greyhound* had been gone for eighteen months, so all considered her lost. John and his father exchanged a few letters, including news that Captain Newton was readying to depart for Canada to become the next Governor of York Fort in Hudson Bay. He desired to take John with him, but the *Greyhound's* repairs delayed John's return to England. Father and son missed seeing each other by a day."

"Two ships that passed in the day, what? I say, did John at least extend his apologies to his father for all he had put him through?" Nigel asked.

Gillamon tightened his mouth. "John was hoping to apologize in person when his father returned in three years after his post was complete, but sadly a tragedy occurred. Captain Newton was swimming and evidently developed cramps and drowned. John never saw him again."

"Oh, how sad!" Kate lamented. "Did they at least have some kind of reunion with their hearts?"

"Yes, Kate," Gillamon answered with a smile. "Captain Newton not only expressed affection for John in his letters but acted on that affection before he sailed for Canada. He traveled to Kent and met with the Catletts, giving them his permission for John to marry Polly."

"*C'est bon!* What a wonderful development despite the tragedy!" Liz exclaimed happily.

"Now that he has his father's approval, he can marry Polly, right?" Jock wanted to know.

"Yes, and no," Clarie answered. "There was still the issue of John's occupation to provide for Polly. He arrived in London to discover that there was no inheritance, and that Captain Gother's promises were all a lie used to trick John into coming home. His father had sailed for Canada, and he had no job. So, while he travelled to see Polly and was encouraged that she had not yet married and still held guarded affection for him, he stopped short of asking for her hand until he had a position and a future to offer her."

"Being a seaman is all he knows, right?" Jock asked.

"Not only a seaman, but a *slaver*, too," Gillamon answered. "Even though John lost his father, the man whose ship brought him home, Joseph Manesty, became like a surrogate father and took John under his wing. He offered the twenty-three-year-old a position as captain of his slave ship, the *Brownlow.*"

"'Never deliberate' were always his method, aye?" Max growled. "Don't tell me the lad took the job."

"Not as *captain,*" Clarie told him. "John showed some maturity in telling Manesty that he lacked enough experience to be captain. He said he needed to learn not only to *obey,* but also to better learn the business side of things. I'm happy to report that he now deliberates before he makes a decision. But he *did* agree to become first mate of the *Brownlow.*"

"You have no idea, Madam," Gillamon told her.

21

EVIL AFLOAT

CHARLATAN'S PARIS HEADQUARTERS

"What. Went. *WRONG?!"* Charlatan screamed, sending shivers up Kakia's spine. "Everything was ssssset up PERFECTLY. We broke Newton's physical health on Plantain Island. We prolonged the trading until the *Greyhound* was rotten. We lured Newton aboard the ship with a lie and then whisssspered blame into the liar's ear that Newton was a Jonah. A little hole is all you needed when the M . . . when *He* sent the ssssstorm."

"But I positioned the ivory tusks perfectly to pierce the timbers and make a hole in the ship, just as you instructed!" Kakia explained in her defense; she had been on board in the shape of a rat. "The hold filled with water and destroyed the food and water, but the humans somehow managed to keep the ship afloat. I did manage to trip Daggdul off the ship just as a wave hit."

"Well, shiver me TIMBERSSSSS!" the snake spat with dripping sarcasm. "It didn't matter how much water poured into the hold, or how fiercely the storm blew, or how cold or exhausted Newton was, or how much Gother wanted to toss him overboard, NEWTON SSSSSURVIVED! That Daggdul's sssssuggestion that they fish for cod saved them. But at least you eliminated *him."*

The cunning snake didn't realize what happened to Daggdul after he went overboard. Unlike the Maker, who is all-powerful (omnipotent), present everywhere (omnipresent), and knows everything past, present, and future (omniscient), Satan and his minions do not. They might be able to study their prey and learn their points of weakness, but they couldn't read minds or hearts. Ever since Satan chose Charlatan as his instrument in the

Garden of Eden, the snake held a high position of stature as a shape-shifter. Even his scales seemed to ooze pride, just like his master. He was used again on the mission of Noah's Ark as a stowaway to kill Noah and wipe out the human race, and despite his failure, he retained his position to counter the effects of the Maker's animal team led by Gillamon. Just as the Maker slowly created and called the Order of the Seven team to work behind the scenes for Him with key humans in history, Charlatan was tasked with creating a team of evil animals to counter them. Kakia was his first recruit, enlisted shortly after Noah's Ark; the new name he gave her meant 'poison,' which she used as a primary weapon. Her skills were gradually increasing and improving, but given the scope of assignments not only with John Newton but also with the birth of America, Charlatan needed more workers. He used other animals across time for singular missions, but he saw the power and necessity of having a cohesive, permanent team. Charlatan recruited and operated by fear alone, and relished tearing Kakia down for her failures, even though he had also failed. Deflection and blame were his forms of self-preservation.

"Now, what?" Kakia asked. "Newton found the Ma . . . I mean, he came back to his faith in the storm." She caught herself before she said the Maker's name. Satan had forbidden any of his agents to speak it.

"His newfound faith is pathetically weak. As long as Newton attempts to 'be religious' and do everything in his own ssssstrength, he will fail just as before, when he became a religious hermit. That is not a threat to usssss. We must keep him isolated from anyone who could show him the way to grow. Confuse him. Tempt him. We must keep evil afloat for Newton," Charlatan told her with a sly grin. "He'll sssssoon know his 'inheritance' was all a lie, and he'll be desperate for a job." He thought a minute, his red eyes darting back and forth as he thought. "Newton sssssailed with cargo on the *Greyhound* that kept him afloat. Let's put Newton on a ssssslave ship and sssssend him right back to the place where P.I. cruelly tormented him. Sssssurely his pride will risssse to be in a position of authority in trading over her, only eighteen months after she tossed him the sssssscraps from her plate. It will sssssstoke his desire for revenge—and from there, he'll be ours again."

"That's a smart idea," Kakia offered.

"Of COURSE it's sssssmart!" Charlatan screeched. "But we must always be sssssubtle, and cunning. Sssssin first deceives, and then it hardens the human heart. We will 'sssssuggest' the wrong moves at the right time. And if necessary, just as he did with our greatest betrayer Judasssss, our master will possess humans involved in Newton's fate."

BROWNLOW, PLANTAIN ISLAND, AFRICA, OCTOBER 1748

"Look familiar, Newton?" Jackson asked with a sick chuckle. "How does it feel to be back, ey?"

John gazed out at the tiny island where only eighteen months ago, he had been chained up as a servant of slaves. He clenched his jaw and raised his chin. "Things are different now. *I* will be the one who tells Evans and P.I. how things will be."

"Go get us the best slaves our trinkets can buy," Jackson ordered as John stepped foot into the longboat to go to shore.

Jackson broke into a broad, yellow-toothed smile. He was extremely pleased with the change that had come over his first mate since they departed Liverpool eight weeks ago. Having himself sailed as first mate of the *Greyhound,* Jackson had watched John start that previous voyage as a profane, blaspheming hellion, but end as some sort of religious fanatic after the storm, always off from the crew with his nose in the Bible. When Manesty offered Jackson the job as captain of the *Brownlow,* he felt slighted that the position had first been offered to Newton. Even though it turned out that Newton wasn't really a "Jonah," and that the *Greyhound* had survived their harrowing ordeal, it concerned Jackson that he would still have a doomsday prophet aboard with all his religious leanings.

As the *Brownlow* slipped from her moorings in Liverpool, Jackson spread his arms wide and declared to Newton, "Now I have a hell of my own!" He was a godless, violent man, and didn't bat an eye at dispensing cruelty and severe punishment to any slave showing the least bit of resistance. Jackson was true to his word. Life aboard the *Brownlow* was a living hell for the ship's human cargo, both below and above decks. On days when the slaves were allowed out of the hold of the ship so the crew could clean and fumigate, Jackson relished chumming the water. Sharks circled the ship while the slaves watched from the deck, clearly understanding their possible fate should they decide to revolt.

From the first night of the voyage, Jackson kept Newton at his table drinking and singing songs. Of course, it bothered Jackson that Newton's language was no longer profane, but at least he could still make up funny, insulting shanties about the crew if asked. As long as the subjects they discussed had nothing to do with God, and everything to do with the evil pursuits of men, Jackson was satisfied with his first mate.

John had brought along his Bible, but by the second day of the voyage, it was buried deep in his sea chest. He stopped reading and quickly grew slack in praying until he stopped regularly having any communication with God. By the time they reached the Guinea coast, John Newton seemed to have forgotten all the Lord's mercies that had been given him. And except for cleaning up his profanity, John was no better than before his dramatic spiritual rescue at sea. He was once again bound in chains—but this time they were around his soul. He had little desire, and no power at all, to recover himself from this backsliding descent. But as he looked out at Plantain Island, he winced, reminded of his ingratitude.

John's primary responsibilities included sailing from place to place in the longboat to purchase slaves. They began trading in Sierra Leone and processed the first slaves to put in chains in the dank bowels of the ship. John's ire now was up as he was rowed in the long boat over to Plantain Island. He looked forward to looking P.I. squarely in the eye.

"Why, isn't this a strange turn of events? Welcome back, John Newton!" P.I. greeted him with a sickly sweet tone of voice. Evans wasn't on the island. She acted as if nothing had ever happened with their inhumane treatment the last time he was there. "Come, have a seat in the shade and enjoy a drink while we serve you."

"I see the lime trees I planted are growing tall," John boasted, holding a refreshing drink and reclining in the comfortable chair under the palm trees that lazily blew in the breeze above him. Servants scurried about, bringing platters of fresh fruit, fish, and other delicious dishes for him to eat.

"Yes! And we expect them to be full of fruit next year!" P.I. reported happily, holding her hand out for him to help himself with the spread of abundant food. "I hope you will return to trade with us again, and you can pick some limes to take with you on your next voyage."

After John made his demands for the slaves he wanted, and negotiated things in his favor, he started to get a terrible headache. He leaned over and put a hand to his head. "I need to lie down."

"Of course, of course! We have the finest quarters ready for you. Go rest in the comfort of our hospitality," P.I. told him, clapping her hands for a servant to escort John to the guest quarters.

When John lay down, a violent fever washed over him. It felt like what he had experienced when he first landed here with Evans. Only this time, he was in a comfortable bed and was the honored guest of these slave traders. All that night, he writhed in a pool of sweat, and everything came pouring back into his heart and mind.

Oh, God! It was You who delivered me from this wretched place! You heard my cries and worked a miracle to save me. It was You who saved me from so many past dangers and heard my prayers in the time of trouble in the storm, John prayed as he wept bitterly with remorse. *Look how easily and quickly I forgot my vows to You that I made at Your Holy table. I've been nothing but an ungrateful wretch in return for all Your goodness to me! Oh, how I wish You had allowed me to sink to the bottom of the ocean when I first came back to Your mercy, so I wouldn't have fallen away again! Surely, there is no hope for me now.*

John rolled over onto his side, unable to sleep. He wept and prayed and wept. In the middle of the dark night, he rose from his bed. He was weak and almost delirious. He made his way to the very spot of the island where he had retreated to be alone and wrote his geometric equations in the sand. He fell to his knees and placed his fevered face into his hands as he pressed his forearms into the sand.

"Forgive me, Lord," John humbly begged. Suddenly, his spirit found a renewed liberty to pray. He felt that he could approach the throne of grace once more. "I dare not make more meaningless resolves before You, but I cast myself before You. Do with me as You please."

As the night went on, with the gentle lapping of the surf against the shore, peace entered John's spirit. He felt the solid embrace of the crucified Savior lifting him from his shame. Suddenly his fever also lifted. He made his way back to bed and fell into a deep, restful sleep.

He spent the next two days regaining his strength and finalizing the details of the trade agreement with P.I. By the time he rowed back to the *Brownlow*, John Newton was not only completely well, but he was a different man. From then on, he was delivered from the power and dominion of sin. He would continue to struggle with his sin nature that was common to every human, but at last the chains that had bound him to a life of moral depravity were broken. He left them there on the beach of Plantain Island. From now on, John Newton would not be a slave to evil or to men, but only to his Lord and Savior Jesus Christ.

THE WAR ROOM

"I haven't been this happy to see a human's transformation perhaps since Saul changed to Paul," Liz celebrated softly, wiping away the joyful tears in her eyes. "How sweet Jesus was to visit John with that fever."

"Indeed, my pet. It has restored my hope in humanity to remember that *no one* is beyond all hope," Nigel agreed.

"Aye, our Jesus were so sweet ta be so tough with John," Kate echoed.

"An' it weren't lost on the lad *where* Jesus chose ta help him br-r-reak fr-r-ree of his bonds," Max followed. "He has a way of puttin' humans in places where they can't miss the meanin'."

"So, does this mean John Newton will be good from now on?" Jock asked hopefully.

"Well, no one is "good," but as far as living fully for the Maker with all his heart, yes, Jock," Gillamon answered. "From that moment on, John never lost his desire to follow Jesus. Of course, he had a great deal to learn. He was still a new believer and had much growing up to do."

"What happened after this point in the voyage?" Liz asked.

"The *Brownlow* spent the next eight months trading for slaves along the African coast. John continued his duties as first mate, but spent his leisure hours now studying Latin, which he had long forgotten," Gillamon relayed. "Before they sailed, I slipped on board a magazine that had a clip of one of the Roman poet Horace's odes. When John saw it, he was determined to once more teach himself Latin. He had no dictionary, but picked up Castalio's *Latin Bible.* Little did John realize it, but this Latin study wasn't just a haven for his mind. He began to develop a mental muscle, putting words together that he had never possessed."

"Jolly good show!" Nigel cheered. "I couldn't be more pleased that he returned to the mother of his mother tongue."

"What aboot any more scary things on his voyage?" Al asked. "Did he see any more . . . zebras?"

Clarie giggled and mussed Al's fur. "No zebras, but plenty of dangers. As John continued his duties along the coast, he experienced burning suns and chilling dews, winds, rains, and thunderstorms, both in the open boat and on shore. He ventured on long journeys through the jungles among hostile natives who poisoned several white men, and he even buried seven men who succumbed to the fevers."

"Poison? I can imagine who was behind that," Liz opined with a frown. "You and Gillamon must have been very busy for those eight months. But were you not on board the *Brownlow?*"

"We were not *visible* aboard the *Brownlow,* but watched over John everywhere he went," Gillamon explained. "We had to rescue him from drowning more than once."

"Wha' happened? He didn't tr-r-ry ta jump overboard an' catch his hat again, did he?" Max asked.

"No, Max. John's heavy drinking days are over," Gillamon answered with a smile. "But several times when riding little canoes in the violent surf, John's boat was overturned. Since he couldn't swim, we had to drag him to shore half-dead, choking up sea water."

"But Gillamon's finest moment came aboard the *Brownlow* when he got Captain Jackson to do his bidding," Clarie reported with a broad smile. "Tell them, Gillamon."

"Ah, yes. Well, after the trading was completed in Africa, John was charged with provisioning the ship with wood and water from shore before they sailed for Antigua," Gillamon began. "They were anchored off the River Cestors, which is three hundred miles south of Sierra Leone. John would take a man and row over in the afternoon with the sea breeze, load the cargo in the evening, spend the night on shore, and then return to the ship with the favorable morning wind. Their longboat was old and nearly unfit for use. He had one more trip to make before the *Brownlow* set sail. After finishing dinner with the captain, he and his mate were about to cast off in the longboat when Captain Jackson ran out of his cabin and called John back on board."

"Why did Jackson do such a thing?" Nigel asked.

"John asked the same thing, but all Jackson would say is that 'he took it in his head' that John should remain on the ship and send another man in his place," Clarie answered. "John was surprised since he always went, and there was no logical reason for him not to go. But Captain Jackson had no reason other than it just came to him as he said."

"Somethin' happened ta the boat, didn't it?" Max surmised.

Gillamon nodded. "Indeed. Sadly, the boat sunk that night, drowning John's replacement. Of course, John immediately knew it was God's

Providence that once again had miraculously saved him, but even Captain Jackson was affected by it. He was rather quiet for a couple of days after that."

"I presume that you 'put it in his head' to order John back?" Liz asked Gillamon.

"It was a silent whisper of such magnitude in his ear that even I was astounded at how quickly he responded," Gillamon told them. "The Maker gave no explanation for my assignment at the time, but I joined John and Jackson in marveling at His protection."

"Utterly astonishing!" Nigel exclaimed. "I dare say our John Newton has been through more dangers, toils, and snares than few humans could ever even *think* of enduring."

"Zebras," Al mouthed to Jock, who rolled his eyes at the daft kitty.

"So, did he have more dangers, toils, and snares crossing the ocean?" Jock asked.

Gillamon and Clarie looked at one another with pained expressions. Clarie shook her head and Gillamon took a deep breath and slowly exhaled.

"I will not show you what took place. You need not see the unspeakable things that happened to some of those slaves at the hand of Captain Jackson when some of them attempted to break free," Gillamon told them somberly. "Never have I witnessed such atrocities. It was as if Jackson were possessed by Satan himself. The voyage was nothing less than sheer evil afloat."

No one said anything for a moment.

"Gillamon, how many slaves made it acr-r-ross the ocean?" Max asked quietly.

"They left Africa with two hundred eighteen slaves. After sailing for ten weeks across the ocean to Antigua, and then another four weeks to Charlestown, South Carolina, one hundred fifty-six remained alive," Gillamon answered.

"C'est tragique. So, sixty-two died," Liz calculated. "How did John handle all of this?"

"He coldly endured it and pressed on with his responsibilities. It did not impact him at the time as much as it did in later years," Gillamon explained. "I have no doubt that he had to push the horrors far back into his mind to cope with the horrific things he witnessed. It would have an immediate impact on what he did when he returned to Liverpool, but we'll get to that later. There is an encounter with one particular slave that I want you to see. This will be hard to watch, but trust that I'm allowing you to see it."

CHARLESTOWN, SOUTH CAROLINA, AUGUST 14, 1749

John Newton made final notations to the roster of slaves as the crew readied them for sale along the wharf. A line of purchasers eagerly waited for the auction to begin. There were no names of the slaves on his roster, only numbers. Nameless, numbered men, women, and children stood in chains, fearful of what would happen next. Their faces bore the pain and fear of being confined in the hellish bowels of the *Brownlow,* some for close to a year. They were in a foreign land and did not speak the language. Captain Jackson proudly presented his "stock" and opened the bidding.

As the humiliating process of inspecting the slaves began, John's gaze drifted to a small, four-year-old boy slave who was softly crying. John had never been affected much by the slaves he purchased, shackled, and brought on board—except for children. Doing his job required emotionless functioning, but it just didn't feel right to see children as slaves. But slavery was the way of the world across all ages, and for every culture on Earth. The series of actions needed to get slaves from one place to another was no more emotional than transporting beeswax. Even when he himself was shackled, John moved on after he was freed, understanding that it was part of the nature of slavery. Every ethnicity had its slaves.

"Sold! Bring those three," Captain Jackson ordered a crew member who took two young men and the little boy away from their mother.

As the family was separated, the little boy futilely shouted and stretched out his arm to his mother while she cried out in anguish, calling his name. "Pompey! Pompey! Pompey!" She was quickly silenced and stood there sobbing as her child was taken from her.

Something happened deep in John's psyche at that moment, even though he didn't realize it at the time. He would feel its effects years from now, and God already knew exactly how he would miraculously use it to change the world for good.

22

Voyages and Vines

THE WAR ROOM

"This is INTOLERABLE! Is Newton BLIND?!" Nigel fumed, pulling out his whiskers.

"Steady, Mousie, or ye'll be just as bald as ye were when Gillafish spit ye out," Max told Nigel with a frown. "Aye, it be a tr-r-ravesty ta see wha' slavery does ta wee ones especially."

"How can humans not see that slavery is evil?" Jock asked, his eyes tearing up over the scene they had witnessed with Pompey in Charlestown.

"Oui, especially for John Newton, who was freed from it *himself,"* Liz agreed.

"Wha' will it take for humans ta stop slavery?" Kate asked with a sigh.

"It will take time and a wedding," Gillamon told them.

"A weddin'?" Al asked hopefully. "I love weddin's!"

"Just as it will take John time to figure it out, so will it take nations. There are two parallel stories unfolding in history that mirror and impact one another—the story of John Newton and the story of slavery," Gillamon told them. "You will see that although John has come to the saving grace of Jesus, he is a spiritual baby. Just as it takes time for a baby to grow and mature, it will take time for John Newton to spiritually grow and mature, especially until he meets a mentor to help him grow."

"I certainly can understand time," Liz stated, wrinkling her forehead. "But I do not follow you on the 'wedding,' Gillamon. Please explain."

"Faith and culture must be wed to bring about the eradication of slavery. It won't work for humans to simply attempt to 'stop bad behavior' just as John repeatedly tried but failed to do at the beginning of his spiritual journey. He was completely blind and had to receive sight to understand grace. It's the same with slavery. As unbelievable as it seems to us, John Newton doesn't realize that he is morally committing crimes against humanity. But he will eventually see what he has done through the lens of faith, and his entire understanding about slavery will change."

"Je comprends. John Newton will then be an *insider* to expose the horrors of the slave trade to a blind world," Liz realized. "Human culture is blind to seeing slavery as evil, so the entire mindset of humans must receive sight to end it."

Gillamon closed his eyes and nodded. "Exactly, Liz. And for the human culture's eyesight, we must be patient. Changing a universal mindset that has existed for thousands of years will take time, but it will be quick compared to history thus far."

"Rome was not built in a day," Nigel posed with a heavy sigh, regaining his composure and straightening his spectacles. "So, how will the Maker bring faith and culture together in wedded bliss?"

"I'm pleased to announce that the wedding plans are underway, and the human chosen to officiate the lengthy ceremony has been selected," Gillamon explained.

"It's not John Newton . . . is it?" Jock asked.

"No, but you will soon see how John Newton will be involved in every part of the ceremony," Gillamon answered with a soft smile.

"Now *that's* the kind of weddin' I like!" Max enthused.

Liz's tail slowly curled up and down as she pondered these things. "I am intrigued, Gillamon. It is becoming clearer why the enemy has been attempting to eliminate John Newton since childhood. Although the enemy does not know everything, if he had any idea that John could be used as an instrument to end slavery, then of course he would want to stop him. And given your hint of the parallel stories, I presume that John will soon marry Polly?"

"Well stated, Liz," Gillamon answered. "Yes, 1750 brought four major shifts into John Newton's life: he married Polly, he lost his father, he began to grow spiritually and intellectually, and . . . I know you don't want to hear this, but . . . he became the captain of a slave ship. He would take three voyages in this position."

"NO!" the animals collectively complained.

"Well, yes, in some regard," Nigel restated. "Of course, marriage and growth are the two bright spots in the middle of this dreadful darkness. I suppose we need to hear the good, the bad, and the ugly, Gillamon."

"Aye," Max agreed, "but let's hear the good first."

"Before we continue, let me tell you a few things about John Newton's time in Charlestown," Gillamon answered. "The *Brownlow* spent a few weeks there being refurbished and loaded with its cargo of goods like tobacco to transport back to England. During that time, John spent his free daylight hours walking and praying in solitude while enjoying the beauty of every park, garden, and field he could find."

"John knew there were many Christians in the city, but he didn't know how to find them," Clarie added. "He supposed that all who attended public worship were good Christians, and that everything spoken from the pulpit was right, so he went to the Independent Presbyterian Circular Church to hear Reverend Josiah Smith. While he enjoyed his sermons, John didn't fully understand them and was too shy to approach Reverend Smith for help."

"The poor dear. It's like he's a little lost lamb in need of a shepherd," Kate observed.

"Aye, sounds like he's got a willin' spir-r-rit, but he's wanderin' aboot in a fog," Max added.

"That's exactly how he was. Young believers need mentors to help disciple them," Gillamon explained. "Especially when surrounded by bad influences. In the evenings, John joined his shipmates, whom he called 'worthless company.' He was more of a spectator than a participant as they acted like typical sailors on shore leave. John's heart was no longer attracted to worldly pursuits, but to the Maker, so he gained peace from not falling into temptation as the Maker gave him strength."

"Can we get to the weddin'?" Al asked. "There's always good food at weddin's."

Gillamon smiled and touched the panel of time to show John and Polly exchanging vows at St. Margaret's Church in Rochester. "John arrived back to Liverpool in December 1749, and he and Polly wed in February 1750."

"C'est très jolie!" Liz exclaimed. "I approve of the venue. This is of course a twelfth-century *Norman* church. I am so happy for them."

"How grand!" Kate exclaimed happily. "John waited a long time ta marry his bonnie lass."

"It took *seven* years for John and Polly to wed from the moment he fell in love with her at first sight," Clarie told them. "And while John was not terribly handsome, had no wealth, social standing or connections, and was rough around the edges, Polly's heart was eventually won over."

"I say, did Polly share John's spiritual leanings?" Nigel asked.

"With time, she did, but at first, she is what one might call a 'polite

Sunday Christian,'" Clarie answered. "She went through the motions, but her heart was not yet inclined to passionately follow the Maker. At first, this had a negative influence on John. He left the deep waters of his growing faith and went back into the shallows, never mentioning his spiritual desires to Polly. He was afraid to even pray with her! He rested in the gift and forgot the Giver."

"This is *not* a healthy way to begin a marriage," Liz declared with a frown.

"The newlyweds stayed with the Catletts in Chatham. John had no job prospects and didn't want to be separated from Polly, so he resorted to buying lottery tickets to try to win money," Clarie added. "He soon found himself seventy pounds in debt."

"The lure of easy money is no way to make a living," Nigel scoffed with his paws clasped behind his back, clucking his tongue. "Plus, it shows a flagrant distrust in the Maker's provision, what?"

"Of course, the Maker knew all this, so He arranged for John and Polly to be separated for a time," Gillamon told them. "Joseph Manesty summoned John from Liverpool and offered him a position. This is when John Newton became captain of the slave ship *Duke of Argyle*. And although he set sail on a voyage for a bad purpose, the Maker used that very ship to bring John back into deeper waters of spiritual growth."

"Sure, and the Maker moves in mysterious ways. But I'm sure the lad missed his lassie enough to make his heart turn blue," Al opined, drawing a smile from Liz.

"Of course, John was saddened to leave Polly, so he wrote her many letters over the course of the fourteen-month voyage," Gillamon told them. "It was in these letters that he was able to begin expressing his spiritual beliefs and prayers for her."

"What happened on his voyage?" Jock asked. "Did he have as much trouble as on the *Brownlow* with that evil Captain Jackson?"

"The good news is that he was able to be a different kind of captain, both to his crew of thirty, and to his two hundred slaves," Gillamon answered. He endeavored to treat them humanely and be an example. He even established public worship twice on Sundays, reading from the common Liturgy of the Church of England for the day."

"Church? On a *slave* ship?" Max asked, wide-eyed.

"Yes, and he spent his leisure time continuing his studies of Latin and mathematics," Gillamon added. "He read Horace, Livy, Caesar, and Sallust."

"Good show!" Nigel cheered. "At least the old boy is making godly and intellectual pursuits rather than drinking rum and singing salty shanties."

"Small progress is still progress, no?" Liz offered.

"But John eventually realized that life was too short for such 'elaborate trifling,'" Clarie noted. "He realized that neither the poets nor historians he read could tell him a word about Jesus, and he decided to apply himself to those who could."

"Indeed, he said he 'grew weary of cold, contemplative truths that could neither warm nor amend the heart, but tended to amplify self,'" Gillamon followed.

"But did he have more dangers, toils, and snares on the voyage while he was slave trading?" Jock asked.

"Let's see if these count," Gillamon replied with a smile. "A violent uprising of some slaves wielding a marlinspike, an attempted mutiny by three crew members, tornados, and an attempted 'poisoning' of the ship's water supply by a slave using African witchcraft by throwing a cursed talisman in the barrel."

"It sounds like nothin' but danger happened!" Al cried.

"Did John go to Plantain Island this time?" Liz asked.

"Yes. John graciously sent a longboat to bring P.I. onto the ship," Gillamon told them. "He even had the crew fire guns over her head in salute."

"Are ye sure he weren't aimin' *for* the wicked woman?" Max asked with a grin.

"John Newton showered his former tormenter with honor, kindness, and gifts," Clarie added with a smile. "He heaped such burning coals of grace on her head that she could hardly stand it!"

"He wrote to Polly that he 'took the noblest kind of revenge' upon her, as he occasionally did with others who ill-treated him," Gillamon shared. "He said that while she didn't intend to do so, P.I. had been an instrument for his good."

"Now that sounds like splendid spiritual growth indeed!" Nigel exclaimed in amazement.

Liz clapped her paws. *"C'est magnifique!* There is nothing more beautiful than when a spiritually blind man finds his sight!"

"What about the other two voyages?" Jock asked. "Did he ever find a Christian friend?"

"He did indeed, Jock. John returned from his first voyage in November 1751, and before he left for his next voyage as captain of the *African* in July

1752, he began to keep a diary," Gillamon answered. "He wrote down his resolutions for spiritual discipline, and his growth progressed slowly, and timidly."

"It was *Polly* who finally suggested they pray as a couple," Clarie interjected.

"Lassie power!" Kate exclaimed happily. "'Tis a grand thing when lassies help their mates."

"Aye, lass," Max agreed, nudging Kate affectionately with his square head.

"Bravo, Polly! And I'm quite pleased that John began the habit of regularly writing down his thoughts," Nigel added. "It does a soul good to make a record of one's journey, and to later look back on its words to see the route traveled."

"John was able to establish more good habits on his second journey," Clarie added. "Since slave ships carry twice the number of men and officers as merchant ships, John had more leisure time while at sea. He divided his day into eight-hour segments: eight hours for sleep and meals, eight hours for exercise and devotion, and eight hours for his books. So, he had a great deal of time with the Maker, which helped him grow."

"So, Jock, the *Maker* was John's friend during this time," Gillamon explained. "His time spent walking in the woods on shore or gazing out at the vast horizon at sea was sweet, but he also had more dangerous encounters."

Al covered his eyes. "I don't want to see stripes."

"Wha's gotten inta ye aboot zebras, daft kitty?" Max wanted to know, rolling his eyes. "Wha' kind of *r-r-real* dangers, Gillamon?"

"Al, there *were* some in the crew who wanted to 'change their stripes' by turning to PIRACY," Gillamon gravely answered.

Al uncovered his eyes and gave Max a confident look. "See?"

"There was a conspiracy in the crew to turn pirate and take over the ship, but two of the plotters became deathly ill. One of them died, and the plot was uncovered right before they were about to carry it out," Gillamon continued. "Meanwhile, the slaves frequently plotted insurrections, but those also were discovered just in time."

"John was also protected from going ashore where his life and character could have been ruined with a fake scandal," Clarie added. "He had a disturbing dream of warning the night before he was to row to shore, but with the assurance that no harm would come to him. So, as he sat in the boat heading to conduct business with the schemers on shore, he felt ill at ease that he should not proceed. The surf was high, so he used that as an excuse to return to the ship. That plot was later uncovered, along with its lies about John."

"The Maker keeps deliverin' John at jest the right time again an' again," Kate marveled.

"He was thus saved from mutinous pirates, insurrections, and conspiracy theories," Nigel exclaimed with a fist raised high. "Remarkable!"

"The Maker must be saving John for something pretty important," Jock concluded. "Did John become angry with his crew?"

Gillamon smiled. "The ill treatment John received only made him want to know better how to minister to his crew. He continued holding 'Sea Sundays' that included fasting and praying with the crew. He sought to always provide a cheery word of encouragement to his twenty-five men. And when he discovered that the *Book of Common Prayer* he read for Sunday services went over their heads, he began to write his own prayers and adapt a service to better meet their needs. He even wrote to his childhood pastor, Doctor David Jennings: *There are few moments of my life affording me a more real pleasure than when I am thus attempting the part of the minister.*"

"Are we talkin' aboot the same John Newton?" Max wanted to know. "The blasphemin' atheist slave ship captain now enjoys bein' a *minister?*"

"C'est incroyable!" Liz explained. "You told us to be prepared to be amazed about John Newton, Gillamon. I, for one, did not see this coming."

"And he's only getting started on the good stuff," Clarie told Jock with a wink. "Just wait."

Jock grinned. "Huzzah! So, what about the third voyage? I'm ready for this bad part to be over."

"Aye, when can he put all zebras behind him?" Al asked.

Gillamon chuckled. "Well, after a change of orders the *African* delivered the slaves to St. Kitt's instead of Antigua. John became physically sick with fear that Polly had died when he didn't hear from her, but all their mail had been sent to the original destination of Antigua. His fears were relieved when he sent a boat to Antigua to retrieve her letters. The Maker used that time to refine John further from putting his unbalanced affection for Polly above Him. John finally returned to Liverpool in August of 1753, but was only home for six weeks. We finally arrive to his final sea voyage." He tapped the panel of time to reveal a scene of John Newton with an unruly sailor in a heated discussion.

"I recognize that sailor," Liz curiously noted. "Isn't that Job Lewis who served with John on the *Harwich?*"

"Excellent memory, Liz," Gillamon told her. "This was a sad reunion for John, but it drove home the gravity and power of how our lives impact others.

If you recall, before Job met John Newton aboard the *Harwich,* he was a solid, clean-living young man and an interested believer, but John's determination to turn him into an atheist unfortunately succeeded. Job became violent, vulgar, and just as much if not more of a blasphemer than John had been. When John brought Job aboard the *African* for this voyage, he attempted to share the change he experienced of turning back to Christ, but it fell on deaf ears."

"Oh, dear! That must have torn up John's heart ta see how he had led a man away from Jesus," Kate lamented.

"It did, Kate," Clarie agreed. "Job wouldn't listen to John's words that urged him to return to Jesus. He even told John that it was *he* who had given him the ideas for living with such godless liberty. His behavior was so terrible that John couldn't control him. John sent Job away on a smaller ship for some trade business, and the young man came down with a horrible fever and died, lost and apart from Jesus."

"Quel dommage!" Liz cried. "John will never forget how his negative influence impacted another's eternity, no?"

"Did *anything* happy happen on this voyage?" Al asked with wet eyes.

"Yes, Al. After this experience, John prayed that he would understand how to better share his faith to save prodigals like Job Lewis," Gillamon told him. "He also prayed that he might be freed from this occupation of being a slave trader."

"Extraordinary progress!" Nigel cheered. "I dare say, I'm quite pleased with our prodigal's about-face despite his inability to bring another prodigal along with him."

"Oui, finalement! I see a glimmer of hope for John to leave the slave trade," Liz injected hopefully.

"After four months of trading, the *African* sailed for the West Indies. Due to over-trading, they only collected eighty-seven slaves instead of the two-hundred-twenty that they were supposed to deliver. Happily, not one of them died on this voyage," Gillamon answered. "John did develop a deadly fever on the Middle Passage, but the Maker preserved his life." He tapped the panel to show John sitting with another man in his quarters, praying. "After several years of trying to learn to walk by faith on his own, the Maker finally gave John a Christian friend and mentor—surprisingly at Saint Kitt's. It was here that John met a Scotsman from London by the name of Captain Alexander Clunie on May 22, 1754."

"He's a Scot just like us, Grandsire!" Jock pointed out happily to Max.

"Aye, that's a gr-r-rand kind of fr-r-riend ta have!" Max cheered.

"Captain Clunie was not involved in the slave trade, but was a merchant seaman. We arranged for them to meet at a social gathering on Saint Kitt's, where they discovered that they both loved the Maker," Clarie shared with a grin. "That was a fun night. For a solid month, they met on one another's ships every night to read, pray, and talk, sometimes until daybreak. Clunie helped John to finally understand so many things about how to boldly live as a Christ-follower, and how to have an intimate relationship with Jesus as the best friend anyone could have. But perhaps most encouraging to John, Clunie helped relieve his new friend's never-ending fear about falling away from Jesus again."

"John Newton's eyes were finally opened to see and understand the security of grace," Liz remarked. "Up until now, he had tried to do everything in his own strength and goodness, no?"

"Aye, the lad learned ta jest abide in Jesus then," Max suggested. "It be so much easier that way."

"Indeed, John Newton finally understood that Jesus is the true Vine," Nigel added. "'*I am the vine, you are the branches. He who abides in Me, and I in him, bears much fruit; for without Me you can do nothing.*'"

"Sounds like he really were like Jonah, not jest with the fish, but with his vines," Al opined.

"How so, Albert?" Liz asked.

"The lad kept sittin' *under* all sorts o' quick growin' vines the Maker gave him for comfort while bringin' him back, but then the Maker kept sendin' worms until John was ready to become a permanent branch," Al explained. "Now he can learn how to grow all sorts o' fruit, maybe even bananas."

Everyone thought for a minute to grasp what Al was trying to say in his simple-minded way.

"Oh, Albert, that is so very profound!" Liz beamed, kissing Al on the cheek, making him wear his goofy grin. "Although bananas do not grow on vines, but on trees."

"Well put, Al," Clarie affirmed the orange cat with a giggle. "Clunie not only helped John there on Saint Kitt's, but he made sure he would have help when he returned to London. *It just so happened* that Clunie lived less than four hundred yards from John's childhood home in Wapping. What's more, he attended an independent church pastored by Samuel Brewer, who was friends with both John's pastor Doctor Jennings and Doctor Watts. He explained to John the 'state of religion,' with its errors and problems between the Church of England and the Dissenters—something that John didn't really grasp before. So, he gave John all he needed to continue his journey with Christian fellowship and guidance once he arrived home later that August."

"Good on ye for settin' up that meetin'," Max echoed with a broad smile.

"Wha' a small world it be!" Kate cheered. "John traveled half-way around the world ta find a Christian friend who went ta church right down the street from where he went as a wee lad."

"Oui, and twenty-one years after Elizabeth Newton died, her son was ministered to by a neighbor and friend of her pastor," Liz marveled. "The answer to Elizabeth's prayers came decades later and over forty thousand miles from home, but the Maker was faithful to answer them. *C'est incroyable!"*

"What goes into the first of life goes throughout all of life, and sometimes leads you right back to where you started," Gillamon shared with a warm smile. "John had seven weeks at sea on the return voyage where he could process all he learned. And I'm happy to report that when the *African* arrived without a single incident, Liverpool couldn't believe it. No ship had ever experienced such success of never losing a single slave or crew member."

Jock sat up and wagged his tail. "Now can John Newton change the world for good like you said he would?"

"Oui, you told us to prepare to be amazed, Gillamon," Liz reminded him. "We have already been amazed to see the transformation of John Newton. When can we witness the transformation of human culture ending slavery?"

"As with all things of lasting value, such a transformation for humanity will take time, Liz," Gillamon told her. "Many things need to happen in time to set things in motion. And in order to fulfill his calling, like Jonah, John Newton first must leave the sea."

23

WILLING TO DELIBERATE

LIVERPOOL, ENGLAND, NOVEMBER 1754

"Tha's wha' I call a bea-u-ti-ful boa', Cap'n New'on, 'ey?" a sailor remarked with a broad smile, revealing some missing upper teeth. He'd just added the final touches of paint to the ship's ornately carved name on the stern. He wiped the yellow oil-based paint from his hands on a rag. "Why'd ye name 'er *Bee?* Are ye 'opin' she'll bring norra bu' 'oney?"

"Something like that," John mindlessly replied, inspecting the ship sitting at Liverpool's Old Dock. He scanned the freshly painted lettering on Joseph Manesty's newest slave ship, that Manesty had allowed John to name. *If only we were sailing to trade for beeswax,* the twenty-nine-year-old thought. Liverpool was one of the world's busiest ports, and it was from this dock that an average of 130 ships sailed per year. Fifty of them were slave ships. How John wished he were going to be captain of a merchant vessel trading for goods instead of trading for human beings! He dreaded another wretched Middle Passage crossing with his forlorn cargo. He had only been home for six weeks with Polly, and now it would be another year or more until he saw her again. He was so weary of this occupation. A pair of seagulls squawked and landed on the main mast overhead, eyeing the bustling port to snag a free bite of food dropped on the quay. John pulled out his watch. "I'm off to meet Doctor Manesty to update him on our readiness. We've got two days to finish outfitting the *Bee* before we sail for the Guinea Coast, so be swift."

"Aye, Cap'n," the sailor answered with a nod.

As John made his way to the tavern to join Manesty for an early dinner, his emotions were on edge. He was eternally grateful to his best friend for how he had repeatedly provided employment over the years. But this slaving profession drained his spirit. He wanted to leave the sea, but what other kind of work could he possibly hope to get? Ships and the sea were all he knew. *No time to think about this now. Put your best face forward in gratitude to Mr. Manesty.*

"Ah, John!" Manesty called with an upraised hand when John stepped inside the tavern.

"Good day, Doctor Manesty," John greeted him, shaking his hand. "The *Bee* now has her name painted in bright yellow on the stern. I hope you'll approve."

"Excellent! I look forward to seeing her," Manesty answered in a broad smile. "Please, have a seat."

John nodded, removed his three-cornered hat and hung it on a peg rack next to the black wooden table. He glanced around at the collection of salty mariners seated at tables, smoking long white clay pipes and drinking from pewter mugs. Men with faces as weathered as their lives laughed and slammed the table over some bawdy joke. *Liverpool has so many lost souls,* he thought as he took his seat. He found himself continually surprised at how he viewed people these days. Everything looked different through the eyes of Christ.

A sketchy tavern maid whose face looked as rough as the cobblestone road she'd walked here approached the table. She set down two overfull mugs on the table, sloshing some of the contents. "A'right, la? Will youse gents be 'avin' some vittles?" she asked. "We jus' go' a deliv'ry of fresh mussels. Dey be propa bosh in butter wif potatoes on de side."

"Aye, that sounds perfect, miss," John ordered, wrinkling his nose against her unappetizing odor. His stomach growled, nonetheless. He had worked hard all morning and was starving. "Please bring me a double portion of mussels."

Manesty laughed, raised his eyebrows, and looked at the tavern maid. "I'll stick with the beef stew." She nodded, turned, and walked off to get their food. "Enjoy your fill before you leave, John. I hope your voyage will be swift and profitable this time. I'm sending extra iron collars and ankle fetters with you in case the tribal chiefs bring us more dangerous criminals this trading season. Let's hope they deliver younger, more manageable slaves to make things easier."

John winced as he thought of young slaves, especially children like Pompey. He tightened his mouth and wrapped his hands around his mug. "I shall do my duty to treat them all well, and pray we have another successful voyage—with no loss of life." He couldn't bear the thought of any soul perishing under his care. And it seemed unthinkable to tear a family apart. *I'm no longer fit to be a slaver. God, please release me from this profession.*

Polly studied John as he sighed and removed his hat, taking a seat at the small table in their rented room here in Liverpool. She brought over a pot of tea and poured a steaming cup to set before him. "How was your meeting with Manesty?"

"Thank you, my dear," John replied, picking up the cup. He shrugged his shoulders. "It was . . . predictable." He took a sip of tea and placed it back on the saucer. "Polly, I feel like I'm nothing more than a jailer. Sometimes I'm shocked that my employment perpetually centers on a discussion of chains, bolts, and shackles. I continue to pray that the Lord in His own time would be pleased to fix me in a more humane calling. How I wish to have conversations with God's people about my newfound faith instead of conversations about iron collars and ankle fetters."

"I know, my love," Polly answered softly, taking a sip of tea.

As John reached for his cup his hand trembled, rattling the cup on the saucer before he shakily lifted it to his mouth. "I also don't want to . . . leave . . . you . . ." he started to say. Suddenly his eyes rolled back in his head, and he dropped the teacup onto the table. His body started convulsing and he fell from the chair to the floor.

"John! John!" Polly cried, reaching for him in fear. His body became rigid, and white spittle appeared at the corners of his mouth. His eyes closed and he lay there in her arms, motionless and appearing to be dead.

THE WAR ROOM

"Is he alright?!" Kate cried, worried sick about John's seizure.

"Never fear! John recovered in an hour," Gillamon assured them as they watched the scene progress. "He was left weak and dizzy with a terrible headache, but otherwise unharmed."

"POISON!" Liz exclaimed in alarm. "It appears to me that John was struck by paralytic shellfish poisoning, no doubt from those mussels!"

"And I suspect that those mussels were poisoned by the sketchy tavern maid who *served* them— that toxic villainess Kakia!" Nigel determined.

"I wish I'd been there ta knock the plate of mussels r-r-right out of John's hand jest like I knocked over them poison peas before George Washington could eat 'em in New York!" Max growled.

Al clamped both paws over his mouth and mumbled. "I'll never eat shellfishies again!"

"Steady, everyone," Clarie told them with a calming voice. "John recovered fully within a couple of days."

"Why did the Maker allow that to happen to him?" Jock asked with a wrinkled brow.

"The seizure was an answer to John's prayer," Gillamon explained. "Not only was John prevented from making another horrid voyage as a slave ship captain, but he was *protected* from doing so." He tapped the panel to show Manesty and a physician standing by John's bedside. "After what happened, they felt it was best for John not to proceed on the voyage. They were uncertain about what was wrong, and did not want to take any chances on it happening again."

"So, John resigned his post the next day, much to his and Polly's relief," Clarie added. "Word came a year later that John's replacement and most of the crew of the *Bee* perished on that voyage from a violent slave uprising."

"Saved again betwixt the jaws of death both on shore and sea!" Nigel cheered. "Brilliant!"

"Sometimes the Maker answers prayers in ways we don't expect," Kate offered. "Look how John were kept from returnin' ta sea."

"Now I see, Gillamon," Liz said. "John was forced to leave the sea, but what became his calling?"

Gillamon tapped on the time panel to show John sitting by Polly's bedside, his head in his hands as he prayed. "John and Polly went to Chatham that winter and spring for John to recover and to figure out what to do next. But just as John regained full health, Polly fell terribly ill for close to a year."

"Did she eat poison shellfishies too?" Al asked worriedly.

Clarie gave Al a tender pet. "No, Al. Polly was traumatized by what happened to John, thinking he was dying. The doctors could not diagnose her ailment, but it appears she suffered a breakdown in body as well as spirit. She became so weak and sensitive to her surroundings that she could hardly bear for someone to walk across the room. All John could do was pray for her and wait."

"But while he waited, John pursued the Maker," Gillamon shared, revealing a panel of John walking in the meadows in Chatham, his hands clasped behind his back as he prayed. "He couldn't find a good church or group of fellow believers in Kent, so he traveled to London in June to meet Alexander Clunie's friends Samuel Brewer and Doctor Hayward. They, in turn, introduced him to someone else." Gillamon next showed them a scene of John standing in a crowd of thousands of people in an open field. John clutched his heart, and joyful tears filled his eyes as he listened to the captivating cross-eyed preacher.

"George Whitefield!" Liz exclaimed. "I would recognize him anywhere! He came to Virginia during the Great Awakening in 1745, when Patrick Henry was a boy! Whitefield spoke at Saint Paul's Parish in Hanover where the elder Uncle Patrick Henry was none too pleased that the Dissenting minister took his parishioners captive with his eloquence."

"That's right, Liz," Gillamon shared. "Whitefield made multiple trips to America, and even Benjamin Franklin attended his sermons in Philadelphia, marveling at how the slender preacher's voice could reach thirty thousand people in an open field."

"Doctor Franklin also made a mint by printing and selling thousands of copies of Whitefield's sermons," Nigel added with a jolly chuckle. "Doctor Franklin has an eye for spotting successful ventures. He and Whitefield are regular pen pals and good friends."

"Indeed, Nigel," Gillamon affirmed with a smile. "So, when John went to see Whitefield in London, he had just returned from his fifth tour of America that June. But the wildly popular preacher was pressed for time to get some letters sent aboard a ship bound for South Carolina that afternoon and couldn't meet with John. Instead, he gave John a ticket to get into the crowded venue the following day. John went to hear him preach, and Whitefield instantly became his hero. You'll soon see how their extensive meetings transformed John's life."

"Meanwhile, John travelled between London and Chatham, going to hear many preachers, communing with the Maker, and praying for guidance," Clarie added. "John's two concerns centered on Polly and his future."

"Somethin' tells me a job came lookin' for the lad," Max surmised with a grin.

Liz nodded. "It is logical to assume that *Monsieur* Manesty found another position for John, as this has been his pattern throughout John's career, no?"

Gillamon smiled and tapped a panel of time to show John aboard a ship in Liverpool. He was inspecting the cargo and going over paperwork with the captain. "You are both correct. A job indeed came looking for John, one that was unsought and unexpected. Mister Manesty arranged a position for John to become the Tide Surveyor in Liverpool at a nice salary of one hundred fifty pounds per year. The Maker once again orchestrated an amazing string of events for John to get the job, which he began in August of 1755."

"Wha' aboot Polly?" Kate asked worriedly.

"Here's the beautiful part, Kate," Clarie interjected. "John was struggling about leaving her in Chatham, so he fully released her to the Maker's care. After he did so, he was filled with peace and strength about Polly. And as soon as he left for Liverpool, she recovered!"

"Maybe she were allergic to the lad instead of to shellfishies," Al pondered. "But why do humans want to know what the tide thinks?"

"Daft kitty," Max huffed, bonking Al on the head. "This be gr-r-rand news, Gillamon. Can ye tell us aboot wha' John does as Tide Surveyor?" He frowned at Al. "And it's *not* aboot askin' the tide questions, lad."

"I can answer that, old boy," Nigel piped up with an upraised finger. "Whenever a ship leaves or makes port anywhere in the world, precise records are used to keep track of the crew and the cargo, with notations made concerning the ship's capacities, sailing dates, etc. Thus, the Tide Surveyor and his officers examine the ship's papers, check that the cargo matches what is listed on its manifest, and collect the required customs duties to deliver goods."

"Oui, and such a position affords a great amount of leisure time, so I presume John used this time wisely," Liz surmised. "Did Polly join him in Liverpool?"

"Polly regained her strength and joined John in October," Clarie told her. "He indeed used his time wisely in September, giving the young couple much to discuss when she arrived."

Gillamon pointed to a scene of George Whitefield and John Newton at a table enjoying a modest meal. "Whitefield came to spend a week in Liverpool that September, preaching to vast crowds in the open fields. John went to hear him preach nine times and dined with him several times. I want you to hear one of the conversations for yourself. John Newton wasn't the only wretch who turned his life around."

LIVERPOOL, ENGLAND, SEPTEMBER 1755

"You must have had twelve hundred people there to hear you today, Reverend!" John exclaimed. "I especially loved how you interspersed hymns throughout your message. You had Baptists, Presbyterians, and Church of England types like me in rapt attention; we all listened with one heart and soul for *three* hours. I'm still trying to understand the mixing of all these faiths and why religion has become so complicated. What does the Church of England make of all that you're doing?"

Whitefield raised his eyebrows and finished chewing a piece of bread. He took a sip of wine, swallowed, and leaned forward with a wink. "They don't like me very much." He wiped the corner of his mouth with a napkin and sat back. "John, my heart is still with the Church of England, although their heart is not with me. I'm too 'enthusiastic' about preaching the Gospel, which they find *dangerous.*" He shook his head and chuckled sadly. "What in the world would they have done if Paul himself dared to preach in their midst? He no doubt would have been escorted past the stained glass windows and ushered out of their imposing doors. I find it ironic that Jesus told his followers to go out into the world to share the good news with joy, yet those in positions of church leadership disapprove if the delivery is too energetic or *joyful.*"

John wrinkled his brow. "But that is precisely why my heart burned within me to hear you speak! It's your *joy* that makes the Gospel come alive! Please help me understand. Did you always know you wanted to preach?"

Whitefield gave a laugh and lifted his hand to a young boy cleaning a table across the room. "Heavens, no! I thought my future was to be an innkeeper! I was a rascal of a boy. I was addicted to lying, filthy talking, and foolish jesting. I broke the Sabbath, preferring to go to the theater, play cards, and . . ." he paused, looking around them with an embarrassed expression ". . . read books about *romance.*"

John's eyes widened. *"You?* You were bad as a boy?" He couldn't believe his ears. *Just like me!*

"Yes, until I was fifteen or so," Whitefield answered. "I received a good education, had an excellent memory, and had an ability to speak well. I especially loved Greek and Latin, but I left school to help my mother run her inn. My father died when I was young, and she was left to raise our family. So, I put on my blue apron, washed cups, cleaned rooms, and in one word, became a professed common drawer for nigh a year and a half. Sadly, my mother's business did not flourish, and she retired from innkeeping. A friend inspired me to attend Oxford, so I returned to the Grammar School to finish my education and entered Pembroke College at Oxford when I was eighteen. It was there that I finally pursued grace and my faith and met some good Christian friends—John and Charles Wesley. I was drawn to their 'Holy Club,' where we soon earned the moniker of being 'Methodists' for how we acted."

John's jaw dropped to hear Whitefield's story—it mirrored his own. Whitefield continued.

"At first, I tried to behave in such a manner of good works that I became more of a legalist, wearing shabby clothes, refusing to powder my hair, and eating the worst food to make me appear 'penitent,'" Whitefield confessed, shaking his head. "I tried to do many things in my own strength to show how *good* I was, but all it did was exhaust me as the *hypocrite* I was. Finally, a friend directed me to some good books on the faith, which helped to open my mind. Ultimately, I began to read the Holy Scriptures upon my knees, laying aside all other books, and praying over, if possible, every line and word." He leaned in and tapped the table with a finger. "This proved meat indeed and drink indeed to my soul. I daily received fresh life, light, and power from above. I got more true knowledge from reading the Book of God in one month than I could ever have acquired from all the writings of men! After that time, I never again returned to legalism or Christian perfection, but only followed the doctrine of free grace."

John smiled and shook his head in wonder. "I thought I was the only one to have been such a rebellious youth who struggled to understand grace, just as you've described it. I also had to lay aside all the classics of literature for purposes of feeding my soul. So how did you enter the ministry?"

"Well, it was unsought and unexpected, but Bishop Bension of Gloucester heard of my character and approached me about ordination," Whitefield explained. "I didn't think I was fit for the ministry, but I began to think that if I held out longer, I should fight against God. So, at twenty-two, I became an ordained minister and preached my first sermon in the very town of my birth! I began to preach at many churches in London and around the countryside. The Lord graced me with favor, and I became a bit of a novelty, I suppose. I traveled to America on the invitation of the Wesleys to visit the colony of Georgia and help with an orphanage there. When I returned to England, the bulk of the clergy here in England did not welcome me. They had had plenty of time to discuss my 'success,' and regarded me with suspicion as a fanatical enthusiast. They were especially shocked that I would dare to preach to large crowds in outdoor spaces where there were idle, godless Sabbath-breakers."

John put his hands on his head in disbelief. "And what about Jesus' preaching to the five thousand in the outdoor hillsides? I assume they would disapprove of Him as well?"

Whitefield gave a quick laugh and nodded. "Indeed. So, from that point on, I started preaching exclusively outdoors, or at churches that will have me. I still love using the Church of England's prayer book and love her. But the Church of England, sadly, does not love me."

"They must be blind!" John exclaimed in disbelief.

"Sometimes Satan does his finest work in the middle of the church," Whitefield told him pointedly. "But I shall continue to do the work that the Lord has called *me* to do, and leave the results to Him."

LIVERPOOL, ENGLAND, FEBRUARY 1756

John sat in the small study of the new house where he and Polly had settled in the last month on Edmund Street. He leaned over his Bible and read from Galatians 1:23–24: *But they were hearing only, "He who formerly persecuted us now preaches the faith which he once tried to destroy." And they glorified God in me.* John slumped in his chair and gazed down at his watch to check the time, sighing.

Polly came into the room and wrapped a shawl around his shoulders, kissing the top of his head. "What insights have you received this morning, my love?"

"This isn't it, Polly," John told her, fiddling with his watch. He was known for being reliable and punctual, and made sure his watch was continually wound and set to the correct time.

"Isn't what, John?" Polly asked, studying his face.

"I'm not doing what I am meant to do. How can I glorify God by collecting customs duties and inspecting ships for smuggled goods?" John answered, slowly shaking his head. He looked up from his watch at Polly. "Did I ever tell you what my dear mother hoped I would become?" Polly leaned forward with a coy grin. "No, what?"

John blushed to even bring it up. "Don't laugh, my love, but she wanted me to enter the ministry. What do you think of that?"

Polly raised her eyebrows in surprise and cocked her head as she studied her young husband's imploring face. "I think . . . she was an unusual woman who was way ahead of her time. And I believe her son is as well. I know how passionate you are about serving the Lord, John. Even as the captain of a slave ship at sea, nothing gave you greater joy."

"I was the blind leading the blind," John told her with a low chuckle, chagrined at his infantile understanding of grace and Scripture then. He took in a sharp breath and his eyes danced with the possibilities. "I don't know if I could ever be of use to the God who saved a wretch like me, but talking with the great George Whitefield gave me hope. He was a wily youth until Jesus got a hold of him—just as he did with me—although Whitefield was not *half* the sinner I was!" He snapped shut the cover of his pocket watch and looked out the window. "I long for a public opportunity to testify to the riches of divine grace." He stood and took Polly's hands into his. "Polly, my life has been full of remarkable turns, including winning your hand—which I didn't deserve. I almost feel like I've been *selected* to show what the Lord can do with a no-good wretch. I am probably more fit than others to show that Jesus Christ came into the world to save the chief of sinners." He dropped his head and sighed. "But I've never been formally trained. I haven't even had a teacher since I was ten years old. I just don't know."

"Time will tell, my love," Polly told him, lifting his chin with her hand. "Pursue it as you pursued me, even if it takes years. The Lord has seen fit to answer your first prayer of a more humane position. And this position affords you the time to ask, seek, and knock. Just be willing to deliberate."

John's smile brightened to hear Polly quote Jesus' words from Matthew. He lifted her hands to his with a smile and kissed them. "I shall be willing to deliberate, Mrs. Newton. If that isn't evidence that I'm a changed man, I don't know what is."

24

Unexpected Encounters

THE WAR ROOM

"This takes the biscuit!" Nigel exclaimed. "Watching the esteemed George Whitefield mentoring young John Newton is all I need see to know that great things lie ahead for our aspiring parson. Greatness begats greatness, what?"

"John even earned the moniker 'the Young Whitefield' after Whitefield's visit," Clarie told them. "John also heard John Wesley preach in Liverpool that year, so just as Patrick Henry was raised in the heartland of the Great Awakening in America, so too was John sitting in the center of the movement in England. Both men were at the right place at the right time."

"When the French and Indian War spread from America to Europe as the Seven Years' War in 1756, John gained even more time to pursue his calling," Gillamon told them. "Because French ships blockaded the coast, John's responsibilities as Tide Surveyor lessened considerably. He and Polly took many trips to the countryside. John developed a close group of pastor friends in Yorkshire who had a big impact on him, especially when he delivered his first sermon there at one of their Dissenter gatherings."

"It must have been *smashing!*" Nigel enthused.

"It certainly was, as John fell *flat on his face* and stepped away from the parlor pulpit when he ran out of things to say!" Clarie chuckled. "He thought he could preach without notes, but he didn't get very far before his mind went blank and his pastor friend had to finish the sermon."

"*Quel dommage!* He must have been terribly embarrassed!" Liz lamented with a paw to her mouth.

"He was, of course, but that is how young apprentices learn," Gillamon pointed out with a chuckle. "John learned from that point on to write out his sermons, which will someday benefit the entire world," Gillamon told them. "You'll be pleased to know that John Newton has quite the gift of writing, and penned numerous letters, sermons, and pamphlets. It was his *pen* that led finally to his becoming ordained, from a totally unexpected source."

"How did he write his way into preaching?" Jock wanted to know.

"Maybe he wrote himself a preaching license," Al suggested, drawing a frown from Max and ducking. "I know . . . I be a daft kitty."

"John was invited to pastor some Dissenting churches in the area. Even John Wesley invited him to become an itinerant preacher. But due to what happened to him when he was a slave on Plantain Island, John just didn't feel that he had the strength of body or mind to endure circuit riding in all weather conditions across great distances," Gillamon explained. "He has a heart for the poorer sort of people—usually Dissenters—but he also felt that he needed to stay with the Church of England. Although he disagrees on a couple of points in belief, such as infant baptism, his desire is to revitalize the Church of England, not break away from it. But his preferred style of preaching is not cold, dull, and rote, but more like that of Whitefield and the Methodists. The problem was that John didn't have a university degree. He couldn't get past the bishops, who considered him to be insufficiently educated. So, he decided to keep at his post as Tide Surveyor until the opportune moment was provided by the Maker. Meanwhile, he escaped more snares that might have killed him on shore."

"Wha' happened!?" Kate asked.

Al opened his mouth to speak, but Max cut him off. "There be *no* zebr-r-ras in England, kitty!"

"John's office was in a very old building at the waterfront called the Watch House, and when a fierce storm blew in, the chimney collapsed and fell directly onto his chair," Clarie explained. "He was out of the office at the time, but was sitting in that very chair two hours before the storm hit. Then there was the time he was delayed in rowing out to inspect a ship. Just as they approached the ship, it blew up, so he missed getting killed by minutes."

"It's vuja de all over again!" Al gasped with his paws to his mouth.

"I do not know what is more remarkable—John's record number of near-death misses, or that he didn't jump at the chance to take the first offer of pastoring. He is truly willing to deliberate, no?" Liz offered. "So how did he use his pen?"

"In the six weeks leading up to his thirty-third birthday in 1758, he penned fifteen thousand words about his thoughts on entering the ministry," Gillamon answered. "He spent time examining his heart and his motives. He wrote this about being a minister:

Who is worthy? Who is able? Who is sufficient? . . .

I confess, O, Lord, there is no one more unfit than me, no one half so unworthy . . .

It if shall please thee, O Lord, to magnify thy mercy to a poor wretch who not long since was possessed by a legion of unclean spirits wounding and tearing himself all about him . . . O Lord, call and I will answer, send and I will go . . . let me know thou has accepted me and encourage me to go forth.

"John determined that humility had to be the most important virtue to be a minister. So, on his birthday, he fully committed himself to be God's servant. But this was just the beginning of John using his pen to become a parson."

"Wha' else did the lad need ta wr-r-rite ta make it clear then?" Max wanted to know. "He seems ta have jest the r-r-right kind of heart now."

"Ordination requires not only examinations, but recommendations," Clarie told them. "Although John had the recommendations, he was flatly rejected when he traveled to London. Not only did he not have a degree from Oxford or Cambridge, but the *real* reason he was rejected was because he was a suspected *Methodist.*"

"The horror!" Nigel shouted sarcastically, pulling on his whiskers. "I assume his style of enthusiastic preaching was too *unseemly.* This is intolerable!"

"Steady, Mousie," Max cautioned, pointing at the little animal's whiskers.

"Right," Nigel answered, smoothing his facial hair.

"Sadly, John's own family felt the same way about the Methodists, so he also had to battle Polly's parents and siblings in their attitude toward his pursuits," Clarie continued. "John continued to pursue ordination but was rejected again and again. Meanwhile, he grew bored of the Tide Surveyor job. He wrote:

My desire to serve the Lord is not weakened; but I am not so hasty to push myself forward as I was formerly. It is sufficient that he knows how to dispose of me, and that he both can and will do what is best. To him

I commend myself: I trust that his will and my true interest are inseparable. To his name be glory forever."

"But finally, this is where John's unexpected pen came into play, along with his remarkable journey that Clarie and I have shown you," Gillamon told them with excitement. "John became fast friends with a young Anglican clergyman in 1762 named Thomas Haweis who was eleven years younger than he. He was dismissed as a curate in Oxford for having 'too much enthusiasm,' like John, and then became the assistant chaplain at the Lock Hospital in London. He began writing to John in 1763. John told Thomas that his heart's desire was to be an ordained minister in the Church of England to tell the world from his 'own experience that there is mercy for blasphemers, for the most hardened, the most complicated wretches.'"

"When they first met, John left Thomas spellbound with his stories of being a slave and a slave-ship captain, and his salvation in the storm," Clarie shared. "Thomas *somehow* got to see eight letters that John had penned to his friend, Reverend Benjamin Fawcett, sharing such stories. He wanted to hear more."

"I assume you arranged this 'coincidence,'" Liz stated with a coy smile. "I am sure John's story would make a best-selling biography, no? It has everything to keep readers from all walks of life turning the pages: adventure, danger, love, tragedy, loss, and redemption."

"Precisely, Liz. This is exactly what Thomas thought," Gillamon told her with a grin. "So, he asked John to expound upon the eight letters of his life story and told him that he intended to publish it. Within a month, John penned a thirty-five thousand word narrative, written in a series of fourteen letters."

"It's jest wha' John had hoped, ta publicly share wha' the Maker has done for him," Kate said happily.

"But before it was published, Thomas sent it to a few people to have them look over the manuscript," Gillamon continued. "One of those people is someone whom you all know quite well, although you might consider him a *villain* in your current mission."

Max gave a low growl. "Who, Gillamon?"

Gillamon eyed the team. "William Legge, the second Earl of Dartmouth."

The animals' jaws hung open.

"You *can't* mean the former Secretary of State to King George the Third!" Nigel protested. "I distinctly remember reading his secret letter to General Gage in Boston in January 1775 about all the trouble brewing in Massachusetts. He wrote: *The King's dignity, and the honor of the Empire, require, that in such a situation, force should be repelled by force.* It was Lord Dartmouth who ordered all the Royal Governors in the Colonies to seize the gunpowder, leading to first shots fired at Lexington and Concord!"

Liz was shocked. *"Oui,* Lord Dartmouth also urged General Gage to arrest and imprison the principal members in the Provincial Congress, such as John Hancock and Samuel Adams, before the situation in Massachusetts reached a 'riper state of rebellion!'"

Al held up his paw. "I were there in the palace when King George gave a tongue-lashin' to Lordy Dartmouth and Hutchinson when news arrived aboot Lexington and Concord. Lordy Dartmouth told London not to worry, that everything were jeeesssst fine in America. But King George blamed the first shots all on Dartmouth and Gage for startin' the war. THEN, when the Americans tried to send their Olive Branch Petition, Lordy Dartmouth took it to King George, who refused to even look at it. Next thing I knew, King George made a speech and declared that the colonies were in rebellion."

Nigel was pacing up and down the table. "And *I* was privy to decoding the British war machine when locked in Gage's trunk on the voyage to London. It was *Lord Dartmouth* who showed Gage how to set up his intelligence-gathering system to position spies and move them in and out of Boston."

"I remember that, Mousie! That's when I broke ye out of the trunk and we went to that Cocoa Tree chocolate house to hear that green dragon brag about going to fight in America, and capture Charles Lee," Al recalled.

"Green *Dragoon,* old boy," Nigel corrected him. "You speak of that *insufferable* Banastre Tarleton who sailed with Lord Cornwallis to America."

Gillamon and Clarie shared a grin.

"Wasn't he that mean soldier who chased General Washington in the Battle of New York, blowing his fox horn to add insult to the defeated Continental Army?" Jock asked with wide eyes.

"Aye, an' Tarleton captured General Charles Lee in New Jersey," Max added. "He even got Lee's horse drunk when the Br-r-ritish soldiers celebrated their prize. He's nothin' but tr-r-rouble!"

Al nodded. "Sure, that's the green dragon! Anyway, before all that, King George fired Lordy Dartmouth and replaced him with Lordy Germain. But of all the Lordy Lads, I have to say Lordy Dartmouth had the least amount of darts in his mouth. He always seemed like a kind human."

"Aye, so we all know who Lord Dartmouth be," Max finally said with a grumble. "Wha's he got ta do with John Newton's letters?"

"Lord Dartmouth was a patron of the Lock Hospital where Thomas Haweis was chaplain," Gillamon began. "What you *don't* know about Lord Dartmouth is that he is a godly man who is very sympathetic to evangelical preachers like Haweis. He was introduced to Whitefield and the Wesleys, and was even accused of Methodism himself. He also has a very tender heart for children, and currently serves as the Vice President of the Foundling Hospital, where Handel's *Messiah* is played annually as a fund raiser to benefit the children."

Liz and Nigel looked at one another in shock. *"Our* Handel's *Messiah?"* Nigel asked.

Gillamon chuckled. "There's only one the last time I checked. Anyway, Lord Dartmouth has a heart for philanthropy and reaching the lost, and acts as a patron of several church parishes located around his estates in Buckinghamshire. One of these parishes is in Olney, and early in 1764, Dartmouth offered the position of Curate in Charge of the Church of Saint Peter and Saint Paul to Thomas Haweis. But unselfishly, Haweis suggested that Dartmouth consider John Newton for the position instead, sending John's letters for Lord Dartmouth to read."

"C'est magnifique!" Liz marveled. "Are you telling us that John Newton became a minister because of Lord Dartmouth?"

"It took a bit of working around the objections of the bishops, but yes, that is exactly what happened," Gillamon answered. "Understand that the title of Vicar of the Olney Church is still held by its predecessor, Reverend Moses Brown, who took another position elsewhere. As Curate in Charge, John will carry out the duties of a vicar but not hold the official title."

"Wha' a str-r-range world of connected humans we live an' work with!" Max exclaimed, shaking his head.

"Huzzah for Captain, uh, I mean, *Reverend* Newton!" Jock cheered. "When did he leave Liverpool?"

"John and Polly left Liverpool the third week of May 1764," Clarie told them. "But before they left, John preached at the local parish church to thousands of people who turned out to come hear the Tide Surveyor-turned-Minister, including the mayor of Liverpool—John Tarleton."

Liz's fur bristled and she sat up straight. "Tarleton? You don't mean . . ."

Gillamon touched the panel of time to reveal the scene of John Newton standing at the door of the parish as people streamed out of the church. They were eager to shake his hand and extend a warm word of congratulations. "John Newton had a brush meeting with someone *else* you know from your current mission."

"Congratulations, Reverend Newton," Mayor Tarleton told John, shaking his hand. "Liverpool is honored that the honorable *Lord Dartmouth* chose one of her citizens for such a position."

"Thank you, Captain Tarleton," John answered the slave ship captain who had made a fortune in the slave trade here in Liverpool. "Excuse me, *Mayor* Tarleton now. Congratulations to you, as well, on your new post. And who is this with you?"

A nine-year-old boy dressed in fine clothes stood beside Mayor Tarleton with his chin raised and his hands clasped behind his back. "Allow me to introduce my son. Banastre, Reverend Newton and I had many discussions when he was a slaver like me. He was quite successful in the trade."

John winced at the memory and the association, especially on this day. "My, what a fine young lad you are," John said warmly, extending his hand.

"You were once a successful *slave* captain, and now you're going to be a *minister?"* scoffed young Tarleton, haltingly shaking John's hand. He gave a sneer. "You won't make any money doing *that."*

John leaned over and gave Banastre a smile. "I have the divine riches of *grace,* which are priceless."

Mayor Tarleton cleared his throat. "Right, well, we'll leave you with it. Farewell, Newton."

As young Banastre Tarleton walked away with his father, John frowned. He could already see the dangerous seeds of arrogance, greed, and shallowness in that boy, and he knew full well the kind of thorny vine that could emerge once those seeds broke through the ground.

PART FIVE

But Now I See

(John Newton 1764–1777)

and Expectation
race! How sweet the sound
t saved a wretch like me!
ce was lost, but now am
Was blind, but now

25

Fish and Lace

OLNEY, ENGLAND, OCTOBER 1764

The small town of Olney was still asleep when John Newton lit his beeswax candle at 5:00 a.m. to begin his morning devotions. He sat down in the red upholstered armchair with his Bible on his lap, tapping it as he smiled and breathed a silent prayer. *Good morning, gracious Lord. Thank You for the night of rest and for this fresh, new day. Please forgive this old African blasphemer his many sins and use me for Your purposes despite my unworthiness. I give this day to You. Please direct my steps to bless those in my care. What word do You have for me today?* This was the first of countless prayers he would utter from dawn until dusk. He spoke to God all day long, just as he would any close friend. John never forgot how God was the only friend he had in his stormiest season of life. God, indeed, had never left him nor forsaken him.

John opened his Bible and turned to Philippians 4. His finger traced down the page as he read. He stopped when he came to the nineteenth verse, reading it quietly aloud: "*And my God shall supply all your need according to His riches in glory by Christ Jesus.*" The thirty-nine-year-old parson leaned his head back on the chair and smiled, absorbing every word. *Amen. Thank you, my good, good God. Oh, how our precious people need to know this! Please help me to live out this verse for them today.*

These past five months in Olney had been marked by much joy despite the difficulties the Newtons faced in ministering to this rural town of two thousand souls. Located in Buckinghamshire, the parish of Olney was four miles long, two-and-a-half miles wide, and nestled in the idyllic landscape of farmland nourished by the Ouse River. The historic town with one long main street had been inhabited by the ancient Romans and boasted an ongoing market dating back to 1205. At the south end of town stood John

Newton's new post, the Church of St. Peter and St. Paul. The 400-year-old gothic church had an iconic spire visible for miles around as it soared 185 feet into the skies above Olney. A stream ran adjacent to the church and frequently overflowed its banks into the green pastureland with its low-hanging mist. John had left the sea, but water abounded here and he loved to take rigorous walks amid the tranquil beauty of this place.

John and Polly were filled with compassion for the poor, undereducated, ragged people of Olney. Half of the town were lacemakers, an industry born in the sixteenth and seventeenth centuries from Huguenots who fled religious persecution in France. They came here seeking a place of safety and brought with them the exquisite artistry of handmade lace.

Upon their arrival in the warm days of spring, the Newtons saw women clustered outside in circles sitting before their straw-stuffed pillows topped with pins and bobbins. The women welcomed the light to better see their work and basked in the sun's warmth. During the cold winter months, they couldn't light indoor fires where the sooty smoke would tarnish the finely crafted thread and lace. They had to huddle close with small earthenware firepots filled with warm embers under their skirts to keep warm. The women of Olney toiled ten to twelve hours a day just to make ends meet. The cold, stale air hurt their lungs, and the laborious work often oppressed their minds as they sang lace-making "tells," many of which had dark, disturbing lyrics, to keep the rhythm. The men of the town primarily worked in the fields, or were shopkeepers or lace factory owners who processed the painstaking lace. Most of the children, including the boys, attended lace schools, where they were supposed to learn to read and write; but it was hard to hold a pencil when you were supposed to hold a bobbin, so education was minimal.

John was disturbed to learn how the unattended boys not in school fell into mischief from roaming the streets. He knew full well from his own upbringing how being left alone or falling into bad company led down the wrong path. He longed to help children avoid making the mistakes he had made. He knew that what went into the first of life went throughout all of life. John recalled young Banastre Tarleton's snide remark about John trading his shackles for the pulpit: "You won't make any money doing *that.*" John smiled sadly at the misguided boy who was correct from a worldly point of view. But the boy didn't realize that all the riches of this world ultimately belonged to God alone. *There is so much I wish to share with children about You and Your grace. But how do I reach them, Lord? Especially those whose families don't attend church?*

John was slowly getting to know the people of Olney and longed to find ways to meet their needs, not only spiritually through the pulpit, but relationally and practically through tangible help. He was determined that his ministry not just be about preaching; it needed to be one of building relationships—family by family, person by person. The cry of John's heart in his preaching was to break a hard heart and to heal a broken heart, and that sentiment spilled over into his relational ministry. Unless he got dirty with the lambs by getting to know them, he felt he couldn't be a shepherd of much value.

John was already serving above and beyond his assigned duties. He settled into a rigorous schedule of preaching two sermons on Sundays: a morning service for faithful believers, and an afternoon service geared more to "sinners." On Sunday evenings he held a small prayer gathering at the vicarage. In the afternoons, he went out to visit the sick and hurting. He saw three or four families a day, not dressed in his clerical attire, but donning his old seaman's jacket. His jolly personality and personal warmth caused the people to immediately fall in love with the newly arrived minister, who practiced throughout the week what he preached on Sundays. The people flocked to him, and his services began to fill immediately. It wasn't that John was a dynamic speaker with a polished delivery, but that he was *real.* He spoke truth from a sincere heart of love, and he taught from a solid foundation of Scripture.

But it wasn't only John Newton's heart and relatable style that made people flock to the pointy- spired church. In August, Thomas Haweis finally compiled John's *An Authentic Narrative*, and Alexander Clunie arranged for its publication. The book was an instant bestseller that would run five editions within its first six months alone. The book was published as an anonymous narrative without John's name, but it didn't take long for people to know who it was. After all, how many former slave ship captains became ministers in England?

John was thrilled to see copies of the book being passed around town. It reached all classes, and painted a picture of grace that people who never darkened the doors of a church could grasp. Those too poor to purchase the book or too illiterate to read even met in small groups to hear the book read aloud. The locals stared at Newton in the streets, for he was a wonder to many, including to himself. Olney's residents were proud of their breath-of-fresh-air clergyman who was anything but cold and stuffy, as were many Church of England vicars. Lord Dartmouth had chosen the perfect man for a parish town heavily populated by Dissenters. Newton wasn't the first one in this area of England to achieve notoriety from his pen. A notable Dissenter from nearby Bedford was John Bunyan, author of *Pilgrim's Progress.* So, the pew boxes filled with regular parishioners, Dissenters, and visitors traveling to see the famed slave ship captain turned minister and bestselling author. John was careful not to allow his early success to go to his head, desiring to always remember his dark days in Africa as a godless wretch and a starving slave.

John needed to read that comforting verse from Philippians today, for while God was faithfully filling his church with people, he needed God to also faithfully fill his purse. His income had drastically decreased to only £40 per year, and he further was losing a small nest egg he had invested in Manesty's shipping business, which was quickly going bankrupt due to crippled trade from the Seven Years' War. While the timely book publication helped supplement their income, he needed far more resources to help his people in tangible ways. *Please, Father, show me how to get substantial funds to help our people. I don't know how, but I know you do. Nothing is impossible with You.*

He continued to pray and read his Bible until daylight crept into the window. A beam of light fell upon a copy of the *Narrative* on his desk and a name came to his mind: *John Thornton.* He was one of the wealthiest men in London, and Governor of the Bank of England. Lord Dartmouth had introduced them when John was in London to finalize his position here at Olney. Thornton was not only a friend of Dartmouth, but was saved through the preaching of George Whitefield. God had undoubtedly given him ten talents, and he used his financial blessings to help his fellow man as a devoted follower of Christ. There was scarcely any public charity that Thornton didn't support.

"I'll send Thornton my *Narrative,* although I do not expect financial assistance. I shall leave it with God to tell him what to do next," John muttered to himself, taking out a fresh piece of paper. He penned a brief letter, packaged up the book, donned his dark blue seaman's coat, and headed out the door to put it in the post.

The morning fog lifted as the sun burned brightly with blue skies overhead, a rarity for the rainiest month of the year in Olney. The summers here were short and comfortable, but the winters were long, windy, cloudy, and very cold. John wanted to enjoy these cool, crisp October days as much as possible before bone-chilling winter arrived. He decided to walk along the Ouse. As he meandered along the river with his hands in his pockets, he noticed a young boy around ten years of age fishing along the bank. He smiled and decided to go meet the young man.

"Are you catching anything?" John asked the boy, slowly walking up to stand next to him.

The boy was dressed in worn clothes, and the arms of his frayed jacket were far too short. His scuffed shoes were a bit too large, and his brown three-cornered hat had holes. He shrugged his shoulders. "Not yet, sir." He turned to look at John and eyed his seaman jacket. He broke out in a grin. "Are you that new preacher captain?"

John gave a jolly laugh and patted his belly. "Indeed I am. I am Reverend John Newton. And you are?"

"Gill," the boy answered with a smile. He had striking blue eyes that haunted John with familiarity.

"What an unusual name. And what a *perfect* name for a boy who enjoys fishing!" John told him with a wink.

"I *have* to fish," Gill explained. "It's just me mum and me, see. She's busy making lace, so I come catch fish for us to eat."

"Ah, I see," John said with a slow nod. He pointed to a second ash branch fishing pole lying on the ground. "May I join you and throw in a line?"

"Sure," Gill answered. "Maybe you'll catch the first fish of the day."

John baited the hook with a worm from Gill's small jar of dirt. "Fishing is an important profession." He threw the line into the water. "Would you believe that fish saved my life more than once?"

Gill's blue eyes widened. "Fish saved your life? I'd love to hear that story."

"The first time was when I was a slave in Africa," John began.

"You were a *slave?*" Gill tried to look surprised.

"Yes, and I was left alone chained to a boat with no food," John explained. "But would you believe I found a line and hook on the deck? I spotted some discarded duck guts to use for bait and caught fish," John recalled, marveling afresh at God's provision at his most desperate hour. "I managed to cook it, and I must say, I've never tasted anything so good, even without any salt or seasoning! Mmmmm-mmmm."

Gill licked his lips. "Amazing! But you said fish saved you more than once? What was another time?"

"Oh, that was when our ship got caught in a storm off of Ireland and left us with a wrecked vessel to drift for a month," John answered. "We ran out of all our food except for *fish.* One of our crew members named Daggdul had suggested that we stop to fish off Newfoundland before sailing across the North Atlantic. That salted cod is the only thing that kept us from starving to death. And would you believe we were down to our last, single fish when we made it safely to port?" He shook his head in awe. "My young fellow, God's grace to me has been nothing short of . . ." He stopped as he felt a nibble.

"Amazing?" Gill interjected, watching John's line grow taught.

"Yes, amazing!" John exclaimed, hooking a fish that splashed on the water's surface as it fought against the line. He carefully pulled it into the bank and lifted it in the air. "We have one!"

"Huzzah!" Gill exclaimed. "You're a fast fisher of fish, Reverend!"

John removed the trout from the hook and put it in Gill's basket. "Let's see if we can catch another," he said as he baited his hook again.

"Your fish stories are amazing!" Gill exclaimed. Suddenly, he felt a fish strike his hook. "I got one!"

"Huzzah! Bring it in, lad!" John cheered. "Ah, that's a keeper."

Together they brought the fish onto shore and added it to the basket.

"Wasn't there something about fish in the Holy Writ?" Gill asked. "Holy mackerels or something?"

John laughed. "Yes, Gill, there are many fish stories in the Bible, but I believe the term, 'holy mackerel' refers to our friends of the Catholic persuasion. They eat fish every Friday." He thought for a moment and studied his line. "Fish are mentioned in the first book of the Bible, in Genesis, when God made them on the fifth day of Creation. Then in Leviticus, fish with scales or fins are identified as good food, while those with shells are considered 'unclean' food."

"I've heard tell people can get sick from shellfish, but I like 'em anyway," Gill added.

John wrinkled his brow. *Mussels,* he thought. "Then of course, there's the epic story of Jonah, who was swallowed by the great fish when he ran away from God."

Gill feigned surprise. "That must have been a big fish to swallow a man! Did Jonah live?"

John smiled sadly. Gill evidently didn't know this Bible story. "Yes, Gill, Jonah lived, and he went on to preach a word of warning to his fiercest enemies."

"His *enemies?* Why would he do that?" Gill asked.

"Because God told him to do so," John explained. Oh, there was so much he wanted to teach this young boy! "God wants us to love our enemies. God loves every soul on earth, even those who act wickedly. But he never gives up trying to reach them. I'm living proof, as I ran from God, just like Jonah. I'm only alive because of God's grace."

"That's amazing," Gill replied.

"Then Jesus called fishermen to be His disciples," John continued. "They dropped their nets and followed him. Jesus told them that from then on, they would be fishers of men. They went on to spread the good news of salvation to people everywhere, catching them with the net of grace. They even used the sign of a fish to identify themselves as Christ followers."

"Fishers of men, hmmm," Gill repeated thoughtfully. "You sure do have a lot of great stories about fish and the Bible. Does that mean you're a fisher of men, too, Reverend?"

"I supposed I am, Gill," John answered with a warm smile.

"I have a couple of friends named Fisher," Gill told him. "Maybe they could come to hear you, and then you'd be a fisher of Fishers!"

"Now wouldn't that be wonderful?" John answered with a hearty laugh. Instantly, both of their fishing poles lunged as fish struck their hooks. Together they laughed, and pulled in their catches, adding the trout to the basket. "Do you or the Fishers attend church?"

"No, since our parents are busy working," Gill answered. "Maybe you could do something for us kids sometime. I think my friends would like to hear your stories."

"I'd like that very much, Gill. I'll pray about how I could make that happen," John promised, smiling at Gill's use of 'kids' from the Old Norse word 'kidh,' meaning a young goat. Over the past century, the term had come into use to describe children who behaved playfully and lively as young goats. "Now, you've got four fish in your basket. Is that enough for supper?"

Gill nodded. "Yes, sir. That's plenty for me and me mum."

"Very well. I can help you carry your basket, as I'm heading home myself," John told him, picking it up. "I'd very much like to meet your mother."

"And she would like to meet you, too, Reverend," Gill answered with a broad smile. "Follow me."

"Pardon mistress, pardon master, pardon for a pin
If you don't give us a holiday, we won't let you in.
Jack be nimble, Jack be quick
Jack jump over the candlestick."

John heard a woman rhythmically singing as they approached the humble thatched roof dwelling off the main square of town.

"That's me mum," Gill told him proudly. "She and the lacemakers sing 'tells' to keep away the boredom and stay on task. She sings them to me all the time, too."

"She's singing to a familiar tune, I see," John noted. "It reminds me of the sea shanties sailors sing as they work together." He frowned as he recalled the bawdy lyrics that he made up for his crewmates to sing. He had been a very clever songsmith, taking whatever familiar tune of the day to teach the lyrics. *My mother used to sing me hymns all the time. It would gladden her heart to see me compose hymns for children, including 'children' who are six feet tall.*

"Needlepin, needlepin, stitch upon stitch,
Work the old lady out of the ditch,
If she is not out as soon as I,
A rap on the knuckles will come by and by . . ."

Gill stopped and together he and John waited outside the door. "I don't want to mess up me mum's work."

"Gill, is that you?" came his mother's voice. "You can come in, love."

"Here we go then," Gill answered, opening the door and walking inside the humble room. "Mum, I brought the new parson. This here is Reverend John Newton."

The mother set down her pillow and stood, offering a clumsy curtsy. "A pleasure to meet ye, Reverend, sir," she replied demurely. "I'm Mrs. Clarie."

"I am most delighted to meet you, Mrs. Clarie," John answered, returning a courteous bow. He lifted the basket of fish. "Young Master Gill allowed me the privilege of casting a line to bring you some fish."

"Ah, what a fine boy he is, hey? Thank ye, Reverend," Clarie answered happily, winking at Gill.

John leaned over to examine Clarie's work. "Your work of lace is lovely, Mrs. Clarie."

"It's amazing lace," Gill chortled.

John chuckled. "Gill and I have enjoyed a wonderful discussion about fish and stories from God's Word. I wish to make a personal invitation for you and Gill to come worship with us," John told her with a smile.

"Perhaps we could," Clarie answered with her gaze to the floor. "But it's hard to get away from work."

"Please, Mum, could we go?" Gill pleaded, pulling on Clarie's skirt.

"We'll see, me wee kid," Clarie answered him with a hug.

"A Sabbath rest is beneficial for the body, mind, *and* soul," John offered. "Well, I shall not keep you from your work. I hope to see you soon, and introduce you to my wife, Mary." He always used Polly's proper name when referring to her in public.

"I look forward to meeting your missus," Clarie said with a smile and a curtsy.

John tapped a finger to his hat. "Very well, I bid you good day."

"I'll see you out, sir," Gill told him as he followed the preacher out the door.

"Thank you for an unexpected, delightful afternoon of fish and lace, young Master Gill," John replied, shaking the boy's hand with a warm chuckle.

"Thank you, Reverend. I enjoyed hearing your stories, and I want to hear more," Gill answered. "I hope you'll be a fisher of kids here in Olney. You've already caught me."

A lump grew in John's throat as young Gill rushed to give him a big hug. He returned the embrace. "The catch is mutual."

OLNEY, ENGLAND, DECEMBER 6, 1764

John shook off the chill as he stoked the fire. It was a bitterly cold day, and he and Polly were ready to sit down to enjoy some hot tea. "Ah, thank you, my dear," he told Polly as she brought in a tray with a teapot and two cups.

"A letter came for you, John," Polly announced, setting down the tray. She handed him the envelope to him. "That is quite the fancy seal."

John took the letter in hand and sat in the red chair as Polly poured the tea. He raised his eyebrows. "An ornate letter T! Fancy indeed!" He broke the red wax seal to unfold the letter and out fell several large banknotes. "Goodness! Who sent this?" he exclaimed, hurriedly reading the letter. He looked up at Polly in astonishment. "It's from John Thornton! He received my *Narrative* and sent this gift to bless us. He plans to come visit us in the spring to see the miracle of God's grace on display in Olney! Praise God!"

"Oh, John! This is *amazing!*" Polly exclaimed. "The Lord is providing all our needs."

Amazing. John immediately thought of Gill. *Mr. Gillamon! He gave me Dr. Watts's book that helped me to memorize God's truths.* "My dear, I wish to use this money for something special. I've been praying about it since October, and the Lord has given me an idea to reach children and young people here in Olney."

"Wonderful!" Polly reacted excitedly, taking a sip of tea. "What kind of idea?"

John's face grew animated as the ideas poured into his heart and mind. "Fishing for kids."

26

Newton's New Year's Habit

OLNEY, ENGLAND, JANUARY 1, 1765

"Happy New Year, my dearest dear!" John whispered excitedly, kissing Polly on the cheek and jumping out of bed to dress. "There's so much to do!" It was 5:00 a.m.

Polly yawned and stretched out her arms, folding them on the pillow above her head as she smiled at her enthusiastic husband. "My love, I believe you are happiest on New Year's Day more than any other day of the year. If you were a Roman pagan, no doubt January's namesake would be your favorite god."

John laughed. "Well, I *was* a blind pagan indeed before I was found by Christ. But Polly dearest, the emblem of the two-faced god Janus *does* afford a bit of instruction that Christians would be wise to consider—looking backward to assess what God has done in the previous year and looking forward in expectation of what He will do in the coming year. What better day could there be for reflection than New Year's Day?"

"Your New Year's habit is one of the many things I love about you, John," Polly told him with a coy grin. "When we first met, you were consistent about getting *into* trouble over the New Year because of your love for me. But now, you are consistent about staying *out* of trouble over the New Year because of your love for the Lord and for me. I much prefer your latter habit."

"And my love for you is even stronger than when I was a complicated wretch!" John exclaimed happily with his arms spread out wide. "I'm so grateful for our lives *now,* because of God's grace. What could be better than new beginnings? I will ever be grateful to start a fresh, clean page for the New

Year, because," he continued, coming over to playfully kiss the top of her head and whisper, "there are no *mistakes* in it yet."

Polly giggled softly, poking him in the chest. "And *you* get to start a fresh, new diary year today with no mistakes in it yet. So, write neatly! There's no telling who might want to read it someday."

John laughed and placed a hand over his heart. "I shall do my best, but it is difficult for my pen to keep up with my thoughts." He grabbed his seaman's coat. "After my devotions I'm going to inspect the Great House."

"What for?" Polly asked.

"I've had an idea for the new meeting with the children. Lord Dartmouth's Great House is not far from the church, and sits there idle. I feel it would be the perfect venue, especially for children who are unaccustomed to attending church. I plan to introduce *hymn* singing. Heaven forbid that we sing anything other than the Church of England's approved hymns whilst in the church building." He chuckled and shook his head. "So, the Great House will alleviate that issue. My friend Alex Clunie graciously provided some Bibles, donated through the Society for Promoting Religious Knowledge, that I can give to children who are without them. I also purchased some booklets to use, including Doctor Watts's *Divine Songs Attempted in Easy Language for the Use of Children*. Once I receive Lord Dartmouth's approval to use his mansion, I will commence the meetings."

"I think this is a splendid idea, John. Do you plan to also teach the children catechisms?" Polly suggested.

"Not so much to teach them a catechism—though I intend to do that likewise—as to talk, preach, and reason with them, and explain the Scriptures to them in their own little way," he explained. "Ah, so much to do! So many kids to fish for!"

"Yes, and you only have three-hundred-sixty-five days left in the year. So, you best get to it," Polly teased with a sleepy smile. "Have fun, my love. I know Jesus will be pleased as you teach his little lambs."

"That is my prayer!" John exclaimed, almost skipping out of the room like a lamb himself.

John lit the candle on his desk and picked up his diary to record his expectations for 1765. He held it up and closed his eyes. "Father, I dedicate this year's diary to you. May it be filled with words and works that give credit to You alone. Amen."

He cracked open the diary and dipped his quill in the ink. "First, I must look back to recall God's goodness in 1764 . . ."

The last year was filled with distinguishing mercy. My introduction to the ministry and my dear's recovery, together with the liberty, acceptance, success, and comfort I have been favored with here, call for special acknowledgement . . .

John finished his summary notes of 1764 and smiled as he dipped his quill in the ink. "Now, looking ahead to 1765."

I propose to establish three meetings—one for the children, another for the young and inquiring persons, and a third to be a meeting with the more experienced and judicious for prayer and conference.

John set down his quill and reached for the small booklets he had obtained to use with the children. One was Mason's *A Little Catechism; With Little Verses and Little Sayings for Little Children.* The other was the hymn book by Dr. Watts, who had died in 1748, but whose words lived on to continue the Lord's work. John smiled, fondly rubbing his hand over the cover of Watts's book. What a privilege it was to have met him as a child. *Thank you, Mother, for faithfully taking me to church and teaching me God's Word. I pray you can somehow see the fruits of your labor.* John opened the booklet to read the preface penned by Dr. Watts:

My Friends,

It is an awful and important charge that is committed to you. The wisdom and welfare of the succeeding generation are entrusted with you beforehand and depend much on your conduct. The seeds of misery or happiness in this world, and that to come, are oftentimes sown very early, and therefore whatever may conduce to give the minds of children a relish for virtue and religion, ought in the first place to be proposed to you.

Verse was at first design'd for the service of God, tho' it hath been wretchedly abused since. The ancients among the Jews and the Heathens taught their children and disciples the precepts of morality and worship in verse. The children of Israel were commanded to learn the words of the song of Moses, Deut. 31. 19,30. And we are directed in the New Testament, not only to sing with grace in the heart, but to

> teach and admonish one another by hymns and songs, Eph. 5. 19. and there are these four advantages in it:
>
> 1. There is a greater delight in the very learning of truths and duties this way. There is something so amusing and entertaining in rhymes and metre, that will incline children to make this part of their business a diversion. And you may turn their very duty into a reward, by giving them the privilege of learning one of these songs every week, if they fulfil the business of the week well, and promising them the book itself when they have learned ten or twenty songs out of it.

John paused. "A reward? My dear Doctor Watts, what a wonderful idea to encourage the children to learn hymns and Scriptures!" He rubbed his chin. "Hmmm, I can give them copies of these booklets, but I think a little money would be an added incentive. It certainly would bless their poor families, too." He looked up to the ceiling. "Lord, I shall need a great deal of money if I am successful!" He returned to the booklet.

> 2. What is learnt in verse is longer retained in memory, and sooner recollected. The like sounds and the like number of syllables exceedingly assist the remembrance. And it may often happen, that the end of a song running in the mind may be an effectual means to keep off some temptation, or to incline to some duty, when a word of scripture is not upon the thoughts.
>
> 3. This will be a constant furniture for the minds of children, that they may have something to think upon when alone and sing over to themselves. This may sometimes give their thoughts a divine turn and raise a young meditation. Thus, they will not be forced to seek relief for an emptiness of mind out of the loose and dangerous sonnets of the age.
>
> 4. These Divine Songs may be a pleasant and proper matter for their daily or weekly worship, to sing one in the family at such time as the parents or governors shall appoint; and therefore, I have confin'd the verse to the most usual psalm tunes.
>
> The greatest part of this little book was composed several years ago, at the request of a friend, who has been long engaged in the work of catechizing a very great number of children of all kinds, and with abundant skill and success.

> So that you will find here nothing that savors of a party: the children of high and low degree, of the Church of England or Dissenters, baptized in infancy or not, may all join together in these songs. And as I have endeavored to sink the language to the level of a child's understanding, and yet to keep it (if possible) above contempt; so I have designed to profit all (if possible) and offend none. I hope the more general the sense is, these composures may be of the more universal use and service.

This perfectly describes our little band of Olney children, both church members and Dissenters! John thought excitedly.

> May the Almighty God make you faithful in this important work of education: may he succeed your cares with his abundant graces, that the rising generation of Great Britain may be a glory amongst the nations, a pattern to the Christian world, and a blessing to the earth.

Amen, Dr. Watts! John thought, thumbing through the selections. He paused at songs that especially caught his eye.

Song 8. Praise to God for learning to read.

1 The praises of my tongue
I offer to the Lord,
That I was taught, and learnt so young
To read his holy Word.

2 That I am taught to know
The danger I was in,
By nature and by practice too
A wretched slave to sin.

3 That I am led to see
I can do nothing well;
And whither shall a sinner flee,
To save himself from hell?
4 Dear Lord, this book of thine
Informs me where to go

For grace to pardon all my sin,
And make me holy too.

5 Here I can read and learn
How Christ the Son of God
Did undertake our great concern,
Our ransom cost his blood.

6 And now he reigns above,
He sends his Spirit down,
To show the wonders of his love,
And make his Gospel known.

7 O may that Spirit teach,
And make my heart receive
Those truths which all thy servants preach,
And all thy saints believe!

8 Then shall I praise the Lord
In a more cheerful strain,
That I was taught to read his Word,
And have not learnt in vain.

Song 12. *The Advantages of early Religion.*

1 Happy's the child whose youngest years
Receive instruction well;
Who hates the sinner's path and fears
The road that leads to hell.

"Yes, yes, yes, a thousand amens YES!" John exclaimed, scanning the song.

4 'Twill save us from a thousand snares
To mind religion young;
Grace will preserve our following years
And make our virtue strong.
5 To thee, Almighty God, to thee
Our childhood we resign;

'Twill please us to look back and see
That our whole lives were thine.

"Ha, now here's one I'll hold in reserve when the children get unruly," John pondered with a chuckle.

Song 16. Against Quarrelling and Fighting.

1 Let dogs delight to bark and bite,
For God has made them so;
Let bears and lions growl and fight,
For `tis their nature too.

2 But, children, you should never let
Such angry passions rise;
Your little hands were never made
To tear each other's eyes.

John smiled and flipped ahead, scanning the songs until he came to Song 21. It felt like a sucker punch to his stomach. "Oh, God! I'm such a wretched sinner! How can I teach these innocent lambs when *I* was the very evil company this song warns about? I know your grace has forgiven me, but the shame I bear for my evil influence on Job Lewis and others crushes my spirit. Help me, Lord."

Song 21. Against evil Company.

1 Why should I join with those in play
In whom I've no delight;
Who curse and swear, but never play;
Who call ill names, and fight?

2 I hate to hear a wanton song:
Their words offend my ears:
I should not dare defile my tongue
With language such as theirs.

3 Away from fools I'll turn my eyes,
Nor with the scoffers go:
I would be walking with the wise,
That wiser I may grow.

4 From one rude boy, that's used to mock,
They learn the wicked jest:
One sickly sheep infects the flock,
And poisons all the rest.

5 My God, I hate to walk or dwell
With sinful children here:
Then let me not be sent to hell,
Where none but sinners are.

YOU WERE NOTHING BUT POISON THEN, AND YOU ARE NOTHING BUT POISON NOW! YOU'RE NOT WORTHY TO TEACH CHILDREN, YOU HYPOCRITE!

John had to pause a moment and pray to shield his mind and heart from the enemy's accusing thoughts that came pouring into his spirit like fiery arrows. He closed his eyes and recalled 2 Corinthians 10:5: *We take captive every thought to make it obedient to Christ.*

He then felt Jesus softly whisper to his heart: TELL THEM, JOHN. TELL THE CHILDREN YOUR STORY AND SHOW THEM WHAT CAN HAPPEN WHEN THEY RUN FROM ME. TELL THEM HOW I FORGAVE YOU. TELL THEM THE BIBLE STORIES OF OTHERS WHO ALSO RECEIVED MY GRACE. BUT ABOVE ALL TELL THEM MY STORY. TELL THEM HOW MUCH I LOVE THEM, AND THAT I WILL FORGIVE THEM, TOO.

He then opened his eyes with grateful tears, overwhelmed anew by the forgiveness he had received. "Thank you, Lord. I will tell them my story. And I will teach them Jonah's story of running, Joseph's story of slavery, Legion's story of grace, Paul's story of conversion, but above all, *Your* story of salvation."

John picked up his Bible. "I am not what I *ought* to be. I am not what I *want* to be. I am not what I *hope* to be. But by the grace of God, I am not who I was."

27

FISHER OF KIDS

GREAT HOUSE, OLNEY, ENGLAND, JANUARY 17, 1765

"Welcome, welcome, children!" John greeted a trio of boys at the entry door of the Great House. "Come in, come inside where it's warm!" he told them happily. Three boys huddled close together, aged eight to twelve, all with similar facial features. It was a bitter cold afternoon, and they blew into their hands to get warm. They eagerly shuffled inside behind John. He walked behind a table at the front of the room to check them in by jotting down their names in a special journal for these new Children's Meetings. "I am Reverend Newton, and who might *you* be?" John asked with a smile, scanning their faces and pointing to them with his quill. "Are you brothers?"

"Yes, Reverend, sir. We're the Howard boys. I'm James, and this here be William and John," the oldest boy offered, pointing to his brothers.

"Splendid, let me note your names and Mrs. Newton will escort you into our meeting room," John explained, extending his hand to Polly. "Welcome the Howard boys, my dear!"

"Welcome, boys," Polly greeted them with a warm smile. "I'm Mrs. Newton. We are so happy you have joined us today. Might I interest you in a shortbread biscuit?" The boys' faces lit up excitedly as they followed her to the table of treats.

John looked up to see a steady trickle of boys and girls pouring into the door. His heart was elated to see so many children. When John and Thomas Fisher gave him their names, he smiled broadly.

"Ah, the Fisher brothers!" John exclaimed. "We have a mutual friend. Did young Master Gill tell you about this gathering?"

"Yes, sir, 'e did," John Fisher answered with a shy grin. "'e said somethin' 'bout fishin' for us."

"'e's always talkin' 'bout fishin'!" Thomas Fisher piped in. "No wonder 'e's named *Gill!*"

John shared a chuckle with the boys. "He's quite the young angler. We'll be talking about fish today, so I hope he'll be along to join us."

"Well, the stream's done froze, so unless 'e's gone ice fishin' 'e should be 'ere," John Fisher offered.

John filled over two pages with the names of forty-nine boys and forty girls, but still no Gill. He scanned the first page and noticed all the similar names. *Five Williams, four Johns, seven Thomases, six Sarahs, seven Elizabeths, and ten Marys! Lord, please help me keep up with them all!*

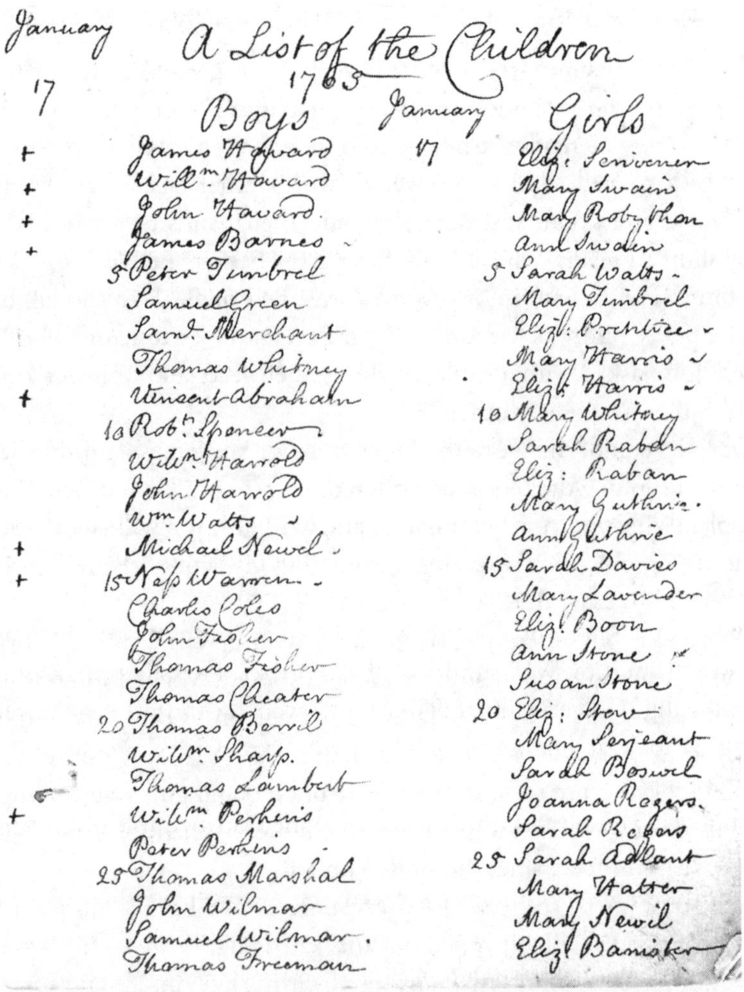

January 17 A List of the Children 1765

Boys	Girls
James Howard	Eliz: Scrivener
Willm. Howard	Mary Swain
John Havard	Mary Robython
James Barnes	Ann Swain
5 Peter Timbrel	5 Sarah Watts
Samuel Green	Mary Timbrel
Saml. Merchant	Eliz: Pritchard
Thomas Whitney	Mary Harris
Vinsent Abraham	Eliz: Harris
10 Robt. Spencer	10 Mary Whitney
Willm. Harrold	Sarah Raban
John Harold	Eliz: Raban
Wm. Watts	Mary Guthrie
Michael Newel	Ann Guthrie
15 Ness Warren	15 Sarah Davies
Charles Coles	Mary Lavender
John Fisher	Eliz: Boon
Thomas Fisher	Ann Stone
Thomas Cheater	Susan Stone
20 Thomas Berril	20 Eliz: Stow
Willm. Sharp	Mary Serjeant
Thomas Lambert	Sarah Boswel
Willm. Perkins	Joanna Rogers
Peter Perkins	Sarah Rogers
25 Thomas Marshal	25 Sarah Adlant
John Wilmar	Mary Walter
Samuel Wilmar	Mary Newil
Thomas Freeman	Eliz: Banister

John stood and went to join Polly in the meeting room. He smiled to see the children sitting in rows on the floor enjoying the buttery shortbread biscuits Polly had lovingly baked for them. He caught Polly's eye, and they shared a look of *I hope we know what we've gotten ourselves into!* They didn't have children themselves, so they would have to learn how to keep these kids orderly and attentive.

"Welcome to each and every one of you," John began, scanning the rows of children to make eye contact. "We are so very pleased and excited that you've come for our very first Children's Meeting here at Olney. Let us begin by inviting the Lord to join us. Please bow your heads and close your eyes."

"Dear Heavenly Father, I thank You for each child who has come to be with us today as we gather to learn about Your Word, Your truth, and Your grace. Please guide our thoughts to all that You would have us know today, and bless each family here represented. Amen," John prayed. When he looked up, he saw Gill standing in the back and they shared a broad smile.

"Welcome, Gill!" John called out, waving him in. "Have a seat. Now, then, how many of you know what this book is?" he asked, holding up a Bible. He wanted to get a feel for his audience and scanned the room for raised hands. He proceeded to ask a series of questions, holding up the Mason's Catechism and Dr. Watts's hymn book to see if any of them had ever learned to memorize verses, hymns, and sayings. A good number of the children were from families belonging to this church, but there were also a good number of Dissenters here, plus a smattering of unchurched children.

"We are going to learn *together,* and you will have the opportunity to earn rewards like books and coins if you work hard to memorize these catechisms," John told them. He held up the Mason booklet. "For those of you who will commit to putting these sayings to memory, I shall give you your very own copy of this booklet. *And* the best boy and the best girl who can best recite from it by Whitsuntide will earn prizes. How does that sound?"

"Huzzah!" Gill exclaimed loudly, followed by the other children, all turning to look at one another with giddy expressions and wide eyes of anticipation.

"Gill, will you please come up and help me read a sample of the kinds of things we'll be learning?" John asked.

"Sure, Reverend," Gill answered, getting up from the floor next to the Fisher boys. He walked up to the front of the room and John squeezed him on the upper arm before handing him Mason's Catechism. "This is amazing!" he whispered excitedly to John.

"Amazing indeed!" John whispered back with a chuckle. "Now, then, I will let Gill, playing the teacher, ask a question of *me,* and I will play the student and recite for *him* the answer. Fair enough?" The kids giggled with delight over this role reversal and eagerly nodded their heads with approval. "Very well, Gill. Please read me a question."

Gill opened Mason's booklet, and proceeded to read a couple of questions, followed by John, who recited the answers by heart.

Quest. If a poor Creature comes to Christ, crying, lamenting
and confessing his sins, will Christ receive him?
Answ. YES, YES: His merciful Arms are spread
wide open to receive him.

Quest. What will the Lord do for such
a one that comes to him?

Answ. 1. He will Pardon all their sins.
2. He will give them Grace.
3. He will give them Peace.
4. He will Comfort them.
5. He will provide for them.
6. He will take their parts.
7. He will bring them to Heaven.

Quest. What is Heaven?
Answ. An everlasting Enjoyment of God in glory.

John teasingly held out his hand as if expecting a coin, and Gill shrugged his shoulders as the children laughed. "Next, I want us to read aloud a rhyme to learn the Ten Commandments from Doctor Watts." He opened the booklet to share the page with Gill as they read aloud:

"The TEN COMMANDMENTS out of the Old Testament
put into short Rhyme for Children.
Exod. 20.

1. Thou shalt have no more Gods but me.
2. Before no idol bow thy knee.
3. Take not the Name of God in vain:
4. Nor dare the Sabbath Day profane.

5. Give both thy parents honor due.
6. Take heed that thou no murder do.
7. Abstain from words and deeds unclean:
8. Nor steal, though thou art poor and mean.
9. Nor make a willful lie, nor love it.
10. What is thy neighbor's, dare not covet.

"Well done, Gill, thank you!" John told him, patting him on the back as he walked back to his seat. "It is important to understand these commandments that God gave us because He *loves* us. They are not meant to keep us from what the world might think is 'fun'; they are meant to *protect* us from the evil that seeks to harm us. You must always be careful of doing even small things that may not seem 'that bad,' but soon grow into harmful habits: disobedience, lying, bad words, petty thefts, and not keeping the Sabbath. I will share in a moment what happened to *me* when I did such things. *Please,* children, I hope you understand how important it is for you to attend church each week so you will better learn these things as you grow." He held up the booklet of hymns. "Now, then, we'll also sing some hymns when we gather, so I will sing a verse and have you sing it back to me, yes?"

While John spent the next ten minutes leading the children in song, Gill scanned the room and smiled. It was a joyful noise.

"Each week, I will bring you a lesson to help you understand God's Word," John told them. "Today, we're going to begin with the most important figure in the entire Bible. Who can tell me who that is?"

Gill elbowed and whispered to Thomas Fisher who raised his hand. "Jesus?"

"Correct, Thomas! The entire Bible points to Jesus as the central figure of history, but do you know to whom Jesus said His kingdom of heaven belongs?"

The children looked around, but no one had an answer.

"Elizabeth, is it?" John asked a young girl sitting on the front row. "Would you help us find the answer by reading today's text, my dear?"

The freckle-faced girl with red hair smiled and walked over to where John had placed the Bible. He pointed to Matthew 19:13–15. She put her small finger on the text and began to softly read: "*Then little children were brought to Him that He might put His hands on them and pray, but the disciples rebuked them. But Jesus said, 'Let the little children come to Me, and do not forbid them; for of such is the kingdom of heaven.' And He laid His hands on them and departed from there.*"

John nodded and clasped his hands together. "Thank you, Elizabeth. You may be seated." He looked around the room into the faces of these little children. Oh, how he wanted them to understand how very loved they were by Jesus! "Jesus was upset with His disciples because they had not *listened* to Him! Did you know that it isn't just children who disobey? In this case it was Jesus' own grown-up followers who disobeyed! Imagine that." He put a hand on his hip and looked around the room with a grin. "The *grown-ups* got in trouble with Jesus!"

The children giggled, happy to hear that they weren't the only ones who got into trouble.

"Jesus had already told His disciples how precious children are to God, a few verses before in Matthew 18." John put his finger on the preceding verses. "*At that time the disciples came to Jesus, saying, 'Who then is greatest in the kingdom of heaven?' Then Jesus called a little child to Him, set him in the midst of them, and said, 'Assuredly, I say to you, unless you are converted and become as little children, you will by no means enter the kingdom of heaven. Therefore, whoever humbles himself as this little child is the greatest in the kingdom of heaven. Whoever receives one little child like this in My name receives Me. But whoever causes one of these little ones who believe in Me to sin, it would be better for him if a millstone were hung around his neck, and he were drowned in the depth of the sea.'*"

John opened his arms wide, acting as if he was carrying a heavy millstone around the room. "How many of you have seen the big millstone here in town? It is massive! Do you see how much Jesus loves you, little children? He says that it would be better for someone to have a *millstone* tied around their neck and they be hurled into the sea than to cause one of you to sin." He acted like he dropped the millstone, wiping his brow. The children laughed, hanging on his every word.

"Did you know that He loves you so much that He even has angels in heaven to watch over you?" He read Matthew 18:10: "'*See that you do not despise one of these little ones, for I say to you that their angels in heaven continually see the face of My Father who is in heaven.*'" John pointed to the children, drawing smiles. "Each of you has a guardian angel! Now then, back to the disciples who were doing the *opposite* of what Jesus had just told them. Instead of welcoming the children, they were turning them away as if they were a bother." John wagged his finger in the air and then waved his hand. "So, when Jesus saw this happening, He called for the children to come back and scolded His disciples. Jesus *valued* the children and wanted them to come to Him. And He did not want *anyone* to stop them from reaching His loving embrace." John wrapped his arms around himself in a hug. "Jesus loves you, children. Wrap your arms around yourself and pretend that Jesus is giving you a big hug!"

The children smiled and fidgeted as they 'hugged' themselves.

"Before we close today, I wish to share something personal with you from one of the shortest books in the Bible. It only has forty-eight verses, and there's something very *fishy* about it." He leaned over with a coy grin as he looked around the room at the smiling children. "Does anyone here know what book I'm hinting at?"

One girl named Mary raised her hand. "Jonah and the whale?"

"Very good, Mary!" John affirmed her. "It is Jonah indeed, but Scripture tells us that God prepared a great *fish.*"

Gill nodded his head in approval to John's clarification. *Bravo.*

"All sin has a storm attached to it. Not every storm in life is of our own doing, but you can be certain that when we choose to run *away* from God, we'll run right *into* a storm," John began. "I know because it happened to me! When I was your age, my mother took me to church, and I learned all sorts of Bible verses, catechisms, and hymns. I knew that Jesus loved me. But when I turned ten, I started getting into trouble by spending time with kids who did not follow God. I slowly drifted away from God, and then I sadly began to *run* from Him. I ran so far from Him that I found myself in ragged clothes, starving as a servant of slaves in Africa!"

All the children gasped, their jaws hanging open.

"I ran so far away from God that I found myself on a ship in the middle of the deepest ocean, in the middle of the darkest night, in the middle of the deadliest storm. The captain blamed the storm on *me,* accusing me of being a 'Jonah!' He even threatened to throw me overboard!" John told the wide-eyed children. He picked up the stack of small Bibles. "If you are able, I want you to read about Jonah's story this week. Who doesn't have a Bible?" Several hands shot up eagerly in the air, and as John handed out the Bibles, he told the children, "If you come back next week, I'll tell you if I was thrown overboard or not."

He's got them right where he wants them, Gill thought with a grin. Little did John Newton know it, but he was pioneering an entirely new way of reaching and teaching children. Someday, fishing for kids with children's meetings would become standard practice for churches around the globe. *Keep fishing, John. And don't let any of these kids get away.*

28

Two Williams of Note

THE WAR ROOM

"What has this kitty always said?" Al posed with a goofy grin. "Fishin' be close to godliness."

"Holy mackerel!" Jock exclaimed with a wide smile. "John Newton has gone from being a good kid to a bad kid, then from a bad adult to a good adult that fishes for good and bad kids!"

"Aye, an' Gillamon's gone fr-r-rom bein' a mountain goat, ta a gr-r-rown man on land an' sea, a gr-r-reen monkey, a gr-r-reat fish ta bein' a wee lad," Max added. "If Newton only knew he'd been talkin' ta ye his entire life!"

"C'est magnifique! What a beautiful way for John to begin his ministry, by trying to reach children," Liz added. "It is of course natural that he would have a heart for children since that is where his heartache and wandering all began. It was very moving to see how *Gill* and *Mrs. Clarie* led John along in his thinking, no?"

"You took the biscuit as a lad, *Gill!* Jolly good show!" Nigel cheered. "I'm eager to hear how these meetings progressed. Did the children keep returning?"

"Indeed, they returned in such great numbers that they had to move the meetings to the chancel of the church where the choir sits," Gillamon told them. "By April, they had over two hundred children regularly attending."

"How grand!" Kate exclaimed, wagging her tail. "Did the wee lads an' lasses start learnin' their lessons from memory?"

"Yes, and by the third meeting, some of the church parish kids were upset because two of the prizes of six pence each were earned by Dissenter children," Clarie answered with a giggle. "John decided to preach on the parable of the Good Samaritan the following week, to drive home how they were supposed to treat one another."

Gillamon smiled, pointing to the time panel of a crowd of two hundred nineteen children singing. "The Newtons got some help with other volunteers who came to lead music and guide the children. John even began writing hymns to match his lessons about the Good Samaritan and Joseph. These meetings were a labor of love, and John sometimes wearily wondered if he was impacting the children as he hoped. But by April, there were twenty children who could recite the whole catechism in front of the two hundred thirty-three children present."

"That's a lot o' wee fishes to catch and biscuits to bake," Al noted, his stomach rumbling again.

Gillamon grinned and brought out a tin of shortbread cookies to set on the table. "Here's a taste of what the children enjoyed. Help yourselves."

"Don't mind if I do!" Al exclaimed, pulling the tin toward him with both paws. "Come to me, me preciouses!"

"Ye got ta share the biscuits, kitty!" Max reminded him with a furrowed brow.

Al stopped mid-bite with an awkward grin, took another biscuit, and shoved the tin to Max. "Here ye go, lad. Ye know, if I were bakin' biscuits for this mission, I think I'd make them into fun shapes, like fish. Just like that Queen o' Elizabeths who made her gingerbread humans look like her courters."

"*Cher* Albert, you mean Queen Elizabeth I, who ordered gingerbread men made to resemble her *courtiers,* meaning her important guests," Liz corrected him with a giggle. "The children would love your fish biscuits, but perhaps a salty kind? For this mission, I would make a *soft* biscuit with something like sweet figs in the middle in honor of the change in John Newton's heart, no?"

Jock watched Max and Kate crunching the shortbread cookies. "I'd make biscuits look like my grandsire and grandmum and me, because kids love dogs!"

"Shortbread Scotties would *literally* take the biscuit!" Nigel agreed with a chuckle, munching on a biscuit. "But *this* mouse would vote for a cheesy biscuit! I say, perhaps we shall endeavor such a sweet and savory biscuit business venture one day, what?"

"I'll eat them all, as long as they aren't shaped like rutabagas," Jock joked.

"Or zebras," Al mumbled, crumbs falling onto his fluffy fur.

"Gillamon, how exactly did John afford to pay for so many booklets, prizes, and treats for the vast school of 'little fish'?" Nigel wanted to know, wiping the crumbs from his whiskers.

Gillamon swallowed before answering. "After visiting Olney that spring, John Thornton wrote to John and pledged £200 per year to use for his ministry expenses. He told John to be hospitable and to help the poor and needy."

"Look how good the Maker was to answer John's prayers in this way," Liz marveled. "That is a great sum of money!"

"Did John have ta use that hymn aboot bitin' dogs?" Max asked with a wink. "I imagine he had some unr-r-ruly lads in that cr-r-rowd."

"Yes, there were some rude boys who disrupted things, so John had to determine the best way to run these meetings," Clarie answered. "Meanwhile, the meetings were paused while they added a new gallery for more seating in the overcrowded church, and to wait for a season of smallpox to clear out of Olney. John finally resumed the meetings in the summer of 1766, but he decided to stop awarding the prizes. He worried that kids were coming for that reason alone. John wanted to attract kids who were truly trying to learn, and whose motives were pure."

"I hope he kept bakin' biscuits, though," Al worried.

"Quite wise of the old boy, I must say," Nigel commended. "It's terribly exciting to see John's church flourishing."

"Everything John touches is growing! He also had such a great number of adults for his Sunday night prayer gatherings that he moved *that* meeting to the Great House," Clarie told them.

"Sure, and John probably has triple the number of Elizabeths and Williams by now," Al supposed with an echoing voice as he stuck his nose into the bottom of the tin to lick up the crumbs.

Gillamon chuckled. "Indeed, Al, which brings us to the point of John Newton's story where you all get to meet two Williams of note. These two Williams will not only bless John, but he will bless *them* in ways that will impact human history."

Jock sat up expectantly. "Since John Newton has changed for good, can he finally start changing the world for good, too?"

"*Oui,* and is it time to see the one who will officiate the 'wedding' of faith to the culture?" Liz followed. "May we assume his name is William?"

"Yes, Jock and Liz, it's finally time for all of that to unfold," Gillamon answered, tapping the panel of time to show a fireplace with a framed inscription above it. "But before I tell you about the two Williams, I want to share an important change that happened at the vicarage where John and Polly live. Lord Dartmouth made some much-needed renovations to the house, and John had these words painted above the fireplace in his study."

Since thou wast precious in my sight
thou hast been honourable,
ISAIAH XLIII. 4th.
BUT,
Thou shalt remember that thou wast
a bond-man in the land of Egypt,
and the LORD thy God redeemed thee.
DEUT. XV. 15th.

"John explained in a letter to Lord Dartmouth that these words would serve to remind him 'from day to day what I was, and by what means I am now undeservedly settled in the Vicarage at Olney." He never wants to forget what happened to him in Africa, how the Maker rescued him, and that it is a *privilege* to serve Him today."

Nigel clapped his paws. "Brilliant! John knows how he repeatedly and easily forgot God's grace. These words shall keep him ever vigilant to remember."

"Aye! If only the children of Israel had r-r-remembered these words when the Maker first said them," Max sighed. "But it's a gr-r-rand thing that John Newton won't forget."

Liz sat there in deep thought, her tail curling up and down. "Gillamon, at the beginning of this briefing you told us to prepare to be amazed, and of course we have been. But I could not help but notice that you repeatedly used the word 'amazing' when you talked with John. I sense that there is more to this word than meets the eye, no?"

Gillamon leaned over to give Liz a tender pet. "Liz, nothing escapes that brilliant mind of yours. I think you will enjoy what comes next. Shall we get on with meeting John's two Williams of note?"

"Aye! I bet they'll be *amazing!*" Jock cheered.

Gillamon tapped the panel of time, and a frail-looking man dressed in a white linen night-cap sat in front of a writing desk holding a white quill feather. Scattered about him were papers filled with inked prose.

"I now bring us to the year 1771. Meet forty-year-old William Cowper. He grew up in a Christian home as the son of an Anglican minister, but experienced several painful events in his childhood," Gillamon shared. "His mother died when he was six years old when giving birth to his brother. In fact, William and his brother John were the only two out of *seven* children that lived past infancy."

"That was the same age that John Newton was when he lost *his* mother," Liz realized with a paw up to her cheek. *"C'est tragique!"*

"William was close to his aunt and uncle, who instilled in him a love for reading, giving him one of his first books, *Pilgrim's Progress.* But at the age of nine, he was sent to boarding school where he was bullied so severely by an older boy that William knew him 'by his shoe-buckles better than any other part of his dress.' This cruel treatment left mental and emotional scars upon the nervous, bashful young William that would follow him throughout adulthood."

"Wha' goes inta the first of life goes throughout all of life," Kate reminded them. "The poor dear! I can't stand bullies!"

Max growled. "Aye! Bullies be nothin' but insecure cowards lookin' for attention. I wish I could bite the br-r-ritches of the bully who harmed the wee lad."

"William's heartache continued with a broken romance while training for a law career for which he was clearly not suited, further filling him with anxiety," Gillamon continued. "He then lost his father and his best friend."

Nigel cleaned his spectacles and held them up to the light. "It would seem that this William has had quite the depressing start in life." He placed the spectacles on his nose. "I can see this leading him down a dark path unless he meets Jesus in the road."

"Exactly right, Nigel. Following these losses, William suffered his first bout of depression, or 'melancholy' as the humans called it. He even tried to take his own life three times and had to be put into a mental institution in Saint Albans so he could recover."

Kate frowned sadly. "How terrible for the poor lad! I don't care how bad it gets, ye should never think of throwin' away the Maker's gift of life."

"Fortunately, a godly physician named Doctor Cotton prescribed *spiritual* care as well as physical care, and William found true salvation as he plunged into reading the Bible," Gillamon told them. "His mental state improved, but he would continue to suffer from bouts of severe depression."

"I'm gettin' depressed meself," Al whined. "I wish I had more biscuits to help me feel better."

"Well, about this time in 1767, William went to live with a Reverend and Mrs. Unwin, who took him in as a kind of adopted son," Gillamon continued. "Although William came from a prosperous, genteel family, he has always been short of money, which makes him dependent on friends and family for support. It was under the Unwins' roof that William first heard of John Newton and read his *Narrative.* It *just so happened* that the Newtons had been invited to visit, courtesy of Clarie serving as courier."

"Ah, bringing humans together with the stroke of a pen is one our favorite and most effective methods," Nigel answered, preening his whiskers back. "Bravo, old girl."

"It was a pleasure to arrange," Clarie told them, her smile falling from her face. "But sadly, just before John and Polly got to the house, Reverend Unwin had tragically been killed. He was thrown from his horse."

"That sounds familiar. Were that evil Kakia kitty in the r-r-road?" Max asked with a furrowed brow.

Kate nodded. "Aye, it sure seems like trouble follows William Cowper wherever he goes. Makes me wonder *who* might be tryin' ta harm the lad, jest like with John Newton. The lad must be destined ta do somethin' grand."

Clarie nodded. "The enemy seeks to afflict *all* humans, but it does seem that those who will use their pens especially suffer a great deal."

"But as we have seen across time, every great book has been written with the author's blood, no?" Liz posed. "Suffering deepens the pen. *Bon,* therefore, I assume that William shall become some sort of poet? And I can only assume that John became a spiritual help to William in the process?"

"Yes, John and Polly went above and beyond in helping William, Mrs. Unwin, and her daughter," Clarie answered. "The Newtons opened their home and invited them all to stay for five months until they could move into a lovely red brick home a stone's throw behind them, called Orchard Side, in Olney in 1768. Here's where things began looking up for William and for John. They became fast friends, and have so much in common—poetry, Latin, reading classic literature, walking the English countryside, humor, and *writing.* Liz, you'll be pleased to know that William Cowper is also an avid gardener. You will enjoy spending time in his garden when it is time for your assignment with Nigel there."

"How lovely!" Liz exclaimed. She and Nigel shared a smile. "Now I am intrigued—and of course, I cannot wait to wander his garden and read what he writes."

"John also nudged William to start visiting the sick and needy with him," Clarie added. "William didn't have a lot of drive to do things, so it helped him a great deal to focus on the needs of others instead of himself."

"Aye, that's the secret when ye're down," Kate agreed. "If ye jest help someone else, ye forget all aboot yer problems, an' ye see that others have problems, too. Some may have it even worse than ye do."

"That's right, Kate. So, as John helped William through his depression, William helped John with his ministry workload, becoming a volunteer curate of sorts," Clarie said. "When they came to see me at the lace shop with 'Gill', I suggested that they write some uplifting songs for the lacemakers to sing, instead of the depressing ones that only serve to make the ladies' days dark and dreary. I started calling William 'Squire' or 'Sir Cowper,' and that brought a smile to his face. Soon, all the people in town called him that."

"It appears that these two men *needed* each other," Liz realized. "I am sure that John did not have anyone in Olney who shared his intellectual interests, and William needed John's nurturing, Christian guidance as he recovered. Friendship is a beautiful thing, no? So, the Maker obviously planned for them to meet, and from what you've told us thus far, what they write will change the world."

Gillamon tapped on the panel to show John Newton walking down a narrow path lined with apple blossoms, a notebook under his arm. "The two friends' houses are separated by a field, and they asked their neighbor if they could pay her a guinea to have the freedom to walk through her property to reach the other without having to walk around the cobblestone road."

Abundant flowers like roses and honeysuckles filled the air with sweet fragrances, and birds flitted from bush to branch while bees buzzed from flower to flower. A small hare scurried under a rosebush. William greeted John with an upraised hand and together the two friends entered William's lodgings to share their writings.

Nigel studied the friends. "What exactly are John and William writing, Gillamon?"

"They have been writing a great number of things since Cowper arrived in Olney," Gillamon answered. "Newton sought to help William through his recovery by encouraging him to express himself on paper."

Nigel nodded. "Bravo! What has John written whilst they have been sharpening each other's quills?"

Gillamon tapped the panel. "John has not only been through his own storm, but he witnessed William's storm as well. He wrote a hymn entitled *The Storm Hushed:*

'Tis past—the dreadful stormy night
Is gone, with all its fears!

And now I see returning light,
The Lord, my Sun, appears.

"Because he had encouraged William to write hymns, John himself grew more and more excited about writing hymns for the plain people of Olney to understand the gospel message, just as he had done for the Children's Meetings," Gillamon explained. "When the Sunday evening prayer meeting moved to the Great House, John and William each wrote a hymn for the occasion. From that time on, John has made it a weekly practice to write a hymn for every Sunday evening gathering, as well as for special occasions such as New Year's services."

"So, the lads each be wr-r-ritin' songs ta sing, which be a good thing an' all, but jest how are these nice tunes supposed ta change the world?" Max wanted to know. "I'm no music expert, but seems like they need ta come up with somethin' big like Handel's *Messiah* ta do that."

"Handel's bestest ora-oreo," Al wrongly remembered.

"Oratorio, old boy," Nigel corrected him.

Gillamon gave them a knowing grin. "Precisely. And just as I reprised my role of the great fish for John Newton that I was for Jonah, so will you, Liz and Nigel, reprise your roles as song compiler and music arranger for John as you were for Handel. While many of their hymns will bless the world, one of them in particular will change it."

"Huzzah!" Nigel cheered with two tiny fists in the air. "Shall I warm up my violin, Gillamon?"

"Not this time, Nigel," Gillamon answered. "You will simply need to find the perfect common tune to put with the lyrics in keeping with John Newton's desired way of doing things. First, you and Liz will need to arrange for the publication of the hymns that John and William will write. Publishing the words with music together will come later. This will be a long-range assignment."

"C'est magnifique!" Liz exclaimed, her eyes dancing with excitement. "So, I take it that William Cowper is to help John Newton change the world with song. And the other William? Is he the one who will oversee the wedding of faith and culture?"

Gillamon smiled and tapped the panel to reveal a tiny, eleven-year-old boy walking in the garden with John Newton. "What goes into the first of life . . ."

29

A Sweet Vine

OLNEY, ENGLAND, 1771

The late afternoon sunshine warmed John Newton and young William Wilberforce as they walked through the garden on this early June day. Polly was in the house entertaining the boy's extremely wealthy guardians, William and Hannah Wilberforce. Hannah was the half-sister of John Thornton, and immediately wrote to John Newton after hearing about his stunning *Narrative*. They soon struck up a friendship, and John and Polly often visited them in London; the Wilberforces, in turn, visited the Newtons in Olney. They also shared a mutual friend in the Reverend George Whitefield, and considered themselves Methodists.

The previous year, after young William's father and sisters had died, his mother became too ill to care for him. She sent the boy to live with his childless aunt and uncle, who had homes in Wimbledon and London. William's family losses, followed by his move away from his mother, devastated the bright, sensitive young boy. The Wilberforces adored their tenderhearted nephew, who was such a considerate child. He once removed his shoes and tiptoed gingerly across the floor to check on an ill guest, concerned but not wishing to disturb them. He was no trouble at all, and he spiritually blossomed as they exposed him to the evangelical teachings of the Great Awakening. William developed an early, strong faith in Jesus. Such fervent faith had been absent in his own family, who adhered to a rote, social church experience in their cold, rented pew. Had William's ardent Anglican mother and grandfather known about the scandalous faith of the Wilberforces, they never would have sent young Billy to live with them. But God had other plans for the young boy, including exposing him to the old African blasphemer, John Newton.

"What kind of vine is this, Reverend Newton?" William asked with the sweetest voice and the most perfect diction John had ever heard from a child. "It smells very sweet."

"You don't know, Billy?" John asked with a grin at the boy's upturned cherubic face. William's expensive silk waistcoat matched the color of the blossoms. "Why, a honeysuckle vine, of course. Shakespeare's 'luscious woodbine.' Honeysuckle is a clinging vine that depends on other plants to grow and flourish as it gracefully binds itself to them with its tiny tendrils, so it is a beautiful symbol of true friendship. Proverbs 18:24 says that '*there is a friend who sticks closer than a brother.*'"

William smiled as he touched a blossom. "I need a friend to help me grow. Can we be sticky friends like this vine, Reverend?"

John smiled at the sweet, fatherless boy and patted his shoulder. "I'd like that very much, Billy. When I needed a friend to help me grow, God gave me a sticky friend named Alex." He reached his hand into the twisting vine, full of trumpet-like yellow-orange flowers, and plucked off a large blossom. "Now, honeysuckles *taste* as sweet as they smell. Would you like to taste one?"

William vigorously nodded his head. "Yes, please!"

"Now watch, Billy. Take a honeysuckle blossom and pinch the bottom green tip just enough to break through the petal, but not all the way through its white stem, like so," he said, leaning over so the boy could see it up close. The boy squinted due to his poor eyesight. "Slowly pull out the white stem and you'll see a drop of sweet nectar. Go ahead—try it."

William leaned in and took the blossom to taste the nectar. His deep brown eyes widened with delight. "It *is* sweet! It's the sweetest flower I've ever tasted." He laughed. "It's the *only* flower I've ever tasted. Can I try another?"

"Of course, of course," John encouraged, pulling off a blossom. "Now, after the bumblebees pollinate these flowers, they produce red berries that the songbirds enjoy. But we can't eat the bitter berries, because they tend to upset the stomach."

William beamed, opening another bloom to relish the sweet taste. "What about the flower? Can we eat that part?"

"Let's see," John answered with a wink. He proceeded to eat the blossom while William watched, giggling. "It's not bad, but it feels like I'm eating paper." John gave an exaggerated swallow and laughed. *"How sweet are your words to my taste; sweeter than honey to my mouth."*

"Is that in the Bible?" William asked. "How can *words* taste sweet?"

"Yes, from the One Hundred Ninety-Ninth Psalm," John answered. "Well, did you know that the Apostle John ate a *book?*"

William's eyes widened. "Why did he do that?"

"In the book of Revelation, an angel told John to eat the little book, saying, '*Take and eat it; and it will make your stomach bitter, but it will be as sweet as honey in your mouth.*' It symbolized John internalizing God's message of warning about things to come," John explained.

"Like the nectar and the berries?" William asked. "Why would the angel tell him to eat something sweet *and* bitter?"

"Well, God's Word is sweet. *Truth* is sweet, but it can also be bitter at first," John explained. "Some truths, like facing our sins, are hard to ingest, but once we also ingest God's truth of grace, He makes everything taste sweet as He brings good from it."

"So, the truth of our sins is like the bitter red berries, and grace is like the sweet honey?" William posed as he studied the vine. "I like this vine, Reverend. It smells, tastes, and even *sounds* sweet the way you describe it."

"I'm glad. There is much to glean from God's natural world to apply to our lives," John told him.

"You seem to know a lot about flowers. My uncle and aunt have large gardens in their houses," William told him. "They even have lime trees! Have you ever seen one?"

John raised his eyebrows and nodded with a sad smile. "I planted a whole grove of them when I was a slave in Africa."

William stopped and gave John a shocked expression. "What do you mean, a slave? And how did you get to *Africa?*"

John cocked his head and studied the boy. "You're from a family of merchants, correct?"

"Yes, Reverend, from Hull," William answered.

"Ah, Hull may be one of the largest ports in England, but it is the only one that doesn't participate in the slave trade," John realized.

"What is . . . the slave trade?" William asked in his soft voice.

John breathed in deeply as he looked upon this face of pure innocence. When he was William's age, John had sailed off with his father to be exposed to all manner of salty sailors, hanging pirates, and docks filled with wicked slave ships. This innocent boy had yet to be exposed to the nightmarish reality of that evil world. But in the moment, John felt God speak in his heart. TELL HIM, JOHN. TELL HIM THE BITTER AND THE SWEET.

"I'd like to show you something in my study above my fireplace," John told him. "Let's walk as I tell you some hard things. But they are bitter truths you should know."

Together John Newton and young William Wilberforce walked among the honeysuckle vines as John told him about the slave trade and what a blind wretch he had been.

William's eyes brimmed with tears as John hung his head with fresh grief from telling the story of Pompey, the evils of the slave trade, and how long it had taken for him to come back to God. John lifted his gaze and pointed to the words painted on the wall above his fireplace. "You see, Billy? I must never forget who I was then, and how Jesus saved me from myself. I was so very blind to my sin."

"Blindness happens in all kinds of ways, doesn't it, Reverend?" William asked him softly. "You were like the blind beggar whom Jesus healed, weren't you?"

John marveled at William's insight. "Yes, Billy. I was spiritually blind."

William smiled and got up from his chair to go put his tiny hand on John's arm. "But now you see," he encouraged in his sweet voice. "Thank you for telling me about your story of grace. And I'm glad to know the bitter truth about the slave trade, even though it breaks my heart. I'm sad the world is blind to it."

John put his burly, shackle-scarred hand atop William's with a gentle squeeze. "Perhaps the Lord will use you to help this blind world see the truth one day."

William's chin quivered and he nodded, getting choked up as he spoke. "Yes, Reverend. That would be . . ."

"Amazing," John finished for him in a whisper.

30

Amazing Grace

OLNEY, ENGLAND, THURSDAY, DECEMBER 31, 1772

Snow softly plinked against the windowpane as John added another log to the fireplace in his study. He stirred the embers with the hot iron poker, careful to hang it on its hook. "If I used you as a *pen,* I could write a big message to the people of Olney out there in that field of snow," he murmured with a chuckle.

John sat down at his desk with his diary, inkwell, and quill. He gazed out the window at the beautiful snowy landscape. The church spire was the only thing visible against the white blanket of sky that hid the sun. *Snow is much like grace. It covers every blemish with beauty. But snow is temporary. Unlike grace it always melts away, like everything else in this world.* He smiled and dipped his quill in the ink. "Very well, let me close this year before *it* melts away."

> *The comforts and trials of another year are finished and can be repeated no more. It is more than sixteen years since I began to write in this book. How many scenes have I passed through in the time? By what a way the Lord led me. What wonders he has shown me!*
>
> *O Lord, accept my praise for all that is past, enable me to trust thee for all that's to come—and give a blessing to all who may read these records of thy goodness, and my own vileness.*

John put his quill in the inkwell and stretched out his arms, wriggling his fingers in the air. He picked up his sermon notes for his annual New Year's Day service. It gladdened his heart that all manner of people came from surrounding areas to darken the doors of the church on a day other than Sunday. He had selected the text of 1 Chronicles 17:16–17, and decided to do with this sermon the same thing he did with his diary each New Year. He would have the people look back on past mercies and look ahead to future hopes. And King David of Israel was the perfect example to show the people how to do just that.

John opened his Bible to reread the full chapter of 1 Chronicles 17. David was living in a palace of cedar in Jerusalem while the Ark of the Covenant was housed in a tent. He lamented to Nathan the prophet that he desired to build a house for the Lord. But God told Nathan to tell David that GOD would build *David* a house.

The house *of David,* John thought, flipping over to Luke 2:4. *Joseph also went up from Galilee, out of the city of Nazareth, into Judea, to the city of David, which is called Bethlehem, because he was of the house and lineage of David . . .* John smiled and shook his head in wonder. "Oh, if David could have fully understood and foreseen what God meant—that *this* House would be built from his bloodline in the city of his birth, Bethlehem. And that the Builder would first appear to the lowliest of the low, the shepherds, just like David. And that He would be laid in the very same feeding troughs where the sacrificial lambs were placed before bringing them to the Temple to atone for the sins of the people. For *my* sins."

John returned to the passage in 1 Chronicles 17 to read how God reminded David where he came from. *"I took you from the sheepfold, from following the sheep, to be ruler over My people Israel. And I have been with you wherever you have gone, and have cut off all your enemies from before you, and have made you a name like the name of the great men who are on the earth."*

The fire popped, and John glanced at the fireplace. His gaze then drifted up to the words painted above it. Perhaps he chose to remember things to a fault. He realized that remembering where he came from often allowed the enemy to shoot fiery arrows of accusation over his past sins and wickedness. But he preferred the constant spiritual warfare and casting down imaginations with Scripture rather than ever returning to the wretched creature he had been. And above all, he knew that God's grace was greater than all of it—greater than his past sins, greater than Satan, greater than any thought, greater than any act.

John returned his attention to the text for his sermon:

> *Then King David went in and sat before the Lord; and he said: "Who am I, O Lord God? And what is my house, that You have brought me this far? And yet this was a small thing in Your sight, O God; and You have also spoken of Your servant's house for a great while to come and have regarded me according to the rank of a man of high degree, O Lord God."*

"I understand how overwhelmed you must have been, David," John whispered. "You went from being a shepherd boy to the King of Israel!" He shook his head, rewinding his own life since boyhood. "Who am *I,* O Lord, that You should spoil me with Your grace? I was a wretch who used to *curse* Your Holy Name! But You rescued me from myself and now allow me to be a shepherd for Your people—even for Your little lambs."

John thought for a moment about the children and how those services began years ago. "Gill," he uttered with a grin. Gill and his mother had evidently moved on, as one day they were no longer found in the thatched-roof house. "If only you could see what God has done since that time, I know exactly what you would say. 'That's *amazing!*'" John chuckled to himself. "But you would be absolutely right, young Master Gill."

He thought of all the Marys and Elizabeths, the Thomases and the Williams. *William Wilberforce.* He smiled to recall that warm summer evening last year with the honeysuckle vine, remembering the boy's sweet voice. *"I like this vine, Reverend. It smells, tastes, and even* sounds *sweet the way you describe it."*

John was happy to have kept in touch with his sweet little "sticky friend," and hoped the Wilberforces would travel to attend the service tomorrow. He reached for his sermon notes. He just needed to write a summary hymn of his three main points to close out the service to be held in the church. Once Lord Dartmouth saw the growth of John's ministry and the need to accommodate increasing numbers of people for services, the prohibition that confined singing to the Great House alone had eased. Tomorrow, the people would sing this new hymn in *God's* House, where it was meant to be heard.

"Now then, what shall I write for the people to sing that summarizes these thoughts of thankfulness for the grace You have shown to us, Lord? We must look back, look around, and look forward." He dipped his quill in the ink and wrote out a title:

Faith's Review and Expectation

John cocked his head to the side to re-read his title. "The title sounds amazing to *me.*" He traced his finger down the sermon notes for the first verse, chuckling as he thought of Gill and Billy, searching for the right words to combine his many thoughts. *Amazing. It even sounds sweet.* "We must first look back and ask ourselves who we were before the Lord revealed His love and grace." He put his quill to paper and began to write.

Amazing grace! (how sweet the sound)
That saved a wretch like me!

John moved his finger down the page of his sermon notes. *We were all rebellious and blinded by the god of this world.* "Blind. What was it Billy said about the blind man Jesus healed?" He turned in his Bible to the scene from John 9:25: *He answered and said, "Whether He is a sinner or not I do not know. One thing I know: that though I was blind, now I see."*

I once was lost, but now am found,
Was blind, but now I see.

Jesus. My healing moment. The storm. John's mind rushed back to that very first moment when he first believed in God and in the grace of Christ. Oh, the elation of that moment! What relief it brought to his heart! His eyes welled up with gratitude, and a lump formed in his throat as he penned the second verse:

'Twas grace that taught my heart to fear,
And grace my fears relieved;
How precious did that grace appear,
The hour I first believed!

John glanced over his second sermon point. *Look around. God protected David from lions, and bears, and Goliath! Wherever he went God cut off all his enemies, and He has also done that for me! I am unable to count high enough to number the dangers, toils, and snares from which God saved me.* His mind raced with scene after scene from his childhood—the bucking horse, his drowned friends; in Africa—slavery, abuse, sickness, starvation, storms, wild animals, near drownings, the shipwreck; in the slave trade—mutiny, attempted murder, violence, and disease; in Liverpool—the falling chimney, the exploding ship, and the seizure.

Through many dangers, toils and snares,
I have already come;
'Tis grace has brought me safe thus far,
And grace will lead me home.

"What was it David said as he ended his prayer about building his house?" John mumbled to himself as he re-read the passage from I Chronicles 17. He scanned down to the end of David's prayer. *And now, Lord, You are God, and have promised this goodness to Your servant.* "Ah, yes. Perfect for point three, to look ahead:

The Lord has promised good to me,
His word my hope secures;
He will my shield and portion be,
As long as life endures.

"And God's promise to Israel after David is gone . . . *'And I will appoint a place for my people Israel and will plant them, that they may dwell in their own place and be disturbed no more . . .'"*

Yes, when this flesh and heart shall fail
And mortal life shall cease;
I shall possess, within the veil,
A life of joy and peace.

John looked out the window at the sunless sky and the falling snow. "Snow never stays, but your grace remains forever, Lord. *Forever.*" John reread the entire chapter. "Forever is mentioned eight times in these verses. *Eight* . . . the eighth day, symbolizing new birth and new beginnings!"

The earth shall soon dissolve like snow,
The sun forbear to shine;
But God, who called me here below,
Will be forever mine.

John laid aside his quill and blew on the ink as he read over the six verses for his new hymn. He nodded and felt pleased with how the Lord had inspired his pen. He would look it over in the morning, and of course would make a brand-new entry in his diary for the first day of 1773. But for now, he would put 1772 to bed.

OLNEY, ENGLAND, FRIDAY, JANUARY 1, 1773

This is the Ninth New Years day I have seen in this place. I have reason to say, The Lord crowneth every year with his goodness. The entrance of this finds me and my dear Mary in health and peace. I am still favoured with strength, and with some liberty for my public work and hope the Lord is still pleased to work by me, for the edification of his people already called, and the awakening of sinners. As to myself, It is given me to trust in the Lord Jesus for life and salvation—I know he is both willing and able to save. Upon him as an All-sufficient Saviour and upon his word of promise I build my hope, believing that he will not suffer me to be put to shame.

My exercise of grace is faint, my consolations small, my heart is full of evil, my chief sensible burdens are, a wild ungoverned imagination, and a strange sinful backwardness to reading the Scriptures, and, to secret prayer. These have been my complaints for many years, and I have no less cause of complaint than formerly. But my eye and my heart is to Jesus. His I am, him I desire to serve, to him I this day would devote and surrender myself anew.

O Lord, accept, support, protect, teach, comfort and bless me. Be thou my Arm, my Eye, my Joy and my Salvation. Mortify the power of sin, and increase the image of thy holiness in my heart. Anoint me with fresh oil, make me humble, faithful, diligent and obedient. Let me in all things attend to thy word as my rule, to thy glory as my end, and depend upon thy power and promise for safety and success. I am now in the 49th year of my age, and may expect in the course of a few years at most to go whence I shall no more return, nor have I a certainty of continuing here a single year or even a month or a day. May thy grace keep me always waiting till my appointed change shall come, and when the summons shall come may I be enabled to rejoice in thee, as the strength of my heart and my portion forever.

John put his quill in the inkwell and nodded. "Amen." With that, he rose from his chair, gathered his sermon and hymn notes, and blew out the candle on his desk. He wanted to go over to the church before the people arrived. He needed to be fully prepared, including determining the perfect tune to use for the people to sing.

After all, he had a new hymn to teach.

31

GRACE NOTES

THE WAR ROOM

"NOW I SEE!" Nigel exclaimed with his paws up in the air. "I see *tremendous* potential for this hymn, Gillamon!"

"Oui, what a wonderful hymn, service, and beginning for the New Year!" Liz added. "I'm sure William Cowper was pleased as well with John's new hymn."

Gillamon furrowed his brow. "Indeed, he was, but tragedy struck immediately following this service. Another mental storm slammed into Cowper, and he once again plunged into the dark depths of depression. As he felt the onset of the mental storm coming, he wanted to get his thoughts on paper before he lost all mental reasoning. He penned a hymn entitled, 'Light Shining Out of Darkness' which begins:

GOD moves in a mysterious way,
His wonders to perform;
He plants his footsteps in the sea,
And rides upon the storm.

"Soon after he put down his quill, William spiraled into darkness, and the next two nights he had nightmares and hallucinations," Clarie added gravely. "He was so delusional that he thought that the Maker was telling him to take his own life! He tried, but Mrs. Unwin stopped him in time. Of course, she sent for John, who had a difficult time caring for his hurting friend over the following weeks."

"Oh, me!" Kate cried. "How horrible!"

Max put his paw around Kate. "Wha' happened ta the poor lad?"

Nigel crossed his arms and shook his head. "What utter madness! Such delusions suggest that he came under spiritual attack."

"It was indeed a severe attack of spiritual oppression," Gillamon answered gravely. "William had experienced more losses, including that of his brother, and new financial difficulties. But the enemy indeed came in like a flood to attack Newton's friend and writing partner after that New Year's Day service. Sadly, that was the last time that William Cowper set foot inside the church. His delusion made him feel that he had failed the Maker, and he felt unworthy. John was dumbfounded as he knew that William was a true believer, but John came to realize that William suffered from severe mental sickness. John sought to simply extend unconditional love and grace to his hurting friend. Although he was in deep darkness and would try to take his life again, William eventually recovered. But this storm took a heavy toll on John."

"This is so sad! What about their hymn writing?" Jock asked.

"The two friends had excitedly discussed compiling their hymns before William became ill, so John has put that project on hold," Gillamon explained. "Liz and Nigel, when the time comes, you two will help John compile all their hymns for publication. So, although this has been a difficult time, know that without William Cowper, John would never have begun writing on the level that he now does. He may never have even written 'Faith's Review and Expectation.'"

Nigel gave Liz a squeeze on the leg. "We shall be ready and up for the challenge."

"I find it beautiful that not only did William Cowper inspire John, but John was able to help Cowper through the darkest storm of his life," Liz realized. "If anyone knows how to survive a storm, it is John Newton, no?"

Clarie smiled. "Yes, Liz. After this time, John wrote one of my favorite hymns in 1774, entitled 'I Will Trust and Not Be Afraid':

Begone, unbelief,
My Saviour is near,
And for my relief
Will surely appear:
By prayer let me wrestle,
And he will perform;
With Christ in the vessel,
I smile at the storm."

"How beautiful, *mon amie!*" Liz exclaimed. "I love this as well, and am so very happy that John Newton's unbelief is indeed gone, no?"

"What about the other William?" Jock asked. "When will William Wilberforce change the world for good?"

Gillamon smiled at the young Scottie. "We must all wait for William Wilberforce to grow up. Everything will unfold at the proper time. When children are betrothed for an arranged marriage, they first must grow up before the wedding can take place."

"Jest like Lafayette an' Adrienne," Kate added.

Nigel raised a finger in the air. "Back to the issue of storms—now that we are past John's storms, I wish to know what he thinks about the storm of war betwixt America and Great Britain."

"Aye, especially with that Lordy Dartmouth bein' the one who got him his church job," Al added.

Jock nodded. "Aye, which side is John Newton on?"

"Allow me to share some of John's words that he penned about the conflict, and then you can tell *me* which 'side' you think he is on," Gillamon answered Jock with a wink. He tapped on the time panel to reveal a letter. "John wrote to Lord Dartmouth about the looming war on January 20, 1775."

> *When historians and politicians descant upon the rise and fall of empires, with all their professed sagacity, in tracing the connexion between causes and effects, they are totally unacquainted with the great master-wheel which manages the whole movement; that is the Lord's design in favour of his church and kingdom. To this every event is subordinate; to this every interfering interest must stoop.*

"Well, he uses a lot of words I don't exactly understand, but it sounds like he's saying so far that he's on . . . the Maker's side?" Jock posed.

Gillamon reached out a hand to scratch Jock behind the ear. "Bravo, little one. John Newton's gaze is on the big picture of what the Maker is trying to accomplish in all nations for His church and Kingdom. Read on a bit further."

> *And I doubt not but some who are yet unborn will hereafter clearly see and remark, that the present unhappy disputes between Great Britain and America, with their consequences, whatever they may be, are part of a series of events of when the extension and interests of the church of Christ were the principal final causes. In a word, that Jesus may be known, trusted, and adored, and sinners, by the power of his gospel, be rescued from sin . . .*

"Bravo!" Nigel cheered with a fist of victory in the air. "The old boy's keeping the main thing the main thing, even in the fog of war."

"Aye, an' did ye notice how he always thinks aboot future generations?" Kate asked. "He's always thinkin' aboot grace."

"Show them what happened after first shots were fired at Lexington and Concord, Gillamon," Clarie asked. Gillamon tapped the panel to reveal Newton's diary.

Wednesday 31 May 1775

The paper this evening brought account of commencement of hostilities in New England, and many killed on both sides. These things I fear are the beginning of sorrows. O that I could be suitably affected with what I see and hear.

"Within two weeks, John called his parishioners to begin meeting for prayer over the conflict on Tuesdays at five o'clock in the morning," Clarie detailed. "Around two hundred people came to the first prayer meeting. They prayed for an hour. John said a few words, and of course, he had written a hymn just for this purpose." Gillamon revealed the words of the hymn.

On the commencement of hostilities in America

The gathering clouds, with aspect dark,
A rising storm presage;
Oh! to be hid within the ark,
And sheltered from its rage!
See the commissioned angel frown!
That vial in his hand,
Filled with fierce wrath, is pouring down
Upon our guilty land!

"Sounds like he's blamin' ever-r-rythin' on the *Br-r-ritish!"* Max interjected with surprise. "I bet Lord Darmouth fr-r-r-owned on *that* hymn!"

"Indeed, it was not to Lord Dartmouth's liking, as you can imagine," Gillamon told him, tapping the panel. "But John had clear opinions, and wrote this letter after the British were defeated at the Battle of Sullivan's Island in South Carolina on June 28, 1776."

"I were there on a ship in the middle of that battle with Lordy Cornwallis and that Green Dragon!" Al exclaimed, covering his eyes. "I don't want to see it again, though!"

> *I am not a politician, much less an American, but I fear the Lord has a controversy with us. I cannot but tremble at the consequences of our present disputes, and lest the disappointment our forces met with at Charlestown should be the prelude to some more miscarriage. The plans of our operations may, for aught I know, be well laid, according to human wisdom, and our generals and admirals well qualified and supported to carry them into execution; but I am afraid the Lord God of hosts is but little acknowledged or thought of in our councils, fleets, or armies. I see the nation in general hardened into that spirit of insensibility and blind security, which in all former ages and nations has been the token and forerunner of judgment; and therefore, I lay but little stress upon the wisdom of the wise, or the prowess of the valiant. I think if our sins were not ripe for visitation, the Lord would have prevented things from coming to the present extremities.*

"C'est magnifique!" Liz marveled. "John is quite bold to take such a stance, especially with Lord Dartmouth in his position with King George the Third!"

"Hear, hear, *bold* is an understatement, my dear," Nigel echoed. "If only more ministers would be so bold to speak the truth about their governments. The *Maker* created government, after all. It's the humans who created politics! The Maker expects His followers to represent His truth in the public square, what?"

"So, you can see that John Newton expressed his bold, clear beliefs that above all, the Maker is the true Sovereign over these unfolding events," Gillamon summarized. "He also believes that Great Britain is trusting in its own power, and not in the Maker. He feels judgment is coming for his nation."

"John says that, 'God deals with us as we do our children; He first speaks, then gives a gentle stroke, at last a blow,'" Clarie shared. "He understands that the Maker chose to use him as 'an unusual proof of His patience, Providence, and grace' through this method, and he feels that the Maker will do the same for Great Britain through this conflict."

"Well put, Clarie," Gillamon said with a nod. "Speaking of the conflict, it's time to bring this briefing to a close. I know we have covered a great deal of time, including our mission with Jonah. You'll be pleased to know that John wrote a hymn about Jonah's vine entitled 'The Gourd.' And in 1776, he wrote to a young lady that, *The work of grace is not like Jonah's gourd, which sprang up and flourished in a night, and as quickly withered, but rather like the oak.* So, his Jonah moniker shall ever remain with him, but he of course uses it to discuss grace. Everything John does from here on out will always center around grace."

"Aye, *amazing* grace!" Jock exclaimed.

Max wrinkled his brow. "Aye, I have ta say though, the lad's title for his tune isn't r-r-real catchy."

"I fear you are right, old boy," Nigel agreed. "Although descriptive of its contents, 'Faith's Review and Expectation' just doesn't quite grab the reader, what?"

Liz nodded and lifted a paw to Gillamon. *"Oui,* so I believe that Gillamon's inspired word provides the simplest, most attractive title. I shall endeavor to publish it under the title 'Amazing Grace.'"

"How grand!" Kate cheered. "That title alone makes me want ta sing it!"

"Indeed, perfectly chosen, Liz," Nigel echoed. "And a hymn with such a name simply begs the use of *grace* notes!"

"What are grace notes?" Jock asked.

"Grace notes are quick, ornamental notes played just before a main note in music," Nigel explained. "They are written as small little flourishes to add flair and expression without altering the overall rhythm of the piece."

"So, gr-r-race notes be small like ye, Mousie," Max noted with a chuckle. "I know where ye can find lots of tunes with them wee notes."

Liz shared a surprised look with Nigel. "Where would that be, Max?" Liz asked.

"Bagpipe music, of course," Max answered with a big grin. "Scottish pipers have ta use gr-r-race notes a lot, with all that extra squeakin' an' such."

"Maximillian Braveheart the Bruce, I am utterly flabbergasted yet thrilled to hear your oppor*tune* insight, old boy!" Nigel cheered, giving Max a tiny fist in the shoulder. "I say, when we locate the right tune to pair with 'Amazing Grace,' we simply must have a bagpiper play a concert."

"Aye, and serve shortbread Scottie biscuits," Al suggested.

"I think you are all on the right track! But this hymn project must be put on the shelf for the moment," Gillamon told them. "Your attention is most urgently needed to continue at your posts in America in the War for Independence."

"Understood, Gillamon," Liz answered with a determined nod. "Kate especially needs to be reunited with Lafayette on North Island. I am sure he will be worried about you, *chère* Kate."

"Aye, ye're right, Liz," Kate agreed.

"Kate, you will be reunited with Lafayette, but in the process, I need you to be 'found' by someone very special who needs to meet the young Frenchman," Gillamon instructed with an expectant look in his eye.

"Who, Gillamon?" Kate asked.

"Who, indeed?" Gillamon replied without an answer.

EPILOGUE

A Fortunate Meeting

MAJOR HUGER'S HOUSE, NORTH ISLAND, SOUTH CAROLINA, JUNE 15, 1777

I have arrived, dear heart, in very good health, at the house of an American officer, and the greatest luck in the world, a French vessel is just about to sail. You can imagine how pleased I am at that. (I have only the time to close this letter.) This evening I go to Charlestown; I shall write to you from there. I have no more interesting news. The campaign has begun, but there is no fighting, or at least very little.

Lafayette sat erect at the small, cherrywood writing desk, casting a frequent glance out the open window to spy *La Victoire* securely anchored offshore. He squinted against the blinding sunshine shimmering like diamonds off the blue water. With two British Royal Navy frigates blockading Charlestown Harbor sixty miles south, he was eager to get going by land while his ship attempted to enter that vital port without the hunted Frenchman aboard. When Major Huger informed him that a French ship anchored in Winyah Bay could take his letters to France, Lafayette hastily penned a few more words to the letter he had been composing to his wife, Adrienne, throughout the voyage to America.

The soft sea breeze offered little relief from the already stifling South Carolina summer morning as it ruffled the gauzy mosquito netting hung over the bed next to him. The sun's rays spilled onto the young Frenchman's paper as if in approval of his glowing, sunny outlook of America:

The manners of the people here are simple, honest, and in every way worthy of this land where everything proclaims the beautiful name of liberty . . .

Ah, *liberté.* That word embodied every reason and action that had brought the French nobleman here. He scanned the earlier entry he had made in this letter on June 7:

Defender of the liberty which I adore, for myself more than anyone, I bring with me only my frankness and enthusiasm, but no ambition, no self-interest; as I work to acquire glory, I am also working for their happiness. I hope that, out of your love for me, you will become a good American; it is a feeling appropriate to a virtuous heart. America's happiness is intimately linked to that of mankind; it will become a safe and respectable refuge for virtue, honesty, tolerance, equality, and a quiet liberty.

Lafayette smiled, thinking of his good fortune in having finally reached these shores following his daring escape from France. He would now make his way to Charlestown, but his ultimate goal was Philadelphia. There, he would join the great Commander-in-Chief of the Continental Army, General George Washington! And there, he would wield his sword in the fight for freedom and independence as a Major General, and all at the age of nineteen.

The young Marquis hoped Adrienne would receive his heartfelt letter with joy. His young sixteen-year-old wife cared for their toddler daughter, Henriette, and would soon give birth to their second child. Lafayette frowned and instinctively gripped the front of his sweaty, open shirt, as if to comfort his conflicted heart. He was filled with agony at being separated from his young family yet equally filled with exhilaration to be in this new world that had captured his heart an ocean away.

It was at that fateful August 1775 dinner with his regiment in Metz where he had first heard of the cause of American independence. It was none other than the black sheep brother of King George III, the Duke of Gloucester, who told the room full of French officers about the defiant boldness of the rebellious colonies. Lafayette was instantly enamored with such news, and stood to his feet, raising his sword dramatically in the air to declare that he would give both his sword and his heart for their glorious cause. Of course, the naive and altruistic teenager was promptly told by his commander to sit down—he wasn't going anywhere, especially not to America where he could ignite a fresh war between France and her longtime enemy, Great Britain.

Lafayette took his seat, but his mind raced with the idea of sailing to America in pursuit of glory and fighting for such a noble cause. He was determined that no one stop him from his quest: not his commander, not the king of France, not the king of England—nor more formidable yet, his father-in-law. And indeed, no one *had* stopped him. The Marquis de Lafayette had persevered and escaped a meaningless life at the court of Versailles and from all those who denied his quest. He purchased and outfitted *La Victoire,* sailing for eight long weeks while "feeding the fishes" with seasickness for much of the journey. But he spent those weeks studying military strategy and learning English—or at least trying to learn the confusing language. He was still very much dependent on his English-speaking fellow sojourners, Baron De Kalb and the American Edmund Brice; but he would overcome the language barrier, too.

So many obstacles to liberty, but wasn't freedom worth such struggle?

"*Monsieur,* are you finished writing to Adrienne? Major Huger's friend from Georgetown is here to take our letters to the French ship, und then to escort us to the mainland," came the deep voice of Baron De Kalb.

"*Oui . . . pardon,* I mean *yes,* my friend. I finish *ma lettre,*" Lafayette answered in broken English mixed with French. "I mean my . . . " he held up the letter, at a loss for the correct word.

"Letter," De Kalb inserted for him with a grin.

"Ah, the word is similar in English!" Lafayette happily exclaimed. "She is almost finished!"

De Kalb smiled at Lafayette's normal French feminine reference to the letter. "*It* is almost finished."

Lafayette chuckled and shook his head at the odd way the English referred to things. He folded the letter and reached for the wax to seal his lengthy missive to Adrienne. He pressed his "L" flourish insignia into the hot wax and held the letter in the air. "IT is finished, and I am finished to go."

The young Marquis tied his cravat, donned his three-cornered hat, and hastily pulled on his coat. He followed De Kalb downstairs and out the main foyer to the courtyard. Lush palm trees, tropical foliage, and sandy soil surrounded the house, as did swarms of mosquitoes. Major Benjamin Huger conversed with his friend from Georgetown, Captain John Buchanan, and lifted his hand to the approaching visitors from France. But there standing off to the side was a slave in his mid-thirties, holding a little white dog covered in mud.

"Bibi!" Lafayette exclaimed, spotting his beloved Westie. He ran up to the slave who handed Kate over to him. *"Où étais-tu, ma petite chienne ?"*

"I found huh runnin' in de swamp," the slave explained. "Looks like she sho loves yuh, suh."

Kate eagerly licked Lafayette's face, and he closed his eyes in delight. "And I love him!"

"Her," corrected De Kalb with a grin.

Lafayette rolled his hazel eyes good humoredly at De Kalb and squeezed Kate tightly before putting her on the ground. He looked the slave in the eye with a wide grin. *"Merci* . . . thank you for bringing Bibi back to me. How are you called?"

"Massa Buchanan calls me . . . Fortune," the slave answered haltingly.

"Fortune," Lafayette slowly answered, raising his eyebrows, and thinking aloud as a word connection struck him. "Fortun*ate,* no? I am very *fortunate* for you." He studied the slave, unconvinced that this was his true name. "Fortune is the name your master calls you, no?" he guessed, leaning in with a grin. "But what do *you* call you?"

The slave looked at the young Frenchman who surprisingly seemed to show genuine interest in him. He didn't remember the last time someone cared enough to know his real name. He lifted his chin and smiled. Kate's eyes welled with happy tears to see these two men meet.

"Pompey, suh. My name is Pompey."

A Word from the Author

PROLOGUE

If you haven't yet read any of the Epic Order of the Seven books leading up to this title, you may be wondering what in the world I'm doing with an opening scene of Lafayette in a book on John Newton and Jonah. I tend to weave multiple plot lines across many books, and this one is no exception. I'm sliding this book into the middle of American Revolution books as an "intermission" of sorts, but I am also establishing several new plot lines going forward in the series, including the abolition of slavery, of which Lafayette was a champion. Just keep reading. You'll catch on in chapter one.

PART ONE: A WRETCH LIKE ME (John Newton 1725–1745)

Chapter 2: What Goes into the First of Life

I pulled from John Newton's own words in telling his story, so much of what you read throughout this book concerning what he was thinking or going through physically, spiritually, emotionally, and mentally is straight from his pen. The dynamic between his parents are true, as is the close relationship he had with his mother and the distant relationship he had with his father. We know that Isaac Watts indeed was a guest at his Dissenter church in Wapping, but the encounter with young John is fiction; however, John did indeed devour and memorize Dr. Watts' book, *A Short View of the Whole of Scripture History.* The events following the death of John's mother are all true. Billy and Edward are fictional names given to personify the true types of mischievous friends John had in Aveley. John's terrible boarding school experience is true, and he did have a teacher who helped him excel in Latin in his second year.

Chapter 3: Missing the Boat

The opening "Drunken Sailor" shanty was sung much later than 1737, but I wanted readers to "hear" the familiar song in their heads to understand what John was singing. Of course, *SpongeBob SquarePants* fans will know the theme song as a variation of the old sea shanty, "Blow the Man Down." John was indeed miraculously saved from a fall from a horse at the hedgerow and by missing the boat (while delayed at church) where his friends drowned, both instances he attributed to Divine protection. St. Michael's Church in Aveley was his family parish. His cycle of trying to live a model life, failing, worsening, repenting, and starting all over was true, including the period of two years leading to depression before he met Polly. I took several spiritual insights, including the "Unholy Trinity," straight from John Eldredge's fabulous book, *Restoration Year.* John's encounter with the Dutchman discussing the 1539 map is fiction, but he did purchase the book he would describe as "poison" (*Characteristics)* in that port. It worked to have the Scandinavian map with serpents for my evil actor interplay.

Chapter 4: The Rings of the Lord

The events with the letter from Elizabeth Catlett reaching John just as he was about to ride to Maidstone on business for his father are true. The Maidstone Inn is a fictional name. The events with Polly and John overstaying with the Catletts to miss his boat are true. From the moment that John Newton saw Polly, it was genuinely love at first sight. She became the only anchor he had for a season of life, and his forthcoming decisions to see her led to severe consequences, but they all stemmed from John's love for her. All the following events with John's voyage to Venice are true. The ring dream is presented using his words recalling the event. Many thanks to John Newton historian Marylynn Rouse for directing me to a letter John penned on July 31, 1773, where he spoke about the Marriage of the Sea ceremony. He may have witnessed, or at least learned about the tossing of the ring, which contributed to his later dream, which occurred in Zakynthos but was set in Venice.

Chapter 5: Pressed for Answers

John amazingly forgot the dream within two or three days. John's second stay with the Catletts, missing his father's arranged ship, and John's capture by the press gang are all true. We're not entirely sure where he was or what exactly was running through his mind at the moment he was seized somewhere along the Thames. He somehow did get word to his father, who came to see him (thank you, Clarie!). The names and operations given of the *HMS Harwich* are true. James Mitchell had a devastating impact on John's thinking and spiritual decisions. Some spiritual serpents walk on two sea legs.

Chapter 6: Never Deliberate

Newton writes of the sad ending of James Mitchell, who was later washed overboard in a violent storm off Lisbon and "swept into eternity." The events of John's behavior as midshipman, violating his twenty-four-hour leave, his personal motto "Never Deliberate," the disapproval of Polly's parents, writing to Polly, his desertion, flogging (likely twelve to twenty-four lashes), demotion, and self-destructive spiral on board the *Harwich* are all true. John wrote that in his despair he indeed had thoughts of ending his life and of murdering Captain Carteret, but "the secret hand of God restrained me."

PART TWO: I ONCE WAS LOST (John Newton 1745–1748)

Chapter 7: The Willing Slave of Every Evil

I took James Mitchell's log entries about Madeira directly from his *Journal of a Voyage to the East Indies (1745–1749),* including all spelling and dates. Other Newton biographers list May 9 as the departure date from Madeira, but Mitchell lists May 14. The descriptions of shark fishing, fly fish, the crew's amusements, and the dead whale all happened after they sailed from Madeira, and of course John Newton was then aboard the *Levant* under Captain Phelps. There has been confusion in the historical record if the Guinea slaver was the *Pegasus* under the command of Captain Penrose, and of the ship's part-owner being Evans or Clow. Newton doesn't mention the ship's name, and only gives "Evans" as the name of the part-owner. Therein lies another mystery, as Evans isn't listed as an owner in the British privateer records for Bristol ships—was "Evans" his middle name? Was he really "Humphrey Fitzherbert" and wanted a cooler sounding name (LOL)? Was his ownership a ruse? Some things we'll just never know. I went with *Levant*/Phelps, per the research by Bruce Hindmarsh in *Amazing Grace* (2023). We know nothing of Phelps, so his appearance and originally being from Liverpool is fiction on my part. I needed to make him "colorful," as John Newton evidently had a lot to work with in unwisely poking fun at him as captain. The Liverpool Scouse dialect is indeed fun and colorful (i.e., the Beatles, yeah, yeah, yeah).

The series of events of Newton oversleeping, being cut down in his hammock, and going on deck in time to see the sailor swap getting ready to take place are all true. We don't know the names of the midshipman who cut him down, or the lieutenant he begged for a transfer, so I made it Lewis and Mitchell. Newton calls the man who cut down his hammock "the messenger of God's Providence." The other sailor who transferred from the *Harwich* to the *Levant* is unknown, so Henry Parker is a fictional name. Of course, "Jonah" (Gillamon) was sure to row over at just the right time. Newton himself says that at this juncture he became "the willing slave of every evil." Gillamon's final paragraph insights were taken from John Eldredge in *Restoration Year.*

Chapter 8: In Hunger, in Thirst, and in Nakedness

Every evil atrocity committed against John Newton by Princess P.I. and Evans is true. The only fiction in the entire scenario is the masked spiritual advisor, but such a character is true to the culture of West Africa. Evil clearly possessed these depraved people on Plantain Island to do what they did, both to John Newton and to the slaves. John never knew who brought him food, but he did hear the clanking of irons, so suspected that slaves took pity on him. A fellow drunken trader of Evans indeed accused John of pilfering their supplies, and Evans responded by chaining John to the deck of the shallop in violent weather for that long trip. Newton writes that catching fish with entrails was the only thing that preserved him.

Chapter 9: A Servant of Slaves

John Newton's self-written epitaph begins:

JOHN NEWTON,
CLERK,
ONCE AN INFIDEL AND LIBERTINE,
A SERVANT OF SLAVES IN AFRICA . . .

I'll finish the rest for you later since it contains a spoiler. He wanted to never forget how low he sank in his depravity apart from God, and frequently referred to himself as "a servant of slaves." Again, everything in this chapter is taken from his *Authentic Narrative,* from washing his one shirt on the rocks at night to hiding from island visitors to sending the letters to his father and Polly. He somehow was assisted in sending letters in the outgoing mail, so of course it was perfect for Gillamon to be the mail-goat. The scene of Evans and P.I. mocking him about the lime trees is exact, as was his self-professed state of being no more changed than a tiger tamed by hunger. His book of Euclid and retreating to write formulas in the sand kept him sane. The exact scene of Patrick Clow first meeting John is unknown, but I wrote what seemed plausible. The discussion of the animals of their evil counterparts Charlatan and Kakia brings out the fantasy portion of the book: The Evil Chaos of the Six vs. the Epic Order of the Seven. This fantasy element in my books serves to portray the true reality of demons and angels, which are very real, and fight unseen to impact human history across time.

Chapter 10: A Fifteen-Minute Miracle

I used much of the imagery and methods for slave trading in Kittam from *Amazing Grace* (Hindmarsh/Bolase). "Grown black" was a term of the day, for the reasons given.

Years later Newton told his beloved Polly: "If I had not known you, perhaps I should have never seen the coast of Guinea. But it seems more certain that if I had not known you, I should never have returned from it!" He also wrote "had the ship passed a quarter of an hour sooner, I had died there a wretch, as I had lived." So, it was indeed a fifteen-minute miracle that changed Newton's life and the course of history. It was a miracle in and of itself that Captain Gother found Newton after being sent to look for him as described. Daggdul, of course, is a fantasy character embodied by Gillamon, but it worked to have him encourage Gother to turn back.

Chapter 11: What If These Things Be True?

The events that Gillamon and Clarie relay about Newton being saved from wild beasts while lost on a wild buffalo hunt in Cape Lopez, the poor condition of the ship, John's profane behavior, and the drinking scene with the shell are all true. A sailor did indeed grab the back of Newton's shirt before he jumped overboard to retrieve his lost hat. The half-day of cod fishing would prove to be what saved the crew (keep reading.) John's account of reading Thomas à Kempis and his exact quote, "What if these things be true?," the night before the storm are true. We don't know the exact passages from *The Imitation of Christ* that most impacted him, so I selected some from an updated edition with easier-to- understand verbiage.

PART THREE: BUT NOW AM FOUND (Back to Jonah)

Liz was, of course, right (she's always right, *n'est-ce pas?)* that at first glance Jonah's brief story isn't very deep. But the more you dig into the Scripture, the deeper you go. I must admit, I've read this familiar Bible story all my life, as I imagine you have, but I have never understood it as I do now. What a joy to take a deep dive into God's Word! He always has so much more to show us than we know even exists below the surface. And given the number of commentaries out there, people have attempted to get to the bottom of *Jonah* since it first rolled off the press. For the factual dialogue of Jonah and the other characters from the book of *Jonah,* I used exact Scripture from the various translations and paraphrases listed on the copyright page at the front of this book. See the bibliography for other sources I used to bring Jonah to life.

There are plenty of unknowns about the book of *Jonah.* We don't know for sure who wrote it. I've read arguments for it being authored either by Jonah himself, or by other authors a century or two after his time, based on little tidbits of wordsmithing here and there. And I can see plausibility for both rationales presented. Of course, we all know that Scripture is inspired by the Holy Spirit, so we know the identity of the real Author (including the One who wrote this book). But the very fact that it paints Jonah in such a negative light convinces me that he himself penned those forty-eight verses. And I think it was the last of God's gut-wrenching instructions for Jonah, after his pouting session when the worm destroyed his vine. It was like he was assigned to write on a chalkboard after school for bad behavior—"Now pick up your pen and write every word of what happened to you. People across time need to learn from your experience and see that they, too, are no different from you, Jonah."

The book of *Jonah* is not only the story of "the prodigal prophet," as Timothy Keller called him. It's the story of Israel, and it's the story of you and me. I hope you can identify yourself, whether you're a pagan sailor, Jonah, or a Ninevite. God loves us so much that He will allow us to run, yet follow us to the depths to reach us and save us anyway. And sometimes He must utilize "severe grace" to get our attention. Then He turns us from our self-absorption toward those who are different from us, or even to others who've hurt us, so we see how much He loves them, too. The best way to truly understand why grace is so amazing is when you must painfully extend it to others; and the only way you can truly extend such grace is after you grasp how it was given freely to you. All of us are murderous, cruel Ninevites to God's heart.

Tarshish: Where was it? No one knows for certain, but many Bible scholars conclude it was southern Spain. If you want a good overview of all the theories of where it could be, see https://en.wikipedia.org/wiki/Tarshish.

Did it really happen, or is it just allegory? The book of *Jonah* has so much depth in its literary construction and poetry, and Jonah's prayer isn't definitive of its meaning, so is it historical fact? Did Jonah drown and get resurrected after the fish swallowed him? Did he die in the fish and get resurrected? Was there a real fish, or was it a metaphor? You'll find all these questions asked in commentaries and sermons. To me, given that Jonah was a real historical person referenced in 2 Kings 14:25, I conclude that Jonah's story is historical as well. I don't know if he died or not, so I'll leave that for you to decide. Was Jonah in the fish for three 24-hour days? Or, like Jesus' death and resurrection, did part of a day constitute a "day" as the Jews reference time? Does it really matter? No, for *Jonah* accomplishes its purposes either way.

Don't get hung up on the fish. There are plenty of true accounts of whales and sharks swallowing humans, the most recent of which was a lobster diver named Michael Packard off Cape Cod, Massachusetts, in 2021. So, we know it's 100% possible. Scripture said that God "prepared a great fish," so I believe He literally created a fish just for this mission instead of using an existing species. This was no big deal for the Maker. Of course, it worked perfectly for me to have the Maker "prepare" Gillamon, who can take any shape or form. I used the effects of a fish's stomach contents on human skin, just as Nigel described. Jonah would have looked like a freak of nature walking through Ninevah. God lit him up like a neon sign to get the attention of the Ninevites! I credit Pastor Jack Hibbs (Calvary Chapel Chino Hills, CA) and his awesome sermon series on Jonah for inspiring me with imagery, especially of the visual of the bobbing idols.

Was there a witness on the beach to see Jonah being spit out of the fish? I believe so. The Assyrian circuit rider system is historical fact. It is astounding that they had developed the fastest mode of communication until the telegraph! Of course, we know nothing about where exactly Jonah landed, but most commentaries assume in the Tyre area. We also don't know how he travelled to Nineveh, but it worked to put the plausibility of these plot lines together with Ninos. The people listened to the skinny, yellow prophet and believed him immediately, so it is certainly plausible that word spread of the incredible event from a witness.

Jonah's recurring childhood dream of the Assyrians attacking his village is fiction. It is true that before they conquered a nation, the Assyrians would make probing raids, and they indeed were doing so in Israel. But we have no record of Jonah having witnessed this. But as Liz so *brilliantly* observed, there is always a reason for driving behavior. I think he was traumatized by some encounter with them to be so adamantly against God's instructions. And as for the end of my story with the child returning Jonah's toy dove, that is fiction as well. But wasn't it beautiful to imagine God doing something like that for Jonah? I believe in my heart that God arranged for a personal one-on-one encounter with Jonah and a repentant Ninevite. God doesn't just teach us His truths to know them. He expects and waits for us to put them into action.

I'm grateful for Timothy Keller's superb book on Jonah, *The Prodigal Prophet*. Jonah's powerful last line, "All sin has a storm attached to it," was taken straight from Keller's pen. The words Jesus said about Jonah stand as the ultimate testimony about the authenticity of Jonah. If you happen to be running from God, I hope you'll stop before He must send a fish, a vine, a worm, or a hot wind to get your attention.

PART FOUR: WAS BLIND (John Newton 1748–1764)

Chapter 19: When a Storm of Terror Surrounds You

Timothy Keller dedicated his book on Jonah, *The Prodigal Prophet,* to John Newton, "whose faith was also born in a storm." This is the big climactic event in the life of Newton, and I sincerely pray I've written it accurately and depicted the transforming scene as true to John's heart. The original date of the storm was March 10, 1748, but due to the eleven-day change in the 1752 calendar, the new date that John Newton recounted each year in his diaries and letters was March 21.

When using Scripture passages, I try to stick to what Newton would have read and quoted from in the King James Version, but usually I pull from the New King James Version. For this chapter, I wanted the verses he gives that first convicted him as he began coming back to God in the storm to be easy for young readers to understand, so I used the Living Bible paraphrase for Proverbs 1:24–31, Hebrews 6:4–6, and 2 Peter 2:20. Although Newton didn't refer to Mark 4–5 as parallel to his storm experience, he absolutely likened himself to Legion when he first returned to Jesus who freed him, even writing a future hymn, "The Legion Dispossessed." The parallels of Jesus' parables and the seeds John's mother planted in his young life worked beautifully in this scene. Newton in later years would write about how his mother's early instruction and prayers over him were the foundation that would lead him back to the saving grace of Christ. He encouraged parents to never stop praying for their children, and to train them up in the way they should go with learning Scripture.

The condition of the ship and the sequence of events by the hour during the storm are just as he wrote them in his *Narrative.* He indeed thought through his spiritual condition throughout the storm and subsequent weeks as he slowly returned to God. It wasn't an instantaneous return, but he was able to say that he was no longer an infidel by the time he reached Ireland. Captain Gother indeed repeatedly accused John of being a Jonah, and although he wouldn't act on his words, those words impacted John Newton deeply. John's quote, "If this will not do, the Lord have mercy on us," instantly struck him as the first time he'd called out for mercy in years. His advice to Gother on using the sails is fiction, but he made some similar comment to the captain. He did indeed attempt to encourage the other sailors with the promise of soon toasting with wine and telling tales of their survival in the storm, but was met with, "No, it's too late."

One sailor was indeed washed overboard just as John set foot on the deck. Of course, it was perfect for our Gillamon as Daggdul to be that sailor (keep reading!).

The cargo was another miracle that saved them after the rotten timbers tore away from the ship. I searched everywhere for a good explanation of the chain pump that John manned in the storm and found a stupendous animated video not only showing the exact pump but also how an eighteenth century warship is built and operated (see my bibliography for "How an 18th Century Sailing Warship Works (*HMS Victory*)". While the *Greyhound* wasn't a warship, nor of the size and scope of the ship in this video, I highly encourage you to check it out. It will give you a fantastic visual understanding of these ships and an appreciation for the ingenuity of eighteenth-century engineers. I took the rate of gallons of water pumped per minute from the video. The creator Jacob O'Neal has many other fun, educational videos on his Animagraffs YouTube channel.

Chapter 20: Saved by the Fish

All events are given as they occurred following the storm. If they had not stopped to fish off Newfoundland, the crew would have starved to death, for they were down to their last fish when they limped into Ireland. They also thought they had more water reserves than they had. The miraculous timing of their arrival into Lough Swilly ahead of the storm (assisted by "Gillafish," of course) is true. The Providential protection across John Newton's life is so blatantly obvious at every turn!

Chapter 21: Evil Afloat

I felt sick more than once in researching and writing this chapter. Captain Jackson was even more evil than I portrayed him, and his successive voyages even more deadly. Newton did indeed return to Plantain Island and did business with P.I., which I find incredible. His fever and return to God are as written. His experiences in Charlestown (Charleston) are as written; however, the delivery of Pompey on the *Brownlow* is plausible fiction. Pompey was a real slave from South Carolina who you'll see in the history to come, but we have no record of his arrival from Africa. It worked to use a real slave to illustrate the real experience that children and families faced in the horrible slave trade. But keep reading, for all that John Newton experienced was ultimately used for good.

Chapter 22: Voyages and Vines

I'm indebted to the brilliant author Eric Metaxas in his stellar book on William Wilberforce, *Amazing Grace,* which was turned into a major theatrical film. (I was privileged to know one of the producers of the film, Ken Wales, and attended a screening/Q&A with him when it released. Little did I know that I would someday write the story! God indeed operates way ahead of us.) The introduction to this book expertly summarizes what happened to human culture to change the mindset on slavery, and I used the "wedding" of faith and culture idea from this work. He wrote about Wilberforce's monumental accomplishment to abolish the slave trade: "What to the people of his day seemed impossible and unthinkable seems to us, in our day, inevitable. . . Wilberforce can be pictured as standing as a kind of hinge in the middle of history; he pulled the world around a corner, and we can't even look back to see where we've come from." It's easy for us, on this side of history, to stand in judgment of how anyone could have tolerated slavery. I hope you will dive deeper into the long-fought-for miracle that was the ending of the slave trade, and appreciate what a handful of God's people did to change human history.

John Newton was slow to grow in his faith because he was on his own. I pray this book will encourage you to either mentor other new believers, or to seek out a mentor if you're on your own. Iron sharpens iron, in spiritual matters. The appointment with Newton meeting Clunie stands as another hinge-turning moment in history (as you will soon see.)

Chapter 23: Willing to Deliberate

All events happened just as written, but the cause of John Newton's seizure is unknown. I used poison, which it may have been, but he recovered quickly, and God used it to prevent him from sailing on the doomed *Bee.* There are far more miraculous details about how Manesty acquired the Tide Surveyor post for John, and there are far more details on the religious circles John and Polly experienced while in Liverpool. I love God's divine appointments, and John's encounters with the giants of the Great Awakening are amazing. Whitefield and John Wesley had no idea what John Newton would become, and how he would impact history.

Chapter 24: Unexpected Encounters

The smallness of this world, with people in history who brushed shoulders with each other, fascinates me. It's incredible that Lord Dartmouth secured John Newton's ordination a decade before he would be in a position of service to King George the Third that ignited the American Revolution. When John preached the sermon before departing Liverpool, he indeed preached to a massive audience, including the mayor. John Tarleton was elected Mayor of Liverpool in 1764, but I was unable to find the exact month to see if he was already mayor by May. Nonetheless, Newton and John Tarleton would have known each other from the slave trade, as well as John's position as Tide Surveyor. It is completely likely that John would have met young Banastre Tarleton as well, so I couldn't resist that scene.

PART FIVE: BUT NOW I SEE (John Newton 1764–1777)

Chapter 25: Fish and Lace

The interactions with John, Gill, and Mrs. Clarie of course are fiction, but the story of the progression of events leading to the Children's Meetings is true, including the depiction of the lace makers. God's provision for John and Polly through the publication of John's *Narrative* and the subsequent patronage of in John Thornton enabled the Newtons to minister greatly to the people of Olney. John Newton was a pioneer in teaching children, twenty years ahead of the Sunday School movement. I highly encourage you to visit two invaluable websites to explore Olney, John Newton, and William Cowper: The Cowper & Newton Museum (https://cowperandnewtonmuseum.org.uk/) and The John Newton Project (https://www.johnnewton.org/)

Chapter 26: Newton's New Year's Habit

John Newton established the habit of looking back and looking forward, which is foreshadowing to the entire premise of *Amazing Grace.* We know from his diary that he did use Mason's Catechism to hand out to the children, and Alexander Clunie did donate Bibles to him. He would have used Dr. Watts's booklets, and although my depiction of his use of them here is fiction, the words from Dr. Watts to parents and children today are worth reading. John often felt convicted and battled the demons from his past as he served in ministry.

Chapter 27: Fisher of Kids

The image of the Children's Meeting list of names is from the Cowper & Newton Museum, which retains Newton's actual journal. We know from his diary the numbers of children who came each week. He preached from Matthew 19:13–15 at the first meeting, and had a child read the passage. John did share his personal story frequently, but my depiction specifically in these meetings is plausible fiction. And no, there is no record of Polly baking shortbread biscuits, but if you've ever served in children's ministry, you know that cookies make for happy listeners! I imagine they would have had something simple for the children of Olney.

Chapter 28: Two Williams of Note

There is so much more history to share about William Cowper, so I encourage you to please study his life, and what happened from this point on in history. He would go on to become one of England's most beloved poets. As the focus of this book is John Newton and "Amazing Grace," I didn't have the bandwidth to expound upon Cowper's life. But God ordained these two men to meet and to share a bond that changed the literary and hymnody worlds. Please visit the Cowper & Newton Museum website to learn more. The animals' hypothetical discussion of fish, shortbread Scottie biscuits, "fig Newtons," and cheese biscuits was pure silliness, but you never know what these animals will do in culinary history.

The painted words above John's fireplace are true.

Chapter 29: A Sweet Vine

This scene is fiction, but John Newton's relationship with William and Hannah Wilberforce and their nephew, little William Wilberforce, is true.

John Newton was William's minister as a child, and we are certain that he was the first one to tell William about the evils of the slave trade. This relationship would change the world in thirty years with the abolition of that horrific practice. Stay tuned for this plot line to continue in my Epic Revolutionary Saga books.

Chapter 30: Amazing Grace

John's diary entries are actual, as are his sermon notes and text for his 1773 New Year's Day sermon. His pattern was to write hymns to summarize his sermons, and "Faith's Review and Expectation" was simply an example of that very thing. You'll have to wait until the next book to see how it was first published, and you'll have to wait for three books from now until Nigel finds just the right tune. If you can't wait and want to understand this wonderful history, please visit the John Newton Project (https://www.johnnewton.org/) for full details of John's writing process, the tune, and the impact of the world's most beloved hymn of all time. I hope this book has given you an understanding of how John Newton's entire life was poured into every word of "Amazing Grace."

Chapter 31: Grace Notes

William Cowper was struck with severe depression right after the service and it became so severe that he even moved into the vicarage with John and Polly for more than a year. "The Storm," as they called it, was very draining to the Newtons, but it was part of their ministry to Cowper. Their hymn publishing partnership was put on hold until 1779, but John proceeded to write on his own in the meantime. John's letters and hymn about the War for Independence are actual. He took a "God's eye view" (if you will) of the conflict.

EPILOGUE: A Fortunate Meeting

Lafayette's letter to Adrienne is actual. Pompey was Lafayette's first servant when he arrived in America. This plot line will continue in the Epic Revolutionary Saga books.

Bibliography

"3D Videos of Slaving Vessels." *Slave Voyages*, www.slavevoyages.org/voyage/ship#3d model/0/en/. Accessed 15 Feb. 2025.

Aitken, Jonathan. *John Newton: From Disgrace to Amazing Grace*. Bloomsbury Continuum, 2023

"Amazing Grace: How Sweet the Sound Online Exhibit." *Museum of the Bible*, www .museumofthebible.org/exhibits/amazing-grace-online-exhibit. Accessed 22 Jan. 2024.

Bass, Robert D. *The Green Dragoon: The Lives of Banastre Tarleton and Mary Robinson*. Sandlapper Press, 1973.

Bernier, Olivier. *Lafayette, Hero of Two Worlds*. E.P. Dutton, 1983.

"Bibliography." *Memorial to the Abolition of Slavery - Nantes (France)*, 11 Dec. 2023, memorial.nantes.fr/en/bibliography/.

Bris, Gonzague Saint, and George Holoch. *Lafayette: Hero of the American Revolution*. Pegasus Books, 2011.

"Bristol Privateers and Ships of War : J. W. Damer Powell : Free Download, Borrow, and Streaming." *Internet Archive*, Arrowsmith, 1 Jan. 1970, archive.org/details /bristol-privateers-and-ships-of-war/page/n213/mode/2up?q=phelps.

"Britain's Role in the Transatlantic Slave Trade." *Cowper & Newton Museum*, 14 Apr. 2024, cowperandnewtonmuseum.org.uk/britains-role-in-the-transatlantic-slave-trade/.

Bruckner, James K. *The NIV Application Commentary: Jonah, Nahum, Habakkuk, Zephaniah*. Zondervan, 2004.

Bull, Josiah. *The Life of John Newton*. Banner of Truth Trust, 2007.

Byas, Jared. *Jonah for Normal People: A Guide to the Most Misunderstood Prophet in the Bible*. The Bible for Normal People, 2022.

bybygoneliverpoolauthors, Posted. "John Newton in Liverpool – from Slaver to Customs Official." *Bygone Liverpool*, 3 July 2023, bygoneliverpool.wordpress .com/2021/03/29/goree-liverpool-part-two/.

_______ Posted. "John Newton in Liverpool, Part 2. Locations and Connections." *Bygone Liverpool*, 3 July 2023, bygoneliverpool.wordpress.com/2022/10/05/john -newton-in-liverpool-part-2-locations-and-connections/.

Cahn, Jonathan. *The Book of Mysteries*. FrontLine, 2018.

Cecil, Richard, and Marylynn Rouse. *John Newton*. Christian Focus Publications, 2000.

Chaffin, Tom. *Revolutionary Brothers: Thomas Jefferson, the Marquis de Lafayette, and the Friendship That Helped Forge Two Nations*. St. Martin's Press, 2019.

Childs, George Tucker. "Pastor Kogba Plantain Island History." *PDXScholar*, pdxscholar.library.pdx.edu/sherbro/119/. Accessed 7 Feb. 2025.

Cowper & Newton Museum, 12 Feb. 2024, cowperandnewtonmuseum.org.uk/.

Disciple's Study Bible: New International Version. Holman Bible Publishers, 1988.

Duncan, Mike. *Hero of Two Worlds: The Marquis de Lafayette in the Age of Revolution*. Perseus, 2023.

"Enduring Word Bible Commentary Ezekiel Chapter 27." *Enduring Word*, 1 Dec. 2022, enduringword.com/bible-commentary/ezekiel-27/.

Franz, Gordon. "Merry Christmas from ABR 2024." *Bible Archeology*, biblearchaeology.org/research/divided-kingdom/4242-nahum-and-nineveh. Accessed 3 Jan. 2025.

"George Whitefield Author Biography." *Banner of Truth USA*, 26 Sept. 2018, banneroftruth.org/us/about/banner-authors/george-whitefield/?srsltid=AfmBOopMqPC-vPNH4B7-CWl2SmnBldB0iLEX7JsROsR0ihW3DDYlUnG8.

Glahn, Sandra. *Kona with Jonah*. AMG Publishers, 2009.

Gottschalk, Louis. *Lafayette in America*. University of Chicago, 1975.

Halley, Henry H. *Halley's Study Bible: New International Version: Making the Bible's Wisdom Accessible through Notes, Photos, and Maps*. Zondervan, 2020.

Harrison, Cy. "Levant Galley." *British Privateer "Levant Galley" (1741)*, threedecks.org/guides/guide_100/index.php?display_type=show_ship&id=32638#ref:1846. Accessed 10 Feb. 2025.

Hart, Stephen. *Cant: A Gentleman's Guide to the Language of Rogues in Georgian London*. Improbable Fictions, 2014.

"Harwich (1743); Colchester (1744): Royal Museums Greenwich." *Harwich (1743); Colchester (1744) | Royal Museums Greenwich*, www.rmg.co.uk/collections/objects/rmgc-object-81580. Accessed 31 Jan. 2025.

Hibbs, Jack. "The Book of Jonah Sermon Series." *Calvary Chapel Chino Hills*, 13 Oct. 2002, calvarycch.org/?sfid=63690&_sft_books=jonah.

Hindmarsh, Craig, and Bruce Borlase.. *Amazing Grace: The Life of John Newton and the Surprising Story behind His Song*. Thomas Nelson Publishing, 2024.

Hodge, Bodie, and Paul F. Taylor. "Doesn't the Bible Support Slavery?" *Answers in Genesis*, 11 Dec. 2020, answersingenesis.org/bible-questions/doesnt-the-bible-support-slavery/.

_______ *Answers in Genesis*, Answers In Genesis, 27 Oct. 2022, answersingenesis.org/bible-history/the-bible-and-slavery/.

_______ "History and Archaeology of the World's Oldest City-Babel/ Babylon and the Tower of Babel." *Answers in Genesis*, Answers In Genesis, 18 Jan. 2023, answersingenesis.org/tower-of-babel/history-and-archaeology-of-worlds-oldest-city/?srsltid=AfmBOoquROcjS6T6dkBpmKf8P1SyYW_C6ObBrUT9r31iHIvUbQf8RbA1.

"John Newton (1725 - 1807)." *Cowper & Newton Museum*, 2 May 2024, cowperandnewtonmuseum.org.uk/john-newton-1725-1807/.

The John Newton Project, www.johnnewton.org. Accessed 31 Jan. 2025.

Keller, Timothy. *The Prodigal Prophet: Jonah and the Mystery of God's Mercy*. Hodder & Stoughton, 2020.

Kramer, Joel P. "Bible Evidence Unearthed at Nineveh!" *YouTube*, Expedition Bible, 2 Dec. 2023, youtu.be/34XBkm4QiLo?si=5efo9ScH6nRYOXEe.

Lafayette, Marie Joseph Paul Yves Roch Gilbert Du Motier, and Stanley J. Idzerda. *Lafayette in the Age of the American Revolution: Selected Letters and Papers, 1776-1790*. Cornell University Press, 1977.

Laurie, Greg. *A Fresh Look at the Book of Jonah*. Kerygma Publishers, 2014.

MacArthur, John. *The Macarthur Bible Commentary: Unleashing God's Truth, One Verse at a Time*. Thomas Nelson, Inc, 2005.

Magnus, Olaus, edited by Antoine Lafréry. *Map of the Sea. | Library of Congress*, www.loc.gov/resource/gdcwdl.wdl_03037/. Accessed 27 Jan. 2025.

Mason, John. "A Little Catechism; with Little Verses and Little Sayings for Little Children." *The Project Gutenberg eBook of A Little Catechism*. 6 Mar. 2025, www.gutenberg.org/cache/epub/13274/pg13274-images.html.

McAlister, Robert. *Georgetown's North Island: A History*. The History Press, 2015.

McGee, J. Vernon. *Jonah and Micah*. Thomas Nelson Pub., 1991.

"Memoir of the Life of Richard Phillips." *HathiTrust*, babel.hathitrust.org/cgi/pt?id=ia.ark%3A%2F13960%2Ft4sj4qk87&seq=54&q1=newton. Accessed 19 Feb. 2025.

"Memoirs of the Rev. John Newton : Some Time a Slave in Africa, Afterwards Curate of Olney, Bucks and Rector of St. Mary Woolnoth, London, in a Series of Letters : Newton, John, 1725-1807 : Free Download, Borrow, and Streaming." *Internet Archive*, London : A. Maxwell, 1 Jan. 1970, archive.org/details/memoirsofrevjohn00newtrich/mode/2up.

Meyer, F. B. *Bible Commentary*. Tyndale, 1987.

Mitchell, James. *Voyage of H.M.S. Harwich to India in 1745-1749: The journal of James Mitchell, Clerk of Captain Philip Carteret, H.M.S. Harwich on a voyage to the East Indies in His Majestys Ship Harwich of 50 Guns and 350 Men*. https://archive.org/details/in.ernet.dli.2015.32677/page/n109/mode/2up?view=theater.

Morgan, George. *The True Lafayette*. Lippincott, 1919.

Motier, Lafayette, Marie Joseph Paul Yves Roch Gilbert Du. *Memoirs, Correspondence and Manuscripts of General Lafayette*. Saunders and Otley, 1837.

Mowday, Bruce E. *Lafayette at Brandywine: The Making of an American Hero*. Barricade Books Inc., 2021.

Newton, John, and Dennis R. Hillman. *Out of the Depths*. Kregel Publications, 2003.

Newton, John, and Marylynn Rouse. *365 Days with Newton: A Unique Collection of 365 Daily Readings from the Unpublished Sermons and the Writings of John Newton*. Day One, 2006.

Newton, John, and William Cowper. *John Newton's Olney Hymns*. Curiosmith, 2011.

Newton, John. *Cardiphonia, or, the Utterance of the Heart: In the Course of a Real Correspondence*. Printed for W.W. Woodward, 1977.

_______ "John Newton's Sermon Notes for January 1, 1773." *Museum of the Bible*, www.museumofthebible.org/john-newtons-sermon-notes. Accessed 22 Jan. 2024.

_______ "Newton, John, 1725-1807. Olney Hymns : Manuscript, 1777-1779. MS Eng 1317. Houghton Library, Harvard University, Cambridge, Mass." *Harvard Mirador Viewer*, iiif.lib.harvard.edu/manifests/view/drs:41261600$12i. Accessed 31 Jan. 2025.

_______ *Olney Hymns: In Three Books*. Forgotten Books, 2022.

"Olney Hymns, in Three Books." *John Newton: Olney Hymns - Christian Classics Ethereal Library*, www.ccel.org/ccel/newton/olneyhymns.TitlePg.html. Accessed 25 Jan. 2024.

O'Neal, Jacob. "How an 18th Century Sailing Ship Works (HMS Victory)." *YouTube*, Animagraffs, www.youtube.com/watch?app=desktop&v=4Nr1AgIfajI. Accessed 21 Feb. 2025.

"People in History Archives." *National Maritime Historical Society*, 28 May 2018, seahistory.org/kids-category/people-in-history/.

Pollock, John. *Amazing Grace: The Dramatic Life-Story of John Newton*. Lion, 1996.

Smith, Billy K. *New American Commentary: Amos, Obadiah, Jonah*. Broadman & Holman, 1995.

Snelling, Dr. Andrew A. "From Where Did the Earth's Water Come?" *Answers in Genesis*, Answers In Genesis, 16 May 2018, answersingenesis.org/geology/rocks-and-minerals/where-did-earths-water-come/.

Staff, BibleStudyTools. "Book of Jonah NKJV - the New King James Bible Online." *Bible Study Tools*, BibleStudyTools, www.biblestudytools.com/nkjv/jonah/. Accessed 4 Jan. 2025.

"State Communications in the Neo-Assyrian Empire." *Wikipedia*, Wikimedia Foundation, 22 Nov. 2024, en.wikipedia.org/wiki/State_communications_in_the_Neo-Assyrian_Empire.

Thompsell, Angela. "The Ivory Trade in Africa." ThoughtCo, Mar. 17, 2022, Thoughtco.Com/Ivory-Trade-in-Africa-43350.

Tsarfati, Amir, and Rick Yohn. *Revealing Revelation*. Harvest Prophecy, an Imprint of Harvest House Publishers, 2022.

Unger, Harlow G., and Matthew Boston. *Lafayette*. Tantor Media, Inc., 2021.

Urbanas, Jason. is a contributing editor at Archaeology. "Features - the Assyrian Renaissance - Archaeology Magazine - July/August 2024." *Archaeology Magazine*, 3 Oct. 2024, archaeology.org/issues/july-august-2024/features/the-assyrian-renaissance/.

Watts, Isaac. "Divine Songs." *Free eBooks*, 6 Nov. 2024, www.gutenberg.org/cache/epub/13439/pg13439-images.html.

Wiersbe, Warren W., and Ken Baugh. *Be Amazed: Restoring an Attitude of Wonder and Worship: Ot Commentary, Minor Prophets*. David C. Cook, 2010.

Wilson, Hazel Hutchins, and Edy Legrand. *The Story of Lafayette*. Grosset & Dunlap, 1952.

Young, Rodger C. "How Lunar and Solar Eclipses Shed Light on Biblical Events." *Bible Archeology*, biblearchaeology.org/research/topics/biblical-chronologies/4517-how-lunar-and-solar-eclipses-shed-light-on-biblical-events. Accessed 3 Jan. 2025.

Glossary of Words and Phrases

Eighteenth Century/Sailor Slang:

Crikey	Expression of amazement, surprise
Fancy some scran and a bevvy?	Would you like some food and a drink?
Flush in the pocket	Has a lot of coin
Huzzah	Hurrah
Keep your hair on	A command not to get excited, or "Keep your hat on"
Liberty-man	Sailor
Miry	Swampy, muddy
Nesh	Frail, tender, especially as regards susceptibility to the cold
Rookie	New recruit
Sink me	To express surprise or disbelief
Sly boots	Cunning fellow
Tibby	A cat
Wolf in the stomach	Hungry
You got a cob on?	Are you in a bad mood?

Select French Terms:

Adieu	Farewell
Ami/amie/amies	Friend (masc./fem./plural)
Allons-y!	Let's go!
Au contraire	On the contrary
Au revoir	Goodbye
Avec plaisir	With pleasure
Bien sûr!	Of course!
Bienvenue	Welcome
Bon	Good
Bon appétit	Enjoy your meal

Bonjour	Hello/Good day
Bonne chance	Good luck
Bonne journée	Good day/Have a nice day
Bonne nuit	Good night
Bonsoir	Good evening
Bon voyage	Good voyage
C'est bon	That is good
C'est ça	That's it!
C'est extraordinaire	This is amazing.
C'est incroyable	It is incredible.
C'est l'amour	It is love.
C'est magnifique	It is magnificient/incredible.
C'est simple	It is simple.
C'est tragique	It is tragic.
C'est un bonne idée	That is a good idea
C'est vrai	It's true.
Cher/chère	Dear
Chocolat	Chocolate (used for hot chocolate)
Comprenez-vous?	Do you understand?
Déjà vu	This has happened before.
Demain	Tomorrow
Dieu	God
Et	And
Exactement	Exactly
Finalement	Finally
Je comprends	I understand.
Je ne comprends pas	I don't understand.
Je ne sais pas	I don't know.
Je regrette	I regret that.
Je sais	I know.
Je suis désolé!	I am sorry.
Je suis vraiment désolé	I am truly sorry.
Je suis très heureuse	I am very happy.
Je vous en prie	You are welcome.
Juste	Just
L'amour	Love
La poupe	Stern of a ship, or "poop deck"
Liberté	Liberty
Ma/Mon	My

Madmoiselle	Miss
Madame	Mrs.
Merci/beaucoup	Thank you/very much
Mes amis	My friends
Messieurs	Misters
Moi aussi	Me, too
Mon ami/amie	My friend (masc./fem.)
Mon Dieu	My God
Monsieur	Mister
N'est-ce pa?	Isn't that so?
Où étais-tu, ma petite chienne ?	Where have you been, my little dog?
Oui	Yes
Quel dommage	What a pity.
Petit déjeuner	Breakfast
Poisson	Fish
S'il vous plaît	Please
Touché	To acknowledge someone has made a clever or witty remark in an argument
Toi aussi	You, too
Très bien	Very well
Très jolie	Very pretty, very nice
Un chat	A cat
Une chienne	A dog
Un moment	Just a minute
Voilà	To call attention, to express satisfaction or approval, or to suggest an appearance as if by magic

About the Epic Scribe...

Award-winning author and speaker
Jenny L. Cote

Jenny developed an early passion for God, history, and young people, and beautifully blends these three passions in her two fantasy fiction series, *The Amazing Tales of Max and Liz®* and *Epic Order of the Seven®*. Likened to C. S. Lewis by readers and book reviewers alike, she speaks on creative writing to schools, universities, and conferences around the world. Jenny has a passion for making history fun for kids of all ages, instilling in them a desire to discover their part in HIStory. Her love for research has taken her to most Revolutionary War sites in the U.S., to London (with unprecedented access to Handel House Museum to write in Handel's composing room), Oxford (to stay in the home of C. S. Lewis, "The Kilns," and interview Lewis' secretary, Walter Hooper at the Inklings' famed Eagle and Child Pub), Paris, Normandy, Rome, Israel, and Egypt. She partnered with the National Park Service to produce Epic Patriot Camp, a summer writing camp at Revolutionary parks to excite kids about history, research, and writing. Jenny's books are available online and in stores around the world, as well as in e-book and audio formats. Her Epic Order of the Seven Podcast and filmed writing workshops are available on the Real Life Network. Jenny has been featured by FOX News on Fox & Friends and local Fox affiliates, as well as numerous op-ed pieces on FoxNews.com. She has also been interviewed by nationally syndicated radio and print media, as well as international publications. Jenny holds two marketing degrees from the University of Georgia and Georgia State University. A Virginia native, Jenny now lives with her family in Roswell, Georgia. Official website: www.epicorderoftheseven.com.

. . . AND HER BOOKS

Same Characters, Two Award-Winning Series

The adventure begins with the two-book prequel series: *The Amazing Tales of Max & Liz®*, where the Maker begins building His team of animals to be His envoys through pivotal points of history. Max, Liz, Kate, and Al launch the adventure in book one, *The Ark, the Reed, and the Fire Cloud*, and are joined by their British mouse friend, Nigel, in book two, *The Dreamer, the Schemer, and the Robe*. With book three, *The Prophet, the Shepherd, & the Star*, the team of seven animals is finally complete, and known forevermore as the Order of the Seven in the *Epic Order of the Seven®* series. Working behind the scenes in the lives of Noah, Joseph, Isaiah, Daniel, those in the Christmas story, Jesus, the Disciples, Paul and the early church, the team will pass through Biblical and world history up to modern times with Patrick Henry and the Revolutionary War, and C.S. Lewis and World War II.

Keep up with Jenny and her latest news by subscribing to Epic E-news at www.epicorderoftheseven.com.

AVAILABLE AT AUDIBLE.COM

BIBLICAL SERIES

AMERICAN REVOLUTION SERIES

The Next Generation of Newtons and Wilberforces to Fight Modern-Day Slavery

As you journeyed through the story of John Newton, you saw the transforming power of God's grace in the fight against slavery. Sadly, slavery still exists today in the form of human trafficking. If you're inspired to take action, consider supporting one of these Christ-centered organizations working to bring freedom, hope, and restoration to modern-day survivors.

Atlas Free: Global https://network.atlasfree.org/

Damaris House: Greece https://amginternational.org/project/House-of-Damaris

Eden's Glory: Maryville, Illinois www.edensglory.org

Mirror Ministries: Kennewick, Washington www.mirror-ministries.org

She is Safe: Africa, the Middle East, and Asia https://sheissafe.org/

Wellspring Living: Atlanta, Georgia www.wellspringliving.org